Akrad's Children

Akrad's Children

Book 1 Akrad's Legacy Series

Jeanette O'Hagan

By the Light Books

Akrad's Children
© Jeanette O'Hagan
Book 1 in the Akrad's Legacy series

Copyright Jeanette O'Hagan © 2017 © 2022
http://jeanetteohagan.com

Cover design: Jeanette O'Hagan © 2017 © 2022
Typesetting and Layout: Jeanette O'Hagan

All events, characters and entities portrayed in the stories are fictional and any likeness to any persons living or dead, events and entities are entirely coincidental.

Cataloguing-in-Publication entry (CIP) is available at National Library of Australia

A catalogue record for this book is available from the National Library of Australia

ISBN-978-0-6481640-1-2
Published through By the Light Books

By the Light Books
Brookside Post Shop, PO Box 2520, Brookside Centre, Qld 4053
Email: Bythelightbooks@gmail.com

To Tony, husband and father, for his love through the fun times and the hard times.

Note to Reader

A map, genealogies and a list of character names are included at the end of the book.

***

This book follows Australian style conventions for spelling, punctuation and grammar.

***

Subscribe to *Jeanette O'Hagan's Newsletter*
at http://eepurl.com/bbLJKT for the latest on new releases, giveaways and other news and receive story set in the world of Nardva.

PART ONE: A REALM AT WAR

Tarka, Royal city of Tamra

Chapter One: Dead

Mannok

Mannok stood paralysed in the doorway of the audience chamber. His heart shuddered against his ribs, the routine palace sounds fading to a distant buzzing.

His father, the Kapok, lay stretched out on the mosaic floor, his strong profile sharp-edged in the harsh sunlight streaming through high arched windows. Big limbs stiff as glacier ice, his face like carved stone. Someone had folded Papa's arms across his broad chest and straightened his cloak. The faint tremble of the long feathers of his royal headdress, the only sign of movement.

It was as though his father was already arrayed in his royal vestments, laid out in state on his funeral bier.

'I wish you were dead.'

Mannok's own words taunted him. Bitter words he'd shouted at the hunting lodge days ago. He had felt so betrayed by Papa's lies, but now he was reduced to a bewildered four-year-old wishing desperately that his father would live...

It had to be a dream, a nightmare distorted by the shattered past. Papa would soon stir, and they'd laugh away the fears as they always did. He scrunched his eyes shut and opened them, but nothing changed.

'Your Highness!'

Madomo Bitjarnan rushed out from an alcove beneath the spectators' balcony, his time-worn face slack and pale with shock.

Usually, it was Uncle Naetok sneering face, not Bitjarnan's

harried brown one that haunted in his night visions.

'Your Highness, I'm so sorry. The Kapok is …' The old Madomo's scrawny voice-nub bobbed. '…He's dead.'

'No,' Mannok glared at the small rotund man. 'You must be mistaken.'

'Your father's not breathing. I…' Sweat beaded Bitjarnan's wrinkled forehead. I'm so sorry, Your Majesty—'

'Don't call me that.' Mannok swung to face the madomo, his heart pumping. 'I'm not…not yet.' He shook his head to clear the buzzing in his ears and tore his gaze from his father's rigid form to scan the empty audience chamber.

An abandoned pen dribbled ink over the open records book spread out on the writing podium. The large wooden chair, where his father usually sat to receive petitioners, tipped over. A small table and a tray of half-eaten food lay overturned beside the chair and a fallen cup spilled guava juice into a crimson puddle on the floor.

Like congealing blood …

A sour taste seared the back of Mannok's throat. Seventeen … he was seventeen, not a child, overwhelmed by nightmares soaked in blood. Blood swirling into lakes drowning him. Blood pooling beneath his father's prone body in the throne room. Bright blood staining Uncle Naetok's hunting knife. His uncle who had been twisted by Akrad's deceit, by his own envy and hate.

But Papa had survived that attack and there was no blood, not now, not here in this place, this time. His father bore no wounds, no bloodied or ripped clothing, no obvious injuries, no clear reason to be lying dead on the floor …

Mannok clenched his teeth against the dark memories and focused on what lay before him.

'What happened?

'He …Your Highness, the Kapok was taking a meal break between petitioners.' Bitjarnan's pudgy hands fluttered like frightened butterflies. 'We were discussing some irregularities in the Palace inventory when Dinnis rushed through the door. Before he could be stopped, he leapt at your royal father and struck him down. Your father fell like a toppled tree. We … I mean the guards grabbed Dinnis …'

The Madomo pointed with his chin to a shadowed alcove where two guards restrained the tall blue-skinned youth. The rangy teenager's smouldering grey eyes pinned Mannok's. He strained against the guards' grip, the burlier guard's hand clamped over his mouth.

A shudder raced through Mannok. What motive could the half-blood Nolmec possess to harm the Kapok. His age-mate could be annoying, but disloyal? Surely, he wouldn't repay Papa's kindness with death.

'Guards, is this true? Dinnis attacked my father?'

The raw-boned, older guard, Lantil, dipped his head. 'Yes, Your Maj ... ah, Highness.'

The other younger guard nodded. 'He said he had something important to tell the Kapok.'

How could he have felled Papa with one blow? Dinnis may be as tall like Papa, but was of narrower build. Nor would Papa be easy to take by surprise. 'He was alone? What weapon did he use?'

Bitjarnan opened his mouth, confusion creeping across his face. 'I ...' He glanced at the guards.

The older guard shook his head. 'We couldn't find a weapon, only his hunting knife, but it was still sheathed ... and the old battered satchel he always carries.'

Rage boiled up inside Mannok. He strode across the audience room, stopping in front of Dinnis. 'I thought you a friend, loyal to the throne. You owe everything to Papa, your life, your home, your position.'

Dinnis' face darkened, his words muffled against the guard's restraining hand.

Mannok gestured impatiently, 'Let him speak.'

'Yes, of course, Your Highness. He wouldn't stop shouting.' Bitjarnan stuttered a reply.

The guard dropped his hand and Dinnis licked his bruised lips. 'Mannok ... Your Highness, you must listen, I didn't kill him. ...'

Mannok raised his eyebrows, his mouth twisting into a sneer. 'Do you deny the claims of three witnesses?'

'No, but you don't understand ...'

'How did you do it? What trick did you use?' What Dinnis lacked in strength and skill, he made up with in subterfuge and wit.

'I didn't... Slide it, Mannu, that's not what's important right now ...'

Mannok gritted his teeth at the familiar contraction of his name. He didn't have time for this. He balled his fist and slammed it into the stone pillar beside the blue-skinned traitor. The pain that shot through his hand was almost a comfort, a kind of clarity. He had to get a grip.

Bitjarnan tugged at his cloak. 'Your Highness, shouldn't we ring the alarm …'

Mannok spun to face the old madomo, nursing his hand. 'No, not yet.' Announcing his father's … incapacity … would only cause panic. 'Fetch my uncle Lukarn and get a physician. And have the guards clear the Great Hall. No one is to enter until we confirm …' Closing his eyes, he swallowed hard. '… that my father is dead and how it was done.'

Taking the Madomo by his richly clad shoulders, Mannok pushed him towards entrance at the end of the audience room. 'Hurry!'

Bitjarnan disappeared through the embossed golden doors. Normal palace sounds drifted from the Great Hall; the measured stamp of the guards' studded sandals on stone floors and the shrill laughter of one of the Palace servants.

Dinnis' strained voice sliced across the eerie silence inside the room. 'Mannok, please, your father …'

Mannok swung around. 'Your excuses and lies can wait.' He spat the words out like bitter seeds. 'Gag and bind him.'

As the guards hastened to obey, Mannok turned his back on the traitor. The room wavered and blurred. Blinking, he dropped to his knees beside his father. Apart from the deep creases between his strong eyebrows, Papa's face was pale and smooth. His mouth, always so ready to curve up in a fierce grin or turn down in displeasure now immobile, the pale lips pressed together with a slight downturn at the corners. His curved nose, a larger version of Mannok's own, stood out like a bronzed buttress.

Mannok lifted one of Papa's cool hands, the tan fingers overlapping his own, heavy and cool against his skin. The anger that had built up since Papa had taken Ista away leached out of him. Papa had kept secrets, betrayed them both, but he'd had his reasons. He was still the man who had taught Mannok to ride and hunt, who knew what to do in every situation, who had always had time for him regardless how busy he was with state affairs. He was still his father. Despite his own heated words, despite all that had happened, he didn't want things to end like this.

Like Naetok, like Akrad, Dinnis, who owed Papa everything had turned on him. Why had his age-mate repaid them all with betrayal?

He let Papa's lifeless hand fall.

Mannok's breath caught. Had Papa's chest moved? Was he imaging it? Spurred by hope, Mannok's heart picked up speed in a thundering gallop. He placed his cheek close to his father's cool lips. The moments slipped by, but then,the softest puff of breath whispered on Mannok's skin. A sob racked through him.

'Alive!' He jumped up and punched the air. 'He's alive!'

But how long before that slight breath was stolen? Once again, his father's life hung on a fragile spider's thread.

NINE YEARS EARLIER

Akrad's Stronghold, North Pass

Chapter Two: Attack

Dinnis

Dinnis spread his lanky limbs along the branch of the sichar tree, careful to keep out of sight of his great-grandfather's soldiers. The spreading mass of small, angular leaves shielded him from unwelcome attention but still allowed him a strategic view over upper and lower wards of the stronghold. Something was about to happen, perhaps a siege or an imminent attack.

Ever since the stranger arrived at dawn and disappeared inside the tower, the air seemed charged with tension. Message hawks came and scouts went out. They returned, panting and wide-eyed, to be secluded with Keloumen Nikoris.

Now, the blue-skinned Nolmec soldiers rushed about with the frenetic activity of a threatened ant-hill; sharpening blades, checking their kit, clearing debris from the spaces abutting the thick stone walls. A long, roped line of overladen yarmas plodded between the massive outer gate towers bringing in stores.

Keloumen Nikoris stood with boots planted on the rutted ground of the bigger lower ward, bellowing in Nolmec at the soldiers and servants unloading the supplies. *'Speudoa, speudoa.'* Hurry, hurry.

A thrill rippled along Dinnis' spine and his lips twitched up. Maybe this was the day his father would rescue him and his sister, Ista. When at last they could escape his great-grandfather, Arkon Akrad, and go home.

'Dinnis, Dinnis, where are you?'

As though conjured by his thoughts, Ista stalked below, a

frown creasing her fine brows. At almost eight, three and a half years younger than he, his sister acted with the highhandness of a princess—a *kiprissa* as the Nolmec called her. Her grey eyes, almond shaped like his own and a legacy of their part-Nolmec mother, were as stormy as lightning fringed summer clouds. She stuck out her sharp you-will-obey-me chin.

'Dinnis, I know you're hiding. Grandfather will be furious if you skip your chores.'

He snorted. When wasn't 'Grandfather' furious with him? Dinnis 'provoked' Akrad's spiteful temper even when he tried to avoid it, and he wore the bruises, burns and scars to prove it. So, what did it matter if he was in trouble again?

He glanced back over the inner wall at the chaos of hurried preparations in the lower ward below. This was their chance, to slip out unnoticed. They were unlikely to find a better one, but would she heed him? When they had first come to this place of horrors three years ago, she had clung to him. He had sung to her and whispered words of hope in the long dark nights. He'd done his best to shield and protect her from Akrad's cruelties. Yet the longer they stayed here, the more she was ensnared by that monster's smooth deceit. Even so, she was still his sister.

He leaned over and called softly. 'Up here, *chia*.'

The branch swayed, sending a few dead leaves twirling onto her upturned face. Her pert nose wrinkled. With a quick glance over her skinny shoulders, Ista hitched up her tunic and scrambled up the tree trunk to perch on the branch opposite him.

'What are you doing up here?'

'Shhh, keep your voice down.' He sat up straighter, his shoulders tense. 'I've been watching. Ista, the gates are open and the guards distracted. We could slip out, escape. Find Papa.'

Emotions flitted across her face—hope, fear, doubt. Her eyes shone then darkened and her knuckles whitened as she gripped the tree. 'We don't know where Papa is.'

'Yes, but somethings happening ... maybe he's come for us at last.' His voice rose, and he bit his lip to contain his excitement.

She scowled. 'It's years since Papa left us ...' her voice faded. She folded her arms tight around her narrow chest. 'What if he's forgotten us.'

He sensed her uncertainty, the longing, though, like Akrad, she was difficult to read. Perhaps, he was getting through to her. 'Papa could have sent the stranger.'

It was possible, after all. While the raven-haired man that arrived in the morning had the same strange silvery-white skin as Arkon Akrad, the two men had eyed each other like adversaries not allies.

She snapped her head up, and he knew he'd made a mistake.

'You don't know anything, Dinnis. The stranger's not Tamrin. He has nothing to do with Papa. Grandfather says that man came to steal his power, so he put narkam in his drink to trap him. Grandfather says Papa doesn't want us. He's never coming back for us. Grandfather says you're stupid and I shouldn't listen to you.'

Heat rushed through him. 'That's a lie. Papa promised he'd come. Anyway, if we get outside the stronghold, we can find—'

Her face hardened. 'You'll get caught, and then you'd be in trouble.'

'Ista …'

'I'm not coming with you. You know what happens when we … you … displease Grandfather. If you were smart, you'd be doing your chores, not skulking around in trees. You're a bad boy, that's why he punishes you.'

With a toss of her long dark hair, she slid down the tree trunk and marched towards the central tower, her back as straight and hard and sharp as crystal.

His shoulders slumped. What should he do now? She was his little sister. Papa had charged him to protect her. He couldn't leave her behind.

* * *

Dinnis jolted awake as a long warning cry split the somnolent midday air.

'Attack! We're under attack,'

He gripped the soft bark with knees and hands to stop sliding off the branch. The cold rush of shock cleared the muzziness of sleep in an instant. He crept along the branch, his breath coming in short, sharp gasps. He had to get a better look over the inner wall.

A long, drawn-out scream. A Nolmec guard plummeted from the outer gate tower to sprawl onto the ground below like a broken toy. Loud war cries came from the top of towers where Tamrin warriors with feathered headdress fought Nolmec. The long-necked yarmas squealed with terror and stampeded, spilling their loads in the wide open outer gate.

A thrill shot through Dinnis. Through some ruse, the Tamrin had captured the gate towers and control of the outer walls. If they could keep the advantage, and make it up the slope and into the inner ward ...

Below him, Nolmec soldiers dropped baskets and crates, rushed to grab shields and weapons. Baskets of potatoes and bags of maize and beans spilled out on the ground. The dogs in the kennels bayed and yowled. Ducks honked and flapped against the bars of the crates.

In the outer ward, Keloumen Nikoris drew his sword, his almond eyes wide.

'Defend the gates. Defend the gates.' His voice echoed off the stout stone walls.

Nolmec soldiers rushed forward. Tamrin arrows fell like deadly sleet from the outer walls, bouncing off bronze chest plates, biting exposed flesh. A soldier slumped to the ground, an arrow through his neck.

Tamrin warriors streamed through the open gates, mouths wide in battle cries, painted faces ferocious.

'For Tamra.'

Dinnis' heart thudded against his ribcage. The battle cry sounded like Papa's deep voice. He clung to the branch and searched the faces of the warriors.

'For Tamra and the Kapok.' Hundreds of voices, full throated and fierce echoed the rallying cry.

The warriors crashed spears and clubs against shields and advanced with the force of an avalanche. The Tamrin parted and a hundred mounted warriors galloped through their ranks, crushing Nolmec soldiers beneath their horses' sharp hooves, thrusting downwards with their spears as they dashed toward the inner gate.

The Tamrin warriors pressed hard against their ragged line of defence and half a hundred Nolmec gave ground. Further back the mounted warriors regrouped, readying for another charge. A black-fletched Nolmec arrow pierced the Tamrin's throat. More Tamrin warriors streamed through the outer gates and surged forward.

Keloumen Nikoris ducked and slashed at a mounted rider with his sword. 'Fall back. Fall back. The outer ward is lost.'

Chapter Three: Close the Gates!

Dinnis

Dinnis leaned forward, the branch swayed beneath him. Though it was hard be sure under the painted patterns and feathered plumes, he glimpsed a familiar face among the riders; the strong nose and chin, the tall broad-shouldered build and confident poise on the dappled grey stallion. His breath caught in his throat. Surely it was Papa.

In one movement, he swung down from the branch and crouched in the shadow of the tree. Taking a breath, he dashed towards the inner gates and the lower ward and his father, then pulled to a stop. He couldn't leave Ista behind. Akrad could use her as a hostage. How could he meet Papa without her?

The clash of spear against shield, of fierce war cries and shouts of pain, the thunder of horses' hooves on the ripped turf rolled closer by the minute, the chaotic sounds shredding his thoughts.

A soldier jostled past. '*Skatua*, son of a slug, get of my way.'

The man backhanded him, sending him sprawling into the dust. Dinnis scrambled backwards into the shade of the spreading sichar tree, his ears ringing, tears smarting his eyes.

Nikoris reversed through the inner gate. Blood streamed from a small gash beneath his bronze helm and his sword lacquered in gore. '*Speudoa*. Shut the gate, get archers on the walls. Why don't you shut the gate?'

'*Keloumen, kuree*, half our troops are still in the lower ward,' Palouma Akillis shouted back.

'*Moros*, do you want to let the Tamrin scum into the upper ward as well? Do it now.'

Two soldiers grabbed the spiked wheel in the gate house. Their back muscles bulged as they grasped the spokes and pulled. The wheel spun with a rattle of the great chains. A Tamrin warrior, his bronzed face distorted in battle rage, rode his horse over two Nolmec retreating toward the closing gate. A swarm of black-fletched arrows pierced him and he slumped forward on the neck of his white-eyed horse.

The heavy bronze-studded doors shivered and juddered together in a slow arc crushing a Nolmec between them. Soldiers rushed to pull her limp body free. The tall gate doors shuddered shut with a hollow boom. Soldiers dropped the heavy bars into place.

The resounding thud echoed in Dinnis' chest with a grim finality.

Keloumen Nikoris waved his bloodied sword. 'Put more archers on the wall? Heat the stones. Defend the inner ward with your honour and your lives.'

Beyond the wall, came a lull in the clash of weapons and a roar of disappointment. A strong bass voice, surely his papa's, shouted in Tamrin.

'Secure the outer ward, warriors of Tamra. We broke the siege at Tavin, we can break down these walls.'

The Keloumen screamed back, 'Barbarian dogs, we will defend the Arkon and the Kiprissa to the last soldier. We are Nolmec and these walls will hold.'

Dinnis rocked back in the long grass beside the sichar tree. He wrapped his thin arms around his legs. The decision had been made for him, unless … he used the confusion to escape through the smaller postern gate between upper and lower wards. He fingered the slim metal pick in the fold of his tunic, the lock wouldn't be a problem, but there would be the guards. If he could devise a way to get past them … He would find Ista and persuade her to come with him.

The inner courtyard seethed with activity. Archers positioned themselves along the walls and other soldiers carried heavy objects to wedge against the massive doors. In the lower ward, the clamour of battle resumed as presumably the stranded Nolmec continued to attack the Tamrin warriors. To do otherwise would be too great a dishonour.

Hecton, one of the Arkon's personal guards, ran from the tower and skidded to a stop in front of the gesticulating Keloumen. Slipping forward, Dinnis slithered on his belly to behind a pile of crates to hear above the battle clamour.

'The Arkon requires your presence to explain the situation, *kuree*.'

Except for a slight blanching beneath his blue skin, Nikoris' flat face remained impassive. His head jerked into a nod. He beckoned one of the officers to him.

'Palouma Akillis, take command. Defend the walls. Keep the gate secure.'

Spinning around, he took off his helm, plunged his hands in a barrel of rainwater and sluiced his face of dried blood and grime. He straightened his scarlet kilt and bronze armour. He wiped his sword of Tamrin blood on the trampled grass and sheathed it. Squaring his compact shoulders, the Keloumen marched towards the Tower, like a proud man going to an execution.

Ista would be in the Tower. Keeping low, Dinnis followed behind the Keloumen. As he passed Hecton, the guard grabbed him and dug thick fingers into Dinnis' shoulder.

'Where do you think you're going, wart. You should be helping on the wall.'

'To do my chores, *kuree*.'

The man squinted his dark eyes. Tall like most Nolmec, he had a moon-like face and heavy eyelids that gave him a deceptively languid look. 'Don't be ridiculous. There's a battle on. Besides, the Arkon doesn't want to be disturbed. He has important business to attend to.'

'But he said I should do them. I'll keep out of his way.' Dinnis lifted his chin. 'Are you going to question the Arkon?' He held his breath. Everyone knew how unpredictable the Akrad was, how severely he would punish anyone who contravened his commands no matter how bizarre.

Hecton gave Dinnis a rough shake. 'Fine, little toad. Do your chores and stay out of the Arkon's way, or you'll get a beating from me as well as him.'

Dinnis ducked his head and sprinted to the well. He filled a wooden bucket with water, grabbed a scrubbing brush, and lugged the bucket toward the tower entrance. He grimaced as water sloshed over the sides and the heavy bucket battered against his shins. High above, an eagle soared in the brilliant blue sky, sunlight gleaming off its white feathered head. If only he could fly out of this prison and be free to find his father.

* * *

Dinnis placed the bucket on the stone-flagged floor and blinked at the dimness inside the semi-circular tower-room. The familiar smells of old parchment, leather, dust, candle wax, herbal concoctions and the stink of strange chemicals lay heavy in the air. Beyond the thick stone walls of the tower and walls of the upper ward, the noises of battle sounded like buzzing flies on a day-old corpse.

Arkon Akrad paced between the long tables, his strange silver skin luminous in the subdued light. His honeyed voice rose and fell in hushed tones. Keloumen Nikoris stood in front of him, plumed helmet held under his arm. Ista was not among the book-laden tables and benches. Maybe she was in the kitchen or the upper rooms or even in the herb garden outside.

Dinnis plunged the scrubbing brush into the soapy water and pushed it across the flagstone floor, edging closer to the spiral stairs and landing that led to the upper levels. With any luck, the Arkon would be too preoccupied to notice him. And if he was challenged, he had an excuse for being there.

Metal chinked against the stone wall in the far corner of the vast room. The silver-white skin of the stranger gleamed in the shadows on the far north wall. The man slouched against the curved wall, chains tight against neck, wrists and ankles in a complicated arrangement. His dark, soulful eyes, so clear that morning, were now swollen shut in a mess of bruises. Not a friend of the Arkon, but nor was he likely to be much help, especially if his wits were dulled by narkam. The stranger had been foolish to place himself in the Akrad's power, but that was not Dinnis' problem. He had to find his sister and escape this tower of nightmares.

Chapter Four: Nikoris' Folly

Rasel of the Forest Folk

Rasel gripped the stone ledge as she teetered on the window sill cut high up, on the second level of Akrad's Tower. From far below came the sounds of battle between the Nolmec and Tamrin, but that was not her immediate concern. Catching her breath, she squeezed through the narrow opening and jumped into the Tower, landing on a wooden floor a couple of tanis below. The thick stone walls cut off the war cries and the violent clash of spears and swords. She wrinkled her nose at the musty smell overlaid with mountainsweet and winterbright. Fine cotton throw rugs, woven blankets and furs draped a large sleeping pallet pushed against the wall. A frayed rag doll lay abandoned in one corner.

Her saba, Kinleader of the Forest Folk, wasn't in this room which appeared to be used for sleeping. He had to be somewhere inside the stone tower for she saw him enter at dawn. Now the sun was high in the sky but he hadn't re-emerged.

She crossed the room in a couple of easy steps to where the arched door pierced the rough grey stone wall. Her slender fingers trembled on the heavy metal ring. She wasn't supposed to be here, she was supposed to be at the Kin Gathering. But she had been the one to warn them of the coming danger. She had to see how things worked out.

A band tightened around her chest. If her brother Semian were here, he'd tell her to find the strike group, for they had to be somewhere close. But that would take time her grandfather may not have. She lifted her chin. She was a pathfinder like her baba, she could do this.

Rasel tugged, lifted and then finally twisted the metal ring. The door opened a crack and she squeezed through onto a narrow landing. Shafts of sunlight sliced through the cavernous space in front of her from the high windows cut into the curve of the wall and disappeared into the gloom. The murmur of voices floated from below. Keeping low, she glided to the edge of the landing and peered through the carved balustrade railings in a large semi-circular room.

It took up one half of the tower, reached from ground level to a flat wooden plank ceiling high above her. A large hearth, the fire banked in its depths, stretched across half the right side of the wall. Two men stood in the middle of the room among long tables cluttered with a chaos of strange equipment, loose parchments and plates of stale food. Melted down old candles teetered in tarnished candelabra. Piles of books haphazardly covered large areas of the stone flagged floor.

The men were as tall as the Kin, unlike most of the younger races. The taller one, half-turned away from her, wore a long charcoal-grey robe edged with twisted gold and silver thread. Long flame-red hair framed the silvery white skin of his chiselled face. A shiver shimmied up her spine. It had to be Akrad, treacherous enemy of her people. If she believed the tales, his smooth silvery-white hands were stained with the blood of thousands.

She turned her head at a soft stuttered swish. In the shadow of an overcrowded table, a rangy lad knelt scrubbing the stone floor. His smoky blue skin, almond shaped eyes and high cheek bones suggested Nolmec bloodlines but his prominent nose seemed more characteristic of the Tamrin. There was something of Akrad in his looks too. An enigma, though no doubt under the Betrayer's thrall.

There was no sign of her grandfather, though she couldn't see into all the nooks about the cluttered room. Maybe she should search the upper levels while the Betrayer was preoccupied here. Rasel shifted and then froze as the Betrayer's mellow voice drifted up in accented but fluent Nolmec.

'Tell me, Keloumen Nikoris, did your scouts not warn you of the Tamrin army's approach?'

'My apologies, Arkon.' The other man, in the bronze armour and the ankle-high boots of a Nolmec army officer, stood rigid as the stone walls that enclosed him. His blue face was a carved mask. 'You said Rokkan would wait—'

Akrad twitched up a red eyebrow and Nikoris' voice-nub bobbed. 'Er ... I mean, we did not expect the Tamrin to regroup so soon after defeating of your tool Naetok or to arrive this quickly. The roads—'

'Yes, yes, always the master of the unexpected, Rokkan brought his army across the high mountain passes, but the outer gates should have held.'

'Yes, *kuree*. According to the scouts, the Tamrin were hours away. We were bringing in food and other supplies from the surrounding villages. Somehow, he's used the confusion as cover to take the gate towers. Or we were betrayed.' The Nolmec commander shifted his feet, his fingers tightening on his helmet. 'Great Arkon, this is a setback, I admit, but my soldiers will defend the inner gate and retake the lower ward.'

Silence settled like a pall inside the tower room, disturbed only by the whisper of Akrad's robes sweeping the flagstones as he paced between the tables. Outside, came sounds muted by the thick stone walls; men shouting, the march of nailed boots, horses whinnying, the clatter of crates being moved, the burr of the smith's sharpening stone and soughing of the wind winding around the outer wall of the tall stone tower.

Then from inside, the cool chime of metal against stone sounded as clear as birdsong in the forest canopy.

Her heart fluttered like flight feathers in the wind. Someone else was in the room. Rasel slid towards the direction of the sound, peered over the edge of the spiral stairs. In a side alcove near a large hearth, someone—her saba—was shackled with dark metal to the wall. Cold pierced her as she took in his battered half-slumped body, stripped bare of all but a clout. His bruised eyes were closed, his breathing erratic. His injuries and the weight of the foul metal would make it difficult for him to use his full power. She had to help him.

As she pulled back, she caught the gaze of the boy below. Her breath caught in her throat. He was staring straight at her. The strange boy flicked his eyes from her to where Akrad paced like a hungry panther in front of the Nolmec Commander and back to her. She put a finger to her lips. The lad's almond eyes narrowed. He tilted his head and went back to pushing foaming water across the flagstone floor as though he hadn't seen her.

She stifled a relieved sigh. Maker be thanked, he hadn't given her away. Could he be an ally sent to help her? He was no friend of the Betrayer's at least. She could take on the Keloumen, despite the Nolmec's ruthless reputation, they were not of the Eldar, but Akrad ... Her muscles tensed. She was of the Kin, the Forest Folk, she would resist his coercive powers and arcane power.

Her heart slowed to a more normal rate, then spiked again when Akrad spun around, his venomous voice sullying the stillness.

'So, to summarise, Keloumen Nikoris, before a siege has even started, the enemy troops have broken into the lower ward. All that stands between us and the Kapok's army is the weaker inner wall and this tower.'

'Yes, great Arkon.' Sweat beaded Nikoris' forehead.

'And how many soldiers did you abandon in the outer ward?'

Nikoris dipped his head. 'Half a hundred men, Great Arkon, but the rest will shield you and the Kiprissa with their lives.'

'Half the garrison lost? You had better. What about supplies?'

The commander looked down. 'Very little apart from what we had already stowed in the storeroom, great Arkon. We were replenishing ...'

'So you said. Hmmm, we have access to water through the well in the upper ward, soldiers to defend the walls and tower, but only enough food to feed them for a five-day at half rations, whereas reinforcements are over half an Alume away. Our position slides toward the untenable due to your blunders, Keloumen.'

The Nolmec touched his fist to the centre of his forehead in salute. 'My honour and my life are in your hands, *kuree*.'

'Yes. Especially your life, Keloumen. I will report your failure to General Nuktis. Unless, perhaps, you redeem yourself in our defence.'

Akrad picked up a book from an unstable pile and ran a finger along its cracked leather spine, a smile creeping across his face.

Rasel took the opportunity to edge over the stairs.

'Despite your incompetence, Keloumen, all is not lost. I've been developing a powerful weapon—an air-borne poison. With the catapults I've designed, we should be able to devastate the Kapok's army in a matter of minutes. As long as the wind doesn't turn, our fatalities should be minimal.'

Rasel paused and chill bumps rippled along her arms. Was this the weapon that had finally stirred the elders of the Kin to act against Akrad? No, surely that was something of more ancient and deadly power.

The Nolmec saluted Akrad again. 'May Kroko grant you victory over all your enemies, Great Arkon.'

Akrad snapped the book shut, a cloud of dust motes rising in the shaft of sunlight. 'A pity.'

'*Kuree?*'

'A pity that ungrateful whelp Rokkan has to be eliminated.'

The bucket clattered against the floor to the accompaniment of a soft gasp.

'We have the Kiprissa, great Arkon.' The Nolmec Commander's voice wavered.

'Ah yes, but our little princess is still too young. If we'd managed to keep Rokkan on our side, we would have beaten the Red Crane faction by now and brought Tamra to heel, defeating both threats to our rule.'

The Keloumen lifted his chin. 'Perhaps, though his loyalties were always divided especially since Kiprissa Gaia died—'

'Either way, Rokkan will regret spurning me! As all ungrateful whelps do in the end.' Akrad twisted and kicked the boy in the ribs. 'Isn't that right, Dinnis dear? Do you think I didn't see you sneaking about?'

The boy flinched back, overturning the bucket. Sudsy water sloshed over the Betrayer's robes.

'*Rakka, moros,* idiot! How is it that two such intelligent and capable parents from such exalted stock can produce a clumsy oaf like you?'

Dinnis righted the bucket, his face empty of expression. 'Perhaps Master, I'm a throwback to some ignoble and boorish grandparent.'

Swearing foully, Akrad booted him again. Rasel almost felt the blow. She clenched her hands, her cheeks flaming.

Nikoris cleared his throat. 'Arkon, excuse me, but shouldn't we deploy the weapon?'

The sorcerer swung round, his glacial gaze pinning the commander. 'Of course, Keloumen. Get the catapults positioned while I prepare sufficient poison. I'll send Hecton when it's ready. Now, leave me.'

The Nolmec's eye-teeth flashed in a grim smile. He saluted the Betrayer. 'The Tamrin's defeat is inevitable.'

Chapter Five: Shackled

Rasel

As the scarlet cloak of the Keloumen disappeared through the door and before Akrad could turn around, Rasel swung over the side of the low railing and dropped to the floor. Her feet connected with cold stone with only a whisper of sound. The boy Dinnis' eyes tracked her, but still he said nothing. She crouched into the deep shadows under the stairs. Now she only had Akrad and possibly the boy to deal with before she could free her grandfather and then warn her kin of Akrad's deadly poison.

Akrad turned and cracked the knuckles in his long tapering fingers, a cruel smile lingering on his chiselled face. Weaving around the benches he sauntered toward the alcove where Saba was shackled.

The Betrayer's sensual lips widened, revealing strong teeth. He grabbed the chains and shook the Kinleader. 'Were you listening, Korak? It is a sweet day that gives two of my enemies into my hands.' He'd switched effortlessly into the ancient speech.

Hot, unaccustomed anger flared within Rasel. How dare he treat the Kinleader with such distain. Saba's tormenter was a good three to four tanis away, too far for her to strike without losing the advantage of surprise, but she tensed her muscles ready to attack.

As though sensing her presence, her grandfather's forest-black eyes snapped open and caught Rasel's gaze. He shook his head a fraction before allowing his eyes to rest on the Akrad. Did he want her to wait?

The chains clanged and chimed as Akrad released them. 'Ah, you are awake, Korak. I hope you are comfortable.'

Saba took a jagged breath and pressed his bloodless lips together. A sheen of sweat covered his face. The purple bruises spread across his chest and abdomen like storm clouds boiling up over the forest. Blood, crimson and maroon, stained a hastily wrapped bandage around his lower abdomen. She had to help him. Keeping close to the wall and the shadows, she edged closer. It took all her will to move slowly, to not attract the Betrayer's attention. When she was close enough, she would attack, whatever Saba thought.

Akrad's voice dripped with disdain. 'You are a fool, Kinleader. When I have both the Nolmec and Tamrin in my fist, I will crush all your kin like rotten fruit—even if I have to burn down the Great Forest to do it.'

'You are the fool, Man of the West.' Saba's voice was faint.

'Ha, I am not the one foolish enough to walk into my enemy's high tower unarmed and alone to negotiate! I am not the one chained to the wall. I am not a dead man.'

'Yet your chains are much stronger than the ones that hold me captive. All tyrants fall in the end and one day you will give an account for all your treacherous and cruel actions to your Maker.' Saba dark eyes brightened and his voice gained strength as he talked.

Akrad let out a long, fluting laugh. '*Skatua*! What a heap of yarma droppings, *rakka*. You are deluded. You should have come to kill me, not to parley. Platitudes and trust get you chained to the wall to die, old man.'

'We are not assassins, Man of the West, but it's time we stopped looking the other way,' Saba took a shuddering breath, 'while you rampage and destroy at will among the younger peoples. The council has given you a chance to leave the Five Lands, to return to wherever you came from.'

'Fool, I'll leave when I'm ready. I am so close to discovering what the power I need. And you, Korak, Kinleader, you will tell me what I want to know.'

'No.'

'When I'm finished with you, you'll beg me to hear your secrets. Another interruption will not save you. But our ... conversation ... will have to wait until I deal with these Tamrin fleas. Count this as an appetiser.'

Akrad struck Saba across the face with a loud crack

Now! The foul man was a jaguar's leap away. She couldn't let him abuse her saba any longer. She tensed her tingling muscles and stilled her mind, readying to spring.

Akrad turned, and before Rasel could pivot and adjust the angle of her attack, bounded up the stairs. His taunting voice carried back in his wake.

'I have poison to brew, Kinleader, poison that works as effectively against your people.' His footsteps paused. 'Oh, and Dinnis, my dear, don't think I've forgotten your clumsy accident with the water bucket. I'm looking forward to our little chat after dinner.' A moment later, a door slammed behind him.

Rasel shot out from under the stairs and rushed to her grandfather.

'*Saba*, are you alright?'

Kneeling beside him, she grabbed one of the shackles and tried to prise it open.

'Rasel, what are you doing here? You should be at the Kin Gathering.' He grasped her wrist, his grip still strong though his eyes widened in pain. 'Go fetch your baba. He's with the others at the large marosa tree north of the wall. Tell him what you have heard. He will know what to do.'

'No, I need to get you out of here. If I could find something to smash these iron bands...'

'There is no time. Commander Nikoris could return or some other of Betrayer's servants. My wounds would make shifting difficult, even dangerous. It is vital the others are warned of the Betrayer's plans.'

Tears flooded her eyes. 'I can't leave you to die.'

'You were ever the wild child, daughter of Jazadek. Refusing to heed older and wiser voices; rushing into danger without a second thought. What do you plan to do, sit here with me until Akrad comes back and takes you captive? Do you think that would bring me any comfort?'

She sat back on her heels, her ringlets falling across her face like a waterfall. How could she leave him? She had to save him! Prickles rippled across her shoulders. She was being watched. Pushing her hair out of her eyes, she looked up.

The strange, sullen boy stared at them, his grey eyes soaking up every detail he saw. She sat up straighter. He could help.

'Where is the key?'

'Did my father send you?'

She crinkled her brow. Who was this boy's father? 'No, but—'

Saba laughed shakily. 'You will get no help from him, child. Can't you see Akrad's blood in him.'

A strong emotion flashed across the boy's face—anger, revulsion, hate—she wasn't quite sure which. Whatever his connection to Akrad, she didn't think the boy was on his side. He could have betrayed her presence, but he hadn't done so. She reached across the space between them and touched his arm.

'Dinnis? Is that your name? If you help us, we will take you with us.'

His nostrils flared. 'Why would I go with you? Papa is coming for us.'

'He is here?'

'With the Tamrin army.'

'Then you should warn him of the poison!'

The boy narrowed his eyes, but he did not move or speak.

She allowed her hand to drop to her knee. 'At least tell us where the key to the shackles is?'

'Akrad keeps them fastened to his belt.'

Her shoulders drooped. Maker help them, there had to be a way out of this. If she found something heavy, some other way to remove the shackles before Akrad or one of his lackeys returned.

Her grandfather leant forward, straining against the chains. 'Rasel, not all songs have happy endings—at least not this side of the Composer's undying Song. You must leave.'

Chapter Six: Unchained

Dinnis

Dinnis fingered the hard metal edge of the bucket handle. What the young woman said was true. Akrad's plan to release lethal poison against the Tamrin warriors would put Papa in peril unless it was stopped. A shiver swept through him. After three long years, Papa was in the lower ward, here to rescue him and his sister. He had to find and warn him. Perhaps these strangers would help, but could he trust them?

Dinnis tightened his lips. Korak had dismissed him as an offspring of the Monster, but he was no one's *pioni* ... Besides, the two strangers had the same strange luminous silver skin as the monster Akrad—and Ista. His own skin had followed his mother's Nolmec blue hues.

He looked at the young woman with her dark eyelashes and smooth cheeks awash with tears. Rasel looked younger than the man, perhaps in her late teens, a young woman. Like this Korak, her eyes and hair were the velvet black of midnight, though his was streaked with grey. She was tall and shapely, with a haunting beauty that inspired Dinnis ... and she had noticed him, and not just as a tool to be used. It was a long time since anyone had looked at him in the eye with warmth, as though he mattered.

Dinnis dropped the bucket, the water sloshing over the sides onto his feet.

'I'll help.' If nothing else, they might provide a distraction.

He hunched down in front of Korak and slipped his lock pick

into the keyhole of the neck shackle. Rasel shot him a wary look. The lock mechanism was like that on the doors to the storerooms and Akrad's library he practiced on when no one was watching. Within a few heart beats of probing, the lock clicked open. He moved on to the ankles and then the hands. As the last shackle released, the man swayed. Rasel wrapped her slender arms around and eased him to the floor.

'Thank you, Dinnis.' Her smile lit the room. 'Thank you, friend.'

A soft, warm feeling stirred inside him, like a small animal emerging after a storm. Her luminous eyes were like dark pools flooded with moonlight. He had never seen anyone more beautiful.

Korak coughed. 'We have to get out of the tower, Son's daughter. If I lag, you must go.'

Dinnis' neck flushed. He stood up. 'Hide behind the stairs until I call you.'

Korak searched Dinnis' face, a slight vee dipped between the man's dark eyebrows. After a moment, he nodded.

Squaring his thin shoulders, Dinnis walked towards the tower entrance and pulled open the large metal-studded door. He squinted against the sudden light. The tumult and stench of battle clamoured from the outer ward.

Hecton stood in the covered alcove outside, an embrasure, the Arkon called it. He turned towards Dinnis, his hand brushing the hilt of his sword.

'What do you want, wart?'

Dinnis dipped his head. 'The Master needs your help, *kuree*.' Akrad used him as a messenger often enough to make his claim credible.

The Nolmec sneered. 'Not up to one of your pranks, are you?'

'You know how the Master rewards tardiness, but it's your skin not mine, *kuree*.'

The soldier's thick eyebrows furrowed in his moon face.

'If you are playing a trick, the Arkon will take it out of your hide and so will I!'

Dinnis stared back, not blinking. The Monster would give him more than a whipping when he found the prisoner missing, but it was too late to worry about that. 'He is in the high tower room, *kuree*. He said to hurry.'

He flinched back as the guard shouldered past on his way into the Tower. Dinnis trailed close behind. Hecton didn't even glance at the alcove where Korak had been shackled, hurrying up the stairs to the balcony and to the spiral stairs that led to Akrad's workshop and library at the top of the tower.

When the heavy footsteps had faded. Dinnis peered into the shadows. 'It's safe. You can come out now.'

They appeared like wraiths from behind the stairs, Korak propped against the girl. Dinnis beckoned them to follow him. Beyond the embrasure, the afternoon sun hammered down on the churned-up ground, bouncing off the inner curtain wall. The loud clash of weapons and squeals of war horses, the shouts of soldiers indicated where the trapped Nolmec fought the besieging Tamrin on the other side of the gate. The soldiers on top of the wall had their backs turned as they threw missiles down at the Tamrin troops in the lower ward. The area in front of them was clear.

Dinnis lowered his voice. 'The main gate is to the left, but there is a small postern gate on the right, behind the storerooms and stables.'

'What are you doing?' A shrill voice demanded from behind him.

Ista stood in the tower doorway, skinny arms akimbo. She stared at the wounded man and his granddaughter, her grey eyes wide and accusing.

Dinnis felt his face relax, for now he'd found her. 'Ista, you have to come with us.'

'I'm telling Grandfather that you are helping the prisoner escape.'

As she spoke, the measured tramp of feet came from around the tower from the left.

She would ruin everything. He caught hold of her arm and clamped his other hand over her mouth as she opened it to scream. She struggled against his hold, but it was for her own good.

Pulling Ista into the shadows, he hissed to the others, 'Quick, get back. Guards.'

The strangers blended into the shadowed wall of the alcove with disturbing ease.

Ista kicked out, pain seared along his shins. Twisting and writhing, she clawed at his hand, but he muffled her cries. 'Be still,' he hissed, his mouth to her ear.

Heart beats later a couple of Nolmec guards raced past lugging a basket of rocks and barrel of arrows.

When the soldiers had disappeared around the other side of the tower, he eased his hand off her mouth. 'You've got to come with me, Ista. Papa is in the lower ward. He has come to rescue us.'

'Idiot boy, you're deluded. Papa's not coming, Grandfather said so.'

'He's a liar ...'

'No!' Ista stamped down hard on his foot and twisted out of his hands. She dashed through the doorway, back into the Tower.

He was torn. He didn't want to leave her behind, but he couldn't drag her kicking and screaming through the inner ward without getting them both caught. And he had to warm Papa about the poison.

'Boy, will your sister give the alarm?'

'Yes, but it will take her a long time to climb the stairs to the top of the tower. Best make your escape while you can.'

A soft flurrying sound came from behind him. Spinning around, Dinnis saw a man standing in the open archway of the embrasure. His resemblance to the other two strangers obvious.

'Semian!' Rasel's face lit up like sudden sunshine on new fallen snow.

'You have led me a fine chase this time, youngest sister. What are you doing here in the middle of our enemies?' He turned toward the older man. 'Saba, what has happened? Are you...'

'No time for stories, son of Jazadek.' Korak turned to Dinnis. 'How many others are in the tower? I've only seen the guard and the girl so far.'

'At present? Probably no more. The Arkon doesn't like people trampling over his secrets.'

The three strangers looked at each other. Rasel caught Korak's hand. 'Saba, we need to get you to mother so she can treat your injuries.'

Korak's face hardened. 'Rasel find your baba. With Semian's help, I have an opportunity to fulfil the council's directive.'

Rasel stiffened. 'I am not a child anymore, Saba.'

Dinnis fingered the lock pick. 'I have to go.' What these strangers did was no business of his. Though he wished the girl would come with him.

He flinched as a hand touched his shoulder. Rasel bent down and his pulse slowed as her eyes met his.

'Thank you for your help, Dinnis. I hope you find your father. You are brave, smart and kind.'

If only ... 'You are the only one to think so.'

There was only sincerity in her gaze. 'I know you are not bewitched by Akrad's lies. You hate his cruelty, as we do. If you would tread a different path than he, then remember this, hate leads down into darkness and, in the end, love wins over hate.'

Tears smarted his eyes. Her words unsettled him, yet resonated. But what good was the softness of love against monsters like Akrad?

With a curt nod, he turned and headed towards the postern gate with a new lightness in his steps. He would find his father, after three long years of fragile hopes.

Chapter Seven: Akrad's Folly

Rasel

Rasel sighed as the strange lad ducked and weaved in the shadows of the buildings close to the wall, not once looking back.

The Kinleader squeezed her hand. 'Rasel, go and inform the others.'

She lifted her chin. 'Saba, I am not leaving you ... if you go, I go; if you stay, I stay. You will need both Semian and my help in whatever plan you're hatching.'

Her grandfather's brow wrinkled. 'You are even more stubborn and wild than your baba.'

Semian chuckled. 'Tell me about it. But she does have a point.'

The Kinleader looked from Rasel to her brother and sighed. 'Then let's not waste time. Back into the tower before the Nolmec see us.'

He wasn't going to send her away. Some of Rasel's tension eased, though her stomach churned at the thought of facing Akrad. She took a deep breath and followed Saba and Semian into the high-ceilinged tower room.

The sound of booted feet on the stairs thundered from above them.

'Good, the Betrayer is on his way.' Grandfather clutched his side, the other hand gripping on her brother's shoulder. 'Block the outer door. We don't want his Nolmec allies interrupting us.'

Rasel turned, pulled the heavy doors shut and dropped the beam in place. She helped Semian push and shove a large table across the doorway. 'Where should we confront him, Saba?'

'Here, where there is space. He comes to us. Distract him and immobilize any Nolmec guards and the girl. I will take the Betrayer. Then we destroy the poison.'

'Poison?' Semian shook his head. 'You can barely stand, Kinleader. I should take him.'

'No, Semian, I have enough strength left for this. Follow my lead.'

Rasel bit her lip. All her grandfather's energy must be directed toward the broken tissues and organs, to staying alive. If he fought or changed form, the damage might be irreparable ...

One of the doors off the balcony banged open. Akrad burst through. The guard Hecton and the girl, Ista, followed close behind. Akrad slowed to stand against the railing, a blackthorn staff in one hand.

'What still here, Korak?' he sneered. 'And is this your rescue party? You disappoint me.'

'You will not take me captive so easily this time. I give you this one last opportunity to save yourself. If you return to your own people or live under surveillance with us, the council's judgement will be stayed.'

The Betrayer laughed. 'I fear my own people's judgment and their punishments more than yours.' He walked down the stairs, his robes swishing on the tread. 'This will be fun. The girl alone ....'

Rasel shivered at his suggestive tone. She could feel his mind, like the drenching cold of the ocean, probing at her defences, flooding her mind with images. She gathered her strength, felt Semian and Saba joining with her, deflecting the mental attack.

A liquid smile spread over Akrad's smooth features. 'Do you think I fear you? You are weak—hiding like frightened children in the forests. All words and no action, all roar without teeth and claws.'

Saba pulled away from Semian. 'You would do well to fear. I gave you the council's message, Man of the West and you ignored it. Your plans begin to unravel—Martal, Gaia, Naetok, Rokkan have slipped your grasp. Now three of your most feared enemies stand within your high tower. The time for talking is past. All that is left is to act.'

The Betrayer strode towards them, swinging his polished staff. He stopped three tanis away. Hecton halted beside him, sword held steady in front of him. Ista hovered a pace or two behind the Betrayer, her grey eyes watchful.

Rasel pushed back the cloying force of Akrad's coercive power, glad to feel Saba's strength entwined with hers.

'Ah Korak, you are so entertaining,' Akrad chuckled. Amused tears squeezed out of the corner of his eyes. 'Three of my most feared enemies — a dying man who can barely stand and two lost children, unarmed and unused to fighting? Please, you insult me.' The amusement dropped from his face. 'Naetok was a disappointment, I'll allow. But my Nolmec allies and other Tamrin nobility wait to do my bidding. Today is the day you die.'

Akrad's mouth twitched as he flicked his left wrist. A small knife spun straight towards the Kinleader's chest. Quicker than sight Saba reached out and caught the knife by its hilt. He sent it flying back.

Akrad stumbled in his hurry to avoid the blade, almost tripping over the girl, and the mental pressure faltered.

The Saba's lips pressed into a flat line. 'For such a clever man, you have a very short memory. We are normally a peaceful people, but not today.'

For the first time, fear flickered in the depths of the Betrayer's silver eyes. He licked his lips. Grabbing hold of Ista, he dragged her in front of him like a shield. 'Give yourselves up, or I'll hurt the child.'

The girl's eyes widened her fine brows veered down into a scowl, but she did not struggle. On the other side of Akrad, Hecton lowered his sword, uncertainty flashing across his face.

Rasel's pulse raced as the mental pressure strengthened, more insinuating and subtle. How could they allow harm to a youngling?

The Kinleader did not flinch. 'Isn't Gaia's daughter far more important to your grandiose plans than she is to us?'

Akrad snarled and shoved the child away. Rasel let out a slow breath. Praise the Maker, the child was at a safe distance. The Betrayer had bought the Saba's bluff.

Saba gave the hand signal. Semian leapt, stretching and morphing into eagle form. He flew at Hecton, evading his blade and driving the Nolmec guard backwards.

Rasel's muscles tingled as her body changed in unison with her brother. She flew at Akrad, drawing his attention and the swing of his staff. The blast of his mind hit her like a gale and her grip on the eagle form wavered. She pushed back, diving at Betrayer's face and shielding herself against his mind's force.

Semian swooped in from the other side, sharp beak raking the man's face and grappling the blackthorn staff with his curved talons.

With a deep shudder, Saba stretched out into jaguar form. He leapt, his blade-sharp claws unsheathed, his mouth open in a deep, bone-shaking roar.

Akrad had no defence against his weight and power. The Betrayer fell backwards with a dismayed shriek. He hit the floor with the crack of crushed bone, dead and silenced forever.

Rasel fluttered to the ground, the tower-room filled with smell of bloody death and Ista's terrified screams.

Chapter Eight: The Battlefield

Dinnis

Dinnis walked at a normal pace but kept to the shadows as much as he could without looking suspicious. He skirted the stables, the clamour of battle raging between the walls of the stronghold swelling in volume. Once he reached the corner of the storeroom, he crouched down behind a stack of crates.

Two Nolmec guarded the postern gate. His stomach tightened. This wasn't going to be easy.

Taking a deep, steadying breath, he sauntered towards the guards, halting a couple of tanis in front of them.

'What do you want?' The female with a scarred face barked, though she wasn't the worst of the guards.

'Keloumen Nikoris requires your help in unloading some vital supplies, *kura*.' He kept his head down and his eyes on his scuffed sandals. 'At the stables, *kura*,' he added.

'Are you serious, boy?' The other Nolmec soldier with the receding hairline spat on the ground. 'And leave the gate unguarded?'

'I only convey the orders, *kuree*. It's locked, isn't it? The Arkon alone has the key. What could happen in a few minutes?'

They scowled at him before looking at each other.

'Should I tell the Keloumen that you doubt his commands?' Dinnis turned to go.

The woman grabbed him by the shoulder. 'Don't be so hasty, boy.'

The other guard scratched his blunt nose. 'Maybe one of us should check?'

Dinnis smothered a smile. They might buy his story.

'The Keloumen requires two soldiers. It's urgent ... something about the Arkon's secret weapon to annihilate the Tamrin army. But if you don't believe me ...'

'No, no, we're going. Stay here and watch the gate. If we find out this is one of your tricks...' The bald guard clipped his ear. 'You will rue the day you were born, you ugly wart.'

Dinnis waited until their scarlet cloaks disappeared around the corner of the storeroom. He rubbed his stinging ear and glanced around. No one was watching. Hunkering down, he pulled out the pick from his frayed tunic and probed the lock. Like the shackles and unlike the chests and doors in Akrad's upper rooms, it was a simple one; a soft clunk, a twist of the metal ring, a shove and the thick door swung in an arc through the uncut grass. Running his hands down the side of his tunic, he slipped through the gap and flattened himself against the side of portico on the other side.

From every direction sounds, smells and movement assaulted his senses. A large rock thudded close beside him. Screams, war cries and the squeals of horses came from all sides. The clash of sword and spears against shields filled the air. Dinnis gagged at the riot of odours; dust, spilt blood, sweat and excreta.

Breathe. He just had to breathe. Gradually the tension subsided and a semblance of order emerged from the chaotic scene in front of him.

The steep grassed slope led down to the long oblong of the lower ward. To the left, bloodied and dishevelled Nolmec soldiers clustered together in front of the closed inner gate. Their interlocked rectangular shields forming a metal wall, and they slashed their swords at spear-wielding Tamrin warriors. Behind the front line, Tamrin archers released a flock of arrows at the ramparts while flaming arrows, huge rocks and streams of steaming liquid rained down on any of the stranded Nolmec and the Tamrin attackers standing too close to the inner wall. The Tamrin army had tripled in numbers, filling the outer ward. Broken bodies, mostly Nolmec, lay strewn across the fouled ground.

His stomach churned. Crossing the battlefield in search of his father would be risky, but he couldn't stay here. The Nolmec guards would soon return.

A bright splash of colour caught his eye about midfield. A green and orange banner with a fierce jaguar emblem rippled in the steady wind over a tightly clustered group of mounted Tamrin warriors. A tall, broad shouldered man on a grey dappled stallion rode at their front. They pivoted and lined up as though preparing to charge a faltering group of Nolmec. Dinnis' face split into a grin. The leader's profile was familiar. It had to be Papa. He would tell him about the postern gate and the poison.

Dinnis sprung forward and slid down the steep grassed slope on his bottom. A missile hissed past his ear, bouncing off the stone of the portico with a dull clunk. Another embedded in the mud a pace to the right, the shaft quivering in the grass. Arrows! His hands tingled. He slid faster almost colliding into a broad-chested bronzed Tamrin warrior with startling green eyes. The warrior blinked at him, then hefted his massive spiked club as though uncertain whether to strike or not.

Dinnis dodged and weaved around him, yelling, 'The gate to the inner ward is unlocked.' He waved his arm toward the top of the slope.

The Tamrin stared at him then followed his arm. The man's eyes popped open, a fierce grin spread across his battle-grimed face.

He grabbed the shoulder of a young warrior nearby. 'Kulan, run to the Kapok. Tell him, 'The postern gate is open. Lutan Jakan is taking a unit to secure it. Reinforcements would be welcome. Quick man.' He turned to face the cluster of warriors following him and bellowed. 'To me, warriors, follow me.'

In short order twenty or so men had formed into a compact group. With their shields covering the front line, the sides and forming a makeshift roof over their heads, they rushed up the slope towards the covered door.

Dinnis turned away, not waiting to see if the charge was successful. He headed towards midfield, where he'd last seen Papa. The Tamrin seemed uncertain what to make of an unarmed part-Nolmec boy wandering through their lines. Some raised weapons against him, but he had become used to dodging blows in the last three years of living with the Arkon. The trickiest part was avoiding the bodies underfoot, most of them Nolmec, many of them deathly still with horrific wounds, some groaning.

Horses' hooves and the warriors' boots stirred up dust in thick swirling eddies. Clouds of flies settled on the motionless figures sprawled in the dirt. Above the filth and stench, in the cloud wreathed sky, a condor and other carrion birds circled like black spots before Dinnis' eyes. His skin crawled at the thought of their strong beaks ripping through flesh and organs beneath blue and tan skinned bodies. Nausea pushed up into his throat, sour and bitter. He clamped his teeth shut and stumbled forward.

He had to warn his father.

Looming out of the mass of warriors, a grey stallion reared up in front of him. Kulan, the soldier sent as messenger to the Kapok, jogged beside the great horse. The rider's gold-plated helmet was capped with burnt-orange and gold feathers that matched his intense golden eyes. Rust coloured blood seeped and clotted about a gash on his broad shoulder and another on his cheek and a great orange cloak swirled behind him.

Dinnis faltered. The elaborate headdress and gold embossed chest plate confused him. Dinnis remembered Papa as an ordinary man, a simple soldier perhaps, but not a resplendent commander. The warrior had his father's look and build, though somehow harder, more forbidding. The man looked right through him. There was no flicker of recognition or acknowledgement. Had he been mistaken?

The rider pushed himself up against the great horns at the front of the saddle and called in a large booming voice, 'To me, to Rokkan Kapok, to the postern gate in the west wall. To me, warriors!'

Rokkan. It had to be him. Then in a flurry of horse hooves and the swish of a long tail, he had passed, and the next rider was abreast.

That rider stared at Dinnis with coffee-brown eyes, the eyebrows pulled together at the top of his strong nose. He lifted his arm, the muscles bulging, and hurled his spear. Dinnis threw himself to the side, rolled, then jumped to his feet. The weapon whistled past him and embedded into the ground a hand's breadth away. As more Tamrin horsemen cantered past, he turned and saw the Kapok's orange cloak receding in the distance.

Putting his hands to his mouth, Dinnis called out 'Papa, Papa, beware Akrad's deadly poison in the high tower.'

The Tamrin Kapok didn't look back. The band galloped towards the postern gate. He ran after them and tripped, jarring his chin and grazing his shins on an abandoned shield.

He lay sprawled out in the blood-slicked dirt and muck, surrounded by corpses and the wounded. Hot tears pricked and stung. Perhaps, Papa hadn't heard him, hadn't seen him. Dinnis screwed up his eyes and clenched his fists.

This was the day that he had clung to through all the dark nights and darker days. This was the day when his father had come to rescue him.

He clung to the memories of his father's laughing smile, his strong shoulders, and the big hands that could toss his children high in the air and catch them again as though they were light as feathers. Dinnis remembered the pleasure of snuggling into Papa's strong body as he taught him to read or to play Conquest or told wonderful tales of magical places and stories about his beautiful mother who had died giving birth to his sister. He remembered the sadness of the frequent partings and the sudden joy when his father rode up the hill, sometimes alone, sometimes with a friend, but always with laughter, presents and promises to stay a little longer. Papa had a duty to fight. When the battle was over he would come for him and Ista, and then things would be all right again.

The thrum of strong wings soared past him. Heart pounding, he sat up. A white crested eagle wheeled and glided above the battle field. It turned and swooped by him again, the forest-dark eyes staring straight at him. It climbed high into the cobalt sky where two other eagles soared on the wind, one bloodied and listing. With a dip of the wings, as if in salute, and a long whistling call, the three eagles looped round then soared northwards past the Tower.

His eyes widened. Thick greenish smoke roiled out of the top room of Akrad's high tower. He grinned. The monster's workshop was on fire. He couldn't be sure but it was as though there were five more white crested eagles rising beyond the farthest wall to greet them.

Chapter Nine: Taken

Ista

Ista lay huddled on the floor where Grandfather had thrown her. She squeezed her eyes shut against the horror creeping up inside her and screamed. Not a frightened squeak at the sight of a snake or the scream of rage when someone displeased her. The sound came from a deep pit within her, a long drawn out wail that rolled through her like the roaring of the wind until she was the scream fraying into the shadows and breaking up against the hard stone walls of the Tower.

She wanted to stop, but she couldn't. She wanted to banish the sight of the stranger attacking, his red mouth open and gaping, his teeth big and sharp, but she couldn't. She wanted to block out the threatening cough, the sickening wet crunch, the flurry of wings pressing down on her, but she couldn't.

If only she could wake up and find herself in her bed in the tower room knowing it had to be an illusion. Dinnis would console her, and Grandfather would scold her for being so silly. Her fingers clawed into the hard floor. The unyielding cold of stone seeped through her tunic, stiffening her flesh.

'Kiprissa, are you hurt?'

Large but gentle hands took hold of her shoulders. She lashed out scratching and kicking, her training eluding her. 'Don't touch me, don't touch me.'

She clamped her hand over her mouth and swallowed the scream welling up from the pit in her stomach. The hands gripped tighter, pulling her up. 'Forgive me, my Kiprissa, but I need to get you to safety while I can.'

The hoarse voice was strained but familiar. One of Grandfather's guards. Hecton. She prised her eyes open. His round blue face floated a ninas from hers. His blunt nose almost touching, his dark, oblique eyes creased in concern. Long shallow scratches racked across his cheek and forehead, a large, livid bruise purpled his temple. But he was alive. So, her grandfather must be also, and it was all the dream …

She swivelled her head, searching the room for the Arkon's face. Dust motes trembled in the shafts of sunlight spearing down from the high windows. Tables were overturned, books and parchments scattered on the floor among smashed glass and scattered tools. Pungent odours of bruised herbs and things far less pleasant hung like a miasma in the room.

She shuddered as Hecton pulled her to her feet. 'Where's the Arkon. We can't go without him.'

His face went blank as if a shutter had been banged shut. She could sense his unease beneath the mask, the chaos of his emotions. He was hiding something from her.

'Come on.' He hustled her along the trestles toward the door. She resisted, her feet dragging on the ground. His body hunched around her as though blocking her view.

She squirmed and looked back. There was something, a long low bundle lying on the floor, a body. Someone had placed a cloak over it, a dark red pool spreading out and tracking between the stones. At one end, red hair, matted and darkened poked out, the blackthorn staff laid beside him. A tremor raced through her, racking her body.

She pulled away. 'No, no. Grandfather.' She scrabbled at Hecton's arms, trying to stop him. 'You have to help him.'

Hecton's grip tightened on her arm. 'There's nothing we can do, Kiprissa. The Arkon is dead, his magical arts can't help him now. The cursed Adelphi have killed him.'

She pummelled his muscular chest. 'You were supposed to die for him, to protect him.'

The Nolmec guard's shoulders slumped. 'I have failed you, my Kiprissa.'

'You will be punished for this.'

'As you wish, my Kiprissa. I am dishonoured, but first let me take you to safety to your uncle Timon and General Nikoris in the north. We must leave before the Tamrin overwhelm the stronghold.'

When he swept her up in his strong arms, she went rigid but did not fight back. He was right. She must escape to make her revenge.

Hecton stumbled outside and ran toward the stables. Ista squinted against the strong sunlight. Hooves drummed an angry rhythm close by. In an instant, large horses encircled them, their nostrils flared and teeth bared as they squealed and snorted. She pulled back, eyes wide at the circle of spears pointing at them.

'Halt, in the name of the Kapok.'

Hecton faltered. He crushed her tighter against the bronze breastplate with one hand and pulled his sword free with the other. He spun around in a slow circle.

Hecton's lips pulled back into a snarl. 'I'll defend my Kiprissa, and I'll take as many of you with me as I can.'

'Commendable, Pioni Hecton, but not very practical,' a deep voice drawled, casual and amused. The tone hardened. 'Where is Arkon Akrad—hiding in his Tower while men spill their blood and guts for him?'

Rage seared through her. How dare he mock her grandfather? The barbarian would regret it when ... but Grandfather was dead.

Ista tipped back her head and glared at the warrior on the dark grey horse with the orange and gold headdress. 'Your demon allies killed him.'

His head tilted, surprise mantling across his strong face. 'Dead?'

'Could be a trick, Rokkan.' The scowling warrior beside him leant forward on his horse. 'To get us off guard.'

Rokkan. She stiffened. Then this was the Kapok, the Tamrin ruler.

'Maybe, Lukarn.' He glanced up at the Tower and moistened his cracked lips. 'Yet, I don't feel his presence.'

Hecton shifted, his sword steady in front of them. Her eyes slid from the Tamrin's commanding face to the sharp bronze spear heads pointed at her. Beyond the circle of horses, Nolmec soldiers rushed towards them, some jumping from the walls in their haste to protect her. But they were intercepted by the Tamrin pouring into through the side gate. Everything was unravelling, like a tapestry with a pulled thread or an errant ball of wool.

The Kapok turned in his saddle and yelled, 'Jakan, get the inner gate open. Kulan, take five men and search the Tower for Akrad.

If you find him, keep your distance. Don't speak to him. Signal us at once that you've found him.'

The Tamrin rushed to follow the orders.

Hecton wobbled and straightened himself. The lump on his head had grown. His thick lips brushed her ears. 'My Kiprissa, when I charge the warrior on the red horse—no, don't look—you must run past to the Palouma Akillis near the stables. He'll get you to safety.'

She gulped at the restless legs of the steeds with their sharp hooves. 'The spears ...' He'd be impaled but ... She squared her narrow shoulders. She was a Kiprissa of the Nolmec, a daughter of the Dawn Sun. She would match her loyal soldier's courage. She squeezed his arm, acknowledging she'd heard him.

Hecton's muscles tensed beneath her. He dropped her to the ground and threw himself at the young warrior on the red horse, as if to impale himself. She hitched her tunic, ready to run between the horse's legs.

All at once, the Kapok's horse was between them. He leant forward and smashed the hilt of a wicked knife into the back of Hecton's shoulders. Hecton sprawled out into the mud, groaning. Hemmed in, there was nowhere for her to run.

Rokkan looked straight at her. 'Too many good men have died today, Kiprissa Ista. Order your soldiers to stand down.'

The horses neighed and shied as a muffled whoomph came from above. A shivering tinkle as shattered glass rained down from the windows in the highest room, Grandfather's workshop. Thick, acrid smoke roiled out.

'What sorcery is this? Is it Akrad's doing?' Lukarn shortened the reins as his spooked horse sidestepped.

The greenish wisps of smoke congealed and thickened. Ista's eyes stung from the foul stench like rotten eggs and metal that enveloped her. Grandfather's new weapon, but it wasn't meant to be deployed like this.

Kulan burst out of the Tower. 'Akrad is dead, his skull crushed. The top room is on fire.'

Rokkan gripped the back of Ista's tunic and lifted her into the air as though she was her rag doll, Armina. She screamed and struggled. He plonked her down between him and the neck of his horse. A faint whiff of chilli and stronger scent of leather and acrid sweat enclosed her. She felt cocooned, safe, but he was the enemy.

She couldn't, shouldn't trust him.

He called out in fluent Nolmec, 'Soldiers of Nolmec. The Arkon is dead. I claim custody of the Kiprissa. I am now your Arkon. Stand down.'

She twisted around, hissing at him. 'You aren't Nolmec, you don't have the right. They won't listen to you.' Her soldiers would fight to the death to save her.

All around the upper ward, the sounds of conflict stilled. Wind whistled around the tower, gusting cloying green smoke into their eyes, burning her throat.

The tall figure of Keloumen Nikoris emerged from the gate house and strode towards them. He ignored the Tamrin warriors, his face impassive. He came to a standstill a couple of tanis away. 'Do you swear to protect her by your gods, on your honour? If so, then we will concede.'

She strained forward. 'No, no you cannot yield.'

Lukarn growled, 'Rokkan, Your Majesty, you can't ...'

Rokkan sat straighter. 'By the Maker and the honour of my house, I give my word. I will.'

Nikoris dropped to his knees and held out his sword to the Kapok. 'Then we yield, Suguzos. May the gods feed on your entrails if you break your promise.'

Weapons clattered to the ground as the Nolmec soldiers knelt in the mud. The blood-grimed Tamrin warriors in inner courtyard erupted in wild cheers.

Why had her soldiers given up so easily? Angry tears burned her eyes.

She was lost—a captive, an orphan at the Tamrin warrior's mercy, taken and bereaved.

Chapter Ten: Warriors and Healers

Dinnis

Dinnis wasn't sure how long he sat in the middle of the battlefield. Hours, perhaps. The sounds of fierce fighting hammered his ears, the Nolmec in the lower ward fighting to the bitter end. Surrender would bring disgrace and ostracism worse than death. Afternoon shadows stretched across the churned-up ground, the warmth falling out of the thin mountain air.

He rolled over, sat up and gripped his knees with shaking hands. The lower ward emptied as Tamrin soldiers streamed through the postern gate and then, when opened, through the main gate. The clash and noise of battle subsided into the weak calls of the wounded. Next to him, a Nolmec soldier moaned '*Hidros, hidros*' on and on. Dinnis' legs jumped with tension. He had to move, to do something. Dinnis scrambled up, took a water bottle from one of the dead, poured half of its contents down his own raw, dusty throat then lifted the head of the Nolmec and helped him drink.

'*Karista*, thank you,' the man murmured. Only yesterday he might have cuffed Dinnis around the ears with curses and insults. Now he was too injured to move.

Dinnis left the water bottle within the soldier's reach, then picked his way through the grisly aftermath of battle. Flies buzzed about him and, in the distance, carrion birds squabbled. A healing tent was pitched between a small stand of fruit trees by the eastern walls and the front gate. Now the battle was over, he should find his father—before nightfall if possible—and that seemed as good a place to ask as anywhere. Would Papa be angry because Ista wasn't with him? Is that why he rode past him? Dinnis glanced again at the garish smoke, dark wisping from the collapsed tower roof. Was she alright?

A Tamrin soldier dragged himself along the ground in front of Dinnis, his bloodied hand gripping a seeping wound to his side.

Dinnis hesitated, then placed his hand on the man's shoulder. 'Can I help you, *kuree* … I mean sir?'

The man frowned up at him, his bronzed face pale and drawn. He jerked his head in what appeared to be a nod. Tearing a strip of long cloth from the man's tunic, Dinnis bound the injury before helping the Tamrin up.

A light breeze freshened, edged with the chill of snow topped mountains surrounding them.

As they shuffled along he remembered the words of the girl. 'You are brave, smart, and kind.' Was he really any of those things? He felt the desire to be so for her … and for his father.

'What's your name, boy?' the gruff voice of the Tamrin warrior interrupted his thoughts.

He bit his upper lip then shrugged. 'Dinnis.'

The man's face darkened. 'That sounds like a Nolmec name.'

'I am Tamrin. My father is a brave Tamrin warrior like you.' Was he also the Tamrin commander? The Kapok? 'May I ask your name, sir?'

The man was silent for a few heart beats, his hands gripping Dinnis arm. 'My name is Sachan, young Tamrin warrior.'

'I am not a warrior, sir. But maybe one day I will be a healer.' Better to bring life than the carnage that surrounded him.

Sachan nodded. 'Today I can see the value of a good healer.' His spluttered laugh fizzled into a raw cough.

Dinnis tightened his grip of the Tamrin's shoulders. Together they lurched towards the healing tent. A flustered young man steered Sachan towards the area where the wounded sat or sprawled waiting to be seen.

As Dinnis turned to leave, the young medic caught his arm.

'Thank you, lad. You help is welcome. Why don't you sit down and rest for a bit? There is a bucket of water over there if you wish to wash.' The man's voice was kind.

Dinnis realized that he was filthy. Dust, grime and gore caked his skin and clothes. He stank. He pulled his tunic over his head and sluiced himself down with the water, rubbing his face to rid it of the worst of the filth. Cuts and grazes pocked his skin, but he had survived.

The wind dried the water, sending ripples of chill bumps over him. He stood up and rubbed his upper arms with the inside of his tunic.

Soon it would be evening. Argenti, almost full circle, rose above the jagged mountain peaks in the east. Alumi, the bigger of the two moons, was a mere crescent in the western sky blushed with pink and gold. Further down, the molten orb of the sun sank towards the distant horizon.

The tension eased out of his neck and shoulders. It was going to be alright. He should ask about Papa.

A rough hand twisted his ear. 'What's this Nolmec dog doing here?'

Dinnis twisted round and looked into the snarling face of an older Tamrin surgeon.

The young medic ran up, his eyes rounded. 'But he's not ....' his voice trailed away.

'Are you blind, Fulik? Can't you see he is a blue-skin?'

'He brought one of our wounded soldiers in, sir. He's only a boy.'

'What of it? Guards! A Nolmec prisoner.'

'But my father is Tamrin,' Dinnis said, his heart fluttering.

They ignored his words.

Soldiers ran to bind his hands behind him and tied him to a stake.

'You don't understand, my father is the com—'

'Be quiet, or will I have to gag you too?'

It was a miserable night. Cold, cramped, hungry, the cries of the wounded disturbed Dinnis' fitful sleep. Smoke and the red glow of bonfires lit up the upper ward where bulk of the army camped the night. It didn't matter. Papa would find him.

Chapter Eleven: Word of Honour

Ista

Ista clung to the horses' neck, her eyes fixed on the charcoal mane in front of her. The ground seemed a long way down. The smell of horse and the coarse mane tickled her nose. She swayed and slid sideways as the horse quickened its gait. The Kapok caught her and she pushed back against his strong body. She should hate him, yet somehow, she felt safe.

A Tamrin led Nikoris and Hecton away, their hands bound with thick cord. All around her, the Tamrin hustled Nolmec soldiers into the yarma pens. Many were wounded, others sprawled on the ground, their eyes staring up at the sky.

Shuddering, she squeezed her eyes shut. She didn't understand. How had this man Rokkan Kapok, a mere Tamrin, persuaded her soldiers to give up, to let him keep her as a hostage? Once again, her world had tilted and changed. Her memories were vague of the night that Grandfather came to Pylonis and taken them to this stronghold at North Pass. She had been five and shaking with fear while Dinnis was defiant, but General Nuktis had reassured them that the Arkon would care for them, as he had once cared for their mother, Gaia.

And he had, hadn't he? If one didn't disobey the rules and was careful not to annoy him, Grandfather was pleasant. He called her the special one, said that she was chosen for greatness——unlike her clumsy, idiot brother who fumbled the simplest of the arcane skills. But she had excelled.

'You are a natural, my sweet,' her grandfather had murmured.

Ista's heart had thrilled at his praise and he rarely punished her. When she did incite his anger, Dinnis' clumsiness would attract Grandfather's ire. She pushed away the memory of the Arkon's eyes blazing with icy fire, the soft venom in his voice, of Dinnis' suppressed whimpers as flesh sizzled or split and bled. Better to please Grandfather, keep him happy, impress him. Dinnis knew Grandfather had a terrible temper, he was stupid to provoke it. Besides, he was deluded, he said Papa would come for them but he hadn't.

Unease stirred in her chest. Had Dinnis gone with that trio of murdering Adelphi? Maybe she'd never see him again. She wouldn't miss his stubbornness. Yet, she felt a hollowness spreading inside. And Grandfather was dead.

The Kapok rode about the upper and lower wards, inspecting the damage and the battle-weary armies, giving orders and encouraging his warriors. It was as if he'd forgotten she was there. Silent tears rolled down her cheeks and her eyes grew heavy with the rocking of the horse's gait.

* * *

Ista jerked awake. Stars sprinkled across the dark sky like grains of rice. Her stomach rumbled. Still she rocked, but she no longer smelt horse. Strong arms carried her. She peeked up through her eyelashes. The profile of the Tamrin Kapok jutted out above her. Looking sideways, she could just make out the curving walls and the dark branches of a sichar tree in the upper ward, before he ducked his head under the billowing entry of a large pavilion.

A tremor ran through her. What did he plan to do to her, an enemy captive? Would she be beaten, tortured, maybe even killed? She would have to escape, find General Nuktis if she could. If only she wasn't so young and untrained, she could use her coercive powers against such simple folk as the Tamrin.

She reached out with her thoughts, as Grandfather had taught, feeling for the texture of the Kapok's emotions, the pattern of his mind—and smashed into a blank wall that sent her thoughts reeling and snapping back into her own head. The strong, muscular arms holding her tightened for a heartbeat, before relaxing again.

She stilled her breath. Had he felt her probe? She wasn't as strong as Grandfather but only he and Dinnis had been able to resist her probing before. She shrunk inside herself waiting for his angry response.

He set her down in the corner of the billowing tent and tucked a woven blanket of yarma wool around her as though nothing had happened.

'You must be thirsty.' His voice was gentle.

He pulled a half empty water bottle off his belt and gave it to her. Aware of the dryness of her throat, she gulped down cool liquid, spilling some in her haste. The Kapok walked to the table and grabbed a hunk of maize bread. Tearing it in half, he swallowed a piece and gave rest to her. Her hands trembled as she gnawed at it, hardly noticing its staleness. His face was cloaked by the darkness inside the tent.

'You should try to sleep, *chia.*'

The sides of the pavilion thrummed in a wind that carried the subdued rustlings of people settling down to sleep, a whinny of the horse and somewhere the mournful hooting of an owl. Despite the fear of seeing her grandfather's murder in her dreams, she drifted into a half-doze.

A burly figure barged into the tent. 'She's with you? It would be safer to confine her in one of the cellars with Nuktis and the senior Nolmec, Rokkan.'

The man spoke in Filane, the language of the Tamrin. If she focused, she could follow his words. Grandfather had made sure she had learnt it alongside Nolmec and Ancient.

The Kapok chuckled. 'Not afraid of a seven-year-old, are you, Lukarn?'

'You know better than anyone, the Nolmec would die for their Kiprissa.'

'Exactly. The Nolmec recognised my claim and surrendered without further loss of lives. I gave my word I'd not harm her.'

Rokkan moved to one side. Striking a firestone, he lit an oil lamp. The flame leapt and shrunk, like a whirling warrior, casting black shadows over the two men's faces.

The other man growled like a wounded mountain bear. 'Would have been better to continue to fight than accept such terms. The northern clans will never accept—.'

'I know, Lukarn.' Rokkan's voice had congealed to ice. 'Don't worry, I'll keep my promise to you and Marra.'

'So, send her far away.'

Ista curled into a ball, any safe, fuzzy feelings scattering like frightened field mice.

Rokkan stood up and faced the man. 'Nuktis won't retaliate while she's my ward.'

'And the boy? You saw him too. Don't deny it.' Lukarn fingered the knife hilt on his broad belt. Ista shivered at the cold intent in the man's voice.

Rokkan threw up his hands. 'By the Maker, Lukku, he's only eleven.' He crossed his arms across his broad chest. 'I promised Gaia ...'

'He's Nolmec and Akrad's had three years to twist them both, like he twisted your brother. You shouldn't allow sentimentality to cloud your decisions. He's a threat. For the sake of the realm, for the sake of peace, you must—

'—must what?' Rokkan's face contorted. 'Don't worry, I will protect your nephew's interests because they align with the interests of the realm.'

Lukarn stared at Rokkan beneath furrowed brows. 'If you— '

'That's enough, Lukarn. Don't push me too far.'

The angry man opened his mouth then shut it with a click. 'As you wish, Your Majesty.' He bowed in an exaggerated way. 'I only hope history doesn't repeat. I will check that your guard is sufficient and that you are, at least, safe from threats outside the pavilion.'

Her hands shook and she tucked her hands under her armpits, relieved when the man shouldered his way out of the tent. The Kapok loomed over her again.

'You heard all that. Don't worry, I'll look after you. Now, get some sleep, *chia*. We have a long journey in the morning.'

He'd switched to flawless Nolmec, with less accent than Grandfather's. He reached out a hand.

She flinched back. 'Don't touch me.'

One flyaway eyebrow twitched up. 'You don't know me, do you?'

She glared at him. 'Yes, I do. You're Rokkan Kapok. Grandfather said I should never trust you.'

He rocked back on his heels and rubbed his hawk-like nose. 'Did he now? And you trust the Arkon?' Before she could answer, he continued. 'I'm tired. I'll be sleeping over there.' He pointed with his chin to the corner of the large tent, where a camp bed was covered in rugs and sleeping furs.

'Aren't you worried I'd sneak up on you and kill you?'

His strong teeth flashed in his golden-brown face. 'No, *chia*, I'm a light sleeper. And in case you're thinking of sneaking out of the tent in the middle of the night, I can assure you, Lukarn will have this tent surrounded with guards in a ring tighter than the string on a Limarian merchant's purse. Now, go to sleep.'

She pulled the sleeping rug up to her chin and stared at the embroidered roof of the pavilion while he settled. His amber eyes had pierced right through her. It was as if he could read her thoughts. She stared at half-seen patterns of jaguars, eagles and koraktils, thoughts and plans teeming through her head. She was young now, but one day she would be as powerful as the Arkon —and then she'd have her revenge.

Chapter Twelve: Loose Ends

Dinnis

At last, the eastern horizon blushed with a gilded red and the army began to stir. Ablutions were made, fires were lit. The mouth-watering aroma of hot bean stew drifted from the cook fires and sleepy soldiers and medics gathered for a simple morning meal.

One of the guards came up with a bowl of beans. He untied Dinnis' hands and shoved the half-filled dish at him. The feeling returned to his hands in a sudden agonising rush. Ignoring the pain and suddenly ravenous, he shovelled the food into his mouth. He hadn't eaten since early yesterday morning.

'Look at the animal eat,' said one of the soldiers in a group by the fire a couple of tanis away.

'Well, what you can expect from a Nolmec?' another said, spitting into the fire.

Heat spread over Dinnis' cheeks. He sat back and slowed his eating.

'If you ask me, it's a waste of food anyway. We should slit the bluey's throat like they do with their prisoners.'

'Prisoners are not to be harmed! Kapok's orders.' Dinnis recognised the younger medic, Fulik's voice. 'Besides he is only a boy and, if I'm not mistaken, he has Tamrin blood in him.'

'Ya think his da would want to admit a bluey for a son? He'd probably pay us to slit the brat's throat.' The men laughed raucously.

Unable to swallow past the tight lump in his throat, Dinnis put the bowl down half eaten. He wrapped his arms around his legs and tried to stop the shivers that racked his thin body. Could his father would be ashamed of him? Is that why he had chosen to ride past him in the battle field yesterday? If it was his Papa.

He closed his eyes and tried to shut out the cruel comments bandied about by the group at the fire. The golden light of dawn swelled around him, gilding the grisly battlefield and tall stone walls of the stronghold, but his hopes darkened and curled into doubt and despair. Had he escaped one nightmare only to find himself lost in another? He barely noticed as the guard roughly retied him to the stake. He squeezed his eyes shut, trying to find oblivion in the forgetfulness of sleep.

A whinny startled Dinnis awake. A horse stomped its hooves from behind him. He stretched as far as the bounds would allow him, his limbs stiff with cold. His breath smoked the cold morning air. It was still icy in the shadow of the wall though the sun was well up in the eastern sky, washing out Alumi's thin crescent. He blew on his numb fingers to warm them.

Tamrin soldiers were already at work burying the dead and clearing the remaining debris on the battlefield. Camp followers, women and children who followed their loved ones in the army, streamed through the gate and moved about looking for their dead and wounded. Some wailed in despair, others expressed joy and relief. Medics continued to work to save or mend the wounded. The Nolmec prisoners, most nursing wounds, sat or sprawled in the yarma pens not too far away.

Dinnis had never really thought of himself as Nolmec despite his blue skin and Nolmec mother. Unlike his sister, the little Kiprissa, they hadn't accepted him as one of their own. Now he was likely to share their fate at the victorious Tamrin, most likely one that was sticky and brief.

A bridle jingle behind him, closer this time. He twisted around, shuffling his legs and straining against the ropes. Several tanis away, past some barrels, Rokkan Kapok sat on his grey charger with another mounted man beside him, the spear thrower, Lukarn. Both men had their backs to him, their colourful cloaks lifting in the chill breeze. The older medic was bowing before the Tamrin ruler.

His heart accelerated. Would they notice him? Did he want them to?

'Your Majesty, this is a great honour ...'

'Yes, yes, Master Surgeon Kimsak.' The Kapok made a dismissive motion with his hand. 'What casualties did we suffer in battle yesterday?'

'Twenty-one fatalities, Your Majesty, and ninety-five wounded, perhaps thirty of these seriously so. The damage was much more substantial among the Nolmec.'

'They are brave and determined fighters. A worthy foe. we have fared much better than I expected.'

The medic's brow creased, 'Cruel and ruthless. I've heard they feast on bab—'

'You shouldn't believe everything you hear,' the Kapok's voice was clipped. His stallion moved sideways and snorted. The Kapok bent down to soothe him. 'Peace, Plume. The Maker was smiling on us over last two days. First we catch Commander Nikoris unprepared—.'

'Your strategy worked well, Your Majesty,' the burly spear thrower said. 'How the postern gate was left open is a mystery.'

'Indeed, Lukarn. And even more a mystery to find Akrad dead in his own tower, his skull crushed. Not another mark on him. Some strange forces are at work here, yet at least for once they are working in our favour.'

Dinnis hunkered down. So, the monster was dead. That at least was good news. Had Rasel and her grandfather killed him? He strained against the ropes. Surely, they wouldn't have harmed Ista also?

Kimsak moved forward, an eager look on his fleshy face. 'Some say that Adelphi—.'

Lukarn hooted, his chestnut stallion arching its neck and shying at the sudden loud noise. 'Yarma droppings, surgeon. You don't believe the tales your nurse told you as a wee child. Evil shapeshifters lurking in every shadow, ready to swallow up bad children and spit out their bones. I thought you were an intelligent man.'

Rokkan rubbed his shoulder where old blood stained his tunic. 'Well, whoever our benefactor is, I'm thankful we didn't have to sit out another siege.'

'Begging your pardon, but perhaps Your Majesty should get your own wounds attended to,' Kimsak said.

'Mere flesh wounds. I'll come by the tent or send for a medic to come to mine later today when everything is in order. Thank you Kimsak. Don't let me detain you any further.'

The surgeon bowed and hurried past Dinnis to the main treatment area. The mounted men stayed where they were looking towards the main gate.

Lukarn looked down at the reins looped about his hands, his gravelly voice casual. 'Even flesh wounds can go bad, my Lord Kapok.'

Rokkan snorted. 'Sometimes I think you are a bigger worrier than your sister. The way she coddles that son of hers, it's a wonder Mannok is not as soft as yarma cheese.'

'Ah, well, mother love is a wonderful thing. I would say he will be a better man—and prince—for it. You should be proud of your son. He—' The Markan stopped as a long, high horn in three long blasts sounded from outside the main gate.

Dinnis closed his eyes, a feeling like a landslide crushing his chest. This man couldn't be his father. He was married, had another son, was a man of substance. How could he have got it so wrong.

'It appears my dear cousin favours us with his august presence,' the Kapok said. 'Good to know my scouts are up to the mark.'

'I wonder what his excuse will be this time. Do you think he comes as friend or foe?'

'That will probably depend on how he strong he thinks our position. I wish he would make a move and get it over with.'

Lukarn grunted. 'His troops are fresher, ours have more battle experience, though only because he commits his troops to the fray after the battle is won. It's a good thing Akillis sent you word—'

'Hush … here he comes.'

The gates swung open and a contingent of Tamrin warriors poured into the lower ward. At the head of the group was a tall man with light silver eyes and flowing auburn hair topped by a gold and aquamarine feather headdress. Markan Haka. He'd been a frequent visitor to the Tower in the days leading up to the war, as had Naetok and a handful of other Tamrin.

The man hauled his bay war horse to a stop, his gaze swept over the lower ward and up the slope to the inner wall. Sitting a little taller, he urged his mount into a trot, stopping again within a pace of the Kapok. He gave the Tamrin ruler a sweeping bow and a wide smile that did not reach his icy eyes.

'Your Majesty, I see you have gained the outer ward.'

The Kapok inclined his head. 'Ah, my dear cousin, it's good to see you, though you have missed all the fun. We gained the upper ward and the tower as well.' He turned and nodded towards faint wisps of smoke and ash ascended in the brilliant blue sky in lazy grey spirals. As he turned, his golden eyes met Dinnis' for a second before sliding past. Had the Kapok recognised him?

Haka's pale eyes widened. 'Then Akrad ...'

'Quite dead. As a matter of etiquette, cousin, do you think we should mourn the death of our great-grandfather or rejoice that a deceitful provocateur can no longer scheme against us or wreak havoc throughout our lands?'

Haka opened his mouth, then closed it.

'Wild celebrations are in order, if you ask me,' Lukarn said. 'But then he was no blood relative of mine.'

'Indeed Lukarn. Well, I'm glad you are here, Haka. I intend to head back to Tarka. Since your warriors are fresh, you can hold this position until I send someone to relieve you.'

'Oh, but Your Majesty surely ...' Haka's voice trailed off. 'Yes of course. I am at your service.'

'Good, good. Come. You have had a long journey—one obviously beset with many delays along the way given the tardiness of your arrival. Join me in the refreshment tent for a morning meal.'

A thin smile stole over Haka's narrow face. 'I'd be honoured, Your Majesty.'

Chapter Thirteen: Left Behind

Dinnis

Wrapping his arms around his legs. A tremor ran through him. Once again, the Kapok gave no sign of recognising him. Or maybe he didn't want to claim him. Half the time he was convinced the man was his father, but he looked more gaunt, grim and hard. Papa had never cared about the colour of his skin or the shape of his eyes. Was he truly ashamed of his part-Nolmec son now?

A slow chill settled in his belly. He closed his eyes and allowed his limbs to still. Perhaps Ista had been right, he was a *moros* to have held on to his faith in his father.

Sunk in his dark thoughts, he turned his back on the scraps of food and cup of water the guards offered him at midday. Soon after, a single long horn blast sounded and, with the rumble of hooves and jingle of tack a contingent of mounted Tamrin warriors thundered through the ward towards the outer gate. Rokkan Kapok and Markan Lukarn rode at the head, resplendent with magnificent headdress and long cloaks.

Dinnis clambered to his feet, pulling against the ropes, and called out until one of the guards cuffed him.

'Quiet, boy.'

No one turned or acknowledged him in any way. He slumped back down on the cold muddy ground.

The last of the Tamrin warriors rode between the towers and the gates swung shut with an echoing boom. He pulled himself into a ball. Papa, if that was he, had left him behind, discarded like shredded hopes.

* * *

Moments later, a heavy hand on his shoulder fell on his shoulder. Dinnis pulled away, a shiver running down his spine. Was this it? Was this when he met whatever fate the Kapok had abandoned him to?

'What's your name, boy?' a rough voice asked.

He looked up. It was the warrior that had led the assault on the postern gate. He could almost imagine kindness in his green eyes.

Dinnis ducked his head. 'Why? Does it matter, Lutan Jakan?'

'You are a strange one. What matters is that you answer the question.'

Dinnis closed his eyes, doing his best to control the trembling in his limbs. 'If you are going to kill me, please, just do it.'

The Tamrin lifted Dinnis' chin with his hand. 'Why would I do that?'

'It's what the guards said would happen ... that ... that my father would pay them to do it.'

'Your father? Who is he?'

'He is a Tamrin warrior. He fought in the battle yesterday, I think, but ... but maybe he does not want to acknowledge me.' Better not to say Papa's name, unless he was wrong or Papa had forgotten him. 'My name is Dinnis.'

The Lutan let go of Dinnis' chin and looked over his back and arms. Suddenly aware of the scars that marked his body, Dinnis squirmed and dropped his eyes.

'You were in the stronghold, boy.' Dinnis nodded. 'They didn't treat you well, did they?'

He shook his head. 'They didn't like Tamrins.'

'I bet they don't. Quick thinking of your part, to open the postern gate. You saved us a lot of trouble.'

The boy looked at the Tamrin warrior, Jakan. 'I wanted to help my father. I wanted Akrad to be defeated.'

'And you did, Dinnis, and he was. Now, the Kapok has asked me to look after you. I'm to find all the orphans and strays among the camp followers and to get you all safely to Tarka.'

A hope stirred inside Dinnis as fragile as a spider's thread. 'But I'm not ... my mother was Nolmec ...' His voice faltered.

'Your father fought in the battle. So, did you, in your own way. That's good enough for me.'

'I have a sister. She is only seven. Her name is Ista. I don't know what happened to her.'

Lutan Jakan nodded, 'We'll look after her. Don't worry.'

Dinnis nodded. Jakan's no-nonsense, blunt but kindly tone reassured him.

'Come on then.' Jakan unsheathed his hunting knife and sliced through the ropes. 'Follow me.'

* * *

Lutan Jakan nodded to the Tamrin guard and pushed open the makeshift door of the stables. A musty smell of old hay, manure and sweaty fear pervaded the dim interior. Patches of light filtered down through the rotted thatch roof and warped walls onto a hardened mud floor. A rag tag bunch of girls and boys ranging from ten to sixteen sat around the on sacks, piles and boxes or sprawled out on sleeping mats.

'Listen up, youngsters. This is Dinnis, another lost waif. Hasuk lad, show him the facilities and a place to doss down for the night.'

Even in the filtered light, it was obvious all present had the bronzed colouring of the Tamrin. No blue-skinned Nolmec here. The palest was the colour of pig ivory, others like dark wood. His sister was not among them.

Dinnis caught the Lutan's hand. 'Ista?'

'Don't worry, lad. She's safe.' He turned and left, the door rocking shut behind him.

'*Karis* ...' No, not Nolmec. Dinnis searched his memory for the Tamrin greeting appropriate for this situation. 'Ah, greetings friends.'

A few glanced his ways, their faces unsmiling. No one moved or spoke. Most of the group looked tough; barefooted with work roughened hands and blunt speech. They gathered in clumps around the fire, dipping their maizebread into bowls of hot bean stew, gulping it down with few words.

'Here, eat this.' The boy Jakan had named Hasuk thrust a clay bowl at him before turning and joining his two friends at the far end of the stalls.

Dinnis ate his meal a little distance from the fire and alone, before finding a spot to sleep.

Next day, as the sun rose in a dirt-smudged sky, Jakan arrived with another officer, a lutan by the shape of his oval chest plate and headdress.

'Okay boys … and girls. I'm leaving with the main army and will arrange for your care once I get to Tarka. You will be travelling with the baggage train. Lutan Zaven will look after you. There will be no free rides—you need to help.'

Lutan Zaven directed the orphans to help dismantle the tents and pack up the heavy equipment and supplies. By mid-morning, the vast bulk of the army had packed up and was streaming through the outer gate heading towards Tarka far to the south, leaving behind the units under Markan Haka command.

By the time the baggage train made its ponderous way through the gates and along the southern road, the pale washed out disc of the second moon Argenti chased the burnished orb of the sun in the western sky.

'We just got here yesterday and have to pack up again,' one of the children muttered.

While the youngest of the orphans perched on the back of some of the heavily laden yarmas, the older children walked. By the evening, Dinnis was relieved that they had left so late in the day. His feet stung with painful blisters and his legs felt like heavy boulders had been strapped to them.

Lutan Zaven strode towards them. 'You older boys, dig latrine trenches for the night—over there.'

'You'd think we were peasants,' a burly boy about eight grumbled.

Dinnis picked up the digging tools and followed.

And then, after another solitary meal, he scrubbed the pots with some of the others. When he rolled himself up in the blanket provided and he fell to sleep instantly, despite his aching limbs.

As the days marched by, his feet toughened and his leg muscles hardened. Despite the ostracism and the teasing from his companions, the long daily trek with the added morning and evening tasks became easier.

The luminous smile of the young woman with the silver skin haunted his dreams and Dinnis' doubts began to melt away. Jakan had said that Ista was safe and the Kapok had instructed Jakan to bring him to Tarka. There would be a good reason why Papa couldn't speak to him at North Pass.

The high mountain vistas and village scenes unfolded before him and Dinnis forgot the pain of blisters, his aching legs and overwhelming tiredness in wide-eyed wonder. In stolen moments at the stronghold, he'd read in Akrad's books of such faraway places and dreamed of visiting them. It wasn't quite as he'd imagined it, but soon he would be in the fabled city of Tarka with Papa.

SEVEN DAYS AFTER
ROKKAN LEFT NORTH PASS
Tarka, royal city of Tamra

Chapter Fourteen: The Strange Girl

Mannok

Prince Mannok fell backwards in the dust of one of the Palace's sparring yards. Garvin whooped in triumph, but before his bigger friend could straddle him, Mannok rolled to the side and sprang lightly to his feet. The move left Garo off balance, his arms flapping. Squinting against the afternoon sun, the Prince darted forward and hooked his feet behind Garo's legs, pulling them out from under him, sending him sprawling. Quick as a jaguar's pounce, Mannok was astride his friend, pinning his arms to the ground.

'I yield,' Garvin yelped, his chocolate-brown eyes wide.

A sustained high-pitched horn blasted from the direction of the front gate. Just one blast. Mannok grinned. Papa was home. At last. Jumping up, he raced past the stables and the kennels towards the entrance gates, Garvin trailing behind him. A couple of days ago, an exhausted rider had arrived with the news that his father's forces had defeated Akrad within days of arriving at the Deceiver's Stronghold at North Pass. The Palace was abuzz with the fact that seemingly invincible Akrad, who had overshadowed Tamrin affairs for more than seventy years, had been killed so quickly. Not that Mannok was surprised. He'd always known his father would return victorious.

As the large golden gates swung open, Rokkan Kapok trotted into the Palace forecourt astride his grey charger, followed by Lord Lukarn the Markan of the North, and a unit of mounted warriors.

The colourful feathers of their headdress fluttered in the breeze and their pennants and long cloaks streamed behind them. Mannok shaded his eyes as the afternoon sun reflected off their gold and bronze accoutrements and weapons, dazzling his eyes. His father sat tall and straight in the saddle even after many days of long travel and despite the scabbed cut on his left cheek and a bandage on his right shoulder.

With a jolt, the Prince realized that a young girl sat behind his father. She was about his age, thin, with long dark hair and unusually pale silvery skin. The girl turned and looked straight at him with strangely shaped grey eyes. Her chin titled, her nose wrinkled in disdain. He glared back at her.

'Who's the girl?' Garo asked.

Before Mannok could respond, Madomo Bitjarnan burst through the front doors of the Palace and rushed toward the Kapok.

'Your Majesty, welcome.' He bowed as low as his short rotund stature allowed. 'The news of your great victory has already reached us.' The Madomo's words tumbled over each other.

Papa swung off his mount and lifted the girl down to the ground beside him. Uncle Lukarn dismounted, his dark eyebrows drawn together in a frown. A couple of grooms lead the horses away.

'My Lord Kapok.' The Madomo bobbed and smiled. 'It is good to have you back. There are so many matters to attend to.'

'Later, Bitjarnan. First I would see the Kupanna.'

Papa strode towards the Palace entrance as the other warriors dismounted behind him. He stopped mid-stride so abruptly that Uncle Lukarn almost collided into him.

'Mannu ... Garo.' Papa gave a wide, joyous smile and beckoned for them to approach. Needing no further encouragement, Mannok ran a couple of strides before remembering palace protocol. He slowed his pace and straightened his posture.

As he reached his father, he bowed low. 'Your Majesty.'

'Ah, Mannu, you are so covered in dust I did not recognise you at once.' Amusement lurked in his father golden eyes. 'And you've grown.'

Mannok stiffened and shot a reproachful glare at Papa. 'Garo and I have been wrestling.'

The Kapok chuckled, the corner of his eyes crinkling. 'Indeed, a worthy opponent. Well, don't let us stop your military manoeuvres

... unless you can spare us some time to guide us to your mother?'

'My Lord Kapok, I can.... that is to say the Kupanna is in the—' Bitjarnan spluttered.

'Of course, Papa, she's in the gardens.' Mannok spoke over the Madomo. He stood taller, ignoring the strange girl's scornful looks and the huffiness of the Madomo.

'Thank you Bitjarnan.' Papa nodded in the Madomo's direction, 'I'm sure you will have more than enough to do for when the rest of the army arrives. Arrange quarters for the commanding officers and see that the Barracks Commander is alerted of the division's arrival. The Prince will show us to the Kupanna.' He waved the fellow off, took a step than stopped. 'By the way, Mannu, Garo, this is Ista. Ista, my son Prince Mannok and Garvin, son of Kaspin, Kaptan of the City Guard.'

Barely glancing at Garo, the girl stared at Mannok, speculation alive in her oblique eyes. Mannok gave her a stiff bow and, to his irritation, she nodded her head as though accepting due homage.

Lifting his chin, Mannok strode across the courtyard towards the eastern gate that led to the formal palace gardens, trusting that his father would follow. Once through the gate he headed along a winding path that revealed the garden's pleasures in carefully planned stages on the eastern side of the three-storey palace.

The garden beds were massed with flowers that scented the dry mountain air and encroached over the edges of the winding paths and around the base of flowing trees. Bright humming birds, scarlet flycatchers and fairy wrens flitted about in the alternating shadows and golden light of the afternoon sun.

Around the corner of the path, stood three women in long tunics, pastel head coverings and cloaks adorned with gold thread and sparkling jewels. His mother, Kupanna Marra, stood with hands clasped in front of her, as Aunt Samara bent forward to snip a long golden lily. Aunt Lakwi carried a basket full of the cut blossoms. Nearby, his younger cousins played under the shade of a blossom-laden marosa tree and the watchful eyes of his old nurse. Their shrill prattle rose clearly above the hums, chirps, rustles carried on the soft sighing of the wind. Behind them the deep blue sky and the snow-covered peaks of the Twins floated above the red painted walls.

'Such sweet beauty,' Papa breathed the words, standing still.

'This scene should grace the tapestries on palace walls rather than harsh exploits of war.'

His mother looked up and smiled, her coffee-brown eyes softening. 'Rokkan, Lukarn, you're back.'

'My Lady Kupanna, as always the most exquisite flower in the garden.' Papa bowed with a flourish.

Mama inclined her head. 'My Lord Kapok, you haven't lost your golden tongue on your forays in the north.' Her tone was more indulgent than cutting.

His aunts bowed deeply before his father. 'Your Majesty.'

At that moment, his cousin Rizanna looked up. Dropping her doll, she ran towards them, her short legs flashing beneath her rucked-up tunic, her plaits flying out behind.

'Papa,' she screamed at the top of her voice, 'Uncle Rokku.'

Rizzi hugged Uncle Lukarn's legs then raised her arms to be lifted. With a sheepish smile at Mama, he lifted his daughter and ruffled her windswept hair. He then slipped his left arm around Markana Samara's waist and bent his head, his lips brushing her light brown cheek. His aunt's gaze was on the ground, but a smile tugged at the corners of her mouth.

Mannok glanced at his parents. A stickler for decorum, his mother's mouth was tucked in primly, but she said nothing. His father looked on with an amused smile, his arms folded across his broad chest.

'Hmm, well Lukku if I didn't know you had been married these ten years, I'd suspect you were newlyweds. Should we leave you two love birds alone?'

Aunt Samara blushed, Uncle Lukarn chuckled. 'Just promise not to drag me away to another battle for a very long time.' He put Rizanna down with a pat on the head.

A grim smile flashed on Papa's face. 'I'll see what I can do. We have won the war, our next challenge is to win the peace.'

His golden eyes softened as he swung to face Aunt Lakwi.

'Lakwi, dear sister, I'm glad you're here. Is that Yalik and little Jati sitting under the marosa tree?'

'Yes, Your Majesty.' Aunt Lakwi beckoned old Suki to bring her children to her. Papa tickled Jati's chubby tummy until she squealed, then he winked at Yalik clinging to Aunt Lakwi's long tunic, a thumb in his mouth.

His father loved to make a fuss of young children. Mama sometimes complained that he behaved more like an avuncular priest than the supreme ruler of Tamra. Today Mama looked on with an indulgent half smile, perhaps because she was happy that Papa had arrived back safely.

His father leant down and gave Aunt Lakwi a peck on the cheek. 'Did mother come with you?'

'No, Rokku. She sends her greetings, but she grieves—.'

'— her son.' The corners of Papa's mouth turned down and he gave a curt nod. 'Of course. We all regret the loss of my half-brother, Naetok.'

'And his treachery,' Uncle Lukarn growled. 'Don't worry, Rokku, what else could you do. She'll see sense in time.'

The fluting birdsong seemed to still and the pink petals of the marosa blossoms floated down in a sudden wind flurry. Mannok shifted his feet, the odour of blood and the image of Papa sprawled out in the throne room following the vicious thrust of Uncle Naetok's knife invading his thoughts. He shook his head. Papa had no choice, but to defend his life, his family and his realm against his treacherous half-brother. Surely, Grandmamma Suraya would understand and return to Tarka.

'What are you doing here?' Rizzi's clear voice cut rang out. His cousin stood nose-to-chin in front of the strange girl, a challenge in her hazel eyes. Mannok had forgotten her presence, she'd been so quiet, hanging in the shadow of the bushes.

His mother's face paled at the sight of her and the warmth seemed to drop out of the thin mountain air. 'Who is she?'

Mannok moved closer, keen to hear the answer. Though he would not say it, she did seem out of place with her strange skin and almond-shaped eyes.

The girl's chest heaved, her slender silvery-white fingers clenched at her sides, her pale lips thinning to a tight line. She glanced at Papa before glaring again at Rizzi.

'Forgive me,' Papa said, 'This is Ista. She's ...' he paused a heartbeat '... an orphan and in need of a new home.'

Mama neck flushed and her nostrils flared. 'She's ... Akrad's spawn, and'

His father raised an eyebrow. 'His great-granddaughter, yes, but she is not alone in that.'

'And you bring her here?'

'My dear Kupanna, there hasn't been time to make other plans, and I could hardly leave her to starve.' Papa crossed his arms across his chest.

Mannok's gaze darted from one parent to the other. Mama pressed her lips together, two red spots blooming in her cheeks.

'She is but a child ...' Aunt Samara's soft voice trailed off, as Mama turned her rock-hard gaze on her.

Mama's lip curled. 'Are we to care for all the waifs and strays this war has produced?'

Papa tilted his head, his face resuming his normal bright expression. 'As to that, I am arranging arrange apprenticeships and places to those without kin to take them in. Come Marra, you would not have children starving in our city streets and the mountain villages because their fathers died defending our land?'

The Kupanna dropped her eyes, her brow creasing. 'No, but this girl. Her father ...' She met the Kapok's unwavering gaze. 'She has been brought up, nurtured, trained by our most decided enemy. She is a threat to our security.'

'She's not yet eight-years-old.'

'The same age as Mannok.' His mother rubbed her temples. 'Even baby snakes have poisoned fangs and cute jaguar cubs grow to be killers.'

The girl, Ista, inhaled sharply as if about to speak, then clamped her lips shut. Her face a silver-white mask except for the grey eyes glimmering with unshed tears. She was reed-thin and there was a bruise on her right wrist. It was old, yellow and brown, faded, spreading like a withered flower underneath her strange silver skin. She was the same age he was and she was alone, with no father or mother to care for her, her grandfather killed for less than the cycle of Argenti, the silver moon.

Were her nights, like his, broken by nightmares? He could see it in her eyes—guarded, proud, cold yet somehow vulnerable and needy. What if Papa had died the day Naetok attacked? Or if he had been killed in battle and Akrad had won? But for the Maker's favour, it might have been him standing in front of hostile eyes, his future in the balance. Maybe he had more in common with this strange girl than he'd first thought. Certainly, more than he did with his carefree cousins.

His father stood looking at his mother as though as though he needed or wanted her permission. The others stood silent around them, Uncle Lukarn tense and frowning with a barely disguised 'told-you-so' expression on his face. Even baby Jati's smile dissolved as she screwed up her chubby face.

A sharp-beaked tarrawong carolled, its melodious arpeggio a parody of what had been, a few short moments before, such a joyous occasion.

'If you fear me so much, then send me away.' Ista's voice was high and cultured but tinged with a slight accent and a hint of scorn. 'I do not care.' The clarity of her tone trembled on the last word.

'I think she should stay,' Mannok said, surprising himself. Emboldened by the ensuing silence, he added, 'We are after all her ... her kin. She is a second or third cousin.'

Did Ista's proud expression soften slightly? He gave her an uncertain smile and then moved to stand beside her, taking her stiff hand in his own grubby one. 'Maybe, she should live with us.'

Mama covered her neck with her hand, her gold and jade necklace chiming. 'Mannu you have no idea what you are talking about.'

He glared at his mother. 'I did get it right. She is our cousin.'

Papa sent him a teasing smile. 'Certainly, Mannu.' His face turned serious as he turned toward Mama. 'Kupanna, I can make other arrangements—my cousin Tannik would be willing to provide Ista a home or ... '

Aunt Samara took a step forward. 'She would be welcome to live with us, Your Majesty. Wouldn't she, Lukarn?' Her tone faltered as she glanced at his uncle's stunned face.

Uncle Lukarn rubbed the back of his neck and shot Papa an aggrieved look.

'That won't be necessary.' His mother rose to her full height and lifted her shapely chin, every ninas a royal Kupanna of Tamra. 'She can stay at the Palace my attendant.'

Papa hesitated for a moment, looking to Ista, then nodded. 'Then that is settled. My gratitude, Kupanna, for your graciousness. I think Lukarn and I need to freshen up from our travels. We will join you for refreshments in a little while. Good day, Ladies.'

He bowed to Mama and strode back towards the Palace entrance, Lukarn hastening after him. Ista's tear-misted gaze followed Papa.

Mannok squeezed her hand, glad to have found a new friend, before letting go and racing after them, Garvin close behind him.

Ahead, the Palace glowed a buttery yellow in the afternoon light as though nothing significant had happened. Yet somehow Mannok felt that the shape of the future had shifted.

Chapter Fifteen: Nightmare

Ista

Ista stood frozen, the air she pulled into her lungs like shards of glass. Once again, she was left alone among strangers.

'Girl, are you listening?'

Ista tore her eyes off the empty garden path and stared at the woman, the Kupanna. 'What?'

'I am the Kupanna, Kupanna Marra. You will address me, as Your Majesty.' She pressed her hands together. 'Maker help me, I've agreed that you can stay—your needs will be provided for.'

Ista nodded, her feelings tampered down like a dormant fire.

'Very well. Now take the basket from Lady Samara and carry it into the Palace.'

The younger taller woman placed a slender hand on the Kupanna's shoulder. 'Marra, she looks exhausted from the journey.'

The Kupanna pressed her lips together. 'She needs to learn palace protocol and not mistake her station. Well girl.'

Ista stirred, while Lady Samara stepped forward and placed the basket into her hands, with a kind smile in her warm brown eyes.

'Come, walk behind us.' The Kupanna turned and stepped after her son and husband. The other ladies scooped up their children and followed.

Ista found it hard to keep up as the women walked through a web of passages and stairs, to a roof top piazza with rich seats, potted plants and bright mosaic floor. Here, she was sent to fetch and carry and hold and follow like a common mud-skin slave.

There was no doubt, despite her tan coloured skin and age that the Kupanna was a beautiful and regal person. Her skin was still soft and smooth and smelt faintly of avocado oil and passion flowers. Her face had a classical beauty with a strong nose, bow shaped lips and large dark brown eyes under arching eyebrows. Exquisite clothes draped her shapely body with style and grace, her neck and arms enhanced by stunning pieces of jewellery of gold and precious stones. She moved with understated dignity. She was every tanis the queen. Ista longed to copy her gestures, her diction, even the timbre of her voice. Yet, the woman made her hostility for her new maid clear in every word she spoke.

As the evening settled in, the Kupanna directed her to stand and serve at the evening meal while the royal family ate at their leisure. Ista's stomach rumbled and her legs ached. If only this long drawn out meal would end so that she could at last snatch something to eat. A small sigh escaped her as she glanced at the Kapok's flinty face and the Kupanna's sullen one.

After a hasty meal, she was required to stand still while her new mistress wound coloured wools around her outstretched arms, and the Tamrin listened with avid curiosity to all the details of her Grandfather's defeat

The young Prince Mannok tried to pry the details from his father, but the Kapok had been reticent and distracted. In the end, it was the horrid Markan Lukarn who had narrated to a rapt audience Rokkan's surprise attack on the outer gate, the fight in the lower ward, the open postern door and finding Akrad dead in the tower.

Of the three languages she spoke, Tamrin was the one she knew the least so it wasn't hard to shut the hateful storytelling out, to lock the tears behind her eyelids, even as her arms ached and cramped. She was thankful when the Kapok decided to retire early, thinking her evening ended.

However, she still had to attend the Kupanna as she prepared for sleep, brushing out her thick curtain of rich brown hair before she was finally dismissed to a spot on the floor in the antechamber.

She'd only had a few hurried moments to eat and rest throughout this long arduous day. Her body ached with tiredness from the long journey from the north and this evening's exertions. The stone floor was hard beneath her hips and shoulder blades.

It was far from what she was used to.

True, sometimes Grandfather needed to chastise her painfully, but for the most part, she was treated as royalty. And that was as it should be. The Nolmec had shown great deference to their Kiprissa. She was used to instant obedience, even if the isolated stronghold at North Pass was not as grand or well-appointed as this magnificent ancient palace. Her brother was the only one who would dare correct or contradict her. But he was an idiot. At least, she wasn't in immediate danger and she had time to think of how to escape back to General Nuktis and Uncle Timon.

Despite the hardness of the floor, the anger that boiled inside her in ever tightening circles, she felt sleep creep over her at last.

* * *

Hands with long taloned fingers grabbed Ista's ankles and pulled her down into the black abyss. She opened her mouth and shrieked, but her words were swallowed by silence. The darks sides of the pit flashed past. She grabbed at the sides, snagged fistfuls of dirt and, at last, a gnarled tree root jutting out. The black monster below her continued to pull on her and her arms screamed with pain.

Above her, white headed eagles with black eyes swooped and dived at her head and shoulders, shredding her with their cruel beaks. Blood and tears ran down her cheeks and her long hair tangled about her. She risked letting go with her right arm, using it to shield her eyes from the vicious flurry of beak and talons.

She licked her dry, cracked lips and screamed. 'Help, help me!' Her voice was cracked and flimsy, it echoed and frayed in the emptiness of the abyss, mocking her.

No one came. Not even her snivelling brother though he had promised to look after her. Not her grandfather who had said she was special. Not the Kapok who had promised to look after her. Terror engulfed her. Her left hand slipped, burning against the rough bark of the tree root. She slid a little further into the darkness before grabbing the root again with both hands. If she fell, she would die.

Arkon Akrad, her grandfather and protector, appeared out of the swirling mist. He paused on the jagged lip of the hole, his pale face strong and noble in a beam of glowing light. He stood tall, leaning on his blackthorn staff as he peered down at her in the pit.

His grey eyes shone like silver stars. He bent towards her, reaching out with his right hand.

He was alive! She sobbed with relief and threw her lacerated left arm out towards him. Even as her fingers touched his, something loomed up behind him—a huge jaguar, eyes black, crimson maw open like a cavern, and long curved fangs dripping with saliva.

Clutching at him, she screamed, 'Beware, Master!'

The huge predator sprung, its powerful paws wrapped around Grandfather, wide jaws enveloping his skull. The nightmarish soulless eyes seemed to focus on her for a moment before the sickening crunch of bone and spray of bright blood.

Grandfather teetered on the edge, before toppling into the abyss. The big cat tumbled after him, twisting, turning into an eagle with bloodied feathers.

As her grandfather dropped, he reached out and grabbed her, pulling her down with him. The root ripped through her hands, twisted into a snake. She let go and plummeted down, down, down.

Cruel mocking laughter reverberated around her, and the darkness swallowed the light above her. She screamed and screamed and screamed.

'Ista!'

She snapped open her eyes, an ear-splitting scream vibrating around her, and a strange room shrouded in a deep darkness. She pulled the sleeping covers tight against her chest until she could feel her ribs ridged beneath her clenched fists. Deep shudders shook her body. It was that stupid nightmare. That's all.

Except it was not just a nightmare. Grandfather was dead, killed by those hateful, evil people. She closed her mouth, biting the inside of her cheek against the terror, the abyss. Scalding tears slid down her cheeks.

'Ista, it's okay. You are safe here.' The rich bass voice was soothing and gentle.

Not her master's silvery tenor or her brother's high alto. She recognised this voice. He was an enemy and her captor. True, he hadn't killed Grandfather, but he had meant to.

A light flared in the darkness, a golden-red flame on a long thin taper in the Kapok's hand. The flame danced in his eyes, illuminated his face and cast spidery shadows around the room. Shielding it with his hand, he lit some candles in their elaborate gold stands.

He came towards her, and she pulled back. He raised his right eyebrow a fraction, gave a slightly lopsided smile and crouched on level with her,

'Amazing how such a slight little thing like you can make a noise that would wake a mountain.' He smothered a huge yawn with his big hand, his eyes creasing at the corners. 'At least you haven't woken the Kupanna. She's a sound sleeper.'

She stared at him, mute.

'It was just a bad dream, child. You are safe here. No one can hurt you.'

'You could.'

His laughter bubbled up, his teeth flashing white in the dark. The faint smell of chilli and simple soap reached her. She felt her heart beat slowing, fingers relaxing their talon grip on the covers bunched at her chest. She wanted very much to trust this man. So big, so powerful. Yet she couldn't. She couldn't trust anyone anymore.

'That's true.' He lifted his strong chin. 'But, I have not yet stooped to killing or torturing children. Nor do I intend to.'

He leant forward and she flinched, but all he did was to brush the tears from her cheeks before prising the crumpled sleeping covers from her stiff fingers and wrapping them around her.

'Not the most comfortable place to sleep—' His voice seemed tight, displeased '—but it's warm and dry. Lie down and get some rest, child.'

She closed her eyes, tried to sleep, but her legs and arms ached from the journey, from playing the servant to the proud Kupanna. And sleep was where the nightmares lurked. She bit down on her lower lip, tasting the salty iron of blood. She despised herself for being so weak. No, she was Kiprissa Ista, the great-granddaughter of Arkon Akrad and daughter of Kiprissa Gaia, a person of power. If the Arkon had won this war, she would be ordering Marra around. And he would've won but for the foul magic of those creatures. She heard her grandfather's voice, 'Ista sweet, with time and patience water wears down the highest mountains. Our plans will take time to come to fruition, but we know how to wait.'

She would wait. She would be stronger even than Grandfather. She didn't need anyone to rescue her. One day she would bring down all her enemies, just as they were now trying to destroy her.

She heard the rustle and looked up with a start. The Kapok

hadn't moved. He looked at her with a faint smile and narrowed eyes. It was as if he could read her thoughts.

'You haven't had a very good day today, have you?'

Her eyes stung with tears at the hint of compassion in his voice. She breathed in sharply but refused to answer. *Why does he care?* And anyhow, he hadn't spoken up in her favour, had barely looked at her all day.

'I'll take that as a yes.' He frowned. 'This isn't quite what I had in mind. It is not too late to accept Markana Samara's offer. Another possibility is my cousin, Princess Sila, wife to Crown Prince Tannik of Silisea. She would take you in if I asked her.'

'Is it true? Are we cousins as Prince Mannok claimed?'

He shifted his position and studied the shadowed mosaic floor. 'I'm distantly related to almost every noble family in Tamra and most of the foreign royal families by marriage or blood.' His face puckered as though eating a sour anka berry. 'But yes, before Akrad began courting the Nolmec, he forced a marriage with my great-grandmother, Princess Sil of Tamra. So yes, we are blood-cousins, as Mannok so ably worked out this afternoon.'

'But ... you're so much older than we ... than me.'

'By the moons, child, you make it sound like I'm in my dotage. There's only a little over twenty years between us.'

'Yes, but Grandfather ...' She stopped. The Arkon was her mother's grandfather, but he didn't ... hadn't looked old.

The Kapok shrugged. 'He was at least ninety. It was part of his glamour, his arcane powers. That and his golden tongue.' He traced the pattern of the rug with his fingers. 'The Kupanna isn't unkind by nature. She is very protective of her son ... our son ... and, like her brother, she perceives you as a threat.' He gave a wry smile. 'She doesn't forgive easily but given time ...'

'She is upset with you, *kuree*, because you brought me here.' It was true, she knew.

He looked at his hands in the spluttering light of the candles. 'There are other matters between us. I should have realised that she would perceive your presence as an insult. So, do you want to leave or stay?'

If she went with the gentle Samara she would be under Markan Lukarn's roof. She would never feel safe with him. If she went to this Sila she may be treated with greater kindness, but it would mean living hundreds of lek away to the south. If she stayed with the Kapok ... and the Prince ... She glanced at Rokkan sitting on the floor talking to her, as though he was not the Kapok, the ruler of Tamra. His sleeping robe was of finely woven yarma wool, but he could have been a serving man for all the finery he was wearing. Yet she could sense the power in him.

'I want to stay with you, *kuree*.'

'Very well then. Now you best get some sleep.'

He rose to his feet, blew out a candle and moved on to the next. She tensed. She stared at the ornate ceiling, her arms stiff beside her sides as darkness once more began to take over the room. She would not give way to terror or the nightmares that clawed at the edges of her vision. At the last candle, he paused as though he could sense her fear.

'What is it, Ista?'

'They might get in,' she whispered.

'They?'

'The assassins who killed my grandfather.'

He smiled and shook his head. 'Any assassin would have to get through the city gate, past the Palace gates and slip by the Palace guards stationed at every door.'

'But what about the windows? They got into the Arkon's Tower.'

He laughed. 'You have such an astute head on your slim shoulders, it's easy to forget you are still a child the same age as Mannu. They would have to fly to get in through those windows.'

She bit her lip, chagrined at the amusement in his voice. What if they could, but who could believe that? 'I don't want to be alone, *kuree*.'

'Hmm.' He ran a finger over the crouching jaguar carved in the mantle support. 'Given I'm now awake as a mountain owl, would it disturb you if I looked over state papers on the other side of the room?'

The tension began to leach out of her. 'No, *kuree*. I think I would sleep better if you were in the room.'

'Indeed. I'll fend off any dangerous assassins, which should give you time to run and get help, or at least get away.'

She didn't care that he was laughing at her. Her eyes fluttered closed and she sank into dreamless sleep.

Chapter Sixteen: Late

Mannok

Mannok pulled the door shut, careful not to wake his parents in the next room. He snuck through the dimly lit antechamber, edging past the heavy furniture outlined in the pale light filtering through the high windows. Halfway across the room, he jerked to a stop. A hulking figure was sprawled across the divan in front of him. His mouth went dry and his hands tingled. He leaned closer, making out the unruly hair, the hawk-like nose and strong chin. Was it Papa?

The man sprung up and grabbed Mannok, strong fingers clamping onto on one shoulders and twisting his arm behind his back. The curved blade of a hunting knife glinted the man's other hand.

'Stop! Papa! It's me!'

'By the moons, Mannu, don't startle me like that. I thought ...' Papa slumped back into the divan, the knife falling beside him. 'I've spent too many years sleeping with one eye open waiting for the next attack.'

'Sorry, Papa. It's just I was surprised to see you here. Did you sleep here all night?'

'No, no ... well ... I suppose I did. Bitjarnan gave me a whole stack of accounts and requisitions to review. He waylaid me after dinner. Three years of palace business and he wanted it all done in one evening. I must have fallen asleep looking at the lists of finery he seems to think necessary to our royal status. Maybe I should just get a new Madomo before he drains the royal treasury.'

'He is very fussy. He tells Garo and me off all the time for getting in the way.'

'Well Mannu, that's probably because you keep tripping him up.' Then Papa sat forward and looked across the room. Lowering his voice, 'Hush, though. We may have woken Ista. She slept poorly last night.'

Torn between being offended at his father's teasing and intrigued at the mention of the mysterious girl, his curiosity won out. 'Why is she sleeping here instead of a room of her own?' he whispered.

'Your mother's idea.'

'Oh, but ...' He frowned. Sometimes he found adults hard to understand. Mama had certainly seemed displeased to see Ista, but she had agreed to give her a home. So why was she making it so difficult for the girl? 'Papa, couldn't you tell Mama to be nicer to Ista?'

'I could. Yet I have a hunch that the more I advocate for her the less your mother will like her. For now, at least, it is probably better I leave the Kupanna to calm down. Anyway, where are you sneaking off to so early in the morning?'

'To the stables. Mirror went into labour just before dinner. She probably has her foal by now.'

Papa's teeth flashed in a quick grin. 'Humph. So Bitjarnan tells me about every broken platter or moth-eaten tapestry and no one bothers to tell me my best mare is foaling?'

Mannok smiled back. It was so good to have his father home again. Papa pulled his boots on and raked his fingers through his dark curls.

He stood up and patted Mannok's shoulder. 'Come, show me.'

They walked towards the door. As his hand rested on the latch, Papa paused and looked to the other side of the room. The girl lay beneath the covers as quiet and motionless as a statue, but her eyes were tracking their movements.

'Sorry to wake you, Ista. Would you like to come with us?'

After a brief silence, the girl sat up, her chin in the air, 'Why would I want to do that, *kuree*?' Her voice was high and scornful. 'I don't see the point of horses. They are big and dangerous and very uncomfortable to ride.'

Mannok stared at the girl, then met his father's eyes, seeing his own surprise mirrored in his face.

Papa laughed. 'You and the Kupanna have something in common

then, lass. Next you will be telling me you don't like dogs. Come on Mannu, you can give me all the news on the way. Somehow I think your report on palace happenings will be far more interesting than the good Madomo's.'

* * *

The stables were heavy with the scent of hay, manure and the sound of horses munching. The foal stood on long shaky legs nuzzling his mother's side. A stray shaft of sunlight picked up motes of chaff and highlighted the white blaze on his sweet nose. Like his mother, his still wet coat was a dark grey.

Best of all, Papa had listened closely to all Mannok's chatter about the stables and the kennels and the minor dramas among of the Palace staff. True, Papa had asked some uncomfortable questions about how well Mannok was doing with his studies, but mostly he listened. By the time, they had completed their informal tour of the stables and kennels, the sun was a couple of hand-breadths above the horizon and the Palace and service areas were bustling with activity. Mannok didn't want the time with his father to end, but his stomach grumbled loudly and he couldn't ignore his growing hunger any longer.

'I think we are late for breakfast, Papa. Mama will not be happy.'

'You could be right.'

They hurried to clean up and entered the morning reception room a little breathless. Several people sat at the table. Mama was sitting at the end of the bright room, with a mostly empty plate in front of her. Her back was straight, her brows creased and the corners of her mouth pulled down. Ista stood like a small, silver statue behind her.

Mama's coffee-coloured eyes rested on Mannok, until him squirmed, before fixing on his Papa leaning against the door jamb.

Papa gave a jaunty smile. 'A beautiful morning Kupanna. I hope you slept well.'

'You are late. The meal is all but over.'

Papa's smile disappeared, his eyes narrowed. 'Late? But my dear Kupanna, surely it is you who started early.'

Palace protocol dictated that a meal only started with the arrival of the Kapok, though Papa didn't normally make a point of it. A red glow crept from Mama's neck to her cheeks. No one else moved, a brittle silence filling the room.

Aunt Lakwi's cheerful voice broke the silence. 'Please forgive us, Your Majesty. I think the war has disrupted a lot of things, and we are out of practice with royal prerogatives.'

A small smile tweaked at the corners of Papa's mouth. He gave a slight bow. 'Of course, Princess, I'm more than happy to forgive what is perhaps a mutual breach of etiquette.' He inclined his head towards the Kupanna and moved into the room.

Mannok relaxed and breathed in the delicious aromas wafting from the half-empty clay serving bowls and trays on the side tables.

Princess Lakwi rose with a natural grace and picked up two clean platters. She piled them half-full of cold meat cuts, maize-bread, yarma cheese, honey and little corn parcels with delicious centres. She presented them both with the loaded plates. Papa took the offering with a quick peck on his sister's cheek and sauntered over to the big chair next to Mama reserved for the Kapok.

Mannok mumbled his thanks and slipped into a corner at the other end of long room next to his cousins. He and his father were the only ones eating. Aunt Lakwi laughed as she settled by her husband, Lord Amaruk who arrived late last night with the army. It was a carefree sound in the tense room, though it made Uncle Amaruk jump.

'Do you remember, Rokku, that day we waited hours for Papa to come to the midday meal only to discover he had decided to spend the day inspecting the mines? He wasn't even in the city. Mama was not at all impressed.'

'Hmm, he used to do that all the time before he married your mother, Lakwi. Sometimes, he would decide to have the morning meal hours before the dawn.' The Kapok gave a wry smile. 'Then, he'd even have dinner in the middle of the afternoon and I would arrive to a room cleared of food and no more to be served till the next meal.'

Mama placed her plate with precision onto the small circular table beside her. The rosy blush had contracted to two spots on her cheekbones. 'Rokkan, you are not suggesting that as Prince Royal of Tarka, you went hungry.'

'No, no, of course not, Marra.' Papa flashed his characteristic fierce grin though it didn't quite reach his eyes. 'But those years between my mother's death and father's marriage to the Lady Suraya were often wild and chaotic. No one would have been foolish enough to suggest that the Kapok was crazy, at least to his face, or to contradict his orders however erratic, but he didn't take my mother's death at all well. His schedule and his moods were as predictable as high mountain weather, and I am certain he sometimes forgot I existed.'

'Really, Rokkan ... you are exaggerating ...'

Papa raised his fly-away eyebrows and his eyes had darkened to a rocky ochre. 'I am not in the habit of exaggerating.'

Mannok put down a half-eaten corn parcel, his stomach fluttered with tension. He shouldn't have kept Papa in the stables.

Uncle Lukarn cleared his throat. 'Rokkan understates the case, sister. Matters were extremely haphazard at the Palace until the late Kapok married Aunt Suraya.'

Papa's eyes softened. 'You are right, Lukku, marriage to Suraya brought stability and order to palace life, definitely an improvement in many ways.'

'But not in all, Rokku?' asked Aunt Lakwi in a teasing tone.

'Indeed. For a start, she banned all animals from inside the Palace, even the dogs, and certainly my collection of critters. She insisted on regular baths and bedtimes and had an obsession about correct manners on every occasion. The rules kept multiplying— no climbing roofs, no climbing trees, no midnight snacks, no riding after dark, no lighting fires—.'

Mama shook her head. 'It seems to me that it was past time such changes were introduced!'

Mannok looked at his plate. A palace routine free of all the rules didn't sound like such a bad idea to him.

Papa raised his eyebrows. 'Life got a lot duller and a great deal more restricted, my dear.'

'Hmmm, life did get a tad more boring, but perhaps a lot safer too,' Lukarn said. 'I was often scared out of my wits tagging along on your wild escapades, Rokku. Not that things have changed all that much when I think about it.'

'Ha! You worry too much. Always did.'

Mama sniffed. 'And you never worry enough, Rokkan.' She turned to Ista. 'A beaker of guava juice, please, then clear the dishes.'

A mutinous looked flickered across the girl's face before it settled into a compliant mask. She glided over to the serving tables and poured the pink juice into a beaker.

Beside him, Rizzi stopped fidgeting with her plaits. 'At last, we can finish the meal,' she whispered.

'Hush Rizzi,' her older brother Waren hissed back. Aunt Samara shook her head at the two of them.

Princess Lakwi leaned over and picked up Jati, cuddled the squirming baby close and kissed her on the head. 'So, now the Nolmec threat is under control and rebel lords defeated, what are your plans Rokku?'

Mama took the beaker from Ista. 'Time for a formal coronation interrupted by your brother's treachery,'

'There are still some loose ends to tie up before we can consider it.'

'I do hope, Rokkan, you don't intend to start another war.' Mama placed the beaker on the table untasted. 'You just got back.'

'Are the Nolmec still a threat, Papa?' Mannok asked, picking up and swallowing the last morsel on his plate. He flushed as the adults in the room turned to look at him.

'No Mannu.' His father leaned back in his chair. 'But not all the rebel leaders were captured or killed when Prince Naetok was defeated.' He stood up. 'Lukarn, I've a few matters to attend to first, if you can get the council together for a meeting at noon. Lakwi, Amaruk,' He turned to Mama, 'Marra, you are welcome as always.'

Mannok let out a soft sigh of relief as Papa indicated the meal was finally over, though he wished he'd been invited to the council.

Chapter Seventeen: Treasures

Ista

The sun-kissed flagstones warmed Ista's skin beneath her thin tunic. A stone wall, hoary with age and covered in lichen, enclosed the herb garden at the back of the kitchens. High above her, long streamers of fleecy clouds raced in the sky. The sun was halfway down in the west, and in east the golden orb of Alumi, lopsided and washed out, hung above the golden tiles of the main palace roof. The snow-covered crown of Younger Twin floated above the kitchen roof, its triangular peak sharp-edged against the lapis lazuli sky. The clash of dishes and shouts of the cooks from the adjoining kitchen were easy to tune out.

Ista allowed herself to relax against the sun-warmed wall. She felt at home in this secluded corner of the bustling palace complex. It provided a patch of familiarity. The comforting scents of meadowsweet, mountain sage and guavamint reminded her of the herb garden Grandfather had kept at North Pass, though he'd also grown thornier, darker plants with more sinister purposes.

Four days had passed since she'd arrived at the Palace, and Kupanna Marra had finally given her an afternoon's respite from her duties. Starting before dawn and finishing well after dusk, she fell into a deep sleep the moment she collapsed onto her sleeping mat. At least, her exhaustion left her nights undisturbed by nightmares.

A small drab bird hopped on the nearby path, while all about her, others chirped, whirred and fluttered. Perhaps Dinnis would've known their names. He was interested in trivial things like that.

She'd not seen him since the day Grandfather died and she wondered if he'd survived or had gone looking for their father.

She pulled out her little bundle of treasures from beneath her tunic, the few belongings that the Kapok had allowed her to gather from the Tower before the long journey south. She unwrapped the fine cloth covering them. Inside was one of Grandfather's leather-bound notebooks scribed mostly in the ancient tongue. She opened the book. Soot smudged on the leather cover, but Grandfather's cramped writing, peppered with arcane symbols and scrawled marginal notes, were unharmed.

There was also a tarnished bronze locket with a painting of her mother that Dinnis had given her on their first night in Akrad's Tower. He had held her tightly and sung her lullabies until his voice had cracked. He seemed so big and strong and able to protect her. She still remembered trying to catch up with him when they ran through the maize fields and the way he would lift her up over the fences or big rocks. That was, until they had tried to escape and were confined behind the walls of the stronghold.

The Arkon Akrad had often been distracted for days in pursuit of his brilliant ideas. He was always unpredictable. Her brother had taken the full brunt of Grandfather's bad moods and sudden tempers and on the lean days when meals were scarce he had a happy knack of producing food to fill both their empty bellies. She had a strong suspicion that he had pilfered those treasured scraps of food, but she had been too hungry to scorn them. She missed him despite his crazy ideas.

Living with Grandfather seemed to have diminished her brother. He had become clumsy and stupid and his promises that Papa would return had proved hollow. Until one day she realized that she didn't want to leave the Tower. She wanted to stay and continue to learn the great mysteries from the Arkon, to be his apprentice, to be cossetted as the Nolmec's little Kiprissa.

Now Grandfather was dead, killed by those hateful Adelphi. She picked up a small bone-handled knife she had purloined from a tray while serving the Kupanna a couple of days ago. While not very sharp or large, it was better than nothing. Not that it would provide much defence against Grandfather's vicious killers if they did decide to track her down.

Putting down the knife, she scooped up the locket and rubbed her slender fingers over the ridged geometric design on the back until it hurt. She peered closely at the shape. It looked like a six-pointed star with a small flower in the centre and a double circle on the outer rim. Dinnis reckoned it was the symbol of their mother's family along with the phoenix.

Then there was the carved bone comb and the small crystal that Grandfather had given her days before he had been killed. He had been excited to find it. Tears pricked her eyes and Ista tightened her hand around the translucent stone. If she could learn its secrets she might use it to forge her own destiny.

The last treasure was the cloth itself. Dinnis said it was silk, an exotic material only the richest Nolmec's possessed. It came from across the sea, Dinnis said. Maybe he had made that up. This too had belonged to their mother, the mother who had died when she was born, the mother she had never known. She looked at the beautiful patterns in bright yellows, reds, greens and blues. She stroked the soft shiny material.

A shadow fell over her.

'What are you hiding?' a muffled voice demanded.

She jumped and jerked the cloth around her treasures. How had she been so careless, engrossed when she should've been alert.

She twisted round and glared. The Prince stood behind her. In his right hand, he held a huge slab of maizebread spread with a sweet tomato jam and his cheeks were bulging. He was dressed in a light-yellow tunic and green breeches with grass stains at the knees, a wooden hunting knife on a belt at his side. His wavy russet hair was messy, his jade coloured eyes shining with interest.

She tilted her chin in the air. 'Why is that your business?'

He blinked at her then gave her a crooked grin.

'I was just asking.'

'Does the Kupanna need me?' Sighing, she put out her hand on the ground to push herself upright.

'No, I've been visiting the kitchens. Thought I'd take this route to the stables rather than go through the Entrance Hall and risk running into Bitjarnan. I didn't expect to find you here.'

'Your mother has relieved me of my duties for the afternoon.'

'Have you no one to play with?'

'I don't want to play. Besides who is there to play with?'

'I dunno ... maybe Rizzi? Baby Jati and Yalik are too little, I guess.'

'Oh them! Rizanna would never play with a Nolmec maid. As if I would want to play with a stuck up Tamrin who can't even read yet. They are all babies.'

He squinted his jade-green eyes. 'So, you can read?'

'Of course, can't you?'

'Oh yes, well I'm learning. Papa says I don't apply myself. Now he's back I'll have to stop skipping lessons.' Mannu took a great bite of the maizebread and chewed.

'Why are you alone? Where is your friend—Garo is it?'

'His grandfather's visiting the family so he had to go home.'

'You could play with Waren.'

'He thinks I'm too young to play with. He says he has important things to do like archery practice and other stuff like that. Anyhow, I'd much rather spend time in the stables. Papa's mare Mirror had a foal a few days ago. He's a real beauty. I thought we could call him Shadow. Papa thought that was a great name. And Tracer had five puppies a couple of weeks ago. Would you like to see them?'

Ista squirmed. 'I ... I don't think so.

The Prince frowned. 'Why not? Oh, I guess you don't like playing with boys. Just like Rizzi.'

'No, *kuree*. It's just that—' she hesitated, then said in a rush, 'I'm afraid of dogs and horses. They are so big and unpredictable.'

Mannok's eyes widened, 'Oh, that's right. Well, Papa's dogs can be a bit unruly. They used to scare me a bit when I was little. What would you like to do?'

She tried to smile. 'Is it true that the Palace has a magnificent library? I would like to see it.'

'The library?'

'Yes.'

'Oh.'

'Is that a problem?' She pressed her lips together. 'I guess maids aren't allowed in the library.'

'No, that's not it. It's just that I've been banned.'

'But you are the Prince, *kuree*.'

'Yes, but ... this one time I was chasing a cavy under a table—'

'What's a cavy? And why was it in the library?'

'A cavy is ... you don't know what a cavy is? It's a little hairy animal with a twitchy nose. It was one of my pets, and it escaped from underneath my tunic so I was trying to catch him before anyone noticed. He went under the table, and I followed him and somehow, I upset the table. All the manuscripts and a couple of old vases went crashing to the ground. The chief librarian said I had ruined several alume of work and it turned out that the vases were very valuable 'cos they were hundreds of years old. They looked rather ordinary to me. Anyhow, books are rather boring, don't you think?'

'No, I like books, *kuree.*'

'Oh.' He looked at her with slightly widened eyes, then frowned. 'Why do you keep calling me *kuree*? Is it Nolmec for 'stupid' or something?'

She laughed then put her hand over her mouth when his frown deepened to a scowl. 'No, I mean, yes, it is Nolmec. It means ... I guess it means something like, sir or honoured person.'

'Oh, that's okay then. I know, I can show you around the Palace.'

She grimaced. 'Thank you, Mannok. but I have run errands around the Palace for her Majesty till my legs are about to fall off.'

'Oh.' He shoved the last thick piece of maizebread into his mouth and chewed, his square forehead creased in thought. As he swallowed the last crumb, his mouth curved into a triumphant smile that reminded her of his father. 'Have you been to the throne room?'

She shook her head. 'Surely—'

He laughed. 'Come on, not afraid, are you?'

He spun around and took off toward the kitchens. With a gulp, she made sure her bundle was safely secured and ran after him.

Chapter Eighteen: Hand of Friendship

Ista

Ista ran as fast as she could, but she had trouble catching up with Prince Mannok. In a few quick strides, he disappeared through the kitchen door. She almost decided to give up the chase, but she'd enjoyed talking to the boy, even though they didn't seem to have many shared interests. Having a close connection to the seat of power didn't always mean that life was easy, but if she was to survive … and escape … making allies was paramount.

She slipped through the back door, dodged a scullery maid and pushed her way through the huge room full of red-cheeked cooks and servants preparing the evening meal.

Ista had quickly learnt that the kitchens not only cooked for the royal family and their visitors, but also for the rest of the Palace staff including the Palace Guard and the barracks. She had to take it slow amongst the bustling activity, dodging servants carrying large steaming pots of chilli beans or baskets full of fruit, vegetables, cheeses and even dried fish from the coast or mountain lakes. On huge spits rotating over enormous fires were peccary and other game. The aromas tantalised her senses and her stomach rumbled. At last, she reached the other side of the room and found the Prince leaning against the frame of the door waiting for her.

He gave her a cheeky grin. 'I was about to send out a search party for you.'

She ignored his jab. 'I expect you can't really show me the throne room. You are just trying to impress me.'

'Follow me and try to keep up.'

This time he walked rather than ran. She followed him along the walkway between kitchen and the main palace building, to an atrium and then turned into a huge room. Large casement windows on the south let in light while tapestries of hunts, banquets and other celebrations hung on the inside wall.

Mannok waved a hand at with high arched ceilings. 'The Royal Dinning Hall for feasts and high occasions.'

She already knew that. She also knew they weren't supposed to be here, or at least she wasn't, unless sent on an errand. They walked past the long low tables stacked against the side of the room. Two warriors with long shafted spears stood in front of the large double golden doors at the far end.

Mannok dropped his voice in a whisper. 'The doors open into the Throne Room. Guards were placed here after Uncle Naetok attacked Papa. He escaped from the Throne Room without being seen, to rally his supporters in the north.'

'How are you going to get past them,' she whispered back. Her heart gave a small tumble and she caught her breath. Maybe this hadn't been a good idea. If they did get into trouble, she would suffer more for it than the privileged Prince.

Mannok strode up to the guards as cool as mountain snow. In a good imitation of his father's casual confidence, he inclined his head. 'The Lady Ista and I wish to view the Throne Room.'

When the guard hesitated, Mannok raised his eyebrows. 'Would you bar the way of your prince?'

After a small pause, the guards bowed and then swung open the doors. 'Forgive us, Your Highness.'

Ista's shoulder relaxed and she followed the Prince through the doors. The Throne Room was more magnificent than the Banquet Hall. Beneath six large casement windows and tapestries with hunting and battle scenes, stood ten large chairs. The two in the middle were larger than their companions and covered in gold. On the other sides of the room was a tiered bank of benched seats.

'That's for the clan leaders and nobles when important decisions are discussed,' Mannok whispered. 'Papa sits in the big golden chair with Mama beside him, flanked by the Markans and Markanas.' He walked a few steps into the room and stopped. 'And here, this is the spot Uncle Naetok attacked Papa.' He looked a little breathless, his bronzed face paler than normal. 'I still have nightmares about it,' he said in a low voice, as though he was speaking to himself. 'I was here, you know, when it happened.'

'Why do you come here then? If it upsets you?'

He looked at her, his green eyes intense, 'Because I will be Kapok one day. Papa is not afraid so neither will I be.' He slowly spun around and looked at the room. 'Before the assassination attempt, I used to come in here to play whenever I could. It was one of my favourite places.'

'I saw them kill my grandfather,' she said in a tiny voice. 'I wish I could stop seeing it happen over and over again.'

He nodded as though he already knew this. He reached out and took her hand in his. His hand was strong, with little nicks and grazes and a little cool. He smelt of grass, dog and horse. He was very like his father.

'We could be friends,' he said, 'You're not silly like Rizzi—always giggling and poking her tongue out and trying to trip me up. I think I like you even if you are a bit stuck up.'

'Maybe I like you too, even though you are not that smart.' She put a hand over mouth. She had not meant to say that.

He dropped her hand and scowled at her. She looked back at him waiting to see what retribution he would take. Suddenly, he threw back his head and laughed.

She scowled. 'What's so funny?'

'We are. I suppose I asked for that for calling you proud.' Then he added fiercely, 'But I'm not stupid. If you want to be my friend, Ista, don't call me stupid again. I don't like it, alright?'

She nodded. 'Alright, Your Highness.'

He relaxed and grinned at her. 'There is something else. I found this secret room that looks down on the throne room. I'll show you where it is, but you must keep it a secret. Promise?'

She nodded. 'Promise.'

'Come on.'

He pivoted around and rushed off towards the big golden doors at a right angle to the ones they had entered by. This time she was not left standing, gaping after him. She was getting used to his sudden moves. They burst through the huge doors, startling a brace of guards on the other side and raced down the dim corridor.

A big man emerged from one of the doors on the right side. Mannok swerved and tried to stop, sliding along the tiled floor.

The man jumped back with a muffled exclamation. 'By the moons, what the...'

Ista's heart quailed as she recognised the deep voice of the Kapok. She knew she couldn't stop in time. The Prince missed colliding with Rokkan by ninas and ended up in a heap against the wall, while Ista ploughed into him, banging her elbow painfully on the wall. She rocked back and sat stunned on the floor for a few minutes, shivering with fear.

Rokkan grabbed the Prince and hauled him to his feet, his eyes narrowed.

'Mannu! Why am I not surprised!'

'Sorry, Papa ... Your Majesty.' The boy's voice was small and he looked down at the floor, his hands behind his back.

'Are you hurt, Mannu?'

'No, Papa.' Leaning forward, Ista could see the grazes on his knees and elbows. His lower lip was trembling and his hands clenched.

'What about you, Ista?'

'No, *kuree* ... I mean, Your Majesty.'

The Kapok gazed at them both for what seemed like a long time, small furrows appearing between his dark eyebrows. At last he blew out a breath.

'How many times have you been told not to run inside the Palace, Mannu? You should know the rules by now and certainly shouldn't be leading others into wrongdoing.'

'Yes, but Papa, the other day you said you didn't like rules.'

'Ha! Don't drag me into this! At seven, yes! But your grandmamma showed me that most rules aren't there merely to make life difficult for young boys. They have good reasons behind them. Which you have just ably demonstrated.'

Mannok squirmed. 'Yes, sir.'

'Hmm, this better be the last time you get caught running inside the Palace. Next time ... I'll let Bitjarnan decide a fit punishment for you'

The Prince groaned. 'But he ...' Rokkan raised his eyebrows and Mannok fell silent. 'Yes, Papa,' he eventually mumbled.

'Now, we best get you patched up before the Kupanna sees you. You too, Ista.'

Chapter Nineteen: Tarka

Dinnis

It was almost half an Alume since Dinnis had watched Rokkan Kapok and his warriors ride out the gate of the stronghold at North Pass the day after the battle. The progress of the baggage train was slow, but at last they were nearing the end of the journey, or so Lutan Zaven informed them.

In the early afternoon, they followed the road round the base of a sharp triangular snow-covered peak. As they crested a rise in the road, the great grey-walled city, perched on the flank of the mountain, loomed up on their right with a suddenness that surprised Dinnis. A smaller snow-covered peak bracketed the city on the other side. In front of the walls, a bowl-like fertile valley stretched out, divided by a glacier fed river and circled by sharp edged cliffs.

This fabled metropolis was his father's city. It was both alien to him and as familiar as the bedtime stories Papa used to tell him— wonderful stories of Kapoks and Kupannas, beautiful princesses and brave warriors, wise priests and crafty merchants, dynastic struggles, betrayals and heroic deeds. How often had he imagined arriving here on the back of his father's charger? His pulse raced with a mixture of excitement and apprehension. What reception would he find inside its ancient walls?

It took what felt like hours to skirt the grey walls towering above them, and it hurt Dinnis' neck when he tipped his head back to see the spear-carrying warriors on the battlements. Escaping from here wouldn't be easy. The serene beauty of that first glimpse was soon shattered as they descended towards the gates. The crowds jostled against him and the other orphans—merchants, soldiers, farmers taking their produce and animals to sell. On occasion. the baggage train shuffled to one side to allow a palanquin or a group of mounted nobles to pass.

The closer Dinnis came to the massive gates, the more overwhelming were the noise and smells. Stall holders, squeezed between the stone-paved road and walls, competed with the calls of the food sellers weaving through the crowds with trays of steaming food. Travelling companions called out to each other, children laughed, babies cried. Mingling with the cacophony of human sounds were the strident hums of the yarmas, the snorts and whinnies of the horses, the excited barking of dogs and the worried cackling of domestic birds. The mingled smells of roasted meats, of chilli, of sweat, animals and manure hung in the air about him, pressing down on him.

Guards screened the people streaming through the massive golden gates. Lutan Zaven hustled the orphans through. A steeply sloping stone-paved street stretched up the hill ahead. On either side, multi-storeyed houses and shops clung together like yarmas huddling for comfort in the rain. Mid-way up the slope, in the centre of the city, a large building sat on the crest of a small hill, dominating the smaller buildings around it. Its high arched casement windows flashed in the sunlight above the crimson walls encircling it. Further up, a huge flat-topped triangular structure, built of massive stone blocks, nestled beneath the snow-capped peaks.

He stopped in awe, drinking in the details, wondering where Papa lived. The other orphans pressed him from behind.

'Move it, bluey.' One of the bigger ones, Uson, shoved him between the shoulder blades.

Some of the other orphans sniggered.

Lutan Zaven turned around. 'Quiet, you lot.' As they reached the other side of the gate, he pointed with his chin to a recess at the base of the massive walls. 'Wait here.'

Sometime later, Lutan Jakan, flanked by two guards, trotted up. He handed a slate to Lutan Zaven.

'Right, after Lutan has counted you, I'm taking you to the Palace. Pipe down over there and listen good.' He glared at Uson and his companions, his horse sidling beneath him. 'You'll be happy to know you'll be looked after. Some of you have kin. You'll be handed over to them.'

'But Lutan, what if we haven't.' This time it was Hasuk who'd interrupted.

'The rest of you? You'll be given food and shelter for honest work. Mind your manners and you won't get into trouble. Oh, and in case some of you is thinking about running away from the Kapok's generous offer ...' the Lutan's green eyes seemed to look straight at Dinnis. He winked. 'We'll hunt you down and find you. Keep up now.'

He wheeled his mount and set it to a brisk walk up the street.

Walled houses lined the main street heading up the hill. After the first few side streets, the congestion eased. The road steepened and Dinnis' calves burned, even after days of walking up and down mountains. Sometime later, tall red walls, topped with carved gilded figures, flanked their left. It was another ten or more minutes before the street flattened out.

'This way,' Lutan Jakan growled and he steered them left into another long street.

The Palace complex loomed on one side, a cluster of buildings, an open plaza and gardens on the other. They passed the huge ornate gates, flanked by guard towers, and entered a smaller gate further along. Walking past stables and practice ranges, they entered towards the back of the massive three-story palace. At last Lutan Jakan ushered them into a big room. Light streamed in from high windows in the western wall and guards stood at the doors.

'Wait here. Eat. Make yourselves comfortable.'

Only moments after the Lutan left, servants arrived with huge trays of food and drink—large rounds of maize bread, creamy yarma cheeses, tomatoes and mounds of fruit. It was more food than Dinnis had ever imagined, much less seen before. Shuffled to the end of the line by the jostling of the Tamrin orphans, he still found plenty to eat when he reached the tables. Dinnis piled his plate high and, as an afterthought, he tucked a few pieces of fruit and some cheese in the folds of his tunic for later. Who knew what lean times might be ahead of him? He found a shaded and relatively unoccupied corner of the room and sat with his back against the smooth lime-washed wall.

He hadn't eaten since the morning meal, but the more he looked around, the more his appetite deserted him. After a couple of bites, he fiddled with the food, his eyes taking in the tapestries on the wall celebrating battles and hunts. Did his father live here or somewhere else in the city? What would happen to him now?

Long shadows had crept into the room by the time footsteps sounded in the corridor outside. Lutan Jakan strode through the huge doors, accompanied by a couple of scribes and a short rotund fellow tottering on small feet. A larger group of adults trickled in behind them. Most with grey hair or lined faces. Many of the men wore thick woven capes, the women were wrapped in woven shawls with yarmas or maize plants patterned on them. Stopping inside the doorway, they shuffled their feet and scanned the faces of gathered children. Dinnis' breath quickened and he leaned forward before slumping back against the wall. None of this broad, sturdy people were anywhere near as tall as Papa.

The Lutan stepped forward. 'Listen up. Step up, if Madomo Bitjarnan calls your name. No dawdling or hanging back now.'

Consulting the slate, the rotund man began calling out names, separating them out by clans. Soon the room was full of a confused babble. The occasional joyous shriek could be heard above the din, as excited kinsfolk hugged children and led them away.

When the Madomo fell silent a dozen children remained unclaimed. Beside him, a girl of about seven began to cry and one of the younger boys soon joined in. Dinnis kept his eyes on the stone-flagged floor, biting down hard on his lip. Perhaps Papa was busy and would come for him later. He almost stuffed his fingers in his ears at the unbidden memory of Akrad's derisive laugh, 'Your father, boy? He's not coming back for a *moros* like you.'

To drown out that mocking voice, he pulled out an empty notebook he'd purloined from Akrad and sketched a rough drawing of the silver young woman at North Pass, Rasel. What had she said? Something about taking a different path.

He jumped as a hand clasped his shoulder. 'Don't worry, we will make sure you are looked after, boy.' Lutan Jakan's voice was gruff but the squeeze he gave Dinnis' shoulder was light.

The Lutan turned to the group of children and read off another seven or eight names. Again, Dinnis was not on the list.

The Lutan cleared his throat. 'I am sorry to say that we have not been able to find your kin. We have arranged apprenticeships for each of you with skilled and honest craftspeople who will also give you a home and teach you their craft. You will be under the Kapok's protection. Be grateful you're not on the streets.' Beckoning to a couple of guards, he continued, 'The Madomo will take you to where you are sleeping tonight. In the morning, you'll be taken to your new situations.'

As the guards and the Madomo guided the children out of the room, the Lutan turned to Dinnis and the other three still remaining. They stood a little apart from Dinnis, their eyes fixed on Lutan Jakan's face. The Lutan nodded as though pleased with what he saw and lifted the slate the Madomo had handed him.

'Hasuk son of Kaptan Maikwi; Uson son of Lutan Yanak and Asik son of Lutan Turak—your fathers fought bravely as officers for the Kapok, giving their lives in his service. Since you now have no kin to care for you, Rokkan Kapok has given you a place at the Palace, to be educated alongside Prince Mannok and to be among his age-mates. This is both a great honour and an opportunity to excel, to win the Prince's favour.'

The eyes of the three boys widened. This was clearly more than they had expected. The tallest one, Hasuk, about Dinnis' age gave a half-smile and stammered, 'Thank you, Lutan Jakan.'

The Lutan's stern expression relaxed a fraction. 'I'll convey your gratitude to the Kapok, Hasuk. Your father and I trained together. He was a courageous warrior.'

Hasuk's serious face split into a grin, though a sheen of tears glinted in his hazel eyes. 'Yes, sir!'

The Lutan cleared his throat. 'Wait here Dinnis, I'll be back for you.' And he guided the other three out of the room.

Outside the great windows, the sky was darkening to indigo. Shadows dimmed the corners and blurred the colours of the huge tapestries on the walls. From other parts of the huge building came the sounds of people's voices, the crash of pots and pans, the march of booted feet and the slamming of a door.

Dinnis stood straight and still and alone, his thoughts dark and tumultuous.

Chapter Twenty: Regret

Dinnis

Dinnis wasn't sure how long he stood in the middle of the rapidly darkening room, but it was probably less than half an hour before Lutan Jakan came hurrying back in.

'Dinnis, I'm sorry to leave you alone in the dark. Come with me.'

'Yes *kur*...sir.'

He hastened after the Lutan, through a hallway and out into a vast hall with great doors leading off it, guarded by Tamrin warriors. On the opposite side, a grand set of stairs led the way to the balconies in the upper levels. Large candelabras around the room cast a flickering golden light on the shining surfaces of the balustrades and floor. Above, the afterglow of the sunset could be seen through the high skylights, giving the room a garish glow. Dinnis barely had time to gape before the Lutan set off, down another corridor and through the second large door on the right. He strode past a smaller atrium with a rectangular pool reflecting the reds and purples of sunset in the middle and turned into a on the other side room brightly lit by smaller candelabras.

'Wait here.' The Lutan disappeared through the door.

A jocular voice floated through the slight opening. 'Ah, Lutan Jakan.'

Dinnis' breath hitched. His father's voice. He edged closer to the slightly ajar door, anxious to hear.

'Your Majesty.'

'Rise, Jakan if you please. How have you fared with your assignment?'

'Sir, most of the children have been reunited with their kin; eight will be placed tomorrow with families offering apprenticeships and three—the sons of Kaptan Maikwi and Lutans Yanak and Turak— are to be companions of the Prince as you instructed. The young lads wished me to pass on their gratitude.'

'And the widows of the fallen, Lutan?'

'I've made arrangements for the compensation you have authorized.'

'Your diligence is impressive, Lutan, as is your quick thinking at North Pass. I've decided to appoint you Kaptan of the Palace Guard when Kaptan Ninak retires.'

'I would be greatly honoured, sir. If you please, Your Majesty, the other boy is outside, as you requested.'

'What boy? Rokkan—' Another voice, as sharp and as brittle as splintered glass. Lukarn Markan's voice.

Dinnis' muscles tightened. It didn't matter, Papa would not listen to this man.

The creak of someone moving in a chair. 'Ah, yes, thank you Jakan. I did say—' Papa hummed. 'Never mind. Send him in. And take an hour's break, get something to eat. And Lutan ...'

'Your Majesty.'

'Shut the door after you.'

Dinnis stepped back as the door swung open. The Lutan reappeared with a wide grin, his green eyes glowing. He swallowed his smile and motioned Dinnis to enter the room.

'Tell the truth, lad. Remember to prostrate yourself before the Kapok. Only speak if spoken to. He is a fair man.'

Dinnis' heart hammered against his thin chest. This was it.

He walked through the door into a cosy room lit by a candelabra hanging from the ceiling. Bookshelves crammed full to overflowing lined the walls. The Kapok sat with his long legs stretched out on an untidy desk. His golden eyes narrowed as Dinnis stepped into the room. Beside the stern-faced Tamrin ruler, Markan Lukarn stood with his arms folded over his chest and a look as hard as basalt on his face.

Dinnis' gaze darted from one unyielding face to the other. The seconds trickled by and Markan's fierce scowl deepened. Worse, there was not a hint of kindness or even mercy in the Tamrin ruler's penetrating eyes. Suddenly, it was hard to breathe.

Remembering the Lutan's instructions, he lowered himself to the floor and stretched out face down. His own erratic breath became a tempest competing with the staccato tap of the Kapok's fingers on the desk. The stone floor pressed against his body. Unshed tears pricked his eyes. This was not how he'd imagined his reunion with his father. Nothing had happened how he'd imagined it from the moment the Tamrin attacked Akrad's Stronghold.

'Rokkan, you can't mean to bring this one into the Palace as well? You can't afford sentiment. After three bitter years of war, surely you can see—'

The drumming of the Kapok's strong fingers jerked to a stop. The chair creaked.

'Rokkan!'

'You forget yourself, Lukarn.' The Kapok brought his feet to the floor with a thump.

'The girl is useful, to keep the Nolmec off balance, but the boy could undermine everything we've fought for. He is what eleven, twelve? Almost a man, and no doubt, Akrad's tool, a baited trap waiting to go off. Hide him deep in the dungeons or give me custody at least, if you can't stomach what must be done—'

The girl? Could that be his sister? Some of the weight pressing Dinnis down into the cold, hard stone floor lifted. And Papa hadn't banished him yet.

'Enough!' The Kapok was up and pacing in the tight space of the room. 'I hear what you say, yet he is just a boy. He cannot help his heritage any more than his sister. I haven't forgotten my promise to you and Marra, to your clan, but what you suggest is unthinkable.'

'I only fear that you will regret this decision, brother-in-law. Not just you, but your family and your realm.'

'Regret? Regret has been my closest companion these last nightmare years. Regret is something I cannot shake whichever path I take.' The Kapok took in a deep breath and let it out slowly. 'You are dismissed, Lukarn.'

'What?' When no answer was forthcoming, the Markan said in a low, rough voice, 'Did you just dismiss me like a common soldier?'

'Apparently not, since a common soldier would have instantly obeyed his superior, something you seem to have forgotten how to do. Your concerns are noted, now go.'

'As you command, Your Majesty. But remember that without my family's loyalty your victory would be short-lived, and I am not the only one you need to persuade.' The Markan stomped past Dinnis and slammed the door behind him.

Dinnis breathed easier and shifted his stiff body. Now Papa could speak to him freely.

Papa's boots whispered against the floor as he paced the cramped space. The tips of the burnt orange boots came to a stop in front of him.

'You may stand.'

Dinnis stumbled to his feet, a smile spreading across his face. He looked up to the Kapok, his Papa, he stepped forward, arms stretched out to hug him. The face in front of him did not soften nor had his father reached out to catch him up. The smile faltered and he dropped his arms.

'Papa?'

'You look even more like her, like Gaia, than when ...' Papa closed his eyes, then opened them, his face hardening, the probing of his mind hard against Dinnis'. 'And do you admire your Grandfather as much as your sister?'

'No, *kuree* .... I mean, sir. You said you'd come back, that you'd take care of us.'

'That was before Naetok rebelled and took half the north...' Papa heaved a breath. 'Look, it's complicated. I loved your mother and I will protect you and your sister, but no one can know of our connection. No one.'

'Our connection? I ... but, Papa—'

'I am not your Papa. Your father is dead to you, boy. Do you understand?'

'Dead?' He frowned, his hopes shrivelling up inside him. 'You mean ...' Hot anger flooded through him until his whole body shook, '... you mean Akrad was telling the truth ... that those stinking guards were right, that I mean nothing ... am nothing but an embarrassment? Because of my mother?' He was shouting, shouting at this stranger, this Tamrin ruler who towered over him, with his big hands and wide shoulders, a powerful man who he did not really know at all. Hot tears began to track down his cheeks. He tried to dash them away with his balled-up fists. 'I suppose it was all a joke? A sick pretence like one of Akrad's tricks to entice trust—'

'Be silent! Just because Lukarn feels free to shout at me, don't think you can take that liberty.'

Dinnis stood panting not trusting himself to speak, his eyes locked onto the Kapok's. He had never felt so angry, so betrayed. All those years of fruitless waiting, of stupidly hoping, of gritting his teeth against the pain and torment, because he thought—he had believed that—he and his sister had mattered to at least one person in this world. A person he had loved and trusted, only to be cast aside like broken pottery.

It had all been a lie.

The Tamrin ruler dropped his gaze, turned away from him. 'Life is not black and white, Dinnis. Your father cared deeply for your mother and for her children. He was young and foolish and did not think of the full implications of his actions. He regrets that others—that you—suffer as a result. Perhaps one day you will understand.'

'No, I never will! Those are just excuses.' He took a jagged breath. 'You would be dead now, all of you, if I hadn't let you into the upper ward. Akrad was making poison; he had machines to deliver it.'

The Kapok's eyes flickered. He turned towards to him, his face impassive. 'Your actions are commendable—'

'I did it all for ... for my ...' He gulped. *Rakka*. How could he be so stupid? Heat coursed through him. Stepping closer, he swept the pile of things jumbled on the desk. Ink pots and papers and books fell to the floor with the tinkle and crash of broken glass and fallen books. Papers fluttered in the air and ink dripped and spread out near the Kapok's burnt-orange boots.

He stood statue still, appalled and thrilled all at the same time. His hands clenched and another book teetered on the edge of the desk and crashed to the floor. He waited for the shouting, the beating. The candles spluttered in their holders. A guard guffawed in the distant. The Kapok folded his arm and said nothing, an unreadable expression on his face.

Dinnis rubbed the tears from his cheeks with the back of his hand. It was time to be done with childish dreams. 'The Arkon, even Ista, thought I was a *moros* to trust my father's promises. Seems they were right. The only good thing in this is that the monster is dead.'

'On that, at least, we are agreed.'

Anger leached out of him. He looked up again into the stony

face of the Tamrin ruler. He wanted nothing from this man, but he had to ask. 'And my sister is … safe?'

'Yes, she attends the Kupanna. Not what I planned, but it will serve.'

'Can I see her?'

'If you are careful. She doesn't recognise me, best it stays that way.'

'And how am I to be … disposed of?' Though, what did it matter what happened to him now?

'Since you are as an orphan with no other kin to care for you—'

'None that cares to acknowledge me.'

The Kapok's knuckles whitened. 'You will join Hasuk, Uson, and Asik in receiving a palace education, which I hope includes some improvement in manners and knowledge of palace protocol. I know this is hard for you, but please don't make a habit of interrupting me. From now on you are to address me as Your Majesty.'

Dinnis took a step back. Had he heard right? 'To be brought up in the Palace? Not prison or—' or death. No, he wouldn't just accept this. 'Why not send us away, back to Uncle Timon at Pylonis if you don't want us?'

'That … wouldn't be wise just now. I want you where I can keep an eye on you and where no one else can use you against the realm. If nothing else, I am in your debt for your actions at North Pass. Lukarn is convinced that anyone under Akrad's sway can only be corrupted, but I will give you a chance to prove him wrong. Do you understand, Dinnis?'

Dinnis' mouth twisted at the Kapok's first use of his name since he saw him on the battlefield. 'Yes, Your Majesty. I understand perfectly.'

Chapter Twenty-One: Interrupted

Mannok

Mannok loped through the small atrium, past the motionless guards, and into the reception room. The duty officer wasn't at his station, but he could hear the rise and fall of his father voice coming from the inner room where Papa often did official business. Mannok pushed against the unlatched door and walked straight in.

Papa stood in front of his desk, feet apart, his face furrowed into a heavy frown. Facing him was a tall thin boy about his cousin Waren's age with silvery-blue skin, high cheek bones and the exotic eyes of a Nolmec. The boy turned his head and looked at him, his oblique eyes flat, his face stony. Yet Mannok was sure he could see the signs of tear tracks down his cheeks. A cold shiver shot up his spine. Everyone knew the Nolmec were ruthless and cruel. Even their women were warriors. Why was the Nolmec boy here, in the Palace? Hadn't Papa said the Nolmec prisoners were being held at Tavin?

Papa turned and gave him such a baleful look that the Prince took a step backwards, suddenly unsure of his welcome. He'd barged in on his father while he was in the middle of an interrogation, not that Papa had worried about being interrupted in the past. Yet Mannok was not a little boy any more, he was almost eight years old. He at once bowed low and dropped to one knee.

'I beg your pardon, Your Majesty.'

He lowered his head and studied the familiar mosaic patterns on the floor. The room was silent except for his father's heavy breathing and the sound of his own heart pounding out a hurried rhythm. The boy standing just tanis away was as silent as a snowstorm. The smell of old leather and candle grease, the mustiness of a room shut up for the many Alume Papa had been away, pressed down on him. Mannok risked a glance and met his father's molten eyes.

Taking a deep breath, he said in a rush, 'I didn't run honest, I was just walking fast. I thought you were with Uncle Lukarn ...'

Papa cleared his throat. 'I don't suppose, Prince Mannok, you have heard of the gentle art of knocking on doors?' His controlled voice was scarier than if it had been hot with anger.

'Yes. I mean, I am sorry, Papa. I just didn't think—'

The Nolmec boy breathed in sharply. Mannok glanced sideways from under his eyelashes, but the boy had turned away, his prolife even stonier than before.

'There's our problem, Prince, you don't think. Action without intelligence is a dangerous thing.'

Mannok's face flamed. The sharp words cut deep. He screwed his eyes shut. It was true, he did have a habit of rushing in first and regretting it later. He wasn't as smart as Papa or maybe even his cousin Waren. He tried hard to be brave, to be good, to fight well and to be as princely as he could be, to make his father proud. His father had praised his efforts ... He swallowed, trying to dislodge the sudden lump in his throat. Why did Papa seem so hostile now?

'Well, things are as they are, and we must muddle along as best we can,' the Kapok said after a long silence, a hint of sadness, even bitterness in his voice.

Mannok stared at the floor. If he spoke, he might cry and Tamrin warriors didn't cry. He flinched as he felt his father's hand on his shoulder, pulling him up.

'So, Mannu, since you are here, I should introduce you to Dinnis. Dinnis, this is my son and heir, Prince Mannok.'

The boy looked up at him and gave a curt nod, a smouldering look in his smoky grey eyes. Papa's lips tightened, then he smiled with a forced cheerfulness.

'Mannu, Dinnis will be one of your new companions. There are three other orphans who will serve in that capacity, who you will meet tomorrow. They are the sons of brave warriors who have died fighting for our realm.'

Mannok's brow wrinkled at the undercurrents he sensed in the room. Who was this Nolmec boy? 'But Papa, isn't he—?' He noticed his father's raised eyebrows. 'Didn't his—?' he stopped shook his head and sighed. Wasn't he the enemy, he wanted to say but somehow couldn't under Papa's level stare. He shuffled his feet and scowled. 'As you wish, Papa.'

'Good. Dinnis and the other boys are new to the Palace. I expect you welcome them and to explain palace protocol and—hopefully—model it.'

'Yes, Papa.' Mannok straightened his shoulders. Why was Papa in such a contrary mood this evening? He'd been acting weirdly ever since he got back from the battle at North Pass. First, he'd introduced the strange girl and now this sullen Nolmec boy. And, besides, Mannok didn't need orphans as companions. He had Garvin and maybe even Ista.

'So, what can I do for you, Prince?'

He lifted his chin. 'I thought you'd want to know that some visitors have arrived. Markana Yuta with her children.'

'By the moons, why didn't you tell me earlier?'

He gave his father an aggrieved glare. 'You were too busy yelling at me.'

'Ah, yes ... so I was. Well, come on then, no time to dawdle.' The strange man with the unforgiving face vanished and his jovial, lively father reappeared.

Papa strode past the boys, waved them to follow, and disappeared through the doorway. Mannok rolled his eyes and raced after him trying to keep up with his long strides. They had traversed the access corridor and were out in the entrance hall when Papa stopped abruptly. He turned and caught Mannok before he collided into him. The Nolmec boy came to a stop a few paces behind them.

'Where are your aunt and cousins, Mannu?'

'Bitjarnan said he would show them into the eastern reception room while he informed you or Mama of their arrival. That's why I went looking for you.'

'I see.' Papa looked at the Nolmec lad standing a few paces behind them. 'Have you eaten yet, Dinnis?'

The boy lifted his head and met the Kapok's eyes without blinking. After a noticeable pause, he said, 'I ate when Lutan Jakan brought us to the Palace, Your Majesty. Besides, I find I've lost my appetite.'

'Humph, you don't look like you have had a decent meal in a ten-day.'

'Not in over three years, not since our father abandoned us.' His voice was soft but edged with an accusation that was reflected in his smoky grey eyes.

Papa nodded and took a step towards the boy. He flinched, moving backwards and ducking his head as though expecting a blow. Papa froze, his hand stretched out with a small ring in his palm. His chest heaved once, his mouth twisted. He cleared his throat.

'Go to the kitchens, boy, and get something to eat. If Lutan Jakan hasn't found you by then, ask one of the guards where the bachelor quarters are. If anyone questions you, show them my token. Do you understand?'

The boy nodded and took the ring as though it were a hot ember. He gave an abrupt bow to Papa and then to Mannok, and headed in the direction of the kitchens, his back as straight as a spear.

'Insolent young pup,' his father muttered. He smiled wryly at Mannok. 'Come on, let's greet our visitors.'

Chapter Twenty-Two: Threads and Arrivals

Ista

Not that one, girl.' The Kupanna's voice bristled with irritation. 'I said I wanted the turquoise.'

Ista bit back a sharp retort, as she bent over the basket and peered at the tangle of threads, imagining the scornful gaze of the others in the room fixed on her. Kupanna Marra sat stitching an elaborate tapestry stretched out on the frame in front of her. The Markana Samara sat close by mending tunics. Princess Lakwi put dainty stitches into baby clothes, a gurgling Jati and solemn Yalik played at her feet. Even Rizanna had spent the afternoon stitching away on crumpled samplers, in between playing with her elaborately dressed wooden dolls.

Ista's finger hovered over the threads. Which of the different shades of blue and green wool was the turquoise? The light was beginning to fade as the big windows of the smaller reception room caught the last beams of the lingering sunlight. Soon the servants would come bustling in to light the finely carved candelabra edging the room.

The flock of servants ensured all the rooms were kept clean, ordered and well stocked, unlike Akrad's Tower where chaotic piles of books and papers, half-eaten dinners and tangled bedclothes were as natural as moonrise and rain. The Palace made Grandfather's Stronghold seem rustic. Ista had to admit that the Palace had been cunningly designed with atriums, balconies, skylights and large windows with their amazing crafted diamonds of glass allowing light and air into even the innermost rooms of the vast building.

'It's that one.' Rizanna placed her tan finger on a skein and gave her a don't-you-know-anything stare.

Ista tilted her chin and used her height to look down at the younger girl. She took the skein of thread to and waited by the Kupanna's chair to be noticed.

'I wish something would happen.' Princess Lakwi covered a yawn with an elegant hand. 'What are the plans for the victory reception and an official coronation, Marra?'

'I need a firmer understanding of Rokkan's intentions.'

'Are the Nolmec still a threat now that both Naetok and Akrad have been defeated?' Lady Samara's forehead creased in a worried frown. 'I'd been looking forward to returning to Nakri to see if my parents are safe.'

Princess Lakwi put down her sewing. 'Rokkan thinks he can broker a peace treaty with Alfeas Timon and General Nuktis. It's the rebel Tamrin lords in the north that remain a concern with family and clan affiliations shattered by the Naetok's rebellion.' She glanced at Kupanna Marra. 'Not to mention the uncertainty of the loyalties of some of the other houses.'

'I know Rokkan distrusts Lord Haka, despite being age-mates as boys. Haka always seems perfectly amenable to me.' Marra picked up a thread and put it down. Where is that yarn, I asked for?'

Ista stepped forward and offered the skein she'd selected. Whatever these women thought, General Nuktis and Uncle Timon would surely not abandon their Kiprissa to servitude.

Princess Lakwi's eyes darkened for a moment. 'Oh, very amenable.' She cupped her chin with her slender hand. 'There is no telling what cousin Haka might to do, but I would imagine it will depend on whether Rokkan can bring peace to the north or not.'

The Kupanna leaned forward, pressing her full lips together. 'Lady Yuta assures me of her husband's loyalty, and Lukarn will soon settle those rebellious lords.' She took the yarn from Ista. 'You took long enough to choose a simple thread. One would think you had never plied a needle before, girl.'

'But I haven't, mistress.'

The women looked up at her in surprise.

Samara smoothed out a small tunic, picking at a loose thread. 'Didn't your mother teach you, Ista?'

'My mother died the day I was born.'

'I am sorry to hear that, Ista. That is a great loss.'

'It is hard to miss what you never had.'

Ista met the gentle eyes of the Markana defiantly. Unbidden, her fingers brushed the locket with her mother's picture nestled under her tunic. Like everyone in her life, her mother had left her to fend for herself. Ista's birth had killed the woman who had given her life. Grandfather was right, only the strong flourished.

'Surely a nurse or a governess to looked after you?' Marra's voice cut in on her thoughts. 'Did she not teach you the womanly arts?'

'There was a nurse, I think, but Grandfather left her behind when he took us in at North Pass after Papa left us. That was years ago.'

She couldn't remember much about her Papa. Just the feeling of being safe, truly safe, in his strong arms, his laughter and the way he would toss her in the air and catch her again. When they first got to the Stronghold, before she stopped listening to him, Dinnis would tell stories of Papa's big horse, his dogs, and his strength. He would tell the stories Papa had told him, sing the songs he sang and assure her that he would come back for them. But he never had. Tears pooled in her eyes.

They were all looking at her with pity now, even Rizanna, even Marra. She bit the inside her lip and blinked back the tears, her cheeks heating at showing them her weakness.

She lifted her chin and stood straight as a needle. 'I can speak three languages, read, count, and identify herbs of power. I know the difference between a feint and a counter attack and how to wield a knife. So, what does it matter whether I know a thread is aquamarine or teal or ... or twirl a spindle?'

Marra looked appalled. 'Your grandfather had eccentric ideas about a suitable education for a young lady. But the less said about that man the better. And I can assure you that, in the Palace, knowledge of the gentler crafts will be much more useful to you than the military arts.'

Ista pushed her lips shut. Stupid woman. What Ista needed was to get back to the safety and homage of her people.

A rap on the door, and the Madomo came bustling into the room.

'What is it Bitjarnan?' The Kupanna sat forward, smoothing down the long skirt of her tunic.

'Your Majesty ... unexpected guests—the Markana Yuta and her children.'

'Show them in and inform the Head Cook we have extra guests and ensure the Western Markan's suite is prepared.'

Dipping his shiny pate, the Madomo backed out the door. Moments later he ushered in a tall stately woman with grey-green eyes and a long face, a sturdy boy about Dinnis' age and a girl with a haughty expression on her face. Their clothes, while of finest yarma wool and adorned with embroidered threads and precious stones, had mud spots were travel-worn. They bowed low to the Kupanna.

Ista twisted the sleeve of her tunic. Not more of these Tamrin to torment her. The girl, standing behind her mother, was pretty in a plump sort of way. Her eyes were silver with an ash-grey ring around them. She gave Ista a cool appraising look, before joining Rizanna at the other end of the room.

Kupanna Marra rose and held out her delicate hands, genuine warmth in her cultured voice.

'This is an unexpected pleasure, Lady Yuta.'

'My dear Kupanna,' the woman drawled, taking the offered hands and pressing her cheek against the Kupanna's. 'I acted on whim. As soon as I heard of Rokkan's brilliant victory, I had to come and congratulate him—and you—in person.'

'You must have travelled with speed to arrive so soon. Rokkan has just arrived from North Pass.'

'The roads were reasonably passable though we ... Did you say North Pass? We heard Prince Naetok's was defeated at the siege at Nakri but ...' Yuta raised her finely arched eyebrows.

'Yes, we defeated the rebels at Nakri ...' A shadow loomed through the open doorway and the Kapok strode in the room, Prince Mannok following behind him. '... and we also dispatched Akrad at North Pass. Not bad for an Alume's work wouldn't you say?'

The Prince glanced at the bigger boy, who rolled his eyes and looked away, before meeting Ista's gaze. His eyes lit up, and he smiled at her with such warmth, she felt a fluttering in her chest. Careful, she needed to make allies without getting entangled herself. She smiled back before composing her face in the solemn mask she'd adopted.

'Your Majesty.' Yuta turned and bowed. 'Then may I congratulate you on two outstanding victories?'

The Kapok inclined his head.

'Your Majesty, is Lord Haka not with you?' Yuta's cool green eyes met Rokkan's golden honey-hued ones, a slight flush to her cheeks. 'He hasn't been injured in the battle, I hope?'

'Ah, I left your husband holding North Pass, Markana. Since he'd again arrived late for the fray, he had the freshest troops. In a little while I will organize another unit to relieve him.'

Yuta's smile faltered for a moment. 'I'm sure he will do his duty by the Throne.'

Ista could feel the undertow of tension even without probing the Tamrins' thoughts. Good, maybe she could use the fissures in Tamrin loyalties for her own gain. That's what Grandfather would do. She smiled.

Chapter Twenty-Three: Token

Dinnis

Dinnis fisted the gold ring, its cold smooth circle seeming to burn into his palm. He gritted his teeth. He wanted to throw it back into the Kapok's face, but he kept walking. He stopped at the southern end of the room. The room divided into two large passageways and there were doorways on either side of him. He spun around. Which of the several doorways would lead to the kitchen?

The Tamrin ruler was bounding up a large sweeping staircase near some large entrance doors, his son hurrying to keep up with his father's long strides. The skylights high in the arched ceiling high above him framed a darkening sky and long purple shadows fell across the flagstones. Along the walls, bunched candles on large stands pooled light on walls and floor. A large junglewood balcony swept around the room, with another tier above that one. This room alone would be as big as Akrad's Tower. The Palace was far bigger than any building he'd encountered before. Tantalising food smells came from behind. That way, perhaps.

He turned and stepped toward the large passageway on his right. A guard swung down the shaft of his spear, barring his way. Grey-threaded eyebrows bristled over dark brown eyes. 'What's your business, Nolmec.'

Dinnis swallowed and uncurled his fingers to show the token. He moistened his dry lips. 'The Kapok told me to find food in the kitchens.'

His broader companion leaned forward. 'Stop playing with him, Lantil. You heard the Kapok.'

Lantil smirked. 'Turn right after the spiral stairs to the library and keep going past through the western atrium until you reach a covered walkway. At the end, you'll find the kitchens, boy. And don't get up to mischief or you could come to a sticky end.' Lantil lifted his spear.

After running the gauntlet of guards at each entrance, Dinnis had finally arrived in the huge kitchen detached from the Palace and with a profusion of storage and preparation areas and large fire roaring along one wall. A blast of warm air and a plethora of mouth-watering smells of roasting food and spices hit him. People stirred pots of bubbling soup, sliced mounds of fruit, pounded spices or rolled maize bread. Others rushed from one areas in the huge room to the other with trays of roasted meats and potatoes or baskets of sweet confections. He hovered at the edge, not sure what to do next.

A young girl carrying a basket full of guavas crashed into him.

'What are you doing standing there, gaping like a right ninny?'

Dinnis stood his ground. 'I was told I could get a meal here.'

Her eyes popped, her gaze swept over him from his cropped head to his worn sandals.

A short, plump man with a red and sweaty face rushed up. 'What are you doing here, bluey?'

'Should we call the guards,' the girl piped up.

Dinnis sighed and flashed the Kapok's token.

The man's face crinkled. 'Didn't steal that, did you? Oh, never mind.' He called over his shoulder. 'Tubak, find this hangon some leftovers. And you, keep out of the way. We've extra nobs to feed tonight, without taking in strays.'

After a few moments, a half-grown youth thrust a bowl of congealed chilli bean stew and a round of stale flatbread into Dinnis hands.

Dinnis found a darkest corner in the noisy, busy kitchen and scooped up the beans with the maizebread. He could feel the stares prickling up his spine and hear the whispered comments. He had nowhere else to go, no one else to turn to. Not General Nuktis, who had handed Ista and him over to the Monster. Maybe, Lord Timon, his mother's bond-brother, but the Nolmec citadel of Pylonis was over a thousand lek away. He had been out of place in the Akrad's Stronghold, like a flagstone not set flush to the others. Here he felt like a cracked tile, dislodged and discarded.

He stayed scrunched in his overlooked corner, his limbs like logs, heavy and reluctant to move. It would be too much effort to fight his way through the crowded kitchen or guarded passageways of the maze-like palace.in search of the 'bachelor quarters'.

Servants bustled out the kitchen with heaped platters of food and trays with decorated dishes. The servers returned with empty platters and dumped them near the tubs where the junior staff washed utensils and dishes with a cacophony of bangs and shouts. At one of the long tables, the kitchen staff sat, or simply leaned against benches, scooping up food before leaving with nods and smiles. The burnished backs of hanging cooking pots reflected the golden flicker of candles and lamps. Soon only a handful of cleaners and the fat red-faced man, lingering over a huge mug of steaming koka and the ruins of his own meal remained.

Dinnis pulled out a sunfruit he'd pocketed earlier in the day and savoured the red flesh and sweet juices, his eyes fluttering with the desire to sleep.

'There you are lad. I've been halfway round the Palace looking for you. Come on.' Lutan Jakan stood over him, an exasperated look in his green eyes.

Dinnis started and stumbled to his feet, shaking out the pins and needles in his legs. He followed the Lutan through long corridors, upstairs, along a balcony encircling another atrium and into a room with tiered beds. Only three of them were taken. Discordant heavy breathing filled the room.

'Find yourself a bunk, lad.' The Lutan clamped him on the shoulder before striding away.

Dinnis crept into the room and fell onto the bed furthest from the door and the other boys.

* * *

Dinnis woke in the half-light before sunrise. Though the wool stuffed pallet was soft—too soft for someone used to sleeping on the hard floor—his skin itched. From outside the latticed windows, the lyrical calls of the tarrawong overlaid the twittering of the smaller birds and the creek-creek of golden jays. The occasional distant clatter indicated that some of the Palace staff were already up and starting the day's tasks.

He lay on his back looking at the ceiling wreathed in shadow, trying hard not to move, not wanting to wake his new companions or attract their attention. The events of yesterday flooded back. The room seemed to darken and a weight, like a grinding stone, pushed down on his chest, making it hard to breathe. His only tie to the Palace had been brutally cut. In a way, the Tamrin ruler had stolen his father away from him. Black fire rose inside him like a beast—hate, anger and despair. He hated the Kapok like he had never hated anyone before, not even that monster, Akrad. The Kapok had taken the one thing from him that Akrad never had—hope.

Staring at the ceiling he saw Rokkan's laughing face, saw the big powerful Tamrin standing poised and confident in all his finery, surrounded by his family, and imagined him dying a thousand times in a thousand different ways.

Suddenly, another figure loomed over his sleeping spot with red flame hair, silvery-grey eyes in a mocking face and the luminous white skin that seemed to shine in the dim light. The man leaned on a sturdy blackthorn staff that bore a carved snake with red ruby eyes. The smell of ashes pervaded the air.

As though pinned by piled stone, Dinnis couldn't move.

A voice echoed through the hollows of his mind. 'You belong to me, Dinnis my dear ... you belong to me.'

Dinnis clenched his hands and felt something cold and hard. With a shudder, he realised it was the token, the ring the Kapok had given him. Even as his fingers felt its round smoothness, the red-haired figure shredded away like clouds before the westerly winds, until nothing was left but the ghostly memory of insane laughter vibrating in his head. He sat up and, pulling his knees into his shuddering chest, and he struggled to calm his breathing. It wasn't real, just a waking dream. What had the silver-skinned woman said? He could choose another path.

A derisive snort came from across the room. 'Look at the Nolmec, he's crying. Reckon he wants his mama. Not so fierce now, are you bluey?'

Three boys lounging on their bed mats stared at him, their derisive eyes glinting in the growing light. The speaker was not the tallest of the three but certainly the biggest, with a broad, nuggetty face and shock of mud coloured hair. Uson, he had heard his friends call him on the way to Tarka.

The other boys sniggered. The smaller weedy looking child, Asik, made a face while the other taller boy, Hasuk, looked down at his hands.

Dinnis rested his chin on his knees. He didn't care what these Tamrin lads thought of him. A great hole could appear in the ground and swallow up the whole of Tarka and them with it for all he cared.

The vision of Akrad shook him to the core. The monster was dead, wasn't he? What did that mean, 'You belong to me'? He had resisted the Arkon with every fibre of his being. Unlike his sister, he had not been tempted by offers of shared power (as if the Monster would ever share power) or cowered by threats of pain and harm. He was nothing like Akrad. He never would be. So why was he still shaking?

Something tickled his ear. He shook his head. A few minutes later the tickling started again. He swotted at whatever it was. He heard suppressed laughter.

Across the room, Uson had a long rough stick in his hands with a feather tied to the end. His muddy brown eyes met Dinnis' and the lad collapsed on his bed and rolled around chortling. Dinnis sighed. This was going to be worse than he thought, though surely not as bad as the Akrad's Tower.

Chapter Twenty-Four: Tour

Dinnis

Dinnis slipped out of the covers, pulled on his tunic and straightened his backbone. No point gnawing on the past like a mouldy bone. He needed to find his sister and work out how to escape from the Palace. It the Kapok didn't want them, Uncle Timon would, especially Ista, as the Kiprissa of the Phoenix faction.

Firm steps approached along the corridor, and Lutan Jakan appeared in the doorway.

'Morning, boys. Good you're up! No sleepy heads among you.'

'Good morning, Lutan,' Hasuk rose to his feet and bowed. The other two mumbled a hasty greeting. Dinnis contented himself with a curt nod.

'Ah, Hasuk, it's good to see one of you has manners,' said the Lutan. 'The rest of you, on your feet quick smart. Stand when your superior addresses you.'

The other two scrambled up. Dinnis gave the Lutan a measured look before complying. When Jakan returned his stare with unblinking green eyes, Dinnis dropped his gaze. Perhaps he shouldn't antagonise the Lutan until he knew how things worked in the Palace.

'Okay lads, the tardy one is Dinnis and the polite young lad here is Hasuk. The little one is Asik, and this ...' The Lutan clapped Dinnis' stocky tormentor on the shoulder, 'great dolt is Uson.'

'But, Lutan, isn't there some mistake. He's Nolmec, a bluey.'

Jakan's bushy eyebrows contracted. 'No mistake, Uson.' He

turned to the other boys. 'Now, you'll find victuals laid out in the next room. I trust you've already found the latrines down the corridor.' He lifted his eyebrows. 'You'll be getting clothes suited to your new positions, hopefully something will fit those long limbs of yours, Dinnis.'

'Pardon me, sir, but what will our duties be?' Hasuk's honest face scrunched with concern.

'To accompany, serve and defend Prince Mannok and to run errands as required. You will be trained in scholastic pursuits, etiquette and the military arts. Does that answer your question?'

Hasuk and the other boys nodded. Dinnis swallowed down bile. Wonderful! He not only was ousted from Papa's favour by the Tamrin Prince, he was supposed to babysit him to?

'Did you have something to say, Dinnis?'

'No, *ku* ... sir.'

The Lutan narrowed his eyes, then nodded. 'Alright then, I'll be back to take you on a tour of the Palace by the second gong. Make sure you're ready.'

By the time the Lutan returned, they had all had eaten, scrubbed themselves clean in the communal bathing room, and dressed in new clothes provided. They jumped to their feet as the Lutan came through the door.

'Good, you're learning. Come, you'll need to know the Palace layout like the inside of your eyelids. The quarters of the royal family are strictly off limits unless invited.' A twinkle in his green eyes belied the Lutan's fierce expression. 'Don't lag behind or we might not find you for days.'

* * *

A chill wind buffeted Dinnis a few hours later, as the group filed out of the barracks and headed towards the stables. The sun was high up in a clear sky, swimming above the slope of the golden roof tiles. Dinnis tucked his hands into the folds of his newly issued, warm cloak. He wasn't that interested in horses, but he was glad to be outside. The tour through the multitude of corridors, chambers, stairs, halls and corners in the Palace seemed interminable.

At least the main rooms were full of light, with high ceilings and fascinating tapestries and artefacts. The only truly redeeming feature of the tour had been the library with its tantalising musty smell, tall shelves of ancient codices, scrolls, scripts and, of particular interest, maps—spread out on lecterns and tables. He could have lingered all day, though the Lutan stopped only to introduce the boys to Ralton, the head librarian.

Shuffling through the stuffy rooms of the barracks, being introduced to warriors of different ranks and being subjected to fond reminisces about his companions' deceased fathers had been beyond boring. The Lutan had not taken them to the armoury.

Now outside, Dinnis was keen to see if there were other ways out of the Palace precinct than the well-guarded front gate and the busy and guarded service gate. And then there were the city gates to get past. Disappearing into a crowd with his blue skin and Ista's silver amongst all these different shades of brown ones was going to be difficult, let alone finding the long way north. He'd need more than maps and weapons to succeed. It seemed impossible, but he'd escaped Akrad's lair. Surely, he could find a way out of the Kapok's golden cage. Dinnis swallowed down the sudden sourness in his mouth. He and his sister were no more than game pieces to this harsh stranger that had replaced the Papa he remembered. They had no future here.

He flinched at the light blow on his shoulder. 'Pay attention lad, we've arrived.'

The stables turned out to be a large complex of buildings, corrals, exercise yards, and workshops with the kennels attached. Dinnis could see the red wall rear upwards behind the low roofs of the buildings. Beyond it, the ethereal bladelike peaks of the Twins floated in the cerulean sky.

Jakan led them towards the holding yards. Four restive horses stood beside the railings, their manes and tails whipped about them in the wind. A couple of grooms slipped saddles and tack on their quivering backs and heads.

A flurry of wind swept up dust and dry grass, swirling around Dinnis and his companions and obscuring his vision.

'Good morning, Lutan,' a young voice piped from in front of him. 'Are these the orphan boys?'

The dust dropped as quickly as it came. The Kapok's son, stood in front of them. Despite his green eyes and reddish-brown hair, the resemblance to Papa was striking, not least in the intensity of his gaze. An acid dislike welled up inside Dinnis for this favoured son of the Kapok. He swallowed down his poisonous thoughts. As he had at North Pass, he would bide his time.

Jakan bowed with deference. 'Prince Mannok.'

He gave a chopping motion and the other boys bowed low. Gritting his teeth, Dinnis dipped at the waist.

'Your Highness, this is Hasuk, Uson and Asik. And this is Dinnis.'

The young Prince accepted their obeisance with a regal inclination of his head. 'Oh, I met Dinnis last night. What are you doing with them, Lutan?'

'I am taking the lads on a tour of the Palace and its grounds.'

The Prince nodded and studied each of the boys with a clear unwavering gaze. 'Very good. Papa and Uncle Lukarn are with Wasuk discussing one of the mares.' He thrust his chin towards the saddled mounts. 'Then, we'll be inspecting the city and the walls.'

'I hear Lady Yuta arrived from Akra yesterday, Your Highness.'

'Yes. Papa kept the visitors up late last night talking. They're still abed.' The Prince stifled a yawn, then his eyes brightened. 'Would the boys like a short ride while we wait?' Spinning round, he set off towards the saddled horses.

'Perhaps, Your Highness, though—' Lutan Jakan swallowed his words, set off after the Prince, waving for Dinnis and the other boys to follow.

Two large hunting dogs darted from the stables and bounded up to the Prince, their tails wagging lazily.

'Ruse, Lead, drop,' Prince Mannok called the dogs. The one with the golden coat settled at his feet, but the black and tan one continued loping towards Dinnis and the boys standing beside him. Uson stumbled back a couple of steps. The dog's upper lip curled in a snarl.

Prince Mannok frowned. 'Lead, come!'

Lead's chest vibrated with a deep growl. Ruse sat up, suddenly interested.

When Uson whimpered, Jakan grabbed his shoulder. 'Stand still, boy, he won't hurt you.'

Without thinking, Dinnis stepped in front of the animal. '*Kaffersa*! Sit! Lead, Sit!'

Lead dropped to his haunches and whined, licking his hand. Ruse raced up with a high-pitched yip, jumping up and putting her paws on Dinnis' shoulders and licking around his mouth. He pushed her off. '*Kaffersa*, Ruse!' When the animal dropped beside her mate, Dinnis squatted down and began to rub both dogs around the muzzle and stroke their silky ears, the touch of the soft fur and their ready acceptance warming him.

He felt the pressure of curious eyes on him. He stood up slowly and shrugged.

The Prince gave Dinnis a puzzled look. 'That's weird. Papa's dogs don't normally take to strangers.' He lifted his shoulders. 'Well, I guess you can ride first,' He moved towards the closest horse, a large grey stallion, and caught its bridle. 'Come on, this is Plume.'

Dinnis hesitated. 'I'm not sure that's a good idea, Your Highness.'

'Why not? Are you scared? Is the horse too big for you?'

There was a challenge in the set of Mannok shoulders, in his gaze. Dinnis looked askance at the magnificent mount. It was skittish, its ears laid back and the white of its eyes showing. He could feel the tremble of fear in its thoughts.

'I don't know how to ride.'

He reached up and stroked the muscular neck. It was a long time since he had been this close to such powerful equine grace. He could feel the quivering of taunt muscles beneath his hand, feel the vibration of the powerful beat of its great heart.

It was true though. As much as he had learnt to handle horses, to groom and stable them, Papa had never found the time to teach him to ride during his all-too-brief stays. He had promised to do so one day but that day had never come. He could feel the horse calming beneath his touch. He looked up into the large, liquid eyes with their long, black fringes, seeing his own reflection in the shining pupils.

'How old are you?'

'Eleven.'

'Papa taught me to ride when I was three, maybe younger. So how is it a big boy like you can't ride? Are you clumsy or something?'

Uson and Hasuk snickered. Jakan shifted his feet, opened his mouth to say something then shut it again with a frown.

'Oh, I know. Nolmec aren't good with horses are they. Guess your Papa never taught you. Or is it...*Paita*? Isn't that the Nolmec word?' The Prince stood arms akimbo, waiting for an answer.

'*Patra* is the Nolmec term for father, Your Highness, but my father was Tamrin not Nolmec.'

'Really? It sure doesn't look like it.'

Dinnis stared back at the hostile prince. What could he say? That they were brothers?

'Well, maybe I should let a real Tamrin—'

'Mannu,' a bass voice, his father's, called, 'Come here, now!'

Chapter Twenty-Five: Provoked

Dinnis

At the sound of Rokkan Kapok's voice, both Lead and Ruse raced past the Prince and Dinnis to where he stood in the shadow of the stable building about ten tanis away. With excited barks and whines, they nuzzled his big hands before settling at his feet. A chill slipped between Dinnis' s shoulder blades. Markan Lukarn stood behind the Kapok, his dark brown eyes firmly on Dinnis.

The Prince waved his hands with an assumed nonchalance. 'I'll ask Papa if we've time for you boys to ride.' He handed the reins to Dinnis, hitched up his leggings and walked toward the stables. 'Yes, Papa?'

'Tell me, is it princely to mock those in a less powerful position than yourself?' The words spoken in a low voice were on the edge of being audible. Perhaps he should move out of hearing range, but where else was he going to go? Dinnis stroked the stallion velvet neck and mane, his eyes on the ground.

'But it's true, Papa. Many boys younger than him can ride.'

'And can you swim?

'Swim? No! Nobody—'

'I am sure if you ask Prince Tolteal of Silisea, you will find he can—even his little brothers and sisters.'

'Yes, but he's Silisean, a flatlander, and everybody knows that—'

'The point is Mannu, that a lack of opportunity to learn something is not the same as the inability to learn it.'

'I guess. But he is a Nolmec!'

'Your grandmother, my mother was Silisean; his grandmother was Nolmec but his father was Tamrin. The lad is only Nolmec to the same extent that you are Silisean.'

'I am not! I can't swim, so that proves I'm not Silisean. How can the Prince Royal of Tamra be Silisean?'

The Kapok chuckled. 'Interesting set of arguments. Your logic is ... unique.'

'Why does he have to stay. He is sullen and rude and I don't need companions. I already have Garvin.'

The Kapok took a moment to answer. 'His father ... was a close friend. This is not just about you Mannok. And in time you will appreciate your new friends. I do expect you to treat those with fewer prospects than yourself with respect. Whatever his behaviour is, I expect better of you.'

Resting his head against the horse's neck, Dinnis tuned out of the conversation. Bitter sorrow welled up within him. He'd become no more than a charity case, a difficult object lesson. He couldn't stay in this city with the reminder of everything he'd lost thrust into his face every day.

A snigger came from behind him. The surrounding noises crashed in on him: the metallic thud of the smith's hammer and the hiss of hot metal in water, the nickers and sighs from the horses, the barking from the kennels, the shouts of the workers, the mindless chatter of his new companions, the whine of the wind as it blustered around the buildings and across the open spaces of the exercise yards.

He turned his head to see Uson grinning at him, showing the gap of his missing front teeth. The boy ambled back to where Lutan Jakan was talking to a long, thin man a little distance away.

Dinnis jumped as the Kapok's voice boomed nearby.

'So Lukarn, are you joining us for the ride?'

'Whatever Your Majesty commands I will instantly obey.'

'Lukku, you are not still sulking, are you?'

The men were walking towards the horses, the wind buffeting up against them and making their cloaks swirl and dance behind them. The boy and dogs trotted close behind the Kapok, each looking up at him with adoring eyes.

'Ha, I'll take your silence for a yes. Well, no need for you to come. Why don't you go romance that sweet wife of yours instead? Or perhaps you can find Marra or Yuta and commiserate with each other on how difficult I am to live with.' A tucked-in smile lurked at the corners of Rokkan's mouth.

Lukarn stopped and glowered at him. 'Difficult? Impossible, more like!' he muttered under his breath.

A wide grin spread across Rokkan's face. He strode up to Plume and took the reins from Dinnis without even glancing at him. Dinnis ducked his head and backed away from the horses to where the Lutan and the other boys were standing.

'Well let's ride.' The Kapok rubbed the stallion's neck. 'Ready, my beauty,' he crooned to the horse, then took hold of the bridle and vaulted up onto its back in one fluid motion.

The instant he came down into the saddle, his mount reared, pawing the air. As the Kapok leant forward, the horse kicked out his back legs and half reared. Rokkan slid sideways.

Dinnis jumped back, his heart racing. He stared, half in horror, half in a wild hope that Papa would fall. But then, if the Kapok died would Markan Lukarn and his sister, the Kupanna, depose of him and Ista? Did he really wish his father's death?

One arm thrust out, Rokkan Kapok twisted and kept his seat. He urged Plume forward, circling the yard until the horse had calmed. Breathing heavily, he brought the horse to a stop in front of Dinnis and the boys. Mannok and Lukarn stood wide eyed and pale faced.

The thin man next to Jakan strode forward and took Plume's bridle.

'Are you alright, Your Majesty?'

'Fine, Wasuk.' With a shake of his head, Rokkan dismounted. 'I wonder what has got into you, Plume. Such bad manners are not your usual style, my beauty.'

He ran his hand over the horse, soothing him and checking the tack.

Wasuk's brow creased in a puzzled frown 'Could be the wind, sir. It's wild today.'

'Hmm, maybe.' Rokkan ran his large hand from beneath the saddle. 'Wait, what's this? I think I've found the problem.'

He held up a large, wicked looking thorn tipped with blood. He looked at it a few seconds, his eyebrows raised, before looking straight at Dinnis.

'Any ideas, boy, about how this got under my saddle?'

Dinnis stared back, his mouth dry. He hadn't put the thorn there.

The Markan's nostrils flared and his lips drew back in a snarl. He strode towards the little group, his fiery gaze locked on Dinnis. Mannok's eyes widened further and he hurried after his uncle.

Dinnis' stomach lurched. Would they all blame him? Why, because he was part-Nolmec, because he was different?

'Well, boy, did you?' The Kapok's asked in flinty voice.

Dinnis gulped air. 'No *ku* ... Your Majesty.' He lifted his chin, meeting his father's accusing glare. Around them the wind keened and lamented. A wet nose pushed up against his hand. He looked down at the Ruse's soft eyes. At least one friend stood by him. He dropped to his haunches and put his arms around the dog, taking some comfort in the animal's warm presence.

'Your Majesty, I saw the Nolmec put the thorn there.' Uson's voice cut through the air.

Dinnis glanced behind him at the boy's smug face. His breathing quickened. Uson had also been next to the horse, but surely the oaf wouldn't sabotage the Kapok's horse—unless ... unless, he thought Dinnis would be the next one to ride it.

He darted a look at Rokkan's unyielding face. The Kapok had shifted his gaze to Uson, his eyes narrowed. The stocky boy looked down and shifted his balance from one foot to the other.

'Are you sure about that,' Rokkan paused a heartbeat, 'son of Yanak? Uson, isn't it?'

The boy shuffled his feet, shifting one hand behind his back. 'Yes, Your Majesty, it was Dinnis.'

The Kapok lunged forward, grabbed the Uson's hand and prised it open. 'What's this, then?'

A knobbly stick lay across the boy's grubby palm. A stick with the oval hollow where the base of a thorn had been, a stark cream against the brown.

Fury flared in the Kapok's molten eyes. Uson whimpered and his face crumpled with fear. His limbs like water, Dinnis buried his head into the spicy musk of Ruse's golden coat.

'I beg your pardon, Your Majesty, I should have kept a closer watch on the boys,' Lutan Jakan said, placing his hand on Dinnis shoulder, the other on Uson's.

'So it would seem ...'

Uson sobs became louder, more desperate. 'Please, sir, Your Majesty, forgive me.' He dropped to his knees and lay flat on his face before the tall ruler.

'He is seven, Your Majesty,' the Lutan said, a slight tremor in his normally gruff voice.

'Rokkan, you could have been badly injured, even killed. The boy should be punished,' Lukarn growled.

'I doubt the prank was aimed at me, Markan. Yet it was maliciously meant.' Rokkan gave a noncommittal sound. 'I might forgive a boyish prank, Uson son of Yanak, dangerous as it was. But a liar and a sneak—that I will find hard to forget. Only due to your inexperience and youth do I choose to overlook this incident.'

Uson rose to his knees, catching the Kapok's hand and attempting to kiss it. 'Thank you, Your Majesty.'

Rokkan shook his hand free, his eyes narrowed. 'If you lie to me or try to fix the blame for your failures on another again, Uson son of Yanak, you will be out of the Palace, or worse. Better keep your eye on this one, Lutan.'

'Yes, Your Majesty.'

'Come Mannu, Lukarn, we've wasted enough time with this foolishness.'

With that the Kapok turned and mounted Plume. Lukarn, Mannok and Wasuk also mounted and they cantered toward the gates.

Uson shot a vicious look at Dinnis, before moulding his features into compliance for the Lutan.

Dinnis rubbed his hands on his tunic, sure he'd made an implacable enemy. He had to leave this place as soon figured out how to reach Pylonis in the far north.

Chapter Twenty-Six: Strategies

Mannok

Mannok stifled a yawn as he watched his cousins Waro and Essu battle it out on the Conquest board. He had enjoyed the morning's ride about the city. He loved to be on his horse and especially spending time with Papa. There had been scant opportunities over the last few years with the realm in upheaval. Now Papa could stay home, unless the northern lords were really a threat to the Realm's safety.

Mama had arranged a gathering of local or visiting nobility in honour of their guests, Princess Lakwi and Lady Yuta, so dinner had been a formal affair requiring stiff embroidered tunics and head gear, and the best palace manners.

Thankfully, most of the visitors had left soon after the long-drawn-out meal finished. Only close family joined them afterwards in one of the smaller reception rooms for a casual supper.

Mannok quickly swallowed another yawn. The women had left their needlecraft to one side and were involved in a noisy discussion with the men about poetry, of all things. Lady Yuta and his own father were the liveliest partakers, quoting verses of their favourite poets and discussing their artistry and import, though Uncle Lukarn made infrequent forays into the field. Ista stood behind his mother's chair. Soft shadows smudged beneath her eyes and her narrow shoulders drooped. Now there was someone who really did need more sleep.

'Seleste, and that's victory, Essu,' Waren said with a wide grin, cutting through an especially long-winded poem by Papa on the beauties of the mountains or was it mountain beauties? Mannok wasn't quite sure though Mama did have a sappy half-smile she sometimes got when Papa said something to please her.

Essu scowled at the board, trying to find a way out of Waro's trap.

Waro laughed. 'Come on, admit it. I've won. Another game?'

'Count me out,' Essu said, 'I've had enough punishment for one night.'

'Come on Mannu, you can play, can't you? Or I guess you're too young.'

'No, I'm not. Of course, I can play.'

'Excellent.' Waren wasted no time in setting up the board with its intricately carved red and blue pieces.

Oh, man. Why had he agreed to play? Hopefully, he wouldn't look the fool. He glanced again at the adults. Papa edged closer to Mama, his hand resting on hers. She didn't seem to mind. In fact, she was leaning towards him. Maybe this poetry business wasn't a waste of time after all.

Waren shook his arm. 'You have to pay attention if you going to play, Mannu.'

Mannok jerked the older boy's hand off his arm and pushed down the urge to wrestle his bigger cousin. He made his first move, pushing forward one of the Foot Soldiers in a classic opening. The game was complex and long. He stifled another yawn and picked up one of his Spearman.

'I wouldn't do that, if I was you,' a high, haughty voice said.

He looked up into Ista's cool grey eyes. She had drifted away from her post behind Mama, to watch the game.

'Well, you're not me,' he retorted, but as he looked at the board again, he realised she was right.

He hated this game. It was a torturous, long-winded battle of logic and foresight. He much preferred Leap-Over, which would have been finished by now. After a pause, he took his fingers off the Spearman. He could move a Horsemen instead though it was only delaying his final defeat.

Now that was a thought. He grinned. If he was going to lose why now and save himself a headache? It was only a silly game after all. He used the Spearman to take on of Waro's Archers, leaving his Kapok open to capture.

'By the moons, Mannu, I know you are just learning, but that was a foolish move.' Papa was leaning forward, a disappointed look on his face.

Mannu's cheeks flamed. This was the fourth time in two days that he had earned a reprimand from his father. Suddenly, he rather wished Mama would send him to bed so he could escape the circle of eyes watching him. The game ended in a rout.

Papa sighed, congratulated Waren before turning back to Yuta and Lukarn to continue their discussion.

'I think you lost that game on purpose,' Ista whispered to him, then smiled before slipping back to her position behind his mother. The back of his neck prickled. It was if she could read his mind.

'It's a question of strategy,' his father's voice intruded on his thoughts. Mannok stiffened, was he talking about his failure in the Conquest game?

Uncle Lukarn grunted. 'Give me some extra levies and I'll hunt them down and bring them to justice.'

No, they were talking about the rebels in the north. Mannok relaxed and edged closer to the conversation.

'I don't doubt it, Lukarn, but half the northern lords and clan leaders sided with Naetok, once Challak took up his cause. Even with extra warriors, it will take you take years, with many lives lost and continuing animosity to the Throne. And it leaves our northern border vulnerable to the Nolmec ...'

'What do you suggest, Your Majesty? Give them a talking to and send them on their way like those kids this morning playing stupid pranks.'

'What pranks Lukarn?' Mama asked.

Papa put his arm around her shoulder. 'Nothing to worry about my dear, just—'

Uncle Lukarn snorted. 'One of those orphans put a thorn under Plume's saddle. It totally freaked him. If Rokkan had fallen ...'

As Mama shot Papa a worried look.

He cleared his throat. 'Really, you are exaggerating the danger, Lukku.'

'Or you're minimizing it, Your Majesty. What's to say both boys weren't involved? Maybe Dinnis put Uson up to it.'

'Dinnis?' Mama's frown deepened and she looked from husband to brother.

Ista gave a small sound and dropped the shawl she was holding for Mama. A faint blush tinged the new maid's silvery cheeks. She ducked down to pick it up, her face once again empty of emotion.

'It's just his style, given whose ...' Uncle Lukarn's voice faltered as he met Papa's eyes. 'That's my opinion, take it or leave it,' he muttered, his head down.

Mannok fingered a discarded Conquest piece, the Brigan. So why was Uncle Lukarn against the half-Nolmec lad? He certainly had a sulky way about him, but the prankster was Uson not Dinnis.

'Thank you, Markan Lukarn.' His father's voice as chilly as mountain ice.

An idea flashed into Mannok's thoughts. 'Uncle Naetok tricked them with all those awful lies he told. You know, like Lord Fulan said he did. That you had killed Grandfather and Uncle had killed me ... Maybe—'

'Mannu don't interrupt.' His mother put a finger to her lips. 'I think maybe it's time these boys were sleeping. Samara, do you mind?'

Aunt Samara put down her stitching and stood. 'Come, children.'

'Mannu does have a point,' Papa said, a faraway look in his eyes. 'Once you are riding the jaguar's back, it's not so easy to jump off without getting devoured.'

'Yes, but could you trust any of them again?' Markana Yuta said.

'Trust? Probably not, but then I am not sure who I can trust anymore.' He drummed his fingers on the divan, his forehead wrinkled in thought. 'Having most of the kingdom, including my baby brother, aiming their spears in my direction—or at least thinking about when might be a judicious time to do so—hasn't helped my peace of mind over the last few years.'

A heavy silence settled over the room. Waren packed up the Conquest board, while Estolik skulked over to Aunt Samara. The younger ones, like Rizzi and Yalik had already been sent to bed earlier. Mannok stayed still and held his breath, desperate to hear more of Papa's plans. He was tired of being left behind.

Papa's fingers stilled. 'I'm going to take a visit north.'

'Rokkan, you can't be serious.' His mother's face was aghast.

'The thought of leaving your brother to pick up the pieces over the next ten years doesn't sit well with me.' He stroked his chin, his face thoughtful. 'If Manu is right, many in the north may regret following Naetok. A general Amnesty in return for swearing allegiance would

134

avert ongoing conflict and strengthen our borders. Besides, easier to deal with the Phoenix Nolmec from Nakri.'

'Let me do it,' Uncle Lukarn said.

'Your support will be valued, Lukku, but I needed to deal with these rebel lords face to face. Besides, we thrashed them on the battle field. They'll think before attacking.'

Waro placed the final Conquest piece in the woven basket. He gripped Mannok's shoulder and pushed him towards Aunt Samara and Essu at the door.

Mannok dug his heels in. 'Papa, if Waren is going, can't I come too?'

He bit his lip, sure that, as on every other occasion, his father would find excuses to leave him behind. He stood as tall as he could and looked as fierce as he could. His father's golden eyes swept over him. He crossed his arms, tapping one elbow with his strong fingers. Then he grinned.

'It was your idea, Prince Mannok. I don't see why not.'

'Yes! Yes!' Mannok punched the air and ran straight at his father, squeezing him tight as far as he could reach. Papa picked him up effortlessly in a massive hug, then placing him down, aimed him at the doorway. 'Now, goodnight scamp. Better go before I change my mind or your mother changes it for me.'

Mannok could hear Mama's voice raised in protest as he followed Aunt Samara and the other boys down the corridor. For once he wasn't concerned. He was going with his father, Rokkan Kapok, on an important mission, and he would show Papa he was worthy.

Chapter Twenty-Seven: Reunion

Dinnis

Leaning back against the red palace wall, Dinnis inhaled the aromatic scents of the flowering plants and sun-warmed soil. Yesterday's gusty wind had dropped overnight and the sky was like crystal. The soft buzz of insects and sweet birdsong surrounded him in this secluded are of the Palace grounds. Silver Argenti wound her way to the western sky. He had walked out of Akrad's Stronghold for the last time an argen ago.

With all the bustle and activity, it seemed a journey of some kind was being planned. So far it didn't involve him and he wasn't sure if he wanted it to, unless it was to the north. He hadn't seen Ista yet, though Pa ... the Kapok had said she served his new wife, the Kupanna. After Uson's prank yesterday, Lutan Jakan had dressed them down with repeated instructions to stay away from the royal family and out of trouble.

He pulled out his notebook and the stick of graphite he'd palmed in the library yesterday. He used to feel guilty about stealing stuff but eventually decided it was the only way to survive in an enemy's domain. And though he would not have thought so even an Alume ago, it was clear that Tarka was as much hostile territory as Akrad's Stronghold had been.

Cracking open the book to a blank page, he sketched the scene before him, especially the birds, making notes about their colours and calls. Then he sketched the outlines ethereal peaks floating above the city with fast, deft strokes. What he really needed was to get back into the library and copy or at least memorise the relevant maps.

The soft scrape of sandals on the path close by jutted into his thoughts. His mouth tightened. Had that annoying wart, Uson found him? He snapped shut the book, tucking it inside his tunic.

Ista's slight figure rounded a bend and walked down the path towards him. His heart missed a beat, then began to race. She was alive, the Kapok hadn't lied. May the powers, be thanked. He hid a smile. She was the most annoying little sister ever, but she was the best thing he'd seen since arriving in this accursed city. Now, they could decide what to do next.

He sat up straighter. 'Hello, Ista.'

Ista's forehead crinkled into a frown as her cool eyes met his. She wore palace cloths, a finely embroidered blue tunic and sash with a cloak of white yarma wool. Her fine black hair was brushed smooth and caught up in an elaborate braid fixed with golden combs. Despite her fine raiment, she looked thinner and her eyes were underlined with bluish shadows.

She stopped a few tanis away and frowned. 'So, you aren't dead.'

'Apparently not.'

'How long have you been here?'

'Maybe an hour or two. It's a pleasant spot. One of the benefits to this place, I guess.'

'No, *moros*. I mean how long have you been in Tarka. I only heard you were here last night, when that Markan mentioned you. I was worried about you.'

He raised an eyebrow. She seemed to mean it. 'Really?'

She turned to leave. 'Be difficult then.'

He stood up and caught her arm. 'Don't go, *chia*. Tell me how they are treating you.'

She shook off his arm and scrunched her pretty nose. 'I'm the Kupanna's maid. I'm forced to run stupid errands all the time. Why are you sitting here sketching? Why weren't you looking for me?'

The accusation stung, as if he was the one who didn't care. 'I have been. Have you seen how many big guards there are around here? And they don't like the Nolmec at all.'

'They don't stop me.'

'You don't have blue skin like Mater, do you, it's silver, like Akrad's.' He sighed. 'Why was my name mentioned? I'm not sure that's a good thing.'

'Oh, something about some childish prank, which is just like you. The Markan Lukarn—the one that frowns all the time—thought you put some other boy up to it.'

'It was kind of funny. I wish I had thought of it but no, Uson takes all the credit for unseating the Kapok on his favourite stallion.'

'Well, the Kupanna was furious. She wasn't happy about the Kapok deciding to take Mannok with him to the north, but your name was mentioned a few more times after they retired for the night. The Kapok decided to go through state papers again like the night we arrived.'

This didn't sound good. 'Listen, with the Kapok out of the city, it might be easier for us to escape.' At least time, he knew which direction to go.

His sister's brow wrinkled. 'Why do you want to escape anyway? It's not like you cared about the Arkon, and you used to rave about all things Tamrin. The Kapok is kind. I like him.'

'Kind?' He didn't think she was being sarcastic. 'That's not how I would describe him. But then you do like the people with power, like the Arkon.' He failed to keep the accusation out of his voice. All the beatings he had taken for her—only to see her turn to the Monster as if he was her saviour—but she was only a child, she didn't really understand. Looking down, he relaxed his breathing, brought his emotions back under control.

'You know, it's your fault that the Arkon is dead.'

He looked up at her. 'He is dead, then?' He'd wondered after the vision or whatever it was the first morning here.

'Yes, *moros*! Those people you helped? They killed him.'

'I didn't know they would do that, but I can't be sorry that they did.'

Their eyes locked.

Hers burned like silver fire. 'I am.'

'I'm sorry Ista, but he was a horrible man.'

'You said father would come and save us.'

He stared at her. The Kapok warned him about telling her and maybe it was better she didn't know what she'd lost. 'I was wrong.'

'Wrong about lots of things.' She hitched her shoulders and walked away. Then she paused and looked back at him, 'So what position have they given you in the Palace? Scullion, stable hand or garden boy?'

'I like the sound of stable hand or garden boy but no, I've been put in with three other snobbish orphans. We are supposed to be 'companions of the Prince'. He is even more stuck up than they are.'

'He's actually rather nice.' She wrinkled her delicate nose. 'How come you get to be a royal companion, while I'm a serving maid? That doesn't seem fair.'

Dinnis snorted a laugh. He picked a marosa flower and shredded the pink petals. 'Sometimes I wonder whether we really are related but we are. It's just us now. We really should work out how to escape.'

Her eyes clouded. 'Where can we go now the Arkon is dead?'

Good question. 'Uncle Timon would help us, even General Nuktis if we could trust him.'

'Have you any idea how far that is, *moros*?'

He clenched his jaw. 'It's a long way, I know, but we could do it.'

Her lips paled. 'Further than North Pass. And even if we could get past the guards and walls, how would we know where to go?'

She had a point, it would be hard to avoid capture over such a distance and then they'd have to get across the border. Besides, what was the difference—Nolmec, Tamrin, they were all the same to him. But Ista, the Nolmec would value Ista.

'I can copy the maps in the library.'

'You probably got it all wrong,' Ista seemed ready to stamp her foot in frustration. 'Why does a stupid boy who can't read properly get to the go to the library and I don't?'

'Who said I couldn't read?'

'Grandfather did.'

Dinnis crossed his arms. 'Well, for your information, there is a lot 'Grandfather' didn't know. If I can, I'll see if I can sneak you some books.'

He almost laughed again as she saw the conflicting emotions chase themselves across her face—doubt, worry and desire. The desire for knowledge he understood. Then she assumed her regal look again. 'I'd like that, but please be discreet. I'm not sure I want anyone to know we're related.'

'What an irresistible offer,' he teased. It was so like Ista to want to keep her distance, but she was all he had left. He caught her into a hug, 'I'm glad you are alright, Ista. I was worried about you.'

She stayed in his embrace for a few heartbeats, even resting her sweet-smelling head against his shoulder, before breaking away and running down the path away from him.

So, the Prince and the Kapok were heading north. Maybe he could make that work in their favour.

Chapter Twenty-Eight: Breaking Point

Ista

Ista hurried down the corridor, her arms full of the linens. Up until the Kapok had announced this latest expedition, the Kupanna was starting to reduce her demands. Now she seemed to relish piling them one on top of the other until Ista could barely catch her breath, rushing from the dawn until late at night. Early this morning, Dinnis had found her in a passageway near the big kitchen and had given her a juicy sun fruit, a wry smile and a ring he said he had plaited out of horse hair. 'For your birthday. It's from Plume's tail. I'm working on an escape route,' he whispered with a cheeky grin. He hadn't given her books from the library and his promises of escape were likely to be a pipe dream, but even she'd forgotten it was her birthday. No one else knew or cared.

She turned the corner of the long corridor and slammed into someone. They careened off each other, her load of linens flying. She skidded along the tiled floor, pain searing scraped hands and knees.

'*Rakka*, idiot. Watch where you are going, you oaf,' she shouted, tears streaming down her face.

When she tried to scramble to her feet, hot spears shot through her right ankle. All about her, the clean, folded linen lay scattered and crumpled, and her tunic was torn. She sat back on the floor, put her head in her bloody hands and howled like she had not done for years. Probably not since their father had failed to return, and they had been taken to Akrad's Tower.

'I am sorry, I didn't mean to do that,' a familiar voice said.

Mannok! What a disaster; the linens were ruined, her tunic of fine yarma wool a mess, she was sure she looked a fright, and she'd shouted at the Prince. She howled even louder.

'Please, I really am sorry. Are you hurt?'

'Go away,' she mumbled through the sobs. Then realised she was making it worse. 'Please.'

He put his hand on her shoulder. 'I don't think I should, Ista.'

She shrugged it off, tried to stagger to her feet and collapsed again with a groan as her ankle gave out under her.

She hiccupped. 'You could have looked where you were going.'

Mannok's brow furrowed. 'You promised not to call me an idiot again, remember. And you banged into me. You could at least say sorry.'

Heat flared inside of her. She was the Kiprissa, she never said sorry. 'I guess you are rather used to everyone bowing and scraping to you.' Except she could feel the warmth of his concern without probing, and despite his irritated tone. And he was the Prince. 'I beg your pardon, Your Highness.

He scowled then suddenly laughed. 'All that bowing can get tiresome at times.'

'I did not mean to call you … those things.'

'And … I should have been more careful.' He kneeled and took her hands in his golden-brown ones. 'You really have scraped yourself. Here, let me help you.'

He picked up one of the linens and used it to dab her knee.

'Not with that you, idio … *kuree*.' Her eyes began to fill with tears again. 'I mean, Your Highness. How am I going to explain that to the Mistress? She'll kill me.'

He wrinkled up his nose. 'Well, I guess it is kinda my fault. I'll come with you and explain it for you,'

'It might work. Can you help me with this mess first?'

Mannok nodded and picked up the scattered cloth, handing each one to her so she could sack them. With a crooked grin, he grabbed the pile, balancing it in one hand and reached out to her with the other.

Gritting her teeth, she let him pull her into standing position. She gingerly put her foot to the ground. If she put most of her weight on his arm, she could hobble. They shuffled along the atrium balcony to the Kupanna's apartments, his breath tickling her ear.

The Kupanna's raised voice met them before they entered the antechamber. 'Even you can't expect me to tolerate ... this ... situation.'

The Kapok stood with legs astride and hands behind, peering out through the balcony, the back of his shoulders stiff. Marra was standing behind him, her arms folded tightly against her shapely chest.

Mannok flushed and looked down. Leaning forward, he rapped his knuckles on the door jamb.

The Kupanna spun around, her eyebrows contracted together. 'What do you want?' Her full lips pursed together. She looked Ista up and down. 'What have you done?'

Mannok cleared his throat. 'Mama, Your Majesty, it's my fault. I ... wasn't looking where I was going ...' his voice faltered at Marra's glassy stare.

Rokkan turned and took them both in with a sweep of his golden gaze. 'An interesting approach to sweeping the young ladies off their feet, Mannu.' A half-smile tweaked at his lips. 'Starting a bit young though, I would've thought.'

'Yes, sir ... I mean no, not at all.' Mannok's tanned cheeks darkened.

'Well, you should know.' Marra gave the Kapok an icy look.

'You may be right, my dear. but I seem to have lost my touch of late.'

Then he strode across the room and picked Ista up. As his strong arms encircled her, she could feel the thumping of his heart beneath her ear. The mixture of woody aromas and chilli calmed her.

'Our thanks, for rescuing our little maid, Mannu. Very gallant and thoughtful of you. However, we can take it from here.'

Holding her with one arm, he placed the other between the Prince's shoulder blades, he pushed him out the door of the antechamber and closed it.

'Rokkan, what are you doing?'

As though he hadn't heard the Kupanna, the Kapok lowered Ista to one of the divans.

'Hmmm, two scrapped hands, two scrapped knees, a scrapped chin, lots of tears and a sprained ankle ... not too much damage it would seem.'

'Yes, but the linens are ruined, I got blood on your tunic and now the divan will be ruined too.' Ista bit her lip. The urge to cry competed with the urge to respond to his teasing smile.

He laughed. 'Well, I've been getting blood on my clothes on a regular basis these last few years, though I generally do spare the furniture.'

'Rokkan, don't ignore me!'

His eyes flared. He spun around and held the Kupanna's eyes with his own.

'This has gone on long enough, Marra. Look at her, thin as a twig, huge shadows under her eyes, barely able to keep them open. You are better than this, taking your frustrations out on a child. She is only eight-years-old.'

'You said she was seven!'

'I am eight. It is my birthday today.' Ista said and the tears started flowing again.

Rokkan had rocked back on his heels and was breathing deeply, his eyes fixed on a point over her head. He brought his gaze back to her face and forced a smile.

'Not the happiest of birthdays.' His voice soft. 'Still want to stay here?'

'I know she hates me and no one cares, but ...' Well, Dinnis had. She had never known him to miss recognizing her birthday with some little token, even though it was a day that often made him sad. For it was also the day their mother had died. Last year she had been impatient at his gift. This year it gave her a sense of stability she had been missing.

'Hardly fair to lose so much at such a young age.' Rokkan grimaced. He stood up and faced the Kupanna. 'I think, Marra, it's about time that you stop punishing the child for the deeds of others.'

'The danger to ...'

'In this case is non-existent.' He sighed. 'You agreed to this. I know you are not heartless. Look after her, please.'

With that he strode across the room and out the door. Ista tensed, waiting for the tirade, the fountain of condemning words. Instead, Marra stood still for a long time fingering the jade pendant at her throat and staring after him. She closed her eyes, her eyelashes flickering against her smooth cheeks and sighed.

'Best lie there, child, for a while. I'll send someone up to see to your injuries and bring you some food to eat. I suppose, given that it is your birthday, you can have the rest of the day off. It is certainly a day to celebrate.'

She gave a wan smile. Picking up a woven throw, she placed it around Ista and walked out of the room. It was as though stones were weighing Ista's eyelids. The door snapped shut and she surrendered herself to sleep.

Tarka and on the road to Nakri

Chapter Twenty-Nine: Distance

Mannok

Mannok rolled onto his back, unable to sleep. Argenti's silver light pushed through the chinks in the shutters turning the familiar furniture in his room into strange humped shadows. Tomorrow they were leaving for Nakri in the north! His limbs were tingling with anticipation. He had never been more than a half a day's journey from Tarka as far as he could remember. The traditional yearly trips to the hunting lodges in the south had ceased during the war years. Despite his pleas, Papa had always refused to include him in any expeditions to north. Maybe he had been too young then, but he was almost eight now and he could fight if he had to, he'd been practicing with Garvin.

The night smells of pine, scented garden plants and snow from mountains peaks floated through his open window. The whirr of crickets overlaid the sound of his parent's voices sparring in the next room. His eyes fluttered shut.

He started. The room was dark. His father's huge form stood turned away from him. Jumping up, he ran towards him, but the faster he ran the further away Papa was. He called out. 'Papa, wait,' but his father kept walking, not even turning to look at him. 'Papa, it's me Mannu.'

All at once, they came to the knife blade edge of a mountain. The tall man ahead stopped, his cloak long, voluminous and red. He turned and smiled. Mannok pulled to a stop in shock, his blood congealing. The man's face and shoulders had narrowed and his sharp teeth gleamed in the silver moonlight. It wasn't Papa. It was his Uncle Naetok.

The rebel's mouth expanded in wild silent laughter. His uncle's cloak began to spread, growing bigger until it covered the white snow in lakes of blood. The tang of the red rusty brine filled his nostrils. Its salty moisture flooded his mouth. Its cloying warmth seeped over him. His eyes wide open, Mannok stretched out his arms in panic, struggling to reach the surface. He couldn't breathe and all he could see was red.

He sat up gasping for breath with the covers twisting around his legs. He searched the room, shadowy in the dim false light before dawn.

His father wasn't there.

'Papa,' he whispered.

He clenched his hands and breathed rapidly. It was a dream, just a dream. It wasn't real.

Only, it had been. The flash of the knife as his uncle had turned a brotherly hug into a nightmare. His father collapsed on the mosaic floor of the throne room, his own small hands trying to staunch the blood with Papa's cloak. The spreading red puddle as Papa had shivered, his voice fading as—even on the edge of death—he gave orders for the protection of his realm and his family. The long days as Naetok led an army of rebels against the capital, Tarka, while Papa lay unconscious before rallying enough to fight back.

Racking shudders ran through Mannok and cold fear crept up on him like a ravaging beast. It had been real, very real. And he hadn't been able to stop it.

Then his father was beside him, engulfing him in a warm hug.

'It's okay, Mannu. Having a nightmare again?'

Mannok clung, burying his head in his father's strong shoulder. 'I'm sorry, Papa, I haven't had one for ages.'

It was true, not since before Papa had ridden back to Tarka half an Alume ago had his nights been troubled by this recurring dream. Many a long night his mother had held him, soothing him, promising that his father was alive, that he would return from the latest battle or manoeuvre. Squeezing his eyes shut, he prayed to the Maker that Papa wouldn't now decide he was too young to go on to Nakri.

Instead, his father said, 'I still get nightmares too, Mannu. Terrifying. I feel as weak as a baby afterwards. Too many deaths, too many friends gone to the Maker's Golden Halls. Replaying Naetu's brotherly affections in the throne room is the worst.'

Mannok's eyes widened. 'Oh, I thought I was the only one.'

His father squeezed him tighter until it almost hurt to breathe. His strong arms were as solid and protective as the city walls.

'Not a chance.' He dropped his voice to a whisper. 'I warrant that even Uncle Lukku has an occasional bad night, but don't you tell him I said so.' His teeth flashed white in the grey light. 'We warriors have to stand together and send those bad dreams back to where they belong.'

Mannok bobbed his head a couple of times.

Mama appeared at the door balancing a tray with a beaker of creamy yarma milk and cornbread spread thickly with honey. Papa patted Mannok's shoulder and stood.

'I have a few things to check with Kaptan Kaspin before we leave. Don't be late Mannu—we have a long day's journey ahead.'

And then he was gone, leaving Mannok to his mother to fuss over him. He wasn't going to tell anyone that he shed some tears too.

* * *

An hour later, Mannok leaned forward in the saddle as the group passed the sharp slopes of the Elder Twin in the pearly dawn light. To their right, behind the jagged outline of Tarka, the bigger moon, Alumi stood out like a golden chest plate in the soft dove grey and pink sky. On the other side Argenti's full disc floated close to the outline of distant mountains on the western horizon.

The jingle of bridles and thud of horses' hooves on the gravel road overlaid the creak of the saddles and soft murmur of voices up ahead. Waren and Estolik rode in front of him and, then, at the head of the line, his father sat casually on Plume, chatting to Uncle Lukarn on his stallion Boulder. Ruse and Lead were running alongside Papa, weaving around the sharp hoofs with practiced abandon.

If only he had been allowed to ride beside his father rather than relegated to the back of the pack with Garvin and the four orphans. Well, not quite the back, as Aunt Samara and Rizanna with Lutan Jakan were riding behind them, followed by the pack-yarmas and servants. With loyal troops already stationed in the north, Papa had decided to take only a brigade of spearmen and cavalry with him, leaving sufficient troops to guard Tarka. He had also decided to travel light, with minimal baggage and staff that might otherwise delay their progress to a frustrating crawl. By sending fast messengers ahead the Royal Way Stations along their route could be prepared and ready for their arrival each day.

Aunt Lakwi and Uncle Amaruk would be returning to Poija and the Eastern March soon. Papa had left Mama in charge to deal with matters of state. He wished she and Ista were coming with them but, whatever happened, this would be an adventure.

The keening whistle of an eagle jerked him back from his daydreaming. It floated in the wind currents high overhead on outstretched wings. The sun warmed his face, though his fingers and toes still felt the bitter cold of the mountain dawn. Glancing behind him, he noticed the Nolmec's grey eyes fastened on him. There was no deference in the boy's stare though perhaps a hint of sympathy about his mouth and eyes. It was as though the fellow could read his mind. Not a reassuring thought. He brushed his cheeks to make sure they were dry. He wished Papa could have placed that Dinnis with someone else.

Garvin flashed his gap-toothed smile. The son of Kaptan Kaspin, Garo grew up in the Palace with him. Even though he was minor nobility, they didn't most days together, and he often slept in the royal quarters with Mannok.

Mannok grinned back. 'I'm glad your papa said you could come.'

'Wouldn't miss it, Mannu. We'll be so close to the border with the Nolmec.'

Mannok whooped. Garo was a much more agreeable companion than his own cousins Waro and Essu, who rode up ahead, too 'grown-up' to take notice of him and Garo.

Mannok glanced behind him at the orphans. Hasuk was handling his horse well and Asik and Uson weren't doing too badly. Dinnis was in trouble though. Hunched forward on his horse, he bounced around with the reins bunched up in his hand. It was a wonder that the horse hadn't bolted with him or tipped him off. So maybe he wasn't kidding when he said he didn't know how to ride. He smirked as he caught Garo's eye.

'He rides like a Nolmec,' he whispered out of the side of his mouth.

Garo grinned at Mannok. 'He will be even bluer tonight, I reckon.' His whisper more like a shout. 'Black and blue.'

They both snickered. More smart comments buzzed through his head. He frowned at a niggle of discomfort. The Nolmec snide demeanour irritated him, but wasn't this what Papa had chided him for doing?

The cinder road stretched ahead of them, seeming endless. Now wide and smooth, soon the road would narrow, with steep drops on one or both sides. His frown deepened. That wasn't his problem, though. Wasn't the Lutan supposed to be looking out for the boys?

He glanced back again. Lutan Jakan was helping with Rizanna and Markana Samara—both not very confident riders. They were probably more used to travelling in palanquins than on horseback. Ahead, Papa and his companions were immersed in conversation. Mannok felt the resentment rising inside of him. He was a prince not a nursemaid. Someone else should help the Nolmec.

Uson's sudden cackle was followed by a twitter of laughter from Asik and Hasuk. Then there was a soft slithering sound, a muffled oath and the snort of a horse behind him. Dinnis had—despite the horns of the saddle—slid to one side and forward on to the neck of the dark grey gelding. He clutched the mane as the young horse broke into a skittish trot, his ears laid back and the whites of his eyes showing. Had the boy been pushed or had he slipped? Uson did have the same smug look on his face as that other day.

'Slide it,' Mannok muttered. He turned his horse Torrent and drew alongside the troubled rider and grabbed the reins of the spooked horse.

'Whoa there, Pumice, it's okay.' He patted the soft pewter neck.

Dinnis sent him a startled look, then managed to right himself. He breathed hard, his pupils so dilated his eyes looked black. He blinked, gripping the horns of the saddle in front of him.

'My thanks, Your Highness.' He squeezed the words out between gritted teeth.

Mannok suppressed a smile. 'You look like you're climbing a tree not riding a horse. Sit back square in the saddle.'

Dinnis shot him a wary look. After a minute or two, he shuffled back but he moved like a sack of potatoes, slouched forward.

'Sit up tall with a strong back but not too tense, grip with your knees.' Mannok eyed his posture. 'Almost. Keep your chin up. Look to where you want the horse to go ... that's better ... you're holding the reins too high ... tuck your elbows in.'

The Nolmec … Dinnis' sat taller in the saddle, as tense as a strung arrow string.

'Relax. You're making poor Pumice nervous.'

The boy gave a shaky laugh. 'He's a lot bigger and scarier than I am.'

'Not to him. If you're afraid, he's afraid. Talk to him. An animal charmer like you can't find that too hard.' It still rankled that Papa's dogs seemed to take more notice of the outsider than him.

'Is that all?'

'More or less. Just move with the horse, not against him, and remember to breathe. Easy as falling out of a tree.' Mannok laughed.

Dinnis gave him a sour look, his eyes squinting against the sun. 'And how many trees have you fallen from?'

Mannok met the boy's flat stare. 'I've fallen off horses often enough. Thing is to roll with the fall, keep your hands and head out of trouble and watch out for the hooves.'

The challenge in the grey eyes flickered and Dinnis looked down with a thoughtful frown. Like ice melting, the tension seemed to seep out of him.

Mannok nodded. 'Much better. See, you can do this.'

He gave Pumice's mane a gentle stroke, thought about moving forward to join Garvin again, then decided to stay beside the novice rider a little longer to be sure he was getting it.

At the front of the column, Papa wheeled Plume to canter towards the back of the line. Uncle Lukarn pulled his horse to a stop, the others clumped up, before moving off to the side of the road.

'I would much rather walk. It's not as if we will get there any faster by riding,' muttered Dinnis. He had settled into the rhythm of Pumice's gait. Maybe he wasn't such a slow learner.

'Horses can go a lot faster than people. Like to see you outrun Torrent!'

'The horse does have the advantage over short or even medium distances,' Papa said, as he approached them. He slowed Plume to a walk. 'Across long distance travel a horse generally travels at about the same distance as a human—about 30 to 40 lek a day, less in the mountains. But where's the fun in walking?'

Papa gave a half-salute as he trotted past on Plume and moved alongside Aunt Samara's mare.

'How are you going, my Lady? We have decided to stop for a meal break.'

Aunt Samara lifted her strained face. 'Thank you, Your Majesty. I am overjoyed to hear that.'

'Hey, Rizzi, chin up. You are doing fine. By the time we get to Nakri you will be a champion rider.'

Rizanna refused to be mollified. 'Girls aren't champion riders. We are supposed to travel in style and comfort in a palanquin, Uncle.'

He laughed. 'Who says? My mother Kupanna Tula could ride rings about my father. She was reputed to be the best rider in all of Silisea, which meant she was the best rider in all the Five Lands.'

'Are you quizzing me, Uncle Rokku? Girls are good needlecraft and boys like riding and fighting. You don't have any girls in your armies, do you?' she asked with a smug smile and the lift of her round chin.

'You would make a grand advocate.' His face was serious but the laughter lurked in his eyes. 'Just like your aunt Marra would make a fearsome general that would strike terror in the hearts of all her enemies.'

Aunt Samara clicked her tongue. Rizzi giggled. 'Uncle Rokku, Aunt Marra is nice and not at all scary.'

He laughed. 'Oh! Maybe it's just me.'

Mannok stroked Torrent. It was already past midday, and Papa rode straight past him to speak to Aunt Samara. This trip might not be as much fun as he expected.

They reined in their horses at the flat area beside the road. Two ancient avocado trees spread out furrowed grey branches near a braided mountain stream winding along the flat-bottomed valley. Under sparse vegetation, dark grey soil was the colour of Dinnis' mount, Pumice. The Lutan supervised the servants setting out the platters and baskets of food and drink on rugs beneath the shady avocado trees.

It would take a few minutes for the rest of the entourage to catch up. Meanwhile, the horses would need watering, feeding and securing. He was just preparing to swing his leg over Torrent's back when he felt a strong hand clap him on the shoulder.

'Hey, champ. You want to see what Torrent can do over a short distance?' Papa challenged, 'Race you to the large boulder over there. You have a five second head start. Beginning now!'

Mannok's heart fluttered and his spirits soared. Five seconds. He reefed Torrent about and spurred the willing horse into the gallop he had been longing for all day. Wind rushed past him, powerful muscles flowed beneath his thighs. Moments later, Plume's hooves thundered after him. Putting every scrap of effort into it, he willed his horse to outpace his father's powerful stallion.

Chapter Thirty: Trap

Dinnis

Dinnis watched the two horses race to the makeshift finish line, the face of the young Prince alive with exhilaration and an indulgent look on the father's face. Dinnis' heart twisted into a painful knot. Mannok had surprised him this morning. He'd resigned himself to a painful and bruising trip, to be black and blue from repeated falls as the Prince's friend, Garvin, had so drolly quipped. The Prince's instructions were timely and only a small amount of his disdain had leaked out in the delivery. Maybe he wasn't quite the shallow, spoilt brat Dinnis had thought him. Yet, seeing the Kapok and Prince together reminded him of what he'd lost. He gritted his teeth. More reason to escape north.

The Kapok whooped as his stallion overtook Mannok's young gelding. At the last moment, he pulled back, allowing the boy to win.

'Seleste, I did it! I beat you Papa.' Mannok yelled, turning his horse in circles and throwing his wooden dagger in the air. Both father and son rode as though riding was as easy and natural as breathing.

Dinnis had been elated when his subtle hints to Jakan that Prince's new companions be included in expedition north seemed to work. Or perhaps that had already been the plan. Dinnis' fingers brushed the map he'd copied down in a few stolen moments in the library and hidden in his tunic. With each step, they moved closer to his mother's people. Though, Ista remaining in Tarka with the Kupanna complicated matters.

Slipping off Pumice, Dinnis walked with his mount towards where the other horses were tethered.

'Here, bluey, take my horse and make sure it's cared for.'

Uson thrust his reins into Dinnis' hands and walked away without a backward look. Asik thrust his arms out stiffly and followed the bully's example. Shrugging his shoulders, Hasuk did the same before sprinting after the other two.

Dinnis stood still, looking at the four horses before looking up into the bright expanse of sky and the smudge of snow-capped mountains on the horizon. Taking a deep breath, he pulled the rein tightly on his own temper.

'Hey, do you need a hand?'

The Prince's friend, Garvin, walked towards him, a friendly smile on his blunt face. Now what? Was this some new kind of joke? His eyes narrowed as he looked the boy up and down. He was probably around the same age as Mannok and Ista. Dinnis hesitated. He had been tricked more than once in the last several days with offers of help or expressions of sympathy or friendliness. All had been opening ploys of a snub or practical joke.

Four large horses were more than he could handle. 'Thank you, yes, Your ...' What address was he supposed to use?

'My Lord.' Garvin took the reins of two of the horses, and they walked them toward the temporary hitching post.

'What?'

'Just kidding. That's how you'd address the Markans' sons like Waren and Estolik, at least on formal occasions. But Garvin's fine for me, or Garo, if you want to be friends. So, what's your name?'

'Dinnis.'

'A Nolmec name.'

'Brilliant deduction, Garvin.'

Garvin shot him a look. Mute, they tethered the horses, loosening their girth straps and making sure they could reach grass and the water.

Dinnis noted that Rokkan and Mannok had ridden past the boulder to a fair distance away. They circled back towards the rest of the travelling party, riding side by side in a companionable way.

The tiresome threesome roughhoused while Estolik and Waren threw pebbles beside the stream. Further down, where the servants were spreading out rugs and food containers, Lord Lukarn fussed over his wife and daughter with an occasional glance towards the Kapok and the Prince. Dinnis felt the pressure of Garvin's eyes on him. He glanced sideways.

The lad's eyebrows pulled together. 'Are you always this prickly?'

'I guess, but at least I didn't pitch headfirst in that cactus beside the road back there. Black and blue and as prickly as a spiny anteater.'

Garvin jaw dropped and then he guffawed, startling the horses. 'Sorry, that was rude of me, but you got to admit it was funny.'

Did he? Then a grin curved up Dinnis' face. Rude or not, he decided he liked the Tamrin lad. Maybe staying in Tamra wouldn't be all bad. Was this what the silver lady meant?

* * *

A small feast was spread out on colourful woven rugs. The Kapok spoke a brief blessing and then he and the Prince filled their plates. Dinnis hung back until all but the servants and guards had helped themselves. He was hungry after riding all morning, and the flat maize bread, cheese, duck eggs and dried inka berries soon vanished. The others pushed away empty plates and lounged back on the mats for a short siesta. Only the six warriors standing guard remained awake.

Except Dinnis couldn't sleep. He tucked a piece of yarma cheese wrapped in avocado leaves into his tunic, for later. Not that he expected to miss a meal on the road with the Kapok, but life was full of uncertainties. His life, at least. Once the convoy had reached Nakri, he'd only be about one hundred lek from the border and another sixty or so lek to Pylonis beyond that. Yet, without Ista, could he be sure of a welcome? His mouth twisted and he stared at the empty sky. When it came down to it, it didn't really matter where he lived. Tamrin, Nolmec—there wasn't much difference. He could tell Uncle Timon where Ista was though it surely be too far for them to mount an expedition. A pity the Kupanna and her entourage decided to stay behind. ... Perhaps, he could pass information about Tamrin military strength. Yet, was he prepared to betray his father, as he had been ... Dinnis shredded the large avocado leaves into tiny pieces, his thoughts circling like vultures, while the rest of the party snored. The glare of the sun bounced off the sharp points of the guards' bronze spears and the pebbles of the river bed, making his head throb.

They were back on the road an hour later. As the day advanced, the roads became narrower and less crowded. Whatever the size of the road, the peasants, merchants, soldiers and other fellow travellers rushed to the side and bowed low as Rokkan Kapok and his entourage passed by. At times the road descended steeply, while at others it spun its way back up towards the heights, opening up to spine-tingling views, plunging waterfalls and steep-sided precipices. And for long stretches it wound across wind caressed highland plains with dry grasses, small cacti and scrubby trees. In between they passed small villages in secluded valleys adorned with duck ponds and wells, and surrounded by ancient trees, maize and bean fields or potato fields. To both the east and the west were the long ridges of blue hazed mountains crowned with snow so white it hurt the eyes. As the sun disappeared behind the horizon for the night, they arrived at one of the wayside houses.

* * *

Five days later, Dinnis settled down on the thin straw palette, trying to shut out the boisterous sounds of the other young people. They arrived in Tarvin in the late afternoon. Though his muscles and backside ached from long hours in the saddle, he was more comfortable riding his borrowed mount, Pumice.

Tonight, they were accommodated in the Clan Leader's house, he and his family vacating their home for the royal guests. It was bigger than the wayside houses they had stayed in along the way. It did mean that the adults would have separate sleeping rooms rather than the one private chamber which the Kapok and his favoured son occupied, everyone else piled in together in the big common room.

Markana Samara, pale and exhausted, had already retired for the night with Rizanna. Asik and Uson were playing knuckle bones. Waren, having just defeated Estolik for a second time that night, enticed Hasuk into a game of Conquest spread out on a low table near the stone fireplace. Hasuk began cautiously, showing a basic knowledge of the pieces and their moves but only a tentative grip on overall strategy. Dinnis stifled a yawn. It would be a short and boring game with Waren dominating play.

On the other side of the room, the Kapok and Lukarn were deep in a spirited discussion on diplomatic strategies, military exploits and political manoeuvrings. Mannok and the dogs curled up at the Kapok's feet—just as he and Ista once did—Garvin beside them.

160

He curled his fingers against his thighs, a hollow ache in his chest. Since the incident with Plume, the Kapok's eyes had glided past him, not once acknowledging his existence. Any hope he had that the Kapok would soften slowly curled up and died a slow death. To think he'd once thought so highly of this hard man who was no longer his father. He turned his shoulder and focused on the boys playing Conquest.

'Your move.' Anticipation edged Waren's muted voice.

Dinnis spotted the trap that only a novice player would fall into. Hasuk leant forward, creases of concentration fanning out above his blunt nose, his fingers playing with his South Markan piece.

'Beware the trap,' Dinnis said then clamped his lips shut. He hadn't meant to say it. Five pairs of boyish eyes fixed themselves on him.

'How so?' Hasuk's light brown eyes narrowed.

Dinnis hitched his shoulder. He should have kept his mouth shut. Too late now. He let out a long, resigned breath.

'Think about it. Would an experienced player like the Markan's son leave his Lutan unprotected?'

Estolik tossed a painted yarma knuckle bone in the air and caught it. 'So, you know something about Conquest? I didn't think a Nolmec would play a Tamrin game.' He gave a lopsided smile; the scorn was no longer concealed in his cool eyes. 'After all, it is a game that requires intelligence and finesse.'

The threesome sniggered. Waren frowned.

Dinnis held Estolik's gaze for a moment then smiled sweetly. 'Of course, they don't. The Nolmec are too busy drinking blood and eating babies to waste their time on board games.'

A chorus of shocked gasps greeted his statement. Waren raised his eyebrows while Estolik's grey eyes rounded in horror, then he scowled.

'Are you saying that you actually saw this?'

Dinnis kept his face neutral. 'Me? Oh no, but I have heard about it just about every time I turned a corner in Tarka. Even the cheese merchant's brat or the girl who scrubs the pots in the kitchen are convinced it's true, so who am I to argue? In my experience, though, Nolmec soldiers spend their evenings belching rowdy drinking songs, lamenting the distance between themselves and loved ones, wishing someone else would wash their smalls for them, complaining about their bunkmates' snoring and trying to avoid the malevolent attention of the Arkon or any superior officer who might put them on an unwelcome duty.'

No one spoke for a few minutes, then Waren chuckled. 'I'm not sure how much to take you seriously Dinnis. I must admit I'd never pictured fearsome Nolmec warriors washing their underwear.'

'Someone has to do it.'

Waren just shook his head and turned to Hasuk.

'Well, what is your move?'

Hasuk hesitated, let go of the Markan, sacrificing a Spearman to block Waren's Lutan piece, thus avoiding the enticing trap laid out for him. He looked over to Dinnis and gave a small smile.

Dinnis returned the smile, then a shiver ran through him as he realized Markan Lukarn's penetrating gaze was fixed on him. Chill bumps mantled Dinnis' skin. He looked down, determined to avoid attracting that man's malevolent attention.

Chapter Thirty-One: Aftermath

Mannok

A scatter of raindrops needled Mannok's face. He pulled his cloak tighter and stepped back under the eaves of the Bent River Way House. The late afternoon sky was shrouded in high grey clouds, bringing a damp chill to the mountain air. The journey from Tarka to Tavin had a festive feel but, five days closer to Nakri, the mood took a grim tone, and not just because of the change in the weather.

A gust of wind swirled about Mannok, bringing the acrid smell of ash, mould and rotting wood. He glanced at the burnt-out houses in this latest village. Beyond them, the fields lay bare and uncultivated, still not prepared for planting. Silent children stood in shadowed doorways, a hungry look in their hooded eyes. Old men and women repaired roofs and moved debris from the narrow street, a part of the Royal Way. Mannok had lost count of how many ruined villages they'd already passed on the road—or broken down defensive towers and walls. Last night they'd had to camp out as the Way House had been trashed and its supplies scattered for the crows and eagles to pick over. The destruction was the result of three years of Naetok's rebellion, so Papa said, but this didn't stop the sense of foreboding seeping into Mannok's every thought.

Inside, the clatter of dishes indicated that Aunt Samara was supervising the preparations for tonight's meal with the meagre supplies available in the storeroom. A few tanis away the sullen part-Nolmec lad, Dinnis, filled a bucket from the Way House fountain.

At least that hadn't been broken, as it was a long walk down hill to the stream. Garo, Hasuk and a couple of the servants were collecting pine cones and fallen branches, the stored wood pile having been scattered down the eastern slope of this high mountain ridge. Uson and Asik hadn't been keen to help, complaining of saddle sores or the like.

'You should come inside and warm up by the fire, Your Highness.' Dinnis dipped his head as he walked past with two wooden buckets brimming with water.

'I will in a moment.'

'As you wish.' Dinnis ducked under the low lintel, disappearing into the Way House.

Mannok turned his attention back to where Papa stood in one of the fields, feet astride, head inclined towards the short headman and village elders. The grey-haired group of men and women gesticulated in animated conversation. Standing close to Papa, Uncle Lukarn rested a hand on his hunting knife. He wasn't happy that Papa insisted meeting up with the various village headmen, local clan leaders or the kaptans of the garrison stationed in the towns or at strategic points. But Papa insisted. He listened to their complaints, made suggestions to overcome shortages and breakages, set garrison troops from their own small contingent to help with repair, promised relief and made notes on what required further attention.

By the time the village elders gave shallow bows and slowly dispersed, the sun was a rusty stain above the mountains in the west. Papa turned and strode toward the Way House, Lukarn and the brace of guards trailing behind him.

'Let's eat, Mannu.' Papa gripped his shoulder and they ducked through the door together.

After a quick and subdued meal, the other boys stretched out on their bed-rolls, fast asleep, even brooding Dinnis. Aunt Samara sat beside Uncle Lukarn with Rizzi asleep in her lap.

Mannok curled up at his father's feet beside Tracer, and hoped Papa wouldn't notice him. The fire crackled in the hearth and outside an owl gave a long mournful cry.

Uncle Lukarn's face scrunched up with worry. 'You should turn back to Tarka, Rokku. As Kapok, your safety and that of your son is paramount.'

Papa's face set in his nothing-is-going-to-move-me look. 'We've come too far to turn back now. I'm glad I came with you, that you are not facing this alone.'

'At least, fall back to Tarvin until we can bring more troops in to protect you.' And when Papa didn't answer. 'Think of the children.'

Papa followed Uncle Lukarn's gaze and rubbed his side. 'Marra was right. We should have left them behind. I will be having words with my Master of Scouts. Maybe I should promote Sparak for the job.' Papa leaned back, his eyes in shadow, his fingers drumming on the seat. 'How many times have we been in a tight situation where the only way out was forward? If we show fear now, we might invite attack. Your brother is stationed at Nakri with a full wing under his command.'

Uncle Lukarn traced the puma design engraved on his chest plate, his eyes lowered. One of the boys was snoring, Uson or Estolik perhaps. A log in the fire cracked and settled in a shower of sparks. Mannok held his breath. Please, don't let him be sent back to Tarka with the other children. He could help Papa, he was sure he could.

Uncle Lukarn bowed his head, then nodded. He slipped to his knees before Papa and touched his forehead with his fist. 'I'd follow your hunches anywhere, Your Majesty, even into the heart of hostile Nolmec territory. This is my own country, the land of my fathers. I only wish I wasn't bringing my family with me.'

'Which is why it isn't an option to fail here. Best get what sleep we can.'

Papa leant forward and pulled Uncle Lukarn into a tight, fierce hug. Releasing him, he bent down and scooped Mannok up as though he were no more than a small child and headed for the sleeping chamber. Mannok glimpsed Uncle Lukarn moving to sit beside Samara, putting his arms and cloak around her, before Papa drew the curtains that separated them from the outer chamber.

He wouldn't fail Papa, whatever new dangers the morning might bring.

Nakri

Chapter Thirty-Two: Amnesty

Mannok

Three days later they rode into Nakri to find a battered city with homes and shops gutted, the walls broken down from the long siege that had finally defeated Uncle Naetok. Brigan Kolik, Uncle Lukarn and Mama's younger brother rode out to greet them with a portion of the garrison troops at his back. People with grim faces lined the street as the royal convoy passed by. There was no sign of the cheering or throwing of flowers that would normally greet the arrival of the Kapok.

Uncle Kolik had already made some of the rooms in the Markan's Stronghold habitable, but the Great Hall was in a dilapidated state. Over the next several days, everyone including Mannok and Papa, pitched in to remove debris, build up gaps in the walls and patch the room. Attendants swept out the dust and leaves, cleared the long strands of dusty cobwebs hanging from the water-stained rafters and scrounged up as many candles as possible for the defaced candelabra.

Messengers were sent far and wide, announcing the amnesty and calling a council on the night of the two full moons. When Papa wasn't riding out, inspecting the damage in the surrounding areas, he and Uncle Lukarn were cloistered together going over plans and leaving Mannok to entertain himself as best he could with his cousins and the orphans. The days passed in a blur. Messengers returned foot sore and weary. One evening, as Mannok was climbing the battlements, he was sure he saw a Nolmec let in the postern door. Yet, when he raced down the stairs and through the corridors he could find no sign of the man, and Papa turned Mannok's questions aside.

As the moons began to wax to full, clan leaders and nobles from the Puma, Grey Fox, and other northern clans started congregating with their troops and levies. The silent streets seemed choked with a growing feeling of menace. This venture could easily end in bloodshed.

* * *

The day of the meeting had arrived. Mannok rubbed his arms to keep warm. Unlike the Throne Room at home, the desolate Great Hall of Nakri didn't have large casement windows or skylights to let in the mid-morning light. Instead, long narrow window slits lined up like sentinels down the length of the outside wall, grudgingly allowing thin slices of golden light to break up the gloom.

Men and women drifted into the large hollow space and settled into the tiered wooden benches that took up one side of the room; clan or village leaders or nobles and their kin. Most had the short, stocky frames of the mountain born while some—probably those from the coast—were taller. A few had the wispy white hair of old age, some the wrinkles or receding hairline of middle age, while others were youths fresh from the manhood Trial of Tears, having barely left their baby names behind them. Only a few were brightly dressed. Most wore brown or grey cloaks and tunics and had the pinched look that only comes from many days of cold and hunger. They glanced at their neighbours with suspicion, starting at the slightest sound, while their hands searched for the haft of spears that had been left outside the door. Even with the troops already stationed here, the royal forces were outnumbered.

Mannok's stomach tightened and he glanced over his shoulder at his father a pace behind him. The Kapok sat in the large wooden chair at the head of the room, an imposing sight in his full regalia of nodding feathers, gold crescent chest plate and arm rings, and long orange cloak embroidered with gold thread. Flanked by spear carrying guards, his face was stern and his golden eyes unreadable. Uncle Lukarn stood behind him, stalwart and dependable. Rizzi and the other boys were under the watchful eye of Lutan Jakan and Aunt Samara to one side.

With a slight gesture of the chin, Papa beckoned Lutan Jakan to his side. Keeping his eyes looking forward and his head up, he said in a low voice, 'If this turns ugly, your foremost duty is to get the Prince, Markana Samara and the other children to safety. Take a unit and follow the low road, keeping off the Royal Way as much as possible.'

'Your Majesty, I could not desert you. Your safety ...'

'Is the Markan and the Brigan's responsibility. Make sure Prince gets back to his mother.'

'Papa!'

'Hush boy. This is not the time for arguments.'

Jakan stepped back and at a subtle hand signal from Papa, a lone horn sounded. The subdued whispering filling the Hall stopped and all eyes watched as the Brigan of the Garrison, Kolik, stepped forward and read out the contents of Papa's declaration of a general Amnesty. A declaration that had been proclaimed across the region to even the remote mountain villages of the rebellious Northern Marches.

'I, Rokkan Kapok son of Martal Kapok, son of Tellek Kapok, Lord of Tamra and Shanta, Overlord of Tarka, mighty jaguar of the North, Protector of widows and orphans, am aware of the falsehoods propagated by my late half-brother, Prince Naetok. Lies by which you, my loyal people, have been deceived. This after he, an unnatural son and brother, betrayed his own loving father, Martal Kapok, striking him down with poison and then attacking my own person. It has been to my great sorrow that, through his actions, my lands have been torn asunder and given over to the ravages of war. Yet, by the Maker's favour, I have been granted full and complete victory over all that oppose me, both my treacherous brother and the evil sorcerer who has long interfered in Tamrin affairs, the Deceiver—Akrad—aided and abetted Naetok in his sedition.

'Nevertheless, I am aware of the great suffering the war has brought upon you, my rightful subjects in the north. You who are close to my heart, not least for the sake of my dear stepmother, Kupanna Suraya, daughter of the Puma clan who you know well, and my beloved wife, Kupanna Marra, her niece and daughter of Derik, formerly Markan of the North before my traitorous brother bore that illustrious title.

'It is my great desire that any enmity and misunderstanding that stand between us be laid at rest, and that we join together in the worthy effort of rebuilding the prosperity of our lands. It is in view of this that I offer an amnesty to all the warriors, great and small, to village heads, clan leaders and nobles who, being deceived by Naetok and Akrad's lies, have fought against me. These treasonous actions worthy of death shall be expunged from my memory and my grace offered towards you on these conditions:

'That you forthwith approach me with suitable humility and swear undying loyalty to myself, Rokkan Kapok, and my rightful son and heir, Mannok, Prince Royal of Tamra, as your rightful rulers and that you place your troops and lands at my disposal within the confines of tradition. If you do this, you will be considered my loyal subjects, friends of the Throne who will receive beneficence from levies established by the Throne to restore our lands.

'If you fail to swear such allegiance by the time silver Argenti has reached her half-cycle within a ten-day, you shall forthwith, without exception or forbearance, be declared my enemy. Such rebels will be hunted down without mercy, your clan lands and property confiscated and distributed as I, Rokkan Kapok, see most fitting to the benefit of our Land.

'Know this, that those who declare their loyalty first shall be the first to receive help to fully restore their lands. This I promise before witnesses and on the honour of my house and in the presence of the Maker of the star-filled skies and the green earth with all its multitudinous inhabitants. May he be ever the judge between you and me and hold all parties accountable for their words and deeds.'

The booming voice of the Brigan Kolik faded. A heavy silence settled over the full Hall.

Kolik smashed the butt of his spear into the stone paved floor. 'The clans may approach the Kapok and their voices be heard as tradition demands.'

Uncle Lukarn at once sprang up.

'I, Lukarn son of Derik and brother of Marra, Head of the Puma Clan and Markan of the North, declare myself the most loyal subject of my royal master, Rokkan Kapok and his son and rightful heir, Prince Mannok. My house and clan stands with you and yours to our last dying breath.'

With this he knelt and touched his fist to his chest, first to Papa and then to Mannok, then stretched himself out full length so that his forehead was within ninas of Papa's boots.

Papa leant forward and touched Uncle Lukarn's head.

'Rise most loyal and treasured brother, Markan of the North. Your oath of fealty is accepted.'

Lukarn stood up and bowed.

Uncle Kolik handed over his spear, and prostrating himself, swore loyalty to the Throne. A trickle of warriors and nobles followed, mostly from the Puma clan, men who had fought for and not against Papa. As each made obeisance and received Papa's acknowledgement, they moved to stand behind Papa's chair.

Most of the people in the Hall did not move from their seats. An uneasy silence settled over the room. The hair on the nape of Mannok's neck prickled.

Suddenly, halfway up the stands a noble with five red feathers in his head-dress jumped up. He had a long thin face with a nose that seemed to droop over his lips.

'Why should we swear loyalty to a perfidious son who killed his own father, the rightful Kapok, Martal son of Tellek, and then hunted down and killed his brother? You are the traitor Rokkan and you shall die like one. Better we follow Lord Haka, or one of our own, Lord Challak.'

A roar filled the Hall as person after person stood, slapping their chests or shaking their fists above their heads. Jakan rushed to Mannok's side, placing his hand on his shoulder,

'Time to go, Your Highness, don't delay.'

Chapter Thirty-Three: In the Balance

Mannok

The horn sounded, cutting across the thunder of angry protests and thumping fists. An uneasy silence fell. Mannok resisted the pull of Lutan Jakan on his arm. His heart raced. His legs felt like water. One thing he knew, he was not going to desert his father. He had to do something.

Pulling away, he grabbed the Brigan's ceremonial spear and bashed it three times into the floor.

All eyes turned toward him.

'What is the name of the base lord who dares slander my father, Rokkan Kapok?' he shouted.

'Mannok, what do you think you are doing?' Uncle Lukarn lunged forward to grab him. Uncle Kolik came from the other direction.

Papa gripped Uncle Lukarn's arm. 'Leave it, Lukarn, Kolik. The move has been made, let it play.'

Mannok stood taller, warmed by Papa's support. His gaze locked on the startled eyes of the protesting lord. 'Are you ashamed to say who you are? You should be, telling lies like that.'

The man's eyes slid away from his. Then he lifted his chin.

'Pirak, son of Kusin, of the Grey Fox Clan. And how would you know, child, about the truth of these great matters? Your father has deceived you.'

'Were you there?'

'No, of course not. But—'

'I was.'

'Nonsense, you must have been a babe in arms when these things happened over three years ago.'

'I was four when my treacherous Uncle Naetok returned Pa ... his brother, the Kapok's embrace with a knife blade. I saw it. I still see the blood in my dreams.' He bit down on his lower lip. Best not go there, 'Naetok killed my grandfather days before. He would have killed my father, because he was greedy to rule. It is you who are wrong, Pirak, son of Kusin.'

Mannok glared at the sea of faces in front of him. He took a deep, steadying breath and shouted one last thing before his shaking knees betrayed him.

'Naetok tricked you. You can redeem your treachery and reclaim your honour, by showing your lo ... loyalty to the throne and to the true and rightful ruler of Tamra, Rokkan son of Martal. As Markan Lukarn did. As I do.'

He spun around and knelt before his father, not daring to look at his face. Then stretched out, his face to the floor.

'A true warrior follows orders, Mannok,' Papa said in a flat voice.

'Yes, Your Majesty, but you gave Lutan Jakan the order not me.'

Papa heaved a gusty sigh. 'Do I have to spell out everything?' Yet despite the rebuke in his words, he could hear the amusement and maybe even a hint of pride. 'Rise, Prince Mannok son Rokkan, most courageous and loyal of sons,' his voice boomed.

Mannok's chest expanded at the words. He walked to stand beside his father as though walking on clouds.

Papa jumped up, placed his hand on Mannok's shoulder, and looked around the high vaulted room.

'Men and women of the north—Pirak, Nawulik, Pawen, Konan, Sarik ...' he named many, catching their eyes, if they dared to look back. 'You are my brothers and sisters, aunts, uncles, cousins, friends. It grieves me greatly that we have all lost those dear to us because of the strife between us, including my own father and half-brother.

'I grieve my beloved father's death, cut down before his time by a painful and deadly poison administered by his favourite son. And yes, I grieve for my treacherous brother though I bear the deep scars of his enmity against me. He listened to the lies of a master Deceiver, Akrad, and in turn learned to weave betrayal and deceit. Did he not tell you that I had killed my father, that Lukarn had killed me and my son, to take the throne as his own? I know he did.

'So, let's look at these so-called truths. Is Mannok dead? Am I? Would I hold fast to a man who tried to kill me? The truth is that Naetok attacked me and, but for the loyalty of my son and brother-in-law, I would not stand before you today. So, if Naetok lied about these things, do you not think he lied about the other, that it was his hand not mine that killed our father? I swear to you before the Maker that my hands are innocent of this foul crime. How many years have I spent among you, eating at your table, a recipient of your hospitality? You know me, surely? '

A hoarse voice hurled across the room. 'You visited Akrad's domain often enough. Maybe it is you who learned to deceive.'

Papa carefully searched the area from where the shout had come until his eyes narrowed.

'Ah, Challak, son of Waruk, is this truly what you believe? Are we not age-mates, did we not take the Test together in our fourteenth year? How often did we hunt side by side or scout the northern border together? Marra was heartbroken when she learnt that you, of all people, her favourite cousin, had sided against us.' Papa's voice broke. He stopped and took a breath. 'Well, there is no need to rush this. I understand it is hard to reappraise the so-called truths you have held to. I will remain here until Argenti is in half-circle. You have until then to make up your minds. I remind you though, that those who swear fealty first will receive help in restoring their lands first.' He paused then gave his daredevil grin, 'Oh, and if you are thinking about attacking me—a dishonourable act under a flag of truce—I give you fair warning, I am used to having the odds against me. Which of you would have imagined as I lay comatose from loss of blood, all but dying, that we would reach this point?

'Maybe, you thought I was a spent force —that Naetok was the future, or even my cousin, Haka, who stayed loyal to me. That is what Naetok thought. He was wrong. You were wrong. I suggest you don't make that mistake a second time, as it will be your last.'

With one last sweep of the faces before him, Papa turned to Uncle Kolik. 'Sound the dismissal, we will reconvene in a ten-day.'

A rustle swept through the Hall.

'But, aren't you giving us a chance to swear fealty? It is not even mid-morning,' someone called out.

Papa raised his eyebrows, 'I am not a beggar, Pawen son of Usak, or a spruiker of a street stall, trying to entice you to buy my day-old maize wraps. I am giving you the opportunity to—as Prince Mannok so ably put it—"redeem your treachery and reclaim your honour". As no one else wishes to avail themselves of that offer today, I have other things to do. Brigan ...'

'Wait.' Challak stood up and limped his way towards the throne. His likeness to uncle Lukarn was striking except for a ragged scar across his face, he was a little shorter and his one remaining eye was more hazel than brown. When he came within two paces, he knelt and then laid face down before Papa.

'I, Challak, son of Waruk of the Puma clan, beg your forgiveness for my lack of faith, my treachery. I do not deserve this amnesty. Yet if you would accept it, I give you, Rokkan Kapok, and your son and heir Mannok, my life and my loyalty.'

Papa stood still for a minute, staring down at the grizzled head with the orange-brown feathered headdress. His golden eyes glistened. Then he knelt, placing his hands on Challak's head and shoulder.

'Rise, cousin, if you would prove your loyalty, then I have a task for you.'

The warrior rose to his feet. 'Whatever Your Majesty commands.'

'Once things are settled here and we have started the process of restoring your lands, I want you to take a brigade of your troops to relieve Markan Haka at North Pass.'

Challak brought his fist to his chest. 'As you command.'

Bowing low, he went to stand behind the throne. Even before he had reached it, the remaining nobles within the chamber were shoving each other aside to be the next in line to swear fealty. By the end of the afternoon, there were few remaining who hadn't done so.

At last Papa, his face pale with fatigue, motioned to Uncle Kolik to sound the dismissal. As the nobles began to file out, bowing low as they went, Papa leant back in the chair and sighed,

'The Maker be praised. There may be one or two loose ends to tie up, but all in all, I think we have won the peace, at least in the north.'

'And here I was thinking I would end up in pieces by nightfall— several of them, all rather bloody,' Uncle Lukarn said.

Papa chuckled. 'But that's your problem, Lukku, you worry too much.' He shook his head. 'No doubt we will all die in our beds long in the tooth and daft in the head. A rather depressing thought, don't you think?'

'Not at all, especially if my wife is at my side. I just hope this drama hasn't affected the baby.'

'Baby?'

'Lukarn,' Aunt Samara was blushing. 'You are not supposed to say anything yet, it's too soon.'

Papa's eyes lit up. He jumped up and wrapped Aunt Samara in a huge hug.

'Congratulations, sweet sister. Such a wonderful way to celebrate a new day with the announcement of the coming of a new life.' He turned to Lukarn and clapped him on the shoulder, 'Not that you seem to waste any time, you old Puma.'

Mannok smiled at the unusual sight of Uncle Lukarn struck speechless. Death and danger had been averted and, even better, he had made Papa proud.

Chapter Thirty-Four: Hostage

Dinnis

Dinnis started awake at a soft scraping sound from the corridor outside the dark room. A band of silver moonlight outlined the scant furniture and the humps where the other boys lay sleeping. Nothing else moved.

The events of the last few days came rushing into Dinnis' thoughts like a flock of ravens. With Mannok's stirring speech, the Kapok had won over his rebellious countrymen and secured the peace. What that meant for Ista and him, he wasn't sure. He thought he'd seen a Nolmec messenger enter the Kapok's quarters some days ago, which was strange as the northern clans hated the Nolmec with even greater intensity those in the south of Tamra. Nothing came of it, though. With the rebel lords taking up the Kapok's offer of amnesty and the return of peace, security might be laxer and it would be easier to find a way out of the Stronghold. Though now his knowledge of Tamrin affairs would now be of less value to the Nolmec.

There it was again, closer this time. The furtive sound of footsteps on the flagstone floor. He sat up, his mouth dry. The door edged open and a dark figure was silhouetted against the light of a flaring wall torch behind him. He had the feathered headdress and short cloak of a Tamrin warrior. The man beckoned. What did the man want? He could ignore the summons, but there was no other door, nowhere to hide. His hands and feet tingling, Dinnis rose and crept around his sleeping companions. As he neared the door, the man reached out, grabbed and pulled him into the corridor, easing the door shut.

'Make no noise.' The man murmured, lips ninas away from Dinnis' ear, the odour of stale chilli beans tickling his nostrils. 'Come with me.'

'Why? Who are you?'

'Hush'. The tall man looked menacing in the muted light of the torch, a puckered scar from eye to chin. Though there was something familiar about him. The man dug his fingers into Dinnis' shoulders and twisted his arm behind his back. The sharp tip of something cold and sharp pressed just beneath Dinnis' jaw. 'What the Kapok orders happens, boy.'

'What—' His chest tightened as if the smoke tainted air had been sucked out of the dim corridor. Hadn't he done all that was asked of him? He'd kept his thoughts to himself.

'Give me an excuse, son of Gaia. I'll enjoy pacifying you.' The man shoved him down the corridor towards tower stairs.

Dinnis' heart hitched against his ribs. Whoever the Tamrin was, he knew his mother's name. He stumbled forwards.

'That's right, young Dinnis, I know where you come from, who you are, and I don't like it. Like Markan Lukarn, I'm not fond of the Nolmec or of those who threaten security of the Throne. Fortunate for you, the Kapok wants you alive. At least for now.'

'Who are you?'

'Sparak, a name you should remember, and one you won't forget.'

The name did seem familiar. Was Sparak one of the friends that came with Papa on his visits to Pylonis?

'Get a move on.' Sparak hustled Dinnis down the stairs, across the courtyard to the postern door and out through a side gate in the city wall. A shadowy figure walked two saddled horses, their soft breaths misting in the chill night air. Above the walls, Alumi and Argenti were two mismatched cats' eyes high against the stars. It had to be near midnight.

Sparak swung up onto one of the horses and pulled Dinnis up in front of him. The other man, a guard by the looks, also mounted.

Sparak clucked his tongue. 'Get on.'

The horses stepped off at a fast walk and were soon cantering north through the rugged countryside and into the unknown. Dinnis' stomach crawled with dread. Nothing about this secretive ride into

180

the dark night felt right, but—he took a deep breath—maybe this was his best chance at escape and find his Uncle.

* * *

The horse pulled to a sudden stop. The moons were slipping down into the western sky, their light sparkling on the small stream winding through a narrow valley but otherwise confusing the eye with double overlapping shadows. The resinous smell of pine and ash carried on the fresh night air. They had to be close to the Nolmec border.

'Who goes there?' Two Tamrin warriors barred their way.

'Our names are none of your business,' Sparak growled. He flashed a token.

'My Lord.' They stood back, grounding their spears.

Sparak grunted and angled his mount toward an adobe building with a broken-down wall and in the deep shadow of a ridge. The chink of metal, stamp of horses' hooves and the creak of leather in the nearby stand of pine trees nearby and dark shapes on the opposite side of the road suggested the presence soldiers. A Tamrin warrior with the short feather headdress of a foot soldier guarded the gate to the courtyard. On the other side stood a tall, Nolmec *pioni* or foot soldier.

His heart lifted. Perhaps, the Nuktis was negotiating for Ista's and his return and—

Sparak swung off the sweating horse and pulled Dinnis to the ground. 'Keep your mouth shut, boy. Do as you're told and stay close.'

Sparak waved the token at the guards. He strode through the low gate, across a small, enclosed courtyard. Dinnis followed close behind.

Sparak rapped a complicated rhythm on a battered door. It swung open. Smoke and stale smells of sweat, fried garlic and familiar Nolmec spices buffeted Dinnis.

'In you go.'

Dinnis swallowed hard. He stepped through into the medium-sized room crowded with several people. They turned and stared as Dinnis and Sparak. A single torch smoked and spluttered on one grimy wall, the room was not much brighter than the landscape drenched in the double moonlight outside.

At the centre of the room, a tall, muscular man sat on an upturned barrel, one ankle resting on his knee. His face was in deep shadow beneath a hooded cloak, but his commanding statue was achingly familiar. It had to be his father. Besides, he was flanked by another stubbier warrior who, but for his plain dress, looked like Lord Lukarn.

Two Nolmec, bareheaded and dressed in flowing silk brocade robes, one old, the other in early middle-age, stood at the far side of the room. To one side, a small table held four flasks and a half-empty tray of small Nolmec delicacies.

In the shadowed corner at the back of the room, two other blue-skinned men knelt, torchlight glinting off their newly shaved heads. The prisoners were familiar, despite their dejected demeanour, Keloumen Nikoris and Palouma Akillis. Not what Dinnis had expected of either officer, to accept such dishonour. Most Nolmec officers would die fighting or even take their own lives than suffer the shame of capture or defeat.

'Thank you, Sparak.' The Kapok's voice was unmistakable.

Sparak hovered just inside the door, his eyes meeting Lord Lukarn's, before he bowed to the Kapok. He nodded. 'I'll be outside ... sir.'

'Is this the boy? How do I know it's him?' The grey-haired man spoke in polished Nolmec, his voice like silk over water. 'He was hardly out of clouts, when last I saw him.'

'Hardly so young, General. Besides,' the Kapok waved a casual hand towards the prisoners. 'I'm sure they can affirm who he is.'

Dinnis stiffened. Since leaving Tarka, Papa—the Kapok—hadn't spoken to him or tried to approach him, even secretly. And now, after all his words of giving him a place in the Palace, the man was going to exchange him like excess baggage. That had been what Dinnis wanted, all that he'd thought about on the long journey north, to escape back to Nolmec. Now, absurd as it was, it felt like he was being discarded all over again.

Nuktis hawked and spat on the packed dirt floor. 'Traitors both. Their word means nothing.'

The other Nolmec, who hadn't taken his eyes off Dinnis from the moment he walked into the room, inclined his head. 'Then take my word for it, General. The boy is Gaia's son.'

Nuktis' lips tightened. Beyond the courtyard, a curlew gave a long aching cry. A few glowing coals hissed and settled in the hearth. The Kapok folded his arms and leaned back against the peeling, water-stained wall, tipping the barrel, a faint smile on his enigmatic, shadowed face.

'Do you doubt my word, General?' The younger man asked, his voice low. 'He has the look of my bond-sister in him.'

Nuktis glanced at his companion and waved a haughty hand. 'No, just your judgment. Are you sure you're not mistaken, Timon?'

Timon. Then it was his uncle, his Mater's bond-brother, her Alfeas. Maybe things were turning for the better.

Timon gave a crooked smile. He beckoned. 'Dinnis, do you remember me? Come closer, lad.' He had switched to strongly accented Tamrin.

He squatted, torchlight falling full across his face. A face like the treasured memory of his mother's, the face that haunted his dreams and eluded him in his waking hours no matter how many times he tried to sketch it. A feeling of loss pierced Dinnis with a suddenness that left him breathless.

He steepled his hands against his chest and bowed, hoping he'd got it right. 'Indeed, *kuree.*'

'Tell me, is your sister alive and well?'

'*Nai*, yes. She was when last I saw her.'

'And when was that?'

'Twenty-five days ago, at the Palace in Tarka, on her eighth birthday.'

'That is good news indeed and confirms what Rokkan claims. Thank you.' Though Timon's quiet face hardly changed, Dinnis felt the tension ease.

Nuktis took a step toward the Kapok, his wrinkled blue hands grasping the silken borders on the front of his robes. 'So, you do have her. I am now her guardian, her Arkon. You must return the Kiprissa to me. Only then will I stand down our troops on the border.'

Rokkan chuckled, a deep rich sound. He stood, his head a couple of ninas from brushing the low rafters. The hood slipped, revealing his dark, unruly hair, the gleam of his golden eyes. 'I think not Nuktis. My claim as *Suguzos* is stronger than yours. I will keep our little Kiprissa safe.'

A dark flush spread over Nuktis' high cheek bones. 'The Kiprissa belongs with her people.'

The Kapok's eyes darkened, his smile vanishing. 'My dear Nuktis, I don't forget you handed over Gaia's children to the Deceiver Akrad's care, despite your sworn word.'

The Nolmec General took a step backwards. 'He was their great-grandfather. I—'

'You know exactly what he was, though I guess I shouldn't blame the puppet for the actions of his master.'

'Nevertheless,' Nuktis swallowed hard, his voice-nub bobbing. 'She should be installed in Pylonis, not Tarka.'

'Turamba, you mean,' Lukarn muttered under his breath, using the Mokkan name for the town.

The Kapok flickered his fingers. 'I disagree, Nuktis. On Akrad's death, Keloumen Nikoris entrusted her into my care. My claim as Gaia's Suguzos is greater. If you object, I have more than a hundred thousand warriors to back it.'

'Tamrin warriors …'

Timon cleared his throat. 'The Suguzos Rokkan has a point, General. And while the Pretender Polema's soldiers continue to attack our towns, the Kiprissa would be safer in Tamra.' He turned to the Kapok. 'But, let us send a *phalanx* to better protect her.'

Lukarn thrust his head forward, his eyebrows bristling. 'Not even a unit will get past Nakri, except over my broken corpse and that of every Tamrin warrior north of Tarvin.'

Nuktis curled his lip, his hand going to the hilt of his sword. 'That could be arranged.

The Kapok held up his hands. 'Friends, please. Only Polema's Red Crane faction will benefit if we fall at each other's throats. Re-establishing the understanding broken by Akrad's treachery is to both your and our advantage.' Standing in front of Lukarn, he bowed in perfect Nolmecan style. 'Thanks for your offer, Timon, but no! I have more than enough warriors to protect her.' Rokkan raised an eyebrow. 'And she will be safe as long as my northern borders remain secure.'

'This is blackmail. You are a bandit, a filthy mudskin.' Nuktis spluttered through barred teeth, his Nolmec aplomb in tatters. 'We give you everything, and you concede nothing?'

'You are not in the position to make demands, Nuktis. Your troops lost, remember.' Lukarn's frown had been swapped for a derisive grin.

'*Moros*, how can I maintain her dominions and keep the loyalty of her soldiers with the Kiprissa a thousand leagues away?'

Lukarn shrugged his muscular shoulders. 'Not our problem.'

'It's a fair point, Lukarn. It's not our wish that the Phoenix faction be devoured by the Red Crane.'

Nuktis spat. 'Pretenders and usurpers.'

'Indeed.' The Kapok stroked his chin. 'As Suguzos and Arkon, I will appoint a regent to manage our affairs among the Phoenix Nolmec.'

'We are not your vassals. Though ...' Nuktis' dark eyes brightened and he clasped his hands behind his back. '... appointing a regent would help. I am happy to acce—'

'I think Timon has the closer claim.'

Nuktis' almond eyes hooded. 'I'm sure Timon would prefer to leave such weighty matters to wiser heads.'

'I'm sure he'd be happy to keep you on as General and advisor. Though perhaps, on second thoughts, Timon, you might consider—'

'Very well, Rokkan. I will remain as General. You have inherited a full measure of Arkon Akrad's deviousness. It will rebound on you one day.'

'Thank you. And I will also return to you the survivors of the *phalanx* at North Pass.'

'Keep them or kill them for all I care. They were weak enough to surrender.'

Rokkan raised his eyebrows. 'That's not how I would put it. They delivered the Kiprissa into the hands of her new Arkon. Besides, you'll need at least two noble witnesses to confirm the appointments I've made.'

Timon spread out his hands. 'We'll accept the prisoners. Take good care of our Kiprissa. If harm comes to her—'

'You will make your appointments in writing,' Nuktis demanded.

'Of, course. Brigan Kolik will arrange the transfer of the other prisoners once you withdraw all but a token group from the border. We can work out the details over the next few days. Will you accept our hospitality for the night, or at what's left of it?'

'Your offer is gracious, but we are anxious to return. We have a great number of things to organise.' The General's jet eyes flickered over at the two silent men before glancing at Dinnis, not troubling to hide the obvious scorn in his dark eyes for both parties.

The General had never been his friend, but his uncle had been kind. Dinnis stepped forward, suppressing the fluttering in his stomach, and tugged on Timon's robe before he could leave the room. '*Kuree ...*'

Timon turned. 'What is it, Dinnu?'

Dinnis swallowed hard at the use of the Tamrin diminutive. 'Take me with you.' He bit his lip. He could have put that better.

The Nolmec paused, then shook his head. 'I'm sorry but, as Ista's brother and Alfeas, your place is by her side. When the time comes for her to return, you will accompany her.'

'But ...'

'No, Dinnis.' His uncle's voice sounded final.

The Nolmec muttered formal words of leave-taking and hustled Nikoris and Akillis out with them.

Dinnis stood still, a deep cold seeped into his bones.

He jumped at the touch of cloth on his shoulder. A heavy cloak redolent with chilli, horse and leather draped warmth over him. He fingered the fine wool and glanced up as the Kapok, now uncloaked, turned his back and stretched. The outer gate clanged. Voices shouted in Nolmec, the sound of marching feet. His mother's people were leaving without him and his hopes of a different future with them.

'So, that went better than I expected.' Rokkan covered a prodigious yawn with his hand.

'Rokkan!' Lukarn glared at Dinnis. 'You can't ...'

'What?' The Kapok turned, his noncommittal eyes resting on Dinnis for a minute. 'Oh, come on, the child is cold. You couldn't have allowed him time to fetch a cloak, Sparak?'

The scar-faced man stood leaning against the doorjamb. 'Not without waking the room. Secrecy being paramount.' He raised one crooked eyebrow.

The Markan's face twisted. 'That child begged to go with the blasted Nolmec. He's like a rotted support rope on a bridge, a disaster waiting to happen.'

'Without a doubt.' Sparak crossed the room and snagged one of the tiny delicacies off the gold-etched tray. His face puckered. 'Gah! I forgot how much I hate Nolmec food.'

'It's an acquired taste.' The Kapok popped two of the concoctions in his mouth. 'Though the quantities often seem wanting.' He offered the plate to Lukarn, who waved it away before setting it beside Dinnis. 'Eat.'

Not that he could with the tightness in his throat.

Lukarn beat a tattoo on this thigh. 'If you'd attacked instead of parleyed, we could have crushed them. They've massacred whole villages, killed without mercy. Our cousins in the north are dead or slaves under their cruel and unrelenting rule.'

'To be fair, it was the Red Crane that took out —'

Lukarn snorted. 'Phoenix, Red Crane ... or whirligig whoopbird, it makes no difference. What they did to our Mokkan cousins, they'd do to us in the thrash of a crocodile's tail.'

'The battle for Mokka was lost a long time ago. And with the Phoenix and Red Crane in a dynastic struggle we buy ourselves breathing space. Not all problems are solved by a spear through the heart, Lukku.'

The Markan's eyes strayed back to Dinnis. 'Some might be.'

'Only a handful of trusted people know—'

'He knows. The Nolmec know. What if they use it—'

'Lukku, please stop interrupting me. It's irritating. Do you think General Nuktis or any of them have the smallest idea of Tamrin customs? To their mind, Gaia's daughter is important, not her son.'

'Well ...' The Markan's hunched shoulders loosened. He let out a guffaw. 'Mudskins and monkeys. They do have an overdose of arrogance.' He rubbed the back of his neck. 'Though Timon—'

'Interests align with ours, for the moment.'

'And when he wants the girl back?'

'We'll work it out when the time comes.'

'And the boy?'

'Is intelligent enough to keep his mouth shut.' But all the same, the Kapok's gaze clouded as he turned away. 'Sparak, better return the lad and see that you treat him with more care. Once we've wrapped things up here and visit the other regions, we can head back home.'

Dinnis didn't resist when Sparak to lead him away. The Nolmec were his last recourse. Now he had nowhere to go, no one who wanted him.

THREE ALUME LATER
On the road to Tarka

Chapter Thirty-Five: Dark of Night

Dinnis

Dinnis wrapped his arms around his knees and stared into darkness. The icy chill of the path seeped into him. His limbs hummed with tiredness from the long days of travel, but he couldn't sleep. When everyone else had settled for the night, he snuck out past the guards to the ridge above the Way House, though he wasn't sure what he planned to do.

Neither of the moons were up and the cold fire of the stars blazed in strings and swirls across the velvet black of the sky. Yet for all their radiance, the stars barely lit the high mountain ridge. The snow on the distant peaks shimmered like floating clouds against the nightshade black and, ten tanis away, the Way House blended into the shadows.

Dinnis picked up a small pebble from the road, rubbing the sharp edges, welcoming the pain.

After the confrontation with the rebel lords in the north and the secret meeting with the Nolmec, Rokkan Kapok decided to tour the realm. Descending from the high mountains, they rode across rolling hills of scrub and swathes of desolated desert to Lord Haka's domains in the Western Marches. Towns huddled in the terraced and irrigated river valleys. New landscapes and population centres spread out before them. At Haka's seat, the port city of Akra, the ocean thrashed and foamed at the base of tall, stark cliff faces and stretching out as far and as wide as the eye could see.

Rokkan had pushed on, taking a royal barge along surging rivers to Lord Durak's domains in the Southern Marches. Then, despite the frequent rain storms, he'd headed northeast to visit his sister and step-mother in the eastern Mist Forests of Poija. Now, after a couple Alume of travel and solidifying clan loyalties, the royal party was heading back to Tarka for the delayed coronation.

The new vistas thrilled Dinnis—the mountains, the vast ocean, the deserts and forests—seeing more places on the maps he pored over in stolen moments among in Akrad's tower room or the Palace library … Yet he was as often plunged into a whirlpool of dark thoughts. The closer he came to Tarka, the harder it was to take pleasure in the novelties and sights and his supposed rescue.

The Tamrin didn't beat him, they fed and clothed him. Not all were scornful or cold. But … the Kapok … the one person he wanted most to please was even more aloof and distant than on the journey to Nakri, if that was possible. And the secret meeting with the Nolmec had made clear, despite his Uncle Timon's sympathy, any position he had with the Nolmec would depend on his relationship to Ista and the Kapok's machinations. That whatever their supposed ranks and connections, he—and she—were both pieces in a game between more powerful, ruthless players.

Akrad's capricious punishments had been physical as well as mental. Dinnis wore the scars on his back and arms to prove it. The difference was that he'd had hope—hope that someday things would be different—and the sure knowledge of his father's love.

Fragile, mistaken, stupid hope.

The stars blurred against the darkness of night. He had been too soft, too stupid, too trusting … He pitched the pebble, watching it skip across the road and tumble down the cliff on its flight to freedom in the ravine far below. The wind whined around him, slapping his cold cheeks and tugging at his cloak. It was as if he heard an enticing voice in its soft fluting.

'Dinnis dear, you are a person of power. Use your hate and anger to destroy lesser folk, these weaker races. Deceive and entrap the Kapok like you did me …'

Words like those the Monster had whispered, when Dinnis had first arrived at the Stronghold at North Pass. Before Akrad had dismissed him as a *moros*. Before he'd made his unshakable loyalty to his father clear. Dinnis shivered, a shudder starting deep inside.

Akrad's fire-singed notebooks were piled in a forbidden corner of the library. He'd seen them when Lutan Jakan had sent him on an errand to the chief librarian the day before they left the Palace. He hadn't told Ista, not sure that he wanted to encourage her admiration of the Monster. He'd learnt the distrust of such dark studies from his father, yet where had his loyalty for Papa got him?

He slipped the ring out from his tunic and rubbed it between his chilled fingers. The token that the Kapok had given him on the first night and failed to reclaim. His father might as well be dead. Something like darkness stirred inside him, Akrad's whispered voice, the taste of bile. 'Deceive and entrap the Kapok like you did me.'

Had he been responsible for Akrad's death, as Ista claimed? Only, indirectly but ... he was good at stealth, at subterfuge ... they all believed him capable of it. He pictured the clouded look in the Kapok's golden eyes, the blatant suspicion in the Markan's coffee brown ones. He could bide his time. Perhaps, he should look at those powerful books. All that was left to him was revenge.

The sky behind him in the east was brightening along the horizon, bringing a grey rose-tinged half-light. Clouds created misty ladders up the dark sky. Pink and gold blushed the slopes of terraced fields with their criss-cross of irrigation channels. The colours spilled over the folds of the mountains and, in the distance, the snowy peaks. All around him was a cacophony of bird song.

Soon the village folk and the royal servants would stir, start their daily chores. He'd better get back to the Way House, before he was missed. He drew back his arm, ready to hurl the useless token over the edge of the cliff and froze at a soft, whispering susurration behind him.

A large bird, a snowy owl, stood on the road. Before his eyes, it transformed into the figure of a woman dressed in a flowing white tunic, one silvery-white shoulder bare. She was young and shapely, long dark hair flowing in waves down her back and deep velvet black eyes. She looked like Rasel, the young woman in Akrad's Tower.

He rubbed his eyes. He had to be dreaming.

'Are you safe and well?' Her voice was as silvery as the night turned dawn.

He sighed, half-convinced he was in a trance. 'No, not really. Nothing is as it should be. It was all pointless.'

Her soft skin smelt of new pine needles, spicy bark, sweet

budding flowers and the wind across the snows. She was too beautiful to be real.

She leant down and touched his arm. Her hand warmed his cold skin, sending shocks through his body. 'I know. I feel the darkness sometimes, the bitter regret and the fear that the losses weren't worth it.' Her voice hitched. 'But Dinnis, you did the right thing.'

He looked up at her, her skin gleaming in the soft pearlescent light, her eyes shining like starshine. His heart stirred in a way he did not fully understand.

He put his chin on his knees. 'No one really cares. I am just a splinter on the banister. A cracked flagstone. A pebble in a boot.'

Traces of tears gleamed in her eyes. 'Nor are you nothing. You belong to the Maker and he values you.'

'I don't know that I believe.' As soon as the words left his lips, he wished he hadn't been so honest.

She laughed, a fluid merry sound. 'That may well be Dinnis, yet he believes in you.'

He smiled at the reply, though he was unconvinced. If this Maker cared or even existed, why had he let his mother die, allowed Akrad to abuse him and his sister, his father to reject him. The Nolmec believed in other deities. Who could know the truth?

'The darkness can only grow when we forsake light and love,' she said, as though she read his thoughts. 'Allow the seeds of love to grow. Kindle the flame. You are brave and strong, Dinnis and I thank you for your help.'

The sky took on a soft purple tone. The horizon star shone bright like a diamond in the east, the others had already faded from sight. He could hear people stirring, pumping water from the well for washing and cooking, preparing the morning meal. He rubbed his face, not sure how to take her words.

The hoot of an owl sounded from the stand of trees behind them.

'I need to go, I'm sorry.' With a soft flurry of sound, her voice seemed to diminish. 'Don't give up hope.'

He dropped his hands and glanced up. The space where she stood was empty. Taking a deep breath of cold mountain air, he slowly let it out.

Perhaps he really was going mad.

Something fluttered in the wind. Something small and light. Dinnis leaned forward and snatched up a snowy feather tinted rosy in the growing dawn light. He slipped it and the ring into his tunic pouch and headed back to the Way House, the Kapok and the choking ties of servitude. He would not give up just yet. Maybe, to his father and the others, he was no more than a minor game piece easily discarded, but he wouldn't let them define his destiny.

Part Two: A Realm at Peace

THREE YEARS LATER
Tarka

Chapter Thirty-Six: Age-Mates

Mannok

And the villages and lands of Shanta destroyed,' Ralton's voice droned on about events of the distant past.

Mannok rolled his eyes at Garvin. It wasn't as if they didn't know this brutal story of their neighbouring realm's demise at Akrad's instigation. Martal Kapok had banned the telling of it, but Papa said history should be told, no matter how painful.

Of course, the carnage hadn't ended there. Some said the Jaguar clan, the clan of the royal house, was cursed. Only peasants and the ignorant believed in superstitions like curses, shape-shifting Adelphi and ... and fire-breathing koraktils. Yet, four generations drenched in bloodshed; brother against sister, father against daughter, son against father, brother against brother.

A splinter of ice slithered down his spine and Mannok shut his eyes against the unsettling image of Papa laying in a spreading pool his own blood, Grandfather Martal poisoned mere days before.

It had to stop!

He clenched his fist under the desk as though he could crush fate like a stinging lowland mosquito. He'd never rebel against Papa, nor would he give reason for his future children to rebel against him. He'd protect his family and the realm. He'd be strong.

Besides, there was no reason for fear ... Over three years since the belated coronation ceremony, held by chance on his birthday and Tamra was at peace—the Nolmec keeping to their side of the border, the northern lords proving themselves loyal to the throne, cousin Haka showed no sign of usurping Papa's position.

'... and if Prince Mannok would grace us with his attention.'

Estolik sniggered beside him.

Mannok sat up straighter. 'Yes, Master Ralton?'

The Head Librarian's long face looked like he'd swallowed a handful of unripe inka berries. 'Yes, thank you, Your Highness. Your attention to your studies is worthy of ... something.' A few more boys smothered chuckles behind their fists. The sonorous palace gong sounded. 'Hmm ... well, off you go. To wrestling practice, I believe.' He flickered his fingers at them, as though shooing off a flock of village ducks.

Dinnis was hunched over the desk writing or sketching, but Mannok didn't need any more urging. He shoved his books on the shelves.

'Come on, Garo.' Clapping Garvin on the shoulder, they headed for the practice yards by the most direct route possible. That is, without jumping out the tall library windows.

The cluster of boys held back as he and Garo jogged down the stairs, along the atrium and through the side door into the practice area. The orphans and Dinnis had been joined by the young sons of noble houses, his age-mates. Some were about his age like Garo and Redrik, old Kaptan Ninak's son. Some were older boys like his cousin Waren, and some were a few years younger, like Challak's second son, Trasin. They were educated at the Palace in book learning and martial skills, returning to their own family's domains twice a year. Except for the orphans, of course. They and Garo were always with him, his constant companions whether he wanted them or not.

* * *

A couple of hours later, Mannok sluiced water on his face. His arms and legs wobbled like custard. Kaptan Jakan was a hard taskmaster, expecting the lutans to push his charges to the edge of endurance. He slumped against the wall next to Garo and rubbed his arm, where Uson had got in a lucky blow. Not that it had helped the young blade in the end. Mannok tucked in a smile, savouring his victory. He ached all over, but he loved the challenge, the thrust and feints, the pull of his muscles and rush of exhilaration. Pushing his dripping hair out of his eyes, he focused on the other bouts.

Asik and Trasin were facing off in the junior practice yard. Both competent if unexciting fighters.

He turned toward the advanced yard. 'Who's matched?'

Garo nudged his with an elbow. 'Waren against Dinnis.'

'Hard to know who to cheer for there.'

Both were irritating. The older lads grappled together. Planting his feet on the ground, Waren used his weight against the taller lad, and Dinnis gave ground.

Garo tilted his head. 'They're evenly matched. Waren has more strength, Dinnis is good on technique and cunning.'

Trasin's older brother, Puran, gave a boisterous cheer. 'Go, Waren, Go Puma, smash the Nolmec mongrel.'

'Smash him good,' Redrik joined in.

Dinnis broke free of a hold. The two combatants circled, but it was hard to see with the crowd of young blades in the way. Mannok stood, dusted off his breeches, and walked toward the ring for a closer look. He edged around Uson, Estolik, Durrin and a bunch of other standing on the sidelines. Just as he got a clear view, Dinnis executed a classic duck under throw and pinned Waren to the ground. A sigh rippled through the boys. Puran, Redrik and a few others hissed. Durrin, son of Lord Durak of the Southern Marches, moved closer to the boundary. Mannok suppressed a snort. Durrin loved a fight.

Lutan Zaven counted the hold before declaring the victory. 'Well done, cadet.'

Waren shot Dinnis a wary, surprised look, then clapped him on the shoulder. 'Seleste, Dinnis.'

Garo jumped and hollered. 'Seleste, Dinnis. One for ... for the Jaguar clan.'

If it had been anyone else, the other boys would be thronging around the victor, clapping him on the back and fist-bumping, but Garo was the only one celebrating Dinnis' victory.

'Way to go, Dinnis,' Mannok shouted. He lowered his voice and turned to his friend. 'But the Jaguar clan? How do you work that out, Garo?' Dinnis was clanless.

'Well, he's an orphan and under the protection of the Kapok.'

Garvin got the weirdest ideas sometimes. The Jaguar tribe was reserved for those of royal blood or strong ties to the royal family. Even if Dinnis' father was Tamrin like he claimed, his father most likely came from the north—not Puma, perhaps, but Grey Fox or Rock Rabbit.

Mannok bumped shoulders. 'If anything, he'd be Yarma clan.'

'Hey, nothing wrong with that.' Garvin bumped him back.

Lutan Zaven tapped a small gong. 'Next bout in five strokes.'

Dinnis stood a solitary figure in the middle of the ring, his expression unreadable. He rubbed his face with his cloak and stretched his back and shoulders. His smouldering gaze sweeping the onlookers when, with the blink of an eye, he seemed to turn to stone, his eyes fixed on something ... no ... someone standing in the shadow of the Palace. It was Papa's Master of Scouts. Sparak's dark, predatory gaze was directed straight at Dinnis, a strange look on his face.

'What's that about?'

'What?' Garo asked. 'Hmmm, Sparak looks like he's seen a puma among the yarma herd.'

Dinnis hadn't shifted his gaze, when Durrin bowled into him, his shoulder connecting, crashing Dinnis to the ground. Mannok could almost feel the impact from where he stood, a couple of tanis away. Durrin was a big, solid lad and he had had no hesitation pressing down on a winded Dinnis with his full weight, a malicious grin on his broad face. 'Not so cocky now, are you.'

Estolik hooted and soon the other boys followed, Uson laughing uproariously.

'One, two ... and ten.' The Lutan stepped forward at the end of the count, his beetling eyebrows drawn together. 'The bout and today's contest goes to Durrin.'

'He wasn't ready,' Garo growled under his breath.

'Courtesy doesn't belong on the battlefield, young scion. The Lutan knows that.' Sparak eyed the boys, his scar stretching. 'Good lesson to remember.' He dipped his head in Mannok's direction. 'Your Highness.'

Mannok wanted to argue, yet a distracted warrior was a dead warrior on the battlefield. Still, it wasn't good form, and Durrin hadn't moved even though the count had ended.

He smirked. 'Going to beg for mercy?'

Dinnis' face was a stiff mask, but he said nothing.

'That's enough, Lord Durrin, son of Durak.' Lutan Zaven grabbed the young blade's brawny arm.

Durrin shook his head. 'Yeah, and how many Tamrin have died at Nolmec hands. They've razed whole villages, killed everyone – man, woman and child.'

'The southerner has a point.' Sparak said from behind them.

Mannok frowned. He remembered Papa's words. Dinnis wasn't responsible for the massacres. 'Durrin, stop.'

Lutan Zaven shook his discipline stick. 'We're not on the border now, Lord Durrin and this cadet is your age-mate.' A tense moment and, then, the lunch gong sounded. 'Son of Durak report to the duty office. The rest of ya ticks, that's it for today.'

Durrin spat to one side, stood and walked away. Uson, Estolik and some others followed, clustering around him.

Dinnis sat up, probing his shoulder with slender fingers, a grimace on his face.

Mannok offered his hand. 'Do you need a medic?'

A slight hesitation, and Dinnis took it. 'Thank you, but no, Your Highness. Bruised, but not broken, I believe.'

He allowed Mannok to pull him up, before bowing and heading off toward the back of the kitchens, in the opposite direction to the rest of the boys. Waren joined Mannok and Garo, shaking his head. 'That was not well done. Durrin acted like a thug, not a warrior.'

For once, Mannok had to agree with his older cousin.

Chapter Thirty-Seven: Walls Within Walls

Dinnis

Dinnis ran his left hand along the red painted palace wall. A wall that were sheer and at least ten tanis high. The gilded carvings of jaguar and koraktils on top, that might have given purchase for fingers and toes, were far beyond his reach. Besides, his shoulder throbbed like festival drum, where Durrin had ground his knee with his full weight behind it this morning.

His fault for not paying attention. The shock of seeing Sparak lurking in the shadows, like a palace cat stalking mountain pigeons, paralysed him for a moment. It wasn't the first time he'd see the man watching him, assessing him—for what? Did he see him as a threat? Dinnis shivered, of course he did. He knew who he was and wanted him out of the way. He'd been foolish to show any military prowess. He'd have to be more careful from now on.

It was like being a captive bird in a gilded cage, except he didn't feel safe or pampered here. He had nowhere else to go, but if living in Akrad's Stronghold had taught him anything, it was the importance of knowing the layout, the routines, the escape routes. Rasel, or her vision, counselled not giving up hope, to build something positive with his life, but how could he when he was stopped at every turn, ignored or reviled.

He pulled out a soft piece of yarma cheese wrapped in vine leaves that Sanak, the Head Cook, had given him before shooing him away. Dinnis allowed himself a grim smile. If he ran errands, helped carry heavy loads, stirred the bubbling pots on the fire, his presence was often tolerated for longer and he seldom went unrewarded. If only he could get on as well with his supposed age-mates.

He bit into the cheese, savouring its creamy texture and the beauty of the day. The sapphire skies were softened by small clouds and a hint of chill in the lucent air. A fitful wind ruffled his hair and needled the back of his neck with premonitions of colder weather. The trees were laden with fruit and, outside the city, the fields grew heavy and ready to harvest.

Picking up a straight stick, Dinnis trailed it behind him as he walked beside the barrier separating the cloistered palace grounds and the bustling city outside. He had traipsed the full circle of the wall on several occasions. There were three gates; the elaborate main gate that opened on the Palace forecourt and a smaller one that opened off the stables, for the pack yarmas and merchants to use, and an even smaller one near the servants' compound at the other end of the Palace grounds. He'd pick the locks except all three were guarded, day and night.

He had tried sauntering through when one or the other had been opened for those on official royal business, but he'd always been turned back. There had to be another way out, maybe a secret passageway or hidden door. After all, Naetok had managed to slip out of the city unseen after his attack on the Kapok, at least, according to Ralton.

He pulled to a stop and stared at the carved gate set in the smaller, inner wall enclosing the Silisean mini-palace. A fourth gate, but it didn't lead outside. According to the gossip in the kitchens, this secluded area held a sprawling single-story building with courtyards and fountains, built to accommodate a Silisean royal bride—maybe Rokkan's mother when she had first arrived in the Palace, or perhaps an earlier future Kupanna. When Prince Tannik and his brother arrived from Silesia for Rokkan's coronation, they had stayed in this isolated building. And it was sometimes used at festivals, when there was an overflow of guests staying at the Palace. But it was not in use at the moment and praise the Maker, or Kroko, today, it wasn't guarded.

He scanned the orchards. The soft twitter of birds, the rustle of leaves, and, faint in the distance, the clatter of the kitchens, but no sight or sound of another human. He walked to the door, the long grass brushing against his calves, grabbed the large bronze ring and pulled. The gates trembled but didn't budge. Locked, of course. He rotated around, confirming that the orchards were deserted. A slow smile stretched unused cheek muscles. Taking out his pick from his tunic, he probed the lock. The mechanism was like those at Akrad's Tower. With a thunk and a clunk, it slid open.

Seleste. He punched the air, wishing he had a partner in mischief.

Pushing open the tall wooden gates, he slipped between their jaws and surveyed a totally unexplored region of the Palace complex.

The gardens were overgrown, giving them a mysterious air. Yet really, they were just another confined area within a larger one; walls within walls within walls.

Ignoring the path that led to the Silesian-styled palace, he pushed his way through the long grass and ducked beneath low tree branches, edging along the curve of the wall. He stopped when he'd come full circle. Another dead end, as he'd expected. He heaved a sigh and sat down, leaning his back against the smooth bark of a marosa tree. Tipping his head back, he looked at the clear sky between the branches of the ancient tree. Branches like clawed fingers stretched out to grasp the peeling paint of the tall red walls. He blinked, then sat up straight. What if ...

Jumping up he traced the route along the wall once again until he found a high branch of a tall tosa tree overhanging the outer wall. He rubbed his hands against his breeches and, ignoring the shooting pains in his shoulder and ribs, shimmied up the trunk until he reached the first branch, five or more tanis above the ground. He pulled himself up to the overhanging branch and edged out over the wall. Gripping the branch with knees and hands, he peered below and grinned.

Long grass and a stand of tall bushes bordered a cobbled road. Two-storeyed adobe houses lined the other side.

It was too far to jump down, but if he had a rope ... And he knew where to find one.

* * *

Half an hour later, Dinnis looped the rope around his shoulder, climbed up the tree and crept out along the overhanging branch. Once well out past the wall, he tied the rope to the branch and pulled. The knot held.

He paused for a moment to look at the rather derelict houses lined up on the other side of the cobbled road. The outside of the ochre houses had no windows, no doubt walls opening out to an atrium or courtyard on the other side. A few small children were playing at the gates, a couple of skinny dogs nosing through a pile of refuse and an old grandmother with a large bundle on her head, lumbering her way down the slope of the road, her back to him. Otherwise, the street was empty.

Taking a deep breath, he grabbed the rope and swung himself down, landing into the middle of the bushes. Startled doves whirred away above him. He dropped flat to the ground, his heart pounding. Had he been seen? Would anyone give the alarm?

The wind whined along the Palace wall interweaving with the reedy voices of the children as they played and the muted sounds of the busy street traffic further down the hill, near the service gate of the Palace. No voice challenged him or shouted a warning. He got to his feet and oriented himself.

On his right, the paved road extended to the Palace service gate further down the hill. At the northwest corner of the Palace wall, it met another road and, beyond it a small knoll. In the distance, the staggered western wall of the distant temple glowed beneath the vertical slopes of the Twins. The barracks for the levy troops were that way as well as some of the administrative buildings. Best to avoid that area if he could. In front of him the shabby houses lined a small valley hemmed in by a spur running off mountain ridges flanking the city.

He turned left, jogging up a small rise. As he reached the southwest corner of the Palace, he crested the slight hill. The road and terrain fell steeply before levelling out to the well-to do houses and shops, the massive city gate towers beyond them. Past the walls, the bowl-like valley spread out in terraced fields, with maize and cheewa plants shimmering in the sunlight.

A laden yarma string accompanied by a convoy of guards laboured along the road, headed his way. His heartbeat quickened. 'Slide it!' There was nowhere to hide close to the wall. Keeping low, he sprinted across the road and dashed down a dirt path snaking through the tumbledown houses.

After a few hundred tanis, he leaned forward, hands on knees, and caught his breath. He continued at a slower pace, keeping to the shadows. More big buildings blocked his way to the south. Best to avoid anything looking too official, but he had the whole day to explore. He wouldn't be missed until the evening meal, and the Palace was such a prominent landmark, he could use it to find his way back.

At the bottom of the small valley, the path ran between two shops before intersecting with another stone paved street. A small public fountain splashed water into a trough with a gurgle, the wind catching and scattering spray like ink stains on the cobble stones. He licked his dry lips, already tasting the coolness of water.

A sudden raucous laugh came from further down the street, followed by shouting.

'Leave me alone, you big ugly bullies.'

'Wotcha going to do 'bout it, orphan girl?'

'I'll tell my ma. She'll make you sorry, you'll see!'

'Oooh, ooh, you'll set the witch on us. We're so scared.'

More hoots of laughter filled the afternoon air.

Dinnis stepped out of the shadows between the buildings and scanned the narrow street. Further along, towards the mountain Twins, three big lads surrounded a girl.

Two long chocolate-brown plaits reached to her waist and she carried a large basket in her arms. She appeared a few years older than he was.

The biggest boy with a flat nose and solid head shoved the girl hard, sending her sprawling backwards, the basket tipping from her arms and upending over the muddy street. The girl gave a cry of pain and distress. The boys cracked up laughing, slapping each other on the back.

'Now look wotcha done, Toban. You good for nothing, peasant. You'll never amount to anything, just like your stupid drunk of a Da,' the girl screeched.

Toban stopped laughing. His face contorted with anger. He lunged, grabbed the girl by the front of her plain blue-grey tunic and pulled her up.

'You take those words back, Tilli, or I'll smash you.'

Chapter Thirty-Eight: Herbal Shop

Dinnis

Toban drew back his fist.

Dinnis did not stop to think. 'Let go of her, you bully.'

He strode towards the group, his heart pounding, the stick held out in front of him.

The lad let go of the girl and spun to face Dinnis. The two companions closed in behind him. Three against one, unless the girl, Tilli, could help. He had shot up in the last few months and, at almost fifteen, was taller than some grown men but thinner than most. The lad in front of him had a muscular build that could easily run to fat, like Durrin or his nemesis Uson. Toban's flinty brown eyes were darkened with rage.

The other boys were smaller, but Dinnis could see the predatory look in their eyes. They were not intimidated by one lone, stick-wielding boy. This could get sticky, but he didn't care. No one was watching him here, and he'd inflict some pain, if nothing else. The taunting after Durrin trounced him still rankled.

He grinned, half snarl, all anticipation. 'Good. Thanks for releasing Tilli. I'm glad to see you are amenable to reason.'

'Ame ... Ame-na ... Listen to the clown, who speaks like that?' Toban spat out. 'Idiot.'

'Cross-eyed bluey, whotcha doing here?' The boy with a face like a yarma wrinkled his long nose in disgust. 'Something smells funny.'

Dinnis tested the balance of the stick. Toban was a couple of tanis in front of his friends. No point waiting until all three could attack him. Whatever happened, these bullies would be nursing bruises tonight.

He stepped forward, bringing the stick down in a feint. Toban raised his arm to shield against the blow. Dinnis changed his stroke, brought the stick across his opponent's shoulders with a thwack. Toban grunted, twisted, grabbed the stick, pulling Dinnis towards him. He let go. Toban staggered back, off balance. Dinnis hooked his left foot behind the other boy's knees. Toban crashed onto his back, winded.

Before the boy could stir, Dinnis was on top of him, kneeling on his chest, his elbow against his windpipe. Toban fumbled, dropped the stick, scrabbled at Dinnis' elbow and hand, his jagged nails digging in. His eyes bulged. Dinnis grabbed the stick, pushed it against the boy's neck. Toban clutched at it trying to breath. Dinnis pulled in deep breaths, his heart racing, the fury mounting inside of him. Tamrin scum. Were they any better, any less savage?

Panicked breathing closed in on him.

'The bluey's crazy mad.'

'He's gonna kill Toban.'

Looking up Dinnis saw the wild-eyed faces of the other two boys.

A shock like cold water went through him. Toban's eyes were rolling back, his lips tinged with blue. What was he doing? This was worse than Durrin. His fingers slackened. The stick rolled with a clatter onto the cobblestones.

With a great gasp of air, Toban coughed and wheezed. He scrambled away on his elbows.

His friends rushed toward him. Dinnis picked up the stick and jumped back, out of their way. Lifting Toban between them, they shot one last look of loathing at Dinnis and fled down the street, disappearing around one of the buildings.

Dinnis caught his breath, trying to calm his tumultuous emotions.

Hearing a suppressed sob behind him, he turned to look at the girl. She was where she had fallen. She flicked him a scared glance, leant forward to grab her upturned basket and began picking up the bundles of what looked like untidy sticks, now scattered over the muddy stones.

He took a couple of steps toward her. Her brown eyes flared wider. He stopped, wiped a trickle of blood from his scraped elbow. 'Can I help you?'

She ducked her head beneath her shawl and turned away from him, speeding up her attempts to pick up the bundles. 'I don't want any trouble, sir.'

He put his stick behind him. 'I won't hurt you.'

Moving closer, he knelt on the road to help her. As his fingers brushed the bundles they released the pungent odour of briarweed, one of the healing herbs Akrad used.

'I wasn't doing anything wrong, sir'

'Sir?' He shook his head, suppressing the urge to laugh. Who called him 'sir'? 'You can call me Dinnis, Tilli.'

Her teeth were a bit crooked with one missing at the top, her hands chafed and calloused with work but, with her rich chocolate eyes, thick hair and rosy cheeks, she was quite pretty. Not beautiful, like the silver mystery of Rasel or even Ista, in a glacial kind of way, but attractive.

He placed the last of the rather crushed bundles in her basket. She stood and limped down the street, angling towards one of the smaller shops. He followed her. She stopped in front of the door then turned to face him. He didn't need the ability to probe her thoughts to feel the waves of fear and uncertainty radiating off her.

He bowed. 'I understand. You want me to go.' His mouth twisted briefly. 'I know, I'm a bluey.' He hadn't really expected thanks for rescuing her.

'No, I mean, that's not it.' Her tan cheeks flushed as dusky pink as a marosa blossom. 'It just that you're a nob. That's trouble for the likes of me. Besides, you scared me the way you took down Toban.'

'Nob? Nobility?' His eyebrows shut up. 'What makes you say that?'

'Your fine clothes, the way you walk, the way you speak, even the way you fight, like a trained warrior. You have to be a lutan or a kaptan's son, maybe even a lord or clanleader's scion.'

He laughed. 'My father was a warrior, a nob I guess, but ... but he died at North Pass. I am an orphan, dependent on charity.' Discarded, unwanted.

Some of the suspicion leached out of Tilli's face. 'My da died in war, at the battle of Nakri, fighting for the Kapok, of course, not that rogue, Naetok. It's been hard on my ma since, trying to keep food on the table, to keep the shop going, at least at first.'

'Didn't the Kapok give some recompense to widows of warriors killed in battle?'

'Yes, yes he did. Ma used it to expand the family shop, but it is still hard with louts like Toban and his thugs feeling free to hassle us. My younger brother Norak is only five with two sisters in between.' She hesitated. 'Would you like a drink of yarma milk? I haven't really thanked you for rescuing me.'

If she thought him a noble, he could play the part. He bowed with a flourish. 'It was my honour to be of service, Tilli.'

She giggled. 'You are funny.'

A small bell tinkled as they walked through the door of the shop. The medium sized front room was dim and full of a wonderful plethora of smells that reminded him a little of the herb garden at Akrad's Stronghold, or the one outside the kitchens at the Palace. His mother had grown herbs too, though her small garden was neglected after she died.

His head brushed bundles of the dried plants hung from the low ceiling, releasing their aromas. Other bundles and sprays sat stacked on shelves or lay on the counters with concoctions and jars of salves and potions. He could feel the power in this place.

Tilli placed the basket on the counter and took him through to a smaller room at the back. It looked like a workroom and kitchen combined. She picked up a jug and poured the blueish milk into two wooden beakers. She took a long drink from one, then handed the other to Dinnis. He savoured the creamy richness.

Draining her cup, Tilli picked up the bucket and poured water into a basin. Dipping in a cloth, she washed the mud off the grazes on her elbows, palms of her hands and left shin.

He took the cloth from her hands. 'Here let me.'

While she sat on a small stool, he cleaned the mud and small stones out of her abrasions. 'You should put some salve on that to stop infection.'

She flicked him with her fingers and laughed. 'I'm the Herbalist Anna's daughter, I think I know how to treat injuries. You have a deft and gentle touch for a boy and a nob at that.'

'I often cleaned up my sister's scrapes when we were little. She was such a madcap and as our mother had died, I had to look after her. Our nurse was hopeless and Papa was gone a lot of the time.'

'See, you say Pa-pa. I say Da. I reckon, your Da was not a common soldier like mine. Not that my Da was really a soldier at all. It was just his levy time in the army. So many da-s did not come back from the war.'

He tensed as he heard a tapping noise out on the street, followed by the tinkling bell as the front door of the shop banged open. It didn't sound like Toban and his mates coming back for revenge, but he had to be wary. Bullies like that didn't like to be bested. This step was slow and uneven, however, and too heavy for the lads. Tilli looked up and he followed her gaze as a stout, matronly figure appeared in the doorway, leaning on a solid looking bloodwood walking stick with an elaborately carved head.

'What's this, girl? You should be working, not sitting around entertaining boyfriends.'

The voice was gravelly. The woman was short but with ample proportions swathed in a brown tunic and red cape. The brown leathery skin of her face was wreathed in wrinkles; laughter lines at the eyes, worry furrows on the brow and small, deep lines, radiating out from her upper lip even now pursed in disapproval. Her prominent nose was hawklike and her fine ebony eyes were fringed in dark lashes, despite the broad strands of white streaked through the hair visible beneath her head scarf.

'A rather scrawny boyfriend at that. Best you give over trying to grow tall till you have the bulk to go with it, boy.' The woman poked Dinnis in the ribs with the end of her stick, and he sucked in a breath as it stirred some bruises from his fight with Durrin.

He stood up and took a step backwards, eyeing her warily.

'This is Dinnis, Ma. He rescued me from Toban and his mates but not before the herbs were tipped over in the street.'

'Humph. Not much of a rescuer then. What you got to say for yourself, boy? You speak Tamrin, don't you?'

'Better than you do, I am sure,' he snapped back then bit his lower lip at his rude response.

She just chuckled, a rich, fruity sound.

'Well, thank you and all, but you best make yourself scarce young man. Young scions like you usually mean trouble, and I'll not have you leading my Tilli astray.'

He stood his ground, lifting his chin though keeping an eye on her stick.

'Are you a sorceress, Old Mother?'

She waved the stick at him. 'I'm a herbalist and a midwife. I reap the benison of nature to heal and make well. I've got better things to do than to meddle with the dark arts. Now get yourself out of my shop before I give you a taste of my stick.'

'Certainly, Old Mother, I would do as you ask except that you are standing in the doorway.'

She clicked her tongue against her remaining teeth but moved aside. He turned to Tilli and gave her a quick smile, bowed ironically to the older woman and sauntered towards the door of the shop without looking back. As he opened the front door to the accompaniment of the tinkling bell, the woman shouted after him,

'And don't come back.'

And suddenly he knew that he would be back, despite her words. There was something about this shop and the old woman with her pretty daughter that drew him. It would take more than a gruff exterior and a solid bloodwood walking stick to stop him.

FIVE YEARS LATER
Tarka

Chapter Thirty-Nine: Prospects

Ista

Ista hurried along the atrium balcony and into the antechamber to the royal sleeping chambers. She paused on the threshold, hand poised to knock. The murmur of voices came through the partially open door, the bass tones of the Kapok mingled with the melodic tones of the Kupanna.

'Your hair is like a curtain of dark chocolate. I could get lost in it.'

'Don't be silly, Rokkan. Next you will be quoting poetry.'

'Or making up my own, inspired by your exquisite beauty.'

The Kupanna laughed, a relaxed sound, long and throaty. She was sitting next to the Kapok, her head leaning against his broad shoulder. One of his arms encircled her, the other entangled in her luxuriant hair, his face relaxed into a soft smile.

Heat flooded Ista's face. This was even more embarrassing than when she found them amid their frequent verbal sparring. She'd better come back later. She stepped back and brushed up against a large ceramic pot holding a rubber plant. It rocked on the tiled floor, and she caught it before it crashed to the ground.

'Who's there?' Marra called.

'Ista, Your Majesty.'

'Come in, girl, don't stand there dawdling.' She pulled away from the Kapok and tucked a few strands of hair behind her ear. 'Rokkan you really should go, I've my hands full with so guests about to arrive for the New Beginnings Festival. I have no idea how I will place everyone and the larders need restocking. Bitjarnan is in an absolute tizzy. Surely you have something useful to do?'

The Kapok caught her hands and kissed them. He gave a lopsided smile.

'I can't think of a single thing I'd rather be doing.'

'Pshaw! You are incorrigible. We have wasted enough time today.'

Marra stood up, adjusting her tunic, her hair floating down her back in a shining, rippling sheet. It was a dark brown, with one single silver strand highlighting the richness of the rest.

'You are so cruel to me, my marosa.' Rokkan leant back against the divan, his lips tugging upwards. 'Would we could waste time more often.'

A blush spread from Marra's neck to her cheeks. Her hands fluttered. 'Rokkan! Are you still here? I don't know why I married such a provoking and obstinate man. Do stop gawking girl and help put up my hair.'

Ista hastened into the adjoining room to fetch the required items. Giving Marra the silver mirror, she took the elaborately carved brush and pulled it through the thick tresses.

'Hmm, maybe it had something to do with our parents betrothing us while we were too young to protest. I remember the day well. You were a beautiful lass just seven-years-old, while I was a clumsy lad of twelve, all elbows and knees and dirt beneath my nails.'

Seeing Marra's secret smile reflected in the oval mirror, Ista quickly looked down and busied herself with the complex twists and curls of the hair arrangement. If love could soften the Kupanna, perhaps there was something to it though it made one vulnerable and weak.

'I'm surprised you remember the day at all. You took no notice of me.' The Kupanna adopted a severe tone. 'To busy mucking around with horses and dogs and oblivious to the trail of broken hearts you left in your wake. Not unlike your son.'

It was hard to imagine these two as children, but she was right about Mannok. Holding hair pins in her mouth, Ista wove the satin strands of hair and piled them into an intricate coiffure the Kupanna favoured.

The Kapok walked towards the balcony and looked out through the open door. 'Ah, yes, Mannok. There was some—'

'And since you won't leave, let's discuss arranging a suitable marriage partner for the Prince.'

Ista struggled to breathe, her chest seized in a cold punishing grip. She forced her fingers to continue twisting and pinning the Kupanna's hair into the elaborate design.

'He's still young, Marra.'

'He is already sixteen. Lord Haka is keen to put past offences behind. It would bring our houses closer, perhaps mend the breach between you.'

'Or give him greater leverage to exploit. Don't you see how he eyes the throne? He would love to claim it as his own.'

The Kupanna frowned. 'You're getting as paranoid as your father was in his last days, Rokkan. Haka stayed loyal to you during Naetok's rebellion, and he would be gratified that his future grandson could one day sit on the Golden Throne.'

'I doubt that would be enough. I know you and Yuta are still tight friends, but Haka is no friend of ours. I will not consider a marriage between Haka's daughter and my son.'

'Our son. You don't agree with any of my suggestions.'

'I am not against Mannu marrying in a few years' time as long as he in agreement, and he is ready to choose—'

'Rokkan, if you are so worried about Haka's designs, then you of all people should understand the importance of securing more heirs. You and Mannok are all that stand between him and the Throne.'

'I'm aware of it. Just give the boy time. Don't you think he should take the Trial of Tears before you marry him off?'

'Rokkan! It's too dangerous. Maybe next year.'

'If we delay much longer he will be a joke throughout Tamra and the Five Lands.' He turned to face them, his face determined. 'I've arranged for his Trial after the Festival.'

Marra gripped the sides of the chair. 'Rokkan! That's only a few days away.'

'Gives you less time to worry.' Rokkan strode over and placed a light kiss on the top of the Kupanna's head. 'Thanks for an enjoyable interlude, my marosa, you should let your hair down more often.'

She swatted at him. 'Impossible man! You never listen!'

'Ah, sweet normality.' He gave a ripple of laughter and disappeared out the door.

'You're insufferable,' Marra called out.

Ista cleared her throat. 'I've finished, Mistress.'

The Kupanna sat straighter and studied at her image in the mirror. 'Splendid, Ista, thank you. If only you could weave cloth with the skill you weave hair.'

'Is that all, Your Majesty?'

'Help me with food selections. When we've finished, check that the Head Cook knows the numbers for dinner. We also should ensure the Guest chambers and the Silisean quarters are ready to receive our guests.'

'Yes, Your Majesty.'

'I sometimes wonder what I would do without you, though I imagine I will have to soon enough.'

Ista breathed in sharply. 'Would you send me away? Have I offended you?'

'No, no, child. You are a young woman of sixteen now and soon enough someone suitable will make an offer for you. Not that oaf Uson, of course.'

'Uson?'

'Yes, he made some insinuations last autumn, but the Kapok soon set him straight. Rightly so. You can do much better than a penniless orphan with the manners of peccary. I saw Lord Challak's second son, Trasin, making yarma eyes at you at Mannok's birthday celebrations last year. You would do well to encourage him when he arrives back with his family for the Festival.'

Ista pressed her lips together. She was not enamoured with the idea of Lord Challak's son. He was personable enough and had a reasonable position yet ... yet he was not what she wanted. His eyes and hair were a common brown and ...With an effort she banished the vision of laughing green eyes, reddish brown hair and a crooked grin that floated before her.

'Wouldn't Lord Challak be disappointed with a penniless orphan like me?'

She had no doubt that the Kupanna would not welcome her as a daughter-in-law. Perhaps she should be practical. Being mistress of her own noble household would be preferable to living as a dependent maid for the rest of her years. Yet her treacherous heart had other ideas. If she could bend Marra to her will ....

Kupanna Marra pursed her lips, then adopted an indulgent smile.

'You are a distant cousin to the Kapok. Rokkan will insist on giving you a decent dowry. I doubt that Haka, Durak or Lukarn would welcome you as a daughter-in-law but, I don't think Challak is in a position to object. Trasin is, after all, his second son.'

Ista started as Marra took her hands into her own. 'I admit, Ista, that I was not pleased when you first arrived at the Palace for reasons ... well, that's old history which we will put behind us. You have grown into a hardworking and capable young woman. You will always have a home here, but it would give me great pleasure to see you well settled.'

Ista could hardly believe what she was hearing. She dropped her eyes and mumbled, 'Thank you, Your Majesty.'

The Kupanna cleared her throat. 'Well, I've wasted more time than I can afford this afternoon. Let's get to work, shall we?'

Chapter Forty: Disgrace

Mannok

Mannok gave the leather shield a vigorous rub. It was cramped in the small armoury room with Garvin perched on the bench beside him. A layer of sweat prickled Mannok's face, the morning already warm and muggy, so unlike a ten-day or so ago when an unseasonable storm had dumped heavy snow across the mountains, threatening livestock and the half-grown crops. That sometimes happened during the rainy season. It hadn't stopped the steady stream of new guests coming for the festival. They'd eaten in the Great Hall last night, Mama, with Ista in tow, fussing about the meal.

Familiar sounds filtered through the window of the armoury; the bangs and taps as the smith and carpenters worked, the creaking of a heavily laden cart, the snicker of the horses, the short yipping of the dogs in the kennels. Why Papa insisted he take care of his own assigned weapons when the armoury assistant could have done it just as well, he wasn't sure. His hands would smell of leather, avocado oil and beeswax all day. Not that he really minded the smell.

Garvin put down his shield and rolled his shoulders. 'Not a raincloud in sky this morning.'

Mannok yawned, his jaw cracking. 'I'm not sorry the never-ending, dismal downpours are over for another season. It's like being hemmed in a yarma pen ready for slaughter.'

Garo ran a hand across the surface of the bench. 'Maybe we

could ride to the Bird's Wing waterfall later today or head out to the South Ridge village—Glacier needs to stretch his legs.'

'So does Shadow, he's getting feisty, but we best keep to the horse paths close to the Palace. I want to check on Sunrise. Wasuk reckons the mare's close to foaling—twins he says.' Born and raised in Silisea, the head groom knew horses better than most men. 'Besides, Papa wants us to stay in the city, with everyone arriving from the clan lands for the festival.' He dipped the cloth in the oil and rubbed the shield in long, smooth strokes. The coming of the dry weather meant Waren, Estolik, Yalik and the other scions of noble houses would be returning.

Garo grimaced. 'Back to lessons soon. History, poetry and statecraft.'

'Yeah.'

Mannok missed the disciplined exercises and training with other lads his age but, like Garo, he hated spending the mornings pouring over books and the dusty past. He dreaded the slight frown, the downward tug of the lip and the soft, suppressed sigh that indicated the Kapok's disappointment at his son's poor scholarship. It wasn't that Mannok couldn't retain the details when he could see the need, like knowing the geographical terrain of Tarka for defence purposes, but did it really matter who was Kapok ten generations ago or which poet wrote about the fall of Mokka to the Nolmec invaders in the north?

'If you rub that spot anymore, you'll wear a hole in the leather.'

Mannok looked up, gave Garo a lopsided grin. 'So, what's the point of piling up pretty words about mountains, or raving in verse about the supposed charms of palace beauties?'

'Or small details like the capital of Silisea is Kuza?'

Mannok punched Garvin's arm. 'Shut up. I knew that answer was Tolka. I just misheard the question.' If Ralton had asked him about Mirror or Sunrise's illustrious pedigree, he could have told him.

'You were daydreaming again, right. Still, girls like poetry, hadn't you noticed.' Garvin waggled his thick eyebrows. 'Lumi looks dreamy when Waren recites Melton. Maybe I could learn some verses.'

The girls? The daughters of all the lords and clan leaders would be at the Festival. And then there was Ista. 'Lumi? Really, Garvin, don't break your heart.'

Garvin deflated. 'I know, I know. My parents will pick out some dutiful daughter of a minor nobleman, but a fellow can dream, right?'

'Hmm, well we haven't even done the Trial of Tears yet. Maybe this year.' He could hear the wistful note in his voice and clenched his jaw. Slide it, it was getting embarrassing. He was sixteen already. Waren had been fourteen when he'd completed it and made Way Maker. So had Papa.

Three long blasts of horns sounded at the main gate, announcing the arrival of a Markan, probably his uncle Lukarn or maybe Haka. When he was younger he used to dash to the gates with the arrival of every visitor.

'Come on Garo, this should do it.' Giving his equipment a last glance, he placed them on the designated shelf.

Garvin's blunt face split into a grin. 'Finally.'

They turned and wandered into the corridor and out towards the exercise and practice yards that stood between the armoury and stables. A rowdy hooting erupted. Mannok raised his eyebrows at Garvin. Who would be making such a din? The raucous laughter climbed in volume joined by an eerie high-pitched scream. Mannok's neck hair lifted at the sound.

Asik, Hasuk and some of the younger stable hands where bunched together in the stable yards. They were leaning forwards, gazes focused to the centre of the group. The wail came in waves, shrill and piercing like a child in pain.

Mannok sprinted towards the sound, his heart accelerating.

'What's going on?' He shouldered through the outer ring. Some of the lads were shaking with laughter.

Uson stood in the centre, his mouth wide open as he yelled, but the eldritch sound came from the object in his hands. It took Mannok a moment to realise that Uson had one of the stable cats, maybe Blackie, by the tail and was spinning the distressed animal in a circle. Mannok tasted a sour rush of anger.

He stepped forward. 'Let it go!'

At the same time, a deep voice slammed through the noise, drowning out his words.

'Uson, son of Yanak, you dishonour yourself.'

The Kapok stood a couple of tanis away, his face like rock. Uncle Lukarn and Waren in travel-worn clothes hovered behind him. Wasuk and another groom were leading the Markan's horses.

The other lads fell silent, shuffling backwards. Uson spun round and stared at the Kapok, eyes as wide as a canyon. The cat flexed its back, grabbing hold of his arm, a biting and scratching ball of fury. Uson yelped and let go. Ears flattened, fur spiking, the cat streaked away.

'Y...Your Majesty, I ... we were only having a little fun. We didn't hurt it,' Uson stammered. Beads of blood formed in lines on his brown arms.

'Fun?' Papa's face contorted. 'This is your idea of fun?'

The blood drained out of Uson's face. Dropping his eyes, he fell to knees in the dirt. 'Your Majesty, I ... forgive me for angering you.'

'You disappoint me, son of Yanak, entertaining yourself by tormenting a weaker creature. Your father was a good warrior, his son disgraces his memory. All of you have disgraced yourselves and your parents this day.'

Papa scanned the group, his eyes blazing and his lips pressed together in a thin line until he reached Garvin and Mannok. The Kapok's face did not soften. Mannok's heart jolted, beating hard against his chest., He shook his head and returned the penetrating glare without flinching, signalling that he was not part of this fiasco, that he tried to stop it. Papa lifted his chin a fraction then turned back to Uson.

'Wasuk.'

The Head groom strode up to the Kapok and bowed.

'Your Majesty?'

'Take this sorry lad and see his scratches are tended to. Then I want him and all the boys involved here to clean out the cesspits for a ten-day. If any shirk the task or do not work to your satisfaction, it will be for an argen.'

'As you say, Your Majesty.'

Some of the lads groaned.

Had he and Garvin been included in the punishment? Should he just accept it? The more he tried to explain, the more he would look like he was just trying to make excuses. From experience, he knew his father would never exempt him from punishment because of his royal status.

Papa turned to go, then swung back.

'Mannok, come with me.'

Letting out his breath, Mannok turned, beckoned Garvin to follow. He passed Uson, sitting back on his haunches, his face, tunic and breeches coated in dirt. The orphan lad arrowed a viscous look at the departing Kapok's back, that vanished as soon as his eyes connected with Mannok. It lasted less than a second, but Mannok was sure he had seen it. He frowned and hurried after his father.

Papa didn't look back. He crossed the sun-filled front courtyard, loped up the wide stairs and past the guards, through the huge doors into the Entrance Hall of the Palace. Only then he turned around.

'Humph, brought your shadow.' He gave Garvin a steady look. 'Son of Kaspin.'

'The Prince had nothing to do with Uson's prank, Your Majesty. We were in the armoury.' There was a quaver in Garvin's normally blithe voice.

'I see,' Papa turned to Mannok. 'So, tell me the truth, Mannu, were you part of that ... that prank?'

Mannok lifted his chin, glancing at Lukarn and the sceptical Waren before bringing his gaze back to Papa.

'No, sir. As Garvin says, we were in the armoury cleaning our gear. We went to check out the uproar and arrived just before you did.'

Once again, he did not flinch away from his father's searching look. His heart pounding in his ear like war drums. It wasn't the punishment so much as losing his father's respect. He remembered the pride that had shone in Papa's eyes, the day he'd stood up to the northern lords and sworn fealty to the throne. In the intervening years, his father had as often seemed disappointed as pleased with him.

'Very well, Mannok, but remember that those lads are your age-mates and you are their leader. You are still young, but ultimately you will be responsible for their actions.'

He stiffened at the hint of disapproval. 'I'll accept pit duty too, if that is what you require, Your Majesty.'

Papa's face softened. 'If I thought for a moment that you were involved in what happened this morning, your penalty would be harsher than that, Prince Mannok. I expect you to reach a higher standard than Uson and his ilk.' He paused, running a hand along his chin. 'Before year's end, you will be seventeen. It's high time you faced the Trial of Tears.'

226

Mannok blinked, uncertain that he'd heard his father right. Then it hit him. The Trial of Tears. He'd been hoping to be judged ready since reaching his twelfth birthday. To prove his mettle. To no longer be considered a boy!

'I am ready, Papa.' As long as Mama didn't suggest they put the test off yet another year.

'Hmm. We will see. In the meantime, you and Garo can take Waren to the Bachelors' Quarters to settle in. Be ready to welcome the other lads as they arrive.'

'Yes, Papa.'

With that, the Kapok walked across the Great Hall towards his study, Uncle Lukarn behind him.

* * *

Mannok and Garvin slipped into the northern reception room, giving the Kupanna a quick bow. She was deep in a conversation with Aunts Samara and Lakwi and barely looked their way. Over the course of the morning, several noble families had arrived and he had been kept so busy settling the boys in that he was late for the midday meal. When the meal was over, Papa had invited the four Markans and some clan leaders to an informal council. The infuriating part was that Waren, Estolik, Durrin and some of the other older lads had been included, but he wasn't because he had not yet undergone the Trial. But that was about to change. Papa wanted him to do the Trial of Tears this year. He had to tell Ista.

With a casual shrug Garvin walked across the room to where Yalik, now eleven, with Waren's little brothers, Iskan and Kimsak, and some others were arm wrestling or playing board games. The women and girls were at the other end of the room with Mama, busy with their needles, looms or spindles while Markana Yuta, Lord Haka's wife, paraded up and down the long room. She yawned, placing an elegant hand over her mouth, the sapphire stone in her rings flashing in the afternoon sunlight.

There she was. Ista sat just a little behind where Rizzi and the other girls huddled in conversation. Whatever the others were gossiping about, Ista gave her full focus to the cloth she was weaving. Illuminated by a shaft of afternoon light, her skin shimmered like the silver moon. Her raven hair was caught up in several exquisite combs with one or two glistening strands floating down her slender neck and over her shoulder. Ista's tunic was simple compared to the elaborately embroidered and gilded robes of her companions, yet somehow, she made them look gaudy and overblown in comparison. When had she become a young woman, as beautiful and remote as a snow-covered mountain peak?

Ista looked up, her grey eyes meeting his, and smiled, the one she reserved for him. His limbs melted.

Chapter Forty-One: Stolen Moments

Ista

Ista glanced up to where the young prince stood in the doorway of the reception room, his unruly hair windblown, his face flushed with exercise. Her heart fluttered at the intensity of his look and a smile spread before she could catch it. She bent her head, hoping the Kupanna hadn't seen the exchange.

He had grown taller and his voice had deepened in timbre over the last few years. He was no longer the gawky boy she had met when she had first arrived in the Palace. He had always been attractive, with his expressive face, cloudy green eyes and russet hair. Now, his nose was—eagle like—like his father's, which was considered a mark of manly beauty among the Tamrin and very ugly among the small straight-nosed Nolmec.

Maybe ... but it was a match the Kupanna would never agree to. Not without persuasion of some kind. Yet, if she was honest, she adored his generous smile, wide shoulders, easy stance and aura of unconscious power that he wore like a royal mantle. None of the other boys or young men could compare. One day he'd be the Kapok.

'Very beautiful,' a tenor voice whispered behind her. She jumped, fumbling the shuttle.

'Mannok, you made me break the pattern,' she hissed, hoping that the trend of her thoughts hadn't been obvious on her face. She certainly didn't want him thinking she fancied him, even if she did.

He laughed, pulled up a stool and sat just behind her, so that he could easily look over her shoulder.

'You have already messed up the pattern. See, here.' He leant over and placed a strong brown finger halfway down the cloth. 'But ... a lovely choice of colours and I like the mountain theme.'

'Oh, why don't you go tease one of the other girls,' she whispered back. 'If your mother sees the mistakes she will lecture me endlessly on the importance of taking pride in one's work and how "a woman's ability to produce cloth is vital for the household's economy." If the Palace was to rely on my ability to weave cloth, we would all have died of the cold in the blizzards last ten-day.'

'And if being a great Kapok depends on learning the contents of dusty old tomes, I'm also doomed to failure.' He laughed, though this time there was a sour edge in it. 'You should hear how Papa goes on and on about that!'

She glanced over her shoulder and quickly placed her hand on his. He leaned closer, the smell of the outdoors still hanging around him, though he'd obviously washed and changed his clothes to attend his mother, the Kupanna. She put a hand to her chest, finding it harder to breathe.

'At least Mama now treats you as a lady of the household and not as a maid, sweet cousin.' He slipped her hand between his two bigger ones. 'You know maybe we could swap, I'll do the weaving, and you can do the book learning.'

She suppressed an unladylike snort. 'Really, Mannok, I'm not at all sweet and you are a tease. You know how much I would love to be a scholar, but you would probably be hopeless at weaving.'

He grinned and gently pulled a strand of hair that had escaped her careful efforts at coiffure.

'Come down to the stables. I'll improve your riding skills and start you with some basic moves with spear, shield and club.'

'Beast. You know I'm afraid of horses and those unruly dogs. Still perhaps you could improve my knife wielding skills. A woman should always be able to defend herself from unwanted attentions.'

'I do hope my attentions are not bothering you.'

She looked down and tucked in her lips to stop smiling. 'Yes, they are. You will get me into trouble,' she said with mock severity.

'Trouble is my other name. I found this horrendously big spider in the stables this afternoon. Whose bed do you think I should sneak it into? One of those oh so superior boys —Waren perhaps—or maybe one of the stuck-up girls like Lumi? I think the girls will

230

make the most noise. Waren would probably just squash the poor thing and not a word said about it next morning.'

She couldn't help giggling. 'As long it's not my bed.' Then a horrid thought struck her. She caught her breath. 'Mannok, where is this spider now?'

'In a fold in my tunic. Would you like a look?'

'No, go away, you horrid, horrid boy. What if it escapes? It could bite you. It could bite me. You are incorrigible.' She pushed him away while he collapsed into a fit of laughter.

'Ista! Is that behaviour becoming in a young lady? Mannok, if you have got nothing better to do you can help me sort my yarn.'

They both cringed at the Kupanna's disapproving tone.

Mannok ducked down and winked at Ista as he picked up his stool and set it back on its legs. He strolled over to his mother, sat down and, with an elaborate sigh, held out his arms. With a tsk, Marra began to wind her strands of wool around them.

Ista almost giggled again at the blatant expression of long-suffering on his face. Maybe if the Prince wanted her enough, his parents would give their assent. After all, she was of noble birth. She worried her lip. Foolish, foolish dreams. She might be able to influence the Kupanna's thoughts, even as strong willed as the woman was, but the Kapok was a different matter. His mind had always presented a blank, hard wall. If only she were stronger. Maybe it was time to put her plan into action during the festival.

* * *

Ista fanned her face, the massive Banquet Hall was insufferably hot, filled with a crush of people, trays piled high with steaming food and the blazing candelabras. Most of the food had been demolished, the remainders to be enjoyed by the Palace staff and their families. Similar scenes of feasting and dancing would be occurring in the streets outside the Palace complex, much of the food and maize beer provided by the Kapok. Tonight was the final day of the five-day Festival of New Beginnings.

The servants cleared the tables and pushed the long trestles up against the wall, and the nobles followed the Prince, dancing to the plaintive mountain music. Mannok cut a fine figure whirling about the floor, teasing the girls with his agile steps and his words, while the other young men flanked him.

The rumble of excited voices, the steady beat of drums, the haunting whine of the pipes and the rhythm of many dancing feet set Ista's pulse skipping. She was tempted to stay, to see if she could attract a smile from her favourite Prince, but this opportunity was too good to miss. With everyone distracted by the celebrations she wouldn't be missed, not even by the Kupanna, who had given her the night off and was deep in conversation with Lady Yuta and Princess Lakwi. It was the moment she had been waiting for.

She pushed her stool back and weaved her way through the crowd, drawing her cloak around her and hunching her shoulders so that her height was less noticeable. She forced herself to walk at a sedate pace. If she did not act suspiciously, the guards would assume she was on an errand for her mistress.

The noise was muted in the Great Hall though the rhythm of feet and drums vibrated through walls and floor. The guards at the doorways followed her with their eyes but did not challenge her, even when she hurried up the stairs that led to the library atrium. She had felt her powers strengthening since the time of red flowers over a year ago, but she had no one to train her. Grandfather was dead, and no one seemed to practice the ancient arts. Kapok Martal had forbidden it on pain of death, and Rokkan hadn't revoked it. Her only hope was the Royal Library.

She stole along the balcony, until she stood before the tall wooden doors, the carvings of the beasts, fish and fowls seeming alive in the flickering light of the walls torches. She put her hand to the door, and it glided open as silent as a dream. Surely, it was normally locked.

The vestibule was a large, square space reaching up two stories to the darkened skylights. Only a couple of guttering candles had been left to burn, one by the door the other deep within the library. The musty aromas of dust, old parchment, leather, glue and candle wax enveloped her, transporting her to Grandfather's Tower. Again, she would think she was dreaming except for the muted sounds of feast and the mosaic floor trembling beneath her feet.

As her eyes adjusted to the dimness, she gaped at the big the maze-like space, more forbidding at night than the quick glances she'd had of it during the day. In an area beyond the vestibule, large tables and writing desks were jumbled together, covered with parchments, bottles of inks, pens, brushes and open books large and small. Rooms radiated out from the central one; codices and scrolls stacked in shelves that lined the walls and formed their own lines, albeit in an irregular pattern. There were so many books, she was paralysed with choice.

Taking up a candle, she lit it from the one flaring on a stand near the entryway. Walking along the stacks, she scanned labels and book titles, attempting to discern if the precious books had been stored by a predictable order. In a tucked away corner, a stack of notebooks bound in black leather and charred at the edges caught her attention.

She frowned at the soft tremor of familiarity, like a ripple spreading in ever wider circles in a pond. A darkness seemed to swirl in the candlelight. She walked to the pile, her steps quickening the closer she got and pulled out the notebook on top of the pile. The subtle worn-out scent of smoke tickled her nostrils. Untidy pages with ragged edges, were cramped full of a spidery scrawl. A scrawl she would know anywhere. Her pulse thundered in her ears.

These had to be Grandfather's notebooks. She'd thought they'd been burned by his murderers.

Her hands shook with the thrill that rushed through her. She had hoped for a trickle and the Powers that be had granted her a flood. Over the last eight years, she'd pored over every small stroke in her salvaged notebook, learning what she could from this single volume. Now a veritable feast lay before her. She wanted to scoop them all up and take them with her but, if she took more than one or two, they would be missed. Perhaps, she could swap one with the book in her room, though who knew when she'd have another chance to plunder the library. For now, she'd absorb as much as she could before daybreak. She sank down on the cold stone floor, pulled down the first volume that came to her hand, and read.

Moments later, a shadow fell over her book. Her heart seized in her chest, before racing away like a stampeding horse. A tall figure loomed over her. The Kapok. No, the man had Rokkan's height, so unusual among these stocky mountain-born people, but he had half his breadth. His cat-like eyes shone in the dark as he swiftly bent forward and took the purloined book from her limp fingers. Crouching down, so that his face was lit by her candle, he studied the cover.

Recognition hit her even as he read the title out in the version of Eldar tongue Akrad preferred to use.

'*Deadly Poisons: Their Preparations, Uses and Antidotes*. So, who is the unlucky sap who has earned your ire?' Dinnis' voice had become surprising deep given his build, though it still held that familiar teasing, sardonic tone.

Recovering from her fright, anger flooded her.

'*Moros*, don't startle me like that. What are you doing here anyway?'

He flicked through the pages, stopping briefly at one or two places before continuing, until he reached the last entry. He looked up.

'Dear sister, it is lovely to see you too. It seems like alume ... or years ... since we last talked.'

He looked back at the book, his eyebrows contracting together. He bit his lower lip and he read the open page in the uncertain candlelight.

'So, that was what he was up to. He'd devised an airborne form of Breathstill.'

'You mean, Grandfather, the Arkon?'

'Who else? A brilliant but risky plan to disseminate deadly and fast acting toxin. A sudden wind change in the wrong direction would mean disaster for the perpetrator. I guess that is why he developed the catapults.'

'He also had an antidote, Dinnis.'

'Hmm,' he flipped a few pages. 'You'd have to take it quickly. Breathstill acts rapidly, especially I would imagine in an aerial form.' He closed the book with a snap. 'And who are you planning to eliminate?' he asked, a false sweetness in his voice.

'No one! It was the first notebook that came to hand. You haven't answered my question, and I asked first.' She stopped. She was beginning to sound like a little child. Realisation struck her. 'You knew these were here all these years, and you didn't tell me.' Her eyes narrowed. 'No doubt you wanted to keep the knowledge to yourself.' She was startled by how much she wanted to hit him, which only made her madder still. How was it he had the power to reduce her to her childhood?

He placed the book down on the ground and looked at her, his face serious.

'This is the first time I've opened a cover of his accursed journals. I'm not sure why the Kapok doesn't burn them. I certainly don't think their dark knowledge would help for you, Ista, or anyone else.'

'You're afraid to use them. A wise choice for one with as little ability to manipulate power as a garden slug.'

Dinnis remained unruffled as ever despite her insults. He never took her seriously. She reached out with her thoughts, but as always found only a stone wall.

With Akrad's notebooks, she would be able to train her gift. It would be as if he were her Master, she the apprentice. A shiver ran up from the cold floor through her limbs. He still haunted her dreams, whispered ideas and thoughts into her mind. Only when she was with Mannok could she push him away.

She wouldn't make the same mistakes Grandfather had. She would be subtle. As a Princess or, her lips parted, as a Kupanna, she wouldn't be cruel or greedy or capricious, but she wouldn't be anyone's servant either.

'As for your prior question,' Dinnis' voice intruded into her thoughts, like a face full of cold water. 'I came here to escape the din outside, and because I often spend nights in the library.' He was sitting on the floor, a slight frown between his fine brows.

'The Head Librarian allows you to use the library at night?'

'No, not exactly.' Then a wide, uncharacteristic smile spread across his face. 'But I don't find a locked door much of a barrier.'

'You were the one who opened the door.' She tensed, her fingers gripping the book in her hand. 'So, are you going to insist I don't look at the Master's books?'

'You are not a child anymore, Ista, and I'm not your keeper. You must choose your own path. I have to ask you though: do you really want to end up like Akrad?'

'I know you think he was evil.'

'He was.'

'He was good to me.'

'Was he? You were just a pawn, a *pioni* in his grand game of Conquest.'

'No, I was his Kiprissa.'

'It's the same thing. The one who holds the Kiprissa wins the game.'

She shook her head, not sure what he meant. 'You're confused. Conquest doesn't have a Kiprissa piece, it's the Kapok that's important.' But maybe he had a point. Mannok was her best friend, maybe her only friend. Manipulating him would warp that friendship.

Dinnis let out a gusty breath, seeming to deflate. 'I think I'll go for a walk. I need some fresh air. Blow out the candles when you leave. I'll lock the door before morning.'

He dipped his head and walked toward entrance.

'Wait. She placed the notebook back on the pile, gave it one long last covetous look. No, she'd try it Dinnis' way. 'You can walk me to the Banquet Hall, I think I'll join the dancing.' She linked her arm with her brother's, feeling of a sudden light and free.

Chapter Forty-Two: Target Practice

Dinnis

Dinnis closed his eyes and felt the soft breeze blowing from the east. The practice yards were quiet as most of the warriors, craftsmen and stable hands had stopped to eat their midday meal. It was his favourite time to practice, away from scrutiny, especially on a day like this. His age-mates would be eating with the Prince and dozing after the festivities last night, which had continued until the sky began to blush red with the dawn. Tonight, they would be taken to the Temple in preparation for the Trial of Tears. This would be his eighth and final year to be chosen but, of course, he never was. Not that it made that much difference. Whatever Anna reckoned, he would never be a nob.

Anna and Tilli would be busy dealing out lotions, poultices and concoctions for splitting headaches, black eyes, bruises and tummy upsets following five days of feasting across the city. He smiled, remembering his first meeting with the herbalist, close to five years past. It required persistence, but he had managed to win Anna's acceptance. He hung around the Herbalist's shop at every opportunity ignoring Anna's curses, threats and even her half-hearted blows with the walking stick. He almost despaired when she had set the City Guard on him, but turned up the next day to ask for salve for the whipping he had received. Tilli gasped at the raised welts on his back and begged her mother to relent. And she had. She'd agreed to take him on as an apprentice even though he wouldn't always be available with his commitments at the Palace.

He would try to slip out of the Palace later in the afternoon to give them a hand. He loved sharing the noisy, cheerful meals with Anna's brood when he could; listening to Tilli, Nikki and shy Aska's banter about the morning's happenings, or Norak's excited chatter about local doings. He guessed that all this was part of normal family life though, before meeting Tilli that fateful day, he had forgotten what that was like.

With everyone in the Palace focused on the Trial of Tears, he wouldn't be missed. Maybe he could see if Wasuk or Jakan needed an errand run to Market Street. Or Ralton might need some more inks. That way he could go through the gate without questions asked. Climbing over the wall, was always a risky business, but even more so with so many guests currently staying in the Silisean Quarters.

Yes, a soft breeze from the east. He felt the weight of the bow and arrow in his hand until he blended with them and, with one smooth motion, opened his eyes, lifted the bow and let the arrow fly to freedom. He smiled even before the bronze tip sliced the middle of the target. He let the second arrow fly. It thudded beside the first one, it's end quivering, when he felt the pressure of someone watching him. Notching the third arrow to the string, he turned and looked across the sparring yards.

The Kapok, Lukarn and Haka stood some distance away, their eyes directed his way. Lukarn, catching Dinnis' eye, strode towards him. Haka followed. They stopped a couple of tanis away.

'Impressive.' Markan Lukarn's eyes bored into Dinnis. 'It seems you are a man to note.'

Like Sparak, the Markan made it clear over the years that he was be watching Dinnis. Any action considered subversive or a threat to the Throne would attract immediate and severe action. Yet the one person's whose acknowledgement would mean something never gave it. Not in eight long years. Rokkan Kapok remained leaning up against the railings, his dogs at his feet, his attention directed at his beloved horses in the nearby holding pens.

Dinnis' heart cramped with a dull familiar ache. He pulled back on the bowstring. It would take a second to send an arrow through Rokkan's heart, though he would not long survive his father, if he did. Maybe it was worth it. Yet, something else, perhaps the simple joys of the stolen life he'd built with Anna and her brood, or Rasel's long ago counsel, restrained him. He steadied his hand, aimed for the edge of the target and let the third arrow fly. He sent next arrows wide and then hit the edge again.

He sighed. 'Slide it, just when I thought I was getting it the wind must have changed.'

Lukarn eyed him, suspicion lurking deep. 'Those first two shots seemed a little more than luck. Though, if you use a bow with same ability that you throw a spear, you would have to be the worst marksman I've ever seen. No offense, Dinnis.'

Dinnis keep his face impassive. 'None taken, sir.'

A sudden burst of Rokkan's good humoured laugh stole Dinnis' attention. The Kapok had moved closer to the stables area and was in a conversation with the head groom, Wasuk.

Lukarn grunted. 'Well, don't let us distract you from your target practice, boy. You seem in dire need of it. And don't forget, I've got my eyes on you,' he added in an undertone, before turning and hurrying down the range towards the Kapok.

Haka followed.

Putting an arrow to the string, Dinnis once again hit the side of the target, then compelled by an impish urge, he tested the wind, took careful aim and let the next arrow whiz past Lukarn. The man spun around, his face was a mixture of rage and shock. Rokkan had stopped talking to Wasuk and stared at Dinnis with narrowed eyes.

A thrill of triumph ran through Dinnis. *Now you notice me.* He shrugged and shouted. 'Sorry, my aim is way off today. I'll wait until you are out of range, my Lord.'

Lukarn scowled, his big hand on the hilt of his hunting knife. Pressing his lips together, he turned and continued walking towards the Kapok.

'Either you have terrible aim, or you are a superb marksman,' a fruity voice drawled beside him. 'Either way you took a terrible risk.'

Dinnis turned. Markan Haka had doubled back and was standing beside him. The man scrutinized him from head to toe as though he were a horse or a slave. His quick smile did not melt the ice in his light silver eyes, eyes so like Akrad's it soured Dinnis' stomach.

'You're one of Akrad's children, aren't you, lad? I remember seeing you around the Stronghold with a knock-kneed brat in plaited pigtails.'

Dinnis suppressed a smile at the Markan's description of Ista, though he cringed at being called a child of Akrad. Haka had indeed been one of the Arkon's regular visitors along with Naetok and a couple of other of the Tamrin nobility.

'He was not my father.'

'Your great-grandfather, then. That makes us cousins, you and me.'

'I seem to recall that one cannot always depend on family for loyalty—cousins, brothers, fathers or sons, for that matter.'

Haka laughed and clapped him on the shoulder. 'I like you, Dinnis. You have spunk. A young blade of hidden talents. You know, if you found yourself able to do me a service, I would reward you well.'

'What sort of reward, a knife between the ribs?'

'You have such a droll sense of humour, my lad. I really don't know why Lukarn hates you, why they all hate you.'

'Because I have such a droll sense of humour, no doubt. Or maybe it's my blue skin.' Dinnis lowered the bow and fitted another arrow to the string. Perhaps, the man could take a hint.

'Prejudice is so depressing. A man of your talents should be rewarded with a position worthy of your ability and birth—perhaps as Markan of the North?'

'That is a position only the Kapok can deliver.'

'Ah, yes, my mistake. Yet I can tell you this, if you pass on things you hear or … ah … remove nuisance obstacles. I would adequately reward your efforts rather than treat you with disrespect you experience from your present master.'

Dinnis frowned, a feeling of unease mantling his shoulders. The Markan's subversive insinuations disturbed him. Pulling back on the bow with his full strength, he sent it quivering into the centre of the target. 'You do me no service with this conversation in full view of my 'present master'.'

'Think about what I've said. If you wish to prosper—' Haka leant forward and dropped a small object into Dinnis' hand. 'Use this token to contact me.'

The Markan of the Western Marches clapped him on the shoulder and headed toward the stables.

Rokkan turned as he approached. His voice drifted over on the wind. 'Ah cousin, I'm glad you finally joined us.'

'My apologies for keeping you waiting, Your Majesty.'

'Some things never change.' Lukarn slapped his thigh and roared with laughter. After a pause, Haka gave a subdued chuckle. The men walked away, their conversation muted by the distance.

Dinnis weighed the gold ring in his hand. Its dolphin crest shone in the white light of the sun. Rebellion exuded a strange allure, but Haka was the last person he'd trust. Not just because he wasn't half as clever as he thought himself. As though either the Kapok or Lukarn would be too engrossed in talking about horses not to see a conversation under their large Tamrin noses.

'Dinnu, there you are.' Garvin's voice startled him.

Dinnis curled his fingers around the token and thrust it into a fold of his tunic, his breath coming faster. What could Garvin want? To gloat about being chosen for the Trial. No that wasn't his style.

'Lord Garvin?'

'I've been looking all over for you.' Garvin paused to catch his breath, his honest face glowing with a sheen of sweat.

Dinnis put down the bow in the rack. 'I thought you'd be getting ready for the cleansing ceremony.'

'Yes, yes, that's just it. Prince Mannok wants you in his party for the Trial of Tears.'

Dinnis rubbed his ears. Did he hear that right? 'What?'

Garvin grinned. 'Come on you dolt, we're late as it is.' Grabbing his arm, he pulled Dinnis along with him. 'Your Prince needs you.'

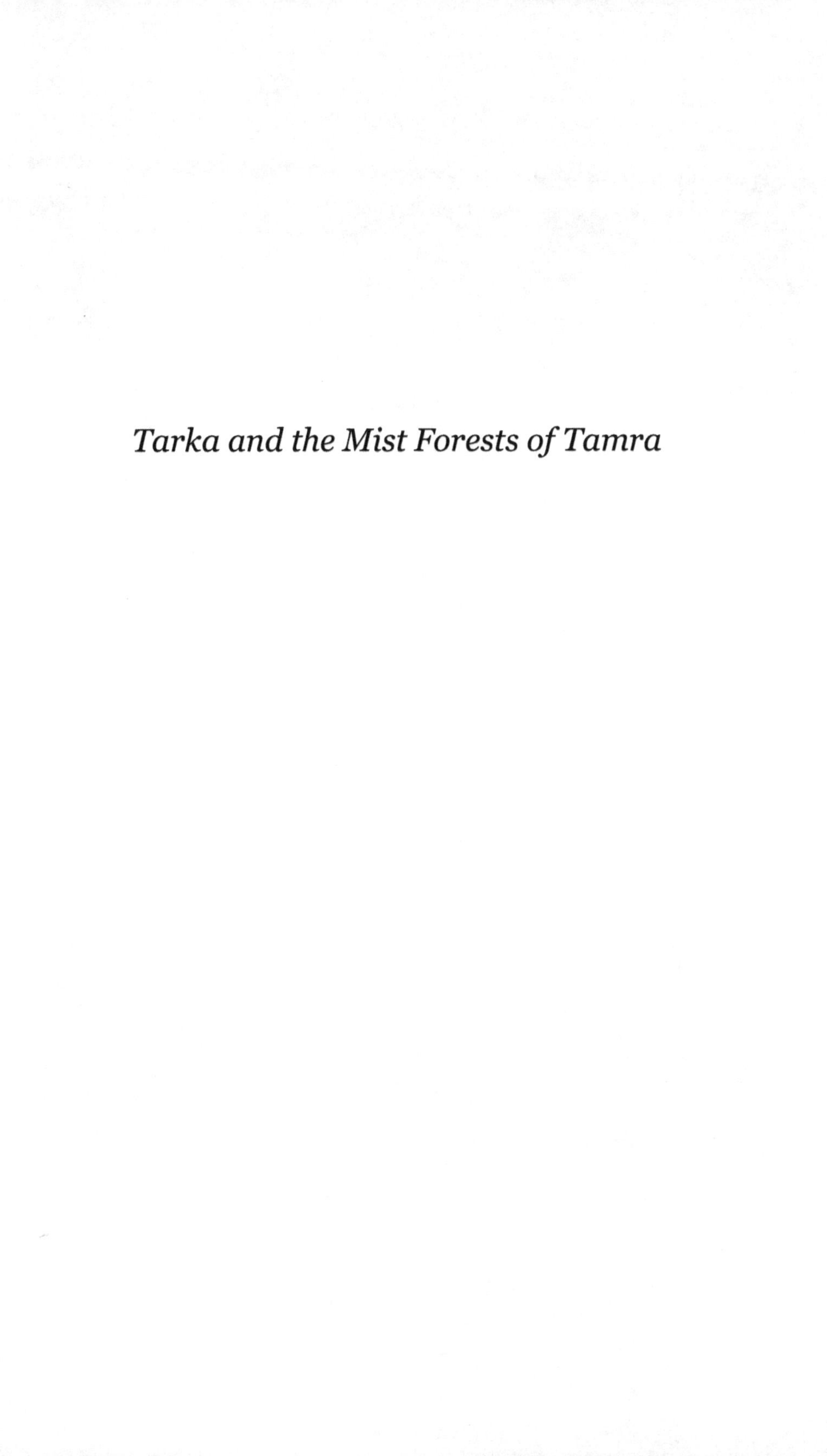

Tarka and the Mist Forests of Tamra

Chapter Forty-Three: Trial of Tears

Mannok

Mannok strained against the subdued candlelight and confusing shadows in the Temple's vast central chamber, his eyes tired. Though every muscle and joint ached from kneeling throughout the long night, he could hardly contain his excitement. Papa overruled all Mama's objections. He was taking the Trial this year.

The meagre meal before sunset, Mama's drawn-out goodbyes, the ritual cleansing were all simple enough to endure, but a long night spent in contemplation was harder than he'd imagined. His stomach rumbled as his thoughts kept flying to a thousand questions about the upcoming test. Would they be taken to the high mountain tundra, a desert area or somewhere in the steamy forests of the lowlands? What equipment would they be allowed? What dangers would they face? Each year the trial was different, but always a test of survival and physical prowess and collaboration.

He stretched his muscles to ease the knots in his shoulders. The main purpose of the test was to survive in the wilderness, but special honour as a Way Maker would be given to those boys who reached the chosen location in time. He didn't just want to pass. He wanted to earn the coveted title, just like Papa had. And Waren.

He craned his neck, peering at the high window on the eastern wall. Surely, it was lighter than before and this ordeal would soon be over.

Garvin elbowed him in the ribs and hissed. 'Mannu, you're supposed to be meditating.'

'So are you,' he hissed back.

Mannok looked down the line at the boys he'd chosen to accompany him in the challenge. Garvin was a natural choice. Waren not so much. Mannok could choose one youth who had completed the Test in recent years as a guide. He had asked Estolik. Essu was a tease, but he was a good hunter and woodsman who had completed the test with honour four years previously. His cousin had come up with some weak-as-water excuse. So Mannok had been forced to fall back on Waren. True, Waren was probably a better hunter than Estolik, but he still treated Mannok as though he was a child.

Trasin, Redrik and Hasuk were decent choices. He was on good terms with Hasuk and Trasin, both of whom were capable. Trasin had endurance and strength and a good eye for tracking game. Then there was Redrik, youngest son of old Kaptan Ninak, strong, loyal and a good runner. Hasuk was adept with bow and arrow, a vital skill when living off what the land had to provide. He was a decent lad, if you got him away from his bellicose friend, Uson. He hadn't been part of the group torturing the cat, so had escaped pit-duty. Anyhow, by then, his cousin Yalik and a few other young nobles had chosen their companions and there weren't many eligible boys left.

Mannok still didn't understand why he'd picked Dinnis; something about the aloof lad with his secretive ways irritated him as much as Waren did.

Garvin had said, 'What about Dinnis?'

He'd laughed. 'You're got to be kidding, right?'

Garvin had shrugged, his smile wilting, then widening again. 'He knows maps.'

'We won't have a map.'

Which might have been the end of it, but something niggled away at Mannok until he blurted out Dinnis' name as his last choice. Maybe it was pity. Without a father or other close male relative to sponsor him, Dinnis' only chance to complete the Trial was being chosen as a companion and once he turned twenty in a few alume, he wouldn't be eligible to take the test at all. Passing the Trial of Tears secured one's position as a man of nobility. Without it, Dinnis' prospects would be severely limited, whatever his talent with maps.

Mannok gave himself a little shake. He was supposed to be thinking noble thoughts about ... well, the meaning of life, his sacred duty.

A spark of sunlight shone through the window and illuminated the altar followed by the long echoing sound of the temple gong.

At last. A thrill raced through Mannok's limbs, and it took all his determination to stay kneeling before the altar. A forest of sighs ran along the line, as other lads relaxed. The doors swung open, thudding against the stone walls. A group of warriors, with painted faces and elaborate feathered headdresses, rushed through the doors towards where Mannok knelt. One of them threw a hood over his face and bundled him towards the entrance. He grinned beneath the burlap. The trial had begun and he would make Way Maker.

* * *

More than a ten-day later, Mannok pulled his yarma wool cloak tight around his shoulders and tried to find a spot in the makeshift shelter that didn't have quite so many drips. After four days of constant, unseasonable rain, the damp had seeped into his clothing, his equipment and his enthusiasm. Even the forest birds, who usually let forth a cacophony of sound at dawn each morning, were subdued. He had known the Trial would be a challenge, but he hadn't counted on it being so wet.

They'd started out somewhere several days travel north-east of Tarka, in the middle of dense forest, on slopes of the Blue Mountains in the Eastern Marches if Dinnis was correct. They were given five days to travel west to the village of Eagle's Rest before the warriors would start looking for them.

That was four days ago. Just one day left.

On the other side of the shelter, Dinnis leaned against one of the stout branches acting as a makeshift post. Cross legged and as still as a bluestone statue, his eyes were closed. He didn't flinch as the water leaking through the roof of branches splashed on his cheek. Despite his morose nature, Dinnis wasn't a complainer. He was a hard worker, knew about plants and maps. And he didn't snore, unlike Garvin.

A loud rumbling came from his closest friend, on his side and slumped against the fragile wall of the shelter. His friend's nasal cacophony, added to the cold, hunger and constant dripping and sudden drumming of rain bursts, kept Mannok awake most of the long miserable night. He wondered how Waren, Hasuk, Redrik and Trasin had fared in the other shelter.

Mannok sat up and scrubbed the sleep out his eyes. It was time to find this village. It would be too humiliating otherwise.

'Come you, sleeping beauties, get up.'

Dinnis flipped open his almond-shaped eyes, a trace of a smile lurking. 'Something to eat, Your Highness? There is cold snake left from last night.'

Mannok repressed a shudder. Last night, he'd been ravenous and desperate enough to eat it, but the thought of cold snake flesh in the morning made him queasy.

'Is there enough?'

'A few mouthfuls each.' Dinnis offered a portion from the food bag. 'So, what now?'

'We have to reach Eagle's Rest Village by sundown tonight to make Way Maker. Papa will expect it.'

Dinnis dropped his gaze, his lips twitching into a brief twisted half-smile. 'Pity we're so thoroughly lost.'

Just like Dinnis to mock him. Mannok ground the rubbery snake between his teeth. The unseasonable torrents of rain made the hunting trails slippery with mud and all but impassable with fast running streams cutting across, or even along them until they were knee deep in fast, turbulent water. When it wasn't raining, a soft drizzle and mist made it difficult to get one's bearings in the more open terrain and impossible in the middle of the forested areas where the tall trees and thick undergrowth obscured the sky. But there had to be a way to find the village.

He picked up a bowl and threw it at Garvin, still snoring blissfully. 'Wake up, Garo.'

'What, what, is it morning?' Garvin opened his bleary, sleep-gummed eyes and gave a prodigious yawn. 'By the moons, I slept a lot better than I expected.' He sat up and, with a grunt, peeled a leech off his arm.

Dinnis snorted. 'Nice to know one of us slept last night, though a little less confirmation of your success would have been welcome.'

Garvin's broad face scrunched up in puzzlement. 'I wish you would speak plain Filane, Dinnu.'

Mannok thumped Garvin on the back. 'You snored louder than a peccary. Is that plain enough?'

'Oh, sorry.' Garvin took the portion of food Dinnis offered and swallowed it with one gulp. 'So, what are we doing today?'

Mannok groaned. He needed time to think. 'Get the others up. We'll discuss plans then, but, first I need to make water.'

Washing down last night's leftovers with a swig of water, he pulled on his mud-caked boots and squeezed through the ragged opening in the shelter. A light drizzle drifted down onto his hair and cloak. Tall forest giants surrounded the clearing. Together with the thick vines and dense understorey wreathed in a cloying mist it was hard to see more than a few tanis in any direction. A loud chuckling sound indicated the direction of the closest stream. Water, at least, wasn't a problem.

When he'd returned, the other lads were sitting on a fallen tree trunk, huddled beneath their cloaks and munching on the scraps of remaining food. No point trying to rekindle the fire.

Waren stood up, looking as wet and miserable as Mannok felt. 'So, we're going to do the sensible thing and sit tight till the warriors find us, right?'

Mannok narrowed his eyes. All very well for Waren. He had already earned his title. 'It could take days for them to find us. This break in the rain won't last long. We should make the best of it while we can.'

'If we don't know which direction to go, we end up further from the village than we started, Your Highness.' Dinnis had a point, though Mannok was loath to admit it.

Redrik twisted the shaft of his spear in his hand. 'Can't see a further than a blind beggar when it rains, we could end up breaking a leg, or something.'

Mannok stared at the ground, thick black mud oozing between matted leaf litter. Not wanting to admit defeat, to fail. A small spray of light glistened at his feet. He looked up, to a frail spear of sunlight filtering between the dripping forest canopy and wisps of curling mist and higher still, the slither of palest blue. But the sun's disk was hidden behind the tapestry of leaves and roiling clouds.

'We could build better shelters, look for game.' Waren wiped his hands on a bush and leant towards him. 'Mannok?'

That was it. If he had height ... Mannok shed his damp cloak and jumped to snag the lowest branch he could see. Slide it, out of reach.

Waren's mouth and brows angled downwards. 'Mannu, what are you doing?'

Mannok turned and beckoned Dinnis, the tallest lad in the group. 'Give me a boost up.'

Dinnis tilted his head then nodded. He cupped his hands, without questioning for once. It was just the lift Mannok needed to grasp the branch. He pulled his legs up and clambered up the tree. The thinner branches towards the crown swayed under his weight. He turned his eyes away from the dizzying drop to the ground and stood up, gripping another branch for balance.

The world was different up here. Screeching birds with rainbow plumage flashed overhead. Butterflies and other insects danced and hovered just above the wet leaves. To the right, a blood-orange hue smudged the horizon. Sunrise and east.

The crowns of the trees in different shades of shrouded green crowded together as they marched down the undulating slope his group had traversed over the last couple of days. In front, more trees stood massed together but some hundreds of tanis away he could see a ravine cutting across the tree line with a mountain ridge perched behind it. On the left, another narrower break in the canopy suggested a path snaking its way down to the ravine and, he hoped, a bridge. Narrowing his eyes, he could just make out what looked like adobe huts with thatched roofs and a spiral of smoke meandering into the clearing sky.

'Seleste.' He whooped in triumph. That had to be Eagle's Rest village. They weren't that far off course. He noted his bearings and any landmarks that might help once he descended beneath the forest canopy, then climbed, slid and jumped his way down the tree.

'Do be careful, Mannu. The last thing we need is for you to break your neck.' Waren stood at the base of the tree, his neck craned backwards. 'This isn't the time for playing games.'

When would his older cousins stop treating him like a child? Unable to resist, he swung off a branch pretending to slip and fall, just catching another well-placed branch before the manoeuvre became dangerous. In fact, all of them except Dinnis were standing stock still with their eyes bulging. He grinned. With a couple of swings and jumps, he landed lightly on the ground in front of them and bowed.

'Slide it, Mannu, you are such a baby,' Waren shouted.

'Oh, oh, and you so scared.'

'Why you—'

Within seconds, the two of them were facing off in a wrestling crouch, ready to take each other on. Waren was older and had begun to fill out, but Mannok was taller and more agile. He knew he could beat his cousin.

'Oh, this should be entertaining. Good use of time.' Dinnis covered a wide yawn with his hand.

Mannok and Waren looked at each other. Dinnis was right, they were wasting time.

Mannok straightened and folded his arms across his chest. 'I've worked out where the Village is. Pack up your things. We're going,'

Waren frowned at him. 'Are you making that up Mannu?'

Mannok made a big effort to keep his temper. He turned and shoved his few things in his pack and hefted his spear in his hand. The other boys followed his lead, Waren last of all, still scowling.

He led them to the west, through the forest. After a while, the undergrowth thinned out and they picked up pace. In a couple of hours, they hit a wider path that looked well used. It was the first path apart from some game trails, that they'd seen in four days.

Garvin clapped him on the shoulder and even taciturn Dinnis smiled. Waren said nothing.

They stepped onto the track and headed north. By midmorning, they came out of the forest and stood blinking in the patchy sunlight at the deep narrow gash in the rock in front of them. Across it was a spidery rope bridge with a carved wooden eagle on top of the entrance posts.

'Seleste! We've done it.' Mannok twirled in a victory dance. They would be in the Village before the midday meal with hours to spare.

'You did,' Garvin crowed.

He and Garvin bumped fists while the other boys slapped him on the back.

Waren shook his head, his hair falling into his eyes. 'Don't know if that was luck, Mannu, but it was impressive.'

Chapter Forty-Four: Chasm

Mannok

Feeling generous, Mannok stepped aside, allowing Waren, as guide, to lead the way.

Waren inclined his head, a new respect in his hazel eyes. 'Your lead, Your Highness.'

A smile spread over Mannok's face but, before he could take a step, Redrik, head down, walked past and out onto the bridge, sending the fragile structure swaying. Waren raised his eyebrows. Mannok shrugged. What did it matter who crossed the bridge first? They'd all earned the title of Way Maker and they had passed the Trial. They were in this together.

He waved Waren on and this time his cousin accepted. The ropes creaked as the bridge took Waren's full weight. The rope bridges did that; it had often made Mannok nervous as a child, but the village elder would have checked and rechecked the ropes in the days leading up to the Trial.

Mannok stepped forward, feeling the sideways sway beneath his boots, feeling something give. The ropes jerked downwards. His spine tingled, his neck hairs lifting. He jumped backwards onto the firm rock behind him, banging into Garvin following close behind.

He yelled. 'Waren, Redrik, off the bridge.'

Redrik, over halfway across, didn't stop, maybe didn't hear him above the roar of the river far below. Waren, a step or two in front of him, sent Mannok a puzzled look and seemed set to argue. Then he shrugged, a tolerant look on his face. As he turned back, a raw, tearing sound sent shivers through Mannok. The bridge jerked again, sliding down and skewing, tipping Redrik and Waren to one side.

Redrik slipped and slithered, grabbed for the guide ropes and arrested his descent.

'Your Highness, Lord Waren.' Dinnis shouted at him.

Taking a shuddering breath, Mannok watched the bridge, twist and swing wildly. Waren clung to the ropes, his legs swinging over a three-hundred tanis drop.

One hand slipped.

Pushing against the inertia of his shock, Mannok yelled to Garvin. 'Hold my waist.' When he felt Garvin's arms around him, he dropped and leant over the ledge, arms stretched out until his shoulders strained.

He couldn't reach. Perhaps if he had a stick or, yes, his spear shaft. The tearing of rope sounded like a death knell. Beside him he felt a shadow. Dinnis leant out past him, over the edge, his longer arms stretched towards Waren.

'Waren, let go of the ropes. Catch my hands,' Dinnis called out.

Waren, face pale beneath the tan, swung himself forward. Dinnis caught his arm.

The ropes snapped, lashing backwards to the other side of the ravine. Redrik shrieked and clung to the ropes. He slammed against the cliff side and hung on over ten tanis deeper into the ravine. There was no way to reach him unless help came from the other side.

'Mannok, Your Highness.' The veins and muscles bulged in Dinnis' neck. Waren's weight dragged him toward the edge. Mannok grabbed him. Garvin's arms tightened around Mannok's waist. Working together, the three of them pulled Waren up out of the chasm and onto the path.

Mannok collapsed beside his age-mates. Relief flooded through his limbs.

'That was close, too close.' Waren pushed his lanky hair out of his face, his hands shaking like leaves in a storm. 'Redrik? Did he make it to the other side?'

'Not yet.' Garvin cupped his hands and shouted. 'Redrik, are you alright?'

The young blade moved his head, but didn't respond, as though stunned. Another crack, the support ropes on the opposite side snapped. The lad began to struggle, kicking out, panicking, the remnants of the bridge twirling and swinging.

'Keep still. Use the rope to climb up the cliff,' Mannok yelled. There might be time.

A creaking and another rope broke under the strain, dropping Redrik lower still. The support post cracked and all slipped over the lip into the gullet of the ravine.

With a harrowing wail, Redrik plummeted like a rock to the river foaming around the sharp boulders far below. The assemblage of ropes and posts hit the bottom of the gorge in a sickening clatter.

'He's …' Mannok peered down to the rocks and white water. No one could have survived that fall. The echoing sounds receded and his heart slammed against his chest. 'He's … gone.'

Water dripped from the canopy of the nearby forest. Overhead, the clouds cleared, sunlight bouncing off the wet surfaces and dazzling Mannok's eyes.

Redrik was dead, a lad he didn't know as well as he should.

'I owe you my life.' Waren gripped Mannok's shoulder. He glanced into the ravine and looked away. 'We'll have to find another way to the village.'

'I wonder why the ropes broke like that,' Trasin said.

Mannok jumped up and leaned over the edge. The ends of the rope attached to the hooks in the rock were frayed. He ran his fingers over the sharp end of one of the ropes and frowned.

'It's as if it's been cut with a knife. So's this one. Garvin, Waren what do you think?'

Garvin crept close to the edge and had a quick look. He nodded then scuttled back a few paces. Waren, taking a deep breath, moved to sit beside Mannok and leaned over carefully.

'I'm sure you are imagining things Mannok. Why would anyone—' He stopped, frowned and ran his fingers over the sheer end of the rope several times. 'Hmm. You could be right. It does look cut part of the way through. This rope looks new too.'

Trasin's brown eyes rounded. 'Who would do such a thing?'

'Dinnis was standing next to the ropes.' Hasuk darted a quick glance in the silent lad's direction. 'When we first got here.'

Dinnis raised his eyebrows. 'Predictable.' His face creased into an ironic smile. He crossed his arms and stared back at them.

Mannok pulled back from the edge. Dinnis had been standing beside the rope bridge. But why would he sabotage the bridge?

'Don't be ridiculous,' Waren said. 'Dinnis just risked his life to save mine. Might as well say that Estolik had something to do with it because he turned down the honour of being Mannok's first choice as guide. Wild speculations won't help us now.'

'There are a lot of fresh tracks on the ground, but it's hard to read them since we've trampled all over them,' Hasuk said.

Trasin crouched down and stared at the churned-up mud in front of what had once been the bridge to Eagle's Rest. He nodded.

'Looks like a small party of men and here, maybe a woman, but it's hard to be sure.' He frowned. 'They must have been here this morning though as the rain would have erased their tracks before then.'

An uneasy feeling stirred in Mannok's stomach. If the area of his challenge was known, then it would not take much to work out that he would need to pass this way to get to the village. Whoever cut the rope might have assumed that, as Prince Royal he would be the first person to cross. Had someone tried to kill him or to harm his group? And if so who? He picked up his spear and walked away from the edge.

'If there are attackers, they must still be on this side of the ravine.' He took a deep breath. 'Whatever. As Waren says, this is all speculation. Maybe the rope was faulty or—I don't know— something. Either way, we need to get to the village. Perhaps there is another bridge, if we walk along the ravine we would find it.'

Dinnis cleared his throat. 'Ah, not up the slope to the east. And not for another fifty lek or more down the slope. If our rescue party is coming from the village, it will take them the same time, unless they can get fresh horses at Cloud Ridge Village.'

Mannok looked at Dinnis. 'How can you possibly know that?'

He lifted a narrow shoulder. 'I looked at the maps in the Royal Library.'

'You couldn't have known the area you would find yourself in. And since when did Ralton allow anyone but his top assistants near the maps?'

'I like maps, I study them to relax, and Ralton likes me.'

Waren snorted. 'The head librarian doesn't like anyone and, no offense, you aren't the most popular of fellows.'

'See, we get on perfectly. Two of a kind.'

Mannok shook his head. He didn't doubt that Dinnis was telling the truth. Two days! It was unthinkable. Then another realisation hit him. If Dinnis knew where they were now, had he known when they were stumbling around in the forest? He looked up and glared at the fellow. Dinnis looked back with his normal insolent aplomb.

Mannok shrugged off the fellow's oddities. 'If only there was some way to get across that ravine.' It was about twenty tanis across, too far to jump and far too steep and dangerous to try to cross without a bridge. It was going to be hard to retrieve Redrik's body for his family to bury, if it was ever recovered. He shook his head, pushing the dismal thoughts away. He needed to focus on the now. He could tell the other blades thought the same. 'If we could get a rope across, we could make our own bridge.'

'Right. Why don't we just walk down to the chandler's shop on Market Street and buy one,' Waren said.

Mannok frowned. 'Hmmm … maybe we could make one from our cloaks.'

Waren slapped a mosquito. 'Even with six cloaks, the rope wouldn't be long enough.'

'Do you have a better idea?'

'Sit tight and wait? We don't know who's out there or how many. They may decide to finish us off.'

Waren had a point. Mannok glanced at the impenetrable forest behind them, tall trees swathed in vines and epiphytes. The Villagers in these parts would have a hard time keeping the paths clear. Vines. 'We could use the lianas vines. I've seen bridges made of them.'

Dinnis said. 'A bigger problem is how to get the rope to anchor on the other side of the ravine.'

'A hook of some kind, maybe.' Mannok warmed to the idea. 'Well, we could at least try it. It will give us something to do.' Keep their minds off their age-mate's shattered body at the bottom of the ravine. 'But Waren's right, we can't assume the miscreants aren't still out there.'

The group looked at him expectation, Hasuk and Trasin clutching their spears.

'Okay, Waren, Trasin and Hasuk try to cut down some strong, pliable lianas along the forest edge. If you can find food, game, berries or plants, that's a bonus. Have one of you on watch at all

256

time. Dinnis, Garvin and I will search for something we can use as a hook.'

'Your Highness.'

Mannok suppressed a sigh. 'Yes, Lord Waren?'

'Perhaps, you should stay with us, close to the bridge. Your safety is paramount and my responsibility.'

Mannok wanted to argue. If anything, he'd welcome a fight right now, but he'd be putting the others in danger as they'd feel obliged to shield him.

Garvin picked up his spear and a jungle slashing knife from the kit. 'Two will make less noise, anyway, Mannu. Come on Dinnis, let's go.'

'Take care, Garo, Dinnu. Keep an eye out for drinkable water. We will need to refill our containers soon enough.'

'Unless it rains again.' Garvin offered.

Dinnis grabbed his gear. 'Right. Thanks, Garo for that cheerful announcement.'

Garvin grinned. 'Let's get moving.'

* * *

It was gruelling work; selecting, slashing down and preparing the vines. Trasin suggested a wave through the fire to make the lianas more pliable. They used some fallen logs to build up a defensive position. They each took turns standing guard, while the others worked, alert both to possible intruders and just in case a villager approached on the other side of the ravine. At a loud rustling in the undergrowth, they dropped tools, grabbed their spears and took cover. It was just a peccary moving in the underbrush.

'Let's get it,' Mannok yelled.

He and the other lads rushed to surround the unfortunate animal, driving it toward Waren. A single spear thrust and soon it was roasting in the coals of their fire.

Hasuk licked his lips. 'Should be well cooked by sundown.'

Waren rubbed his back. 'Better get this rope finished.'

By the time the sun reached its zenith and slipped down the western sky shrouded in high, grey clouds, Mannok was covered in sap, ash, sweat and dirt. His muscles ached and his stomach was as hollow as a festival drum. He inhaled the fragment aroma of roasting peccary, his mouth watering. He and Trasin pulled on the liana rope, testing its strength, hoping that all this effort was worth it. It held.

Trasin punched the air. 'Looking good.'

'Someone's coming,' Hasuk called from the look-out position.

Mannok let go of the rope and gripped his spear. The clear notes of a tarrawong, in the agreed upon sequence, sounded out of place in the eastern Mist Forests.

'It's them.' He whistled back the response.

Garvin and Dinnis emerged from the forest, looking as filthy as he felt.

'Did you find something?'

Dinnis raised a bundle of forked branches trimmed into hooks. 'A fallen cambara tree. The wood is almost as strong and hard as metal.'

'And look what out else we found.' Garvin's grin was wider than the ravine. He opened up his bundle cloak full of knobbly fruit about the size of a fist.'

Hasuk whooped. 'Wild Cream-Heart fruit.'

Waren clapped Garvin on the back. 'Go perfectly with our roasted peccary.'

Mannok smiled. Things were looking up.

They feasted on peccary and the sweet, pulpy flesh of the fruit, though the death of their age-mate was never far from Mannok's thoughts. Dinnis lashed the hooks into a grapple with smaller vines and sap, and attached them to the liana rope.

The sun, a silvery disc veiled by high grey clouds, was now two fingerbreadths above the forest canopy.

Mannok jumped up and wiped his hands on his grubby and mud-splattered tunic. 'Let's do this. Garvin, you're the best caster.'

Waren hesitated, then handed the looped rope with its makeshift grapple to Garvin. 'Aim for the boulders.'

The first few throws fell short. On the fifth, the grapple caught. Garvin and Waren pulled. The rope held. They had just enough length left to loop it around a tree and tie it off. The liana rope spanned the ravine.

'We did it.' Mannok fist bumped Garvin and Waren, though the sudden thought of Redrik's death dampened his feeling of triumph.

'So, who is the poor sap who gets to climb across first?' Hasuk asked. It was clear that he wasn't volunteering.

'Someone agile and not too heavy,' Trasin said.

'I will,' said Mannok. 'I'm the best climber and lighter than Waren, Garvin and maybe even Hasuk.'

Waren's forehead wrinkled into a frown like his father's. 'No, Mannok, out of the question.'

Mannok lifted his chin. 'I can do it.'

'Yes, you've demonstrated your climbing ability today. The point is that my father—and yours—will kill me if I don't bring you back alive.'

'Someone light, agile ... and expendable,' came Dinnis' sardonic voice.

'Oh ... but,' Mannok stopped. How could he again ask his friends to take risks he couldn't, as heir to the throne, take himself? He let out his breath in a steady stream.

He'd so wanted to not just survive this test, but to walk out of the wilderness as a Way Maker. Now, Redrik's death made that obsession seem trivial. All he wanted was to get his group home without further death or injury. They were his responsibility.

'I guess Waren is right. It's too great a risk.' Mannok threw some sticks on the fire, swallowing the bitter taste of his disappointment. 'We should make shelters for the night. I can take first watch.'

'I could do it, Your Highness.' Trasin, just fourteen, looked both scared but determined, his hand clutching on his spear. He had the same coffee brown eyes as Uncle Lukarn and Mama, but the sharper features of his father, Lord Challak. Challak had sided with Naetok, but then it had been his decision to swear loyalty to Papa that had turned the tide of hostility at Nakri, eight years ago. The northern lord had lost two sons and an eye to the war. So why was Mannok's life more important that Trasin's?

Trasin dropped to his knees before Mannok.

'Let me do it, Your Highness, to prove our loyalty.'

'No, Trasin, you have nothing to prove.'

'Where's Dinnis?' Hasuk asked.

Mannok glanced around the circle of lads. Dinnis' blue skinned face was not among them. Well, they all needed to go into the bush from time to time. Or was there another more sinister motive?

He scanned the path and the area along the ravine. His jaw dropped.

Dinnis was halfway across the rope, hanging precariously beneath it and gripping it with ankles and hands in a monkey crawl. He had looped his cloak around him and the line for extra security. The rope sagged beneath his weight, but it was holding.

'Go, Dinnis,' Garvin yelled out. 'You can do it.'

They lined up and watched him move ninas by ninas across the waving line, toward the far edge. Several heartbeats later, he had reached the cliff face. He paused to breathe then rotated to the top of the vine and belly crawled over the edge. Untying his cloak, he collapsed on his back beside the boulder.

Once his chest stopped heaving, Dinnis stood up. Cupping his hands, he shouted, 'I'll tie the vine on this side. Do you want another line across as a handrail? Fasten it about waist height and throw it across.'

Mannok looked at Waren and shrugged. The fellow was so unpredictable. Suddenly he was very glad that he'd chosen Dinnis to be one of the group.

With the two secure lines, one to walk on and the other at waist height to use as a grip, they crossed one at a time. Garvin froze in the middle and took three times as long as everyone else, but he made it to the other side.

It took them just over an hour's walk to reach Eagle's Rest Village. He would never forget his father's grin and glowing eyes as they walked into the village centre, wet, muddy, hungry and tired. Only Redrik's death and the possibility of sabotage lay like shadows across his triumph.

THREE ALUME LATER
Tarka

Chapter Forty-Five: Old Friends

Mannok

Shadow snorted and pranced beneath Mannok as they cantered through the Palace Gates beside Papa on Plume. Garvin rode behind them, followed by a convoy of officials and guards. Mannok leant forward and stroked his favourite stallion's neck. The inspection tour of the mines and timber plantations in the areas surrounding Tarka had taken most of the morning. Within days of Mannok's return following his trial at Eagle's Rest Village, Papa had included him and Garvin in decisions and even council meetings.

Yet his age-mate's untimely death weighed on his mind. One of Sparak's scouts discovered the battered and broken body several tanis downstream from the destroyed bridge. Redrik's family were devastated by his death, but a red-eyed Kaptan Ninak expressed appreciation for the presence of the royal family at funeral.

Sparak had confirmed that the rope bridge had been sabotaged. There were no further incidents and no further clues as to those responsible. Mannok shivered. As if sensing his master's unease, Shadow shied beneath him. Did someone want him dead? Or had there been some other reason to sabotage the bridge? Uncle Lukarn was taking no chances and insisted Papa strengthen Palace security.

Shadow quickened his pace, keen to get back to the stables. Plume nickered and huffed, edging ahead as they clattered into the Palace forecourt. They parted with the officials and headed toward the service area, trotting past the kennels and tack rooms, to bring the horses to a stop in front of the two-story stable lofts. Three grooms rushed up and grasped the bridles. Papa swung off Plume. Mannok and Garo dismounted in turn.

Papa gripped Mannok's shoulder. 'You made some good suggestions this morning, Mannu. It pleases me to see you take an interest in the less glamourous affairs of the Realm.'

'Thank you, Papa.' Mannok's chest expanded. He bounced on his toes, buoyed by his father's rare praise. 'Do we have time to attend to the horses?' Mannok loved the quiet moments in the stables with Papa, as though they were no longer Kapok and Prince Royal but simply father and son.

'Pardon the interruption, Your Majesty.' The Head Groom, Wasuk, strode toward them and bowed.

'No need for formality, Wasuk. What is it?'

A smile spread across the groom's lanky face as he straightened. 'New arrivals from Silisea, Your Majesty.'

'Silisea? Has Tannik sent us some young horses?' Papa rubbed his hands together, his eyes brightening.

'You will be pleased with this batch, sir. Prince Tannik and his brother Prince Atok accompanied them—and a young Prince Tolteal as well.'

Mannok met Garvin's brown eyes and raised an eyebrow. Prince Tannik had been at Papa's coronation. He was related to the Silisean Queen in some way. Maybe he should have paid more attention to Ralton's dry lectures on Filane history.

Papa grinned. 'Cousin Tannik? Even better. We'll inspect the new horses later. Come lads, let's greet our visitors.'

Papa headed towards the front entrance of the Palace with long strides. Handing over Shadow to a waiting groom, Mannok strode after his father, Garvin at his heels. These days, it was easier to keep up with him.

Bitjarnan directed them to the smaller formal reception room. The ladies plied their needlecraft, while the children played nearby. Two men and a tall, gangly lad stood in front of Mama. Looking tired and travel worn, they were dressed in richly embroidered tunics, breeches and cloaks and headdresses of beaten gold.

'Tannik, you old steed, what are you doing here?' Papa burst through the door like a gust of wind. He slapped the Silisean on the back.

The man turned, his uneven teeth flashing in a wide grin. 'Rokku, you haven't changed a bit.'

The two men punched fists. Papa turned to the other more serious young man with deep brown eyes. 'Atok, I believe you have grown taller since I last saw you.'

'That is unlikely, Your Majesty, since I was at least eighteen last time you were in Silisea.'

'No, you were fourteen—it's been over thirteen years. And, yes, definitely a ninas or two taller.'

'Too many years, Rokkan. We wondered if you had forgotten us,' Tannik said.

'Never. I've been rather busy—you know—burying my father, surviving assassination attempts and fighting wars, restoring a devastated kingdom.'

'Small things like that. Seriously though, you have survived much.'

'I was sorry to learn of your father's death last year and regret not being free to attend his funeral. If Silisea hadn't sent the troops to support us in the early dark days of the rebellion, there may not have been a coronation.'

'We were glad to send them. I only wish father had allowed me to come with them.'

Rokkan rubbed his chin. 'Hmm. He was probably worried that I would lead his son and heir into death and danger.'

Tannik grinned. 'Now why would he think that? Do you remember that time you got me to climb the Palace roof with you and I fell off and broke my arm?'

'Now you beginning to sound like Lukarn. I do remember spending many a long dry season riding, hunting, swimming, fishing, climbing, reading, feasting ...'

'... dancing, flirting, breaking the hearts of all the young ladies—'

Papa waved his hand. 'Lies, all lies! Which reminds me how is the lovely Sila? Now, why didn't you bring her with you? You haven't put her in seclusion, have you?'

'What do you take me for, a Limarian Sulkan? No, it's just that our youngest is not yet two-years-old, so my dear wife was reluctant to travel so far.'

'Your youngest? How many do you have now—five is it, or six? At this rate, you will be able to repopulate Shanta.'

'Five. Four boys and a sweet baby girl.' Tannik smiled proudly and gestured to the boy, who looked a few years older than Mannok, standing beside him. 'You remember Tolteal?'

Papa nodded at the lad. 'You, young man, have definitely gotten taller. Last time I saw you, you were tumbling about on bowed legs trying to hug every dog in sight.'

The lad's thin lips tugged upwards before he looked at his feet. 'I remember that you had the biggest dogs I'd ever seen, Your Majesty.'

Papa chuckled. 'The best ones too. And how do you find the journey to Tarka?'

'Rather hair-raising in some parts. After half an alume crossing the high mountain passes, rickety rope bridges and teetering on the edges of precipices, sir, I was beginning to long for flat ground and home. Yet Meltan was right when he said,

> *Between the steep sided mountains,*
> *and treacherous mountain passes,*
> *Grey walled Tarka floats*
> *An ethereal shadow*
> *beneath two heavenly peaks.*

Your city is truly beautiful, Your Majesty.'

Papa clapped the lad on the shoulder, almost rocking him off his feet.

'It's good to see a young man who appreciates scholarship. I was beginning to think it was a forgotten art. Though he lived a couple of hundred years ago, Meltan in my opinion is still one of the most evocative Tamrin poets.' The Kapok rubbed his hands together, his golden eyes alight. 'You must visit the library while you are here. Tannik, you won't believe it but I managed to recover a fully illustrated volume of Herun's history of the Five Lands, complete up until about a hundred years ago. It had been missing from the royal archives for the last forty years, until I discovered it in—of all places—Akrad's Tower. There were several other missing royal treasures in the tower as well.'

Mannok suppressed a sigh. Maybe he wasn't going to like this young Silisean prince who could so easily charm his father by quoting poetry. Soon Papa and these new visitors would be immersed in long winded discussions about long-dead people. Mannok would be hard pressed to produce one intelligent comment. He was glad when Mama, who had been sitting with her hands folded on her lap, cleared her throat.

266

'Rokkan, perhaps our guests would like to freshen up before the evening meal? If you start discussing history or philosophy, we could be here until the middle of the night.'

Tannik laughed. 'Only to midnight? Last time I got into a scholarly discussion with Rokkan we saw the sun peeping over the horizon before I could escape, thoroughly beaten. His relentless logic shredded my theories to tatters, I might add.'

'Was I such a bore? My deepest apologies. It's just that I am famished for intellectual debate. As Socin said, 'A starving man knows not moderation.' Papa waved his hands. 'Come, cousin, let's show you to your chambers.'

Mama frowned. 'Rokkan, I'm sure Bitjarnan can spare the time—'

Papa had already disappeared through the door, the guests in tow.

Chapter Forty-Six: Kiprissa

Ista

Ista held the open book in front of her as she walked along the long balcony of the large northern atrium. Dinnis had 'borrowed' it for her from the Royal Library. It wasn't one of the Arkon's notebooks, but the arrival of the Silisean visitors yesterday made it fascinating. The book contained Tusin's account of the defeat of Shanta by Tamra and Silisea some fifty years ago.

She pulled her brows together. Rokkan's mother had been Silisean and he certainly was friendly with these new arrivals. Was this the family he'd suggested sending her to when she'd first arrived in at the Palace? They seemed harmless enough, though the Kupanna Marra was seemed put out by their arrival.

Still, ever efficient, she had organised a magnificent meal in their honour last night with Ista's help. Marra relied on her more and more since the New Beginnings Festival with only a little nudging of her thoughts. Ista bit down on a smile. She had to be careful. Marra was not easily led. Maybe Dinnis was right about controlling people.

Ista turned the corner of the balcony and someone ran straight into her.

The book banged into her nose. She stumbled backwards. The person caught her arm, preventing her from falling over a potted plant sitting beside the railings.

'Look where you're going.' Her face flamed. She brushed his hand off her arm.

'I beg your forgiveness, my Lady.' The tenor voice had a soft lilting accent.

The young man standing in front of her, apologetic and uncertain, was no other than the visiting Silisean prince. This lad would probably be King of Silisea one day and she had not only collided into him but reproached him. Her eyes widened with horror. When would she learn to hold her tongue? She snapped the book shut, tucked it into her tunic and bowed.

'Beg your pardon, Your Highness. Though you could have looked where you were going.' To be fair though, she had been the one with her nose in a book. 'I ... I'm sorry if I walked into you.'

He laughed, a soft pleasant sound.

'You are right. I should look where I am going. My tutor often scolds me for being a dreamer.'

She bit her lip, not sure what to say. He was attractive; built rather like her brother, maybe not quite as tall or thin, with brown hair, soft brown eyes, a straight nose and skin the colour of cinnamon. Quiet, a bit boring perhaps, but his eyes were kind. Their eyes met, she looked down quickly.

'I had better go. My mistress will need me.'

'Your mistress? I did not take you for a servant.'

She tilted her head, stung by his comment. 'I'm a kiprissa, captured and forced to live here.'

Now why had she said that? She had never told anyone in the Palace her connection with the Nolmec before.

'Forgive me, that's Nolmec for princess, isn't it? But you don't have blue skin of a Nolmec.'

She could see that he only half-believed her, but she could sense no scorn or horror for the Nolmec in his thoughts. The barriers in his mind were soft, easy to read.

'My father was Tamrin.' She jutted out her chin, daring him to doubt her. 'My mother was Nolmec. Royalty follows the female line among the Nolmec, it's matrilineal.'

'Really, I've never heard of that before.'

'Just because women can't inherit royal title among you Filane, doesn't mean it doesn't happen among more civilised peoples.'

He laughed again. 'I thought we of the Five Lands were the civilised ones, but I won't argue the point with you. It's true the girls never inherit in Tamra, but they can in Silisea. My grandmother Suza is the Queen because she was the only child of King Rantil.'

'Well, my grandfather was Arkon Akrad so I'm royal from both sides.'

He nodded. 'That would explain why your skin is silver, not blue. So, you were captured at the Battle of North Pass when Rokkan Kapok defeated the Deceiver.'

'Akrad was not a deceiver! He was a great man.'

'That's not what I've heard.'

'It's only the victors who get to tell their side of the story, isn't it?'

'I've never really thought about it like that.' He frowned. 'Though perhaps some people are just bad.'

She stared at him and pursed her lips. Everyone thought Akrad was evil, especially Dinnis. Grandfather had been harsh at times— and unpredictable—but as he had said, sometimes you needed to be cruel or even ruthless, to inspire people to do their best. Although he did seem to relish the pain he inflicted. She pushed that unwelcome thought away. Grandfather had loved her. What her brother had said about him using her was nonsense. Little people were forever trying to bring great people down to their own level. They were jealous of his brilliance.

'I am sorry, Kiprissa, I have offended you.' The young man executed a courtly half bow. 'Was that a volume of Tusin's 'History of the Shanti Wars' that I saw you hiding away?'

'It might have been.' Was he going to mock her for reading history? As though weaving cloth and looking after a household was all a girl could do?

He took a step back, raising both his hands as if to ward off an attack. His lips tugged up into a diplomatic smile.

'I sue for peace. I seem to be saying all the wrong things this morning. It is just that the Kapok told me last night that I was free to explore the library, but I have no idea where it is. When I noticed you carrying the book, I thought you might be able to direct me.'

'Oh.' And it was true, there was no mockery in his thoughts.

'I admire a young lady with a love for learning. Forgive me. I do not know where my manners have gone. I don't even know your name.'

'Ista, Your Highness.'

'Am I right in saying that Ista means star in Nolmec? The name suits you; you are as beautiful as the horizon star. A beautiful name for an exquisite young woman.'

He looked apologetic and hopeful, almost puppyish in his desire to please her. And both handsome and royal to go with it. A mischievous thought floated into her head. Hadn't she read a charming spell in Akrad's notebooks? Or perhaps a little subtle mind pressure? Then she suppressed a sigh. What good would that be? If the Markans would not consider her as a suitable daughter-in-law, then the Silisean royal house was unlikely to. Besides, he was not nearly as attractive as Mannok.

She bowed. 'You flatter me, Your Highness. Please excuse my sharp tongue. I will show you to the library to make up for my lack of manners.'

She turned and glided away, trusting that the young prince would follow.

Chapter Forty-Seven: Words on a Page

Dinnis

Dinnis loved the atmosphere of the library in the early mornings; the quiet rustle of parchment and subdued whispers of the scribes in the dim recesses of the book stacks. He carefully dipped the stylus into the ink and began to outline a drawing of the briarweed plant he had just finished sketching in graphite. The table was under a skylight, providing clear, crisp light as he worked.

The unexpected arrival of the Siliseans the previous day interrupted normal lessons, which suited Dinnis just fine. He had long since absorbed most of what the tutors could impart. A few free mornings would give him time to finish this project. When Head Librarian Ralton had discovered his wide knowledge of plants, picked up from Anna and his own researches on the annual hunting expeditions, he asked Dinnis to record his findings. He enjoyed transforming his rough field sketches into fully developed annotated drawings, and Ralton was prepared to pay him for his time. Even better he was now granted almost unrestricted access to the library.

He skipped as many of the afternoon military sessions as he could, to pursue his clandestine interests. It wasn't always easy, but it was worth it. Being unpopular had its advantages. He was rarely missed, and he could think up a credible excuse when he was.

A couple of years ago, he'd been digging out the food garden at the back of the shop when Anna had poked him in the ribs with her stick.

'Well boy, I've taught you just about all I know. It's time you moved on.'

He was shocked. Wasn't he almost part of the family? He helped with the household chores or looking after the younger children as often as helping with the pounding, preparing and potting or storing of Anna's herbal concoctions. If he had a home at all, it was in Anna's shop.

'Have I offended you, Old Mother, that I'm no longer welcome?' he'd asked.

She hooted, slapping her thighs with her hands.

'You will always be welcome in our house, boy. But seems to me, you be needing an apprenticeship with a healer to further your skills. You have a talent for it and now little Nikki is older, we can manage the shop on our own.'

His emotions had spiked at the thought, then dampened. 'Who would sponsor me?'

'Healer Laetil be a distant cousin of mine, skilled and looking for an apprentice. I can lend you half the establishment price, if you be finding the rest, just two gold rings.'

He took a while for her words to sink in. 'Why would you do that for me?'

Her eyes sparkled with merriment. 'Well, it's not your pretty face.'

Tilli had taken the spade from Dinnis' slack hands. 'Oh hush, Ma. Don't mind her, Dinnis. What my Ma is too proud to say, is that we couldn't have done without your help over the last four years.'

'You don't need to thank me. I don't need charity,' he said.

'It's not charity, boy. You'll be paying me back. Think about it before you turn the offer down.'

Dinnis re-inked his stylus, shaking his head at the memory of the cantankerous old herbalist's unexpected generosity. At first sight, he had sensed a warm heart beneath that crusty exterior. He had been right.

After thinking about it for a ten-day he'd accepted. He had the metal from running errands and selling herbs he gathered on hunting and other expeditions. One thing he was sure of, he didn't want a third-rate military career as Lutan in the City Guard or one of the minor outposts, even now that he was a Way Maker.

The horror of his walk through the battlefield at North Pass—the cries, the smells, the horrific injuries, the nausea—the despair of it all was as sharp as if it was yesterday. His words to the wounded Tamrin at North Pass, Sachan, still resonated with him. He wanted to heal not kill, wield healing potions and bandages rather than a spear and club like his warrior father. Nothing matched the joy he felt when he watched the fever abate from a listless child, saw the pain ease from the face of a man or woman with gout or stones, bring some comfort to the dying and their grieving families. Redrik's despairing cries as he plummeted to his death added to his resolve.

He stretched his fingers and rolled his shoulders before labelling the parts of the plants and making neat notes of their uses. Would the Kapok ever agree to let him go? Or Lukarn and Sparak? Their suspicions of him only seemed heightened since the Prince had escaped plunging to his death in the ravine. Somehow, he would get free of the Palace and its machinations.

Ralton entered the Library and grumbled a greeting to his assistants. Moving over to where Dinnis sat, he examined the original sketches and the dried specimens then compared them with the final drawing. The man's flinty face thawed into a flat smile. 'Adequate' he said. He moved on to viciously critique the work of the newest apprentice.

Dinnis smiled. From Ralton that was high praise. Dinnis sprinkled fine sand on the page and dusted it off. Now it was off to the kitchen for a bite before heading to Laetil's surgery in Greyhaven Street.

'Here is the Royal Library, Your Highness,' an alto voice caused a rustle of startled sound as the scribes turned to see the woman who had dared to enter their sanctum. It was an intrusion that usually only Princess Lakwi seemed to get away with, though she and Lord Amaruk hadn't arrived from Poija yet.

Dinnis glanced up and raised his eyebrows. Ista stood just inside the entrance doors with a hand on the arm of a tall youth. His little sister looked every ninas a Tamrin lady with a pale sleeveless blue tunic, heavily embroidered in silver thread. Her hair was piled on top of her head in elaborate curls and pearls hung from her shell-like ears and nestled round her slender neck. The lad beside her matched her height and elegance of dress, his brown eyes watching her every move.

Dinnis frowned then laughed silently at himself for feeling so protective towards his little sister. At sixteen-years-old she was well able to protect herself. Certainly, she wouldn't thank him for interfering. He tipped the sand off the page and placed the drawing into a protective folder before packing away his tools.

'Thank you, sweet Kiprissa,' the lad said, with a bow and a Silisean accent. 'You are indeed my guiding star.'

Ista bowed with a gracious smile, borrowed directly from the Kupanna, and gave one last, longing look at the bookshelves. For an instant, her eyes met his. She ducked her head, in a hurried, secretive greeting, before gliding out the double doors.

The Silisean watched her leave and then wandered further into the library with the air of a lost yarma. Well, he might be if he mistook Ista as a form of reliable guidance.

The scribes bent their heads to their work, too worried about Ralton's terse responses to help the stranger. Ralton himself had disappeared into his office on the half-floor above. Dinnis stood up and walked over to where the visitor was hovering.

'Do you need help, sir?'

The lad turned, his brown eyes narrowed.

'Thank you, yes.' He gave a regal inclination of the head. 'My name is Tolteal, by the way.'

Prince Tannik's son, then, if he remembered his Silisean royalty rightly. 'What are you looking for, Your Highness?'

'I am not sure. Maybe some poetry—Meltan, perhaps, or Suza.'

'Suza, an interesting choice. She was an evocative poet though much of her imagery and allusions seem confused.'

'How so?'

Dinnis stretched out his arm and recited.

> *'Emerging from a waterfall of rested delight,*
> *The winsome woman took silvery flight,*
> *Upon dulcet wings of snow and light*
> *Blended into the bright horizon*
> *Diminishing from the prince's eagle sight.*

While this verse reminds me of someone I once met, it seems somewhat fanciful.' He still thought of Rasel and her silvery beauty and gentle words on occasion, though it was years since he'd seen her.

Tolteal laughed. 'It's clear enough to me. The woman is of the Eldar. An Adelphi.'

Dinnis lifted his chin and gave the impudent princeling a cool stare.

'Mythical creatures of ancient tales? Yet Suza writes about events not much over a hundred years ago, well within historical times.'

'Some believe the Eldar are not myths.'

'Really? Is that your opinion?'

'I like to keep an open mind on such things.' Tolteal rocked on his toes. 'Tell me, are Nolmec always so combative?'

'I couldn't say. For a start, my experience is limited. I certainly could not claim to have met—let alone to speak for—the whole of the Nolmec people.'

Tolteal's forehead wrinkled and then he grinned.

'You wouldn't be related to the girl by any chance?'

Dinnis stared at him, shocked. In eight years at the Palace, no one else had made the connection, or at least hadn't voiced it. But then Ista had been so determined to distance herself from him, barely acknowledging him when someone else was around. It rankled, but she was set on ingratiating herself with the Kupanna and had decided he was a liability.

Tolteal's brown eyes widened, then his face crinkled into a happy smile. 'Then I'm right? I was making a poor jest.' He tilted his head. 'You do have something of her look. The eyes are the same and the hair. I wouldn't have picked Ista for Nolmec if she hadn't told me. What's your name?'

'Dinnis. I'm an age-mate of Prince Mannok's. But please, don't go blabbing about my connection with Ista.'

Tolteal inclined his head, his eyes twinkling. 'As you wish. It's a pleasure to meet you, Dinnis. As Helsun says, "A new friend is like soft rain on a hot day.'

'So, he does.' As princes go, this one wasn't half bad. 'Let's find this book for you.' Dinnis walked down the stacks until he reached the right spot. Running his fingers down the soft leather spines, he pulled out a volume of Suza's poetry and handed it to the smiling prince.

Chapter Forty-Eight: Manoeuvres

Mannok

Mannok stifled a yawn, feeling like an insect caught in amber. Waro and Essu battled it out on the Conquest board and, for a second night in a row since the arrival of the Silesians, the adults were involved in a lively discussion about poetry and philosophy. Mama had invited the local nobility to a small banquet in honour of the visitors. Most of the dinner guests had retired, leaving only close family with the visitors in the withdrawing room. Now Papa sang a tragic ballad about Sil, princess of Tarka and Mama looked on with a sheen in her light brown eyes. Aunt Lakwi clapped her hands.

'Hey, Tolteal would you like to play?'

Waren's jaunty voice jolted Mannok's attention away from Papa's melodious rendition.

'You do know how to play Conquest?' Waren asked, his eyebrows raised.

Tolteal shrugged his narrow shoulders, 'Actually I don't. It looks an interesting game.'

'Would you like to learn?'

'Sure.' Tolteal leaned forward. 'What are the rules?'

Mannok rolled his eyes. With another victim to practise on, at least Waren wouldn't drag him into a game tonight. He felt sorry for Silesian prince. Despite his tendency to sprout poetry, Tolteal was growing on him. On their ride this afternoon, Mannok and Garvin struggled to keep up with him on his long-legged gelding, Sea Breeze. At least once they reached a stretch of flat land.

After returning from the ride, Tolteal hadn't ridiculed the suggestion that he join them to check on Ruse's high-energy half-ten of puppies.

'Would you like one?' Mannok had suggested.

Tolteal's eyes brightened. 'That's generous of you, Mannok.'

They spent a happy half-hour or more discussing the merits of each of the excitable, wriggling, round bellied, tail-wagging dogs with their eager pink tongues and scrabbling feet.

In the end, Tolteal said, 'You choose, Your Highness.'

Mannok grinned and captured the fat golden one with the comical face.

'Perfect choice.' Tolteal lifted the puppy up and laughed when it licked his face.

'What will you call it?' Garo asked.

'Alumi after the golden moon.'

Mannok shook his head. Anyone with such an obvious love for animals and unassuming manner had to be alright. Now he was listening to Waren's explanations with a grave and attentive face.

Mannok scanned the room, Garvin and Hasuk played a noisy game of Leap Over. Estolik sat close to a blushing Rizanna, who at fifteen looked a young lady. Ista sat straight-backed and regal, listening intently to Aunt Lakwi recite some romantic tragedy. Beside her, Lumi caught his eye and fluttered her thick eyelashes at him.

He cringed. Lord Haka's daughter was a beauty, but Papa had firmly ruled out a liaison between them. Lord Haka had been livid, Mannok relieved. He would turn seventeen by year's end, increasing the expectation that he produce an heir to the Throne. If only he had as many brothers as Tolteal did. He wasn't ready to tie himself down with betrothals and marriage plans, certainly not with haughty Lumi. His gaze drifted to Ista, her pale skin and calm poise alluring in the candlelight.

Papa sat snug against Mama, his arm around her shoulders. For once, she hadn't shaken it off, the coolness that had followed the days following the Trial of Tears beginning to thaw. Were they still exchanging soppy romantic poetry? No.

'Once in the outer ward,' Papa's bass voice drifted across the room. '... and with the postern gate open it was a matter of time before we defeated the Nolmec. My major concern was that the

Deceiver had to be brewing up some mischief. To then discover Akrad already dead in the Tower by unknown means ....'

Oh, he was retelling war stories for the Siliseans' benefit.

Tannik shook his head. 'I'm glad all turned out well.'

'Without the Maker's favour, I doubt we would have triumphed. I was expecting a siege not a rout. There were other forces at work that day.'

'Mysterious. Yet it's not the first impossible battle you've won, my friend, from all I've heard tell.'

'What about the battle of the Mid Pass in the first days of the war,' Lukarn said. 'That was a true demonstration of Rokkan's sheer stubborn and foolhardy genius.'

'Lukarn, you do exaggerate. Maybe I should make you my chief scribe so you can pile up tall stories about me and call them history.'

Tannik stroked his long chin. 'You do like to put yourself in the forefront of danger, cousin.'

'It's the cost of war, losing friends and loyal warriors, risking your life. Given the alternative of death and destruction of all I love, it was worth the risk I think.'

'Maybe, but surely you don't need to personally carry out every hair-brained scheme you come up with?'

Papa leaned back against the divan and folded his arms. 'Why would I ask my warriors to do something I wasn't prepared to do? Brooding on that cursed golden chair while others go into danger is not at all to my taste.'

Mannok nodded. How could he ask his age-mates to cross the ravine and risk death for him? Yet, had he led the way, it would have been him, not Redrik ...

'Yes, but Rokkan you are Kapok and your only son and heir is still young.' Uncle Lukarn rubbed the back of his bull neck, a frustrated look on his blunt face. 'At least, until he marries and has sons or is old enough to take your place, you should take more care.'

Mannok squirmed, suddenly feeling the warmth of the room. In the end, it came down to him. And what if he failed? He'd made Way Maker, it was true, but only because Dinnis had risked his life. Mannok wasn't as clever as Papa or as wise and, only by the Maker's favour, had Papa had survived Naetok's attack or defeated Akrad.

Mama's rested her hand on her throat, the gems on her rings reflecting the candlelight. 'Speaking of danger, has Sparak found the people responsible for that dreadful accident. Mannok could have been killed.'

A strident tone had entered her voice, the words an echo of his own thoughts. Mannok winced and looked down.

'The evidence of sabotage was ambiguous, my dear.' Papa said. 'Some tracks in the mud, a rope that might have been partially cut. Despite an extensive search, no one suspicious was found in the area.'

Yes, but the ropes had been new. Was there an undertow of concern beneath Papa's reassurances? Mannok swallowed against the tightness in his throat and directed his gaze back at the Conquest game.

Ista was no longer in her seat. She knelt beside the Silisean prince, guiding him in his game against Waren. Mannok stiffened, an unfamiliar feeling kicking his ribs. She'd never shown such intimate interest in any of the other young scions. Surely helping the Silisean interloper didn't require quite so much whispering.

His heart quickened as Ista's silver hands brushed against Tolteal's light brown ones. The fellow turned to smile inanely into her eyes. How had he ever thought he liked the idiot? It was clear that the flatlander was insufferable.

Chapter Forty-Nine: Proposal

Dinnis

Yarma street dozed in the afternoon sun, not even a mouse stirring. Satisfied no one was watching, Dinnis shinnied up the rope then pulled it up and secured it. He crawled along the branch into the Palace grounds. Now that he could often score errands that took him into the city, he didn't need to use the tree so often. Yet, he was sure he had been followed over the last several days. He'd been able to shake them off. He was glad when Markan Lukarn had left with his entourage for Nakri an argen ago. That man was like a hunting dog once he suspected an irregularity. Sparak was still around. It made sense to use the more concealed exit for now.

As Dinnis eased over into the fork of the tree, he froze.

Below him, Tolteal lounged against the trunk with a volume of Meltan's poetry in his hand. Rather than reading, the Prince gazed into the distance with a dopey half-smile on his pleasant face. Now, which of the Palace beauties had stolen the hapless fellow's heart? Not that his suit was likely to be refused when he had the future crown of Silisea to offer. For all his royal position, Tolteal had been friendly whenever their paths had crossed. Dinnis rather liked him. He wished the fellow would move, so he could get out of the tree, though. He pulled his legs into a crossed position and settled down to wait.

Several minutes later a bird landed on the branch beside him, ruffled its feathers and let out a loud, protesting squawk. Tolteal started, glanced up and looked straight at Dinnis as the tattle tale bird flew away.

The Prince shot up, his fine eyebrows close to touching his hairline.

'Dinnis? How long have you been up there?'

Dinnis shrugged, slid forward a little and jumped down to stand in front of Tolteal. 'Long enough. So, who's the fortunate girl?'

'What girl?'

'The one that's stolen your heart, of course.'

The Prince sighed and sat, his back sliding down the tree trunk. He rested his chin in his hand. 'Is it that obvious?'

'About as obvious as a Tamrin's nose.'

Tolteal's mouth popped open, then his face collapsed into a grin. 'Oh dear. That bad?'

Dinnis inclined his head and took a step back. Before he could escape the Prince spoke, 'Can I ask your advice?'

Dinnis nudged a twig with his foot. 'You can always ask.' Pulling out two sunfruit from his tunic, he tossed one to the Prince, sat down and bit into the other. There was still a little time before he had to be at his next duty roster.

'Do you always carry fruit around with you?'

'You never know when you might be kidnapped by an evil monster, or find yourself in the middle of a brutal battle that changes your whole world. So yes, my advice is, never be without food and always be prepared for disaster. You can have that piece for free.'

Tolteal laughed. 'Can I have another piece of advice at the same price? Tell me. Ista is your sister. Do you think she could love me?'

'Ista?' For once Dinnis couldn't think of anything to say.

'Yes, she is exquisite; spirited, talented, cultured, intelligent and ... and womanly. She's been so helpful, showing me the library, giving me hints with Conquest ... I can't stop thinking about her. We leave for Silisea tomorrow and I can't endure the thought of not seeing her again.' Tolteal brought his gaze back from the horizon and frowned. 'You must admit she is beautiful.'

Dinnis smoothed the amazement off his face. He took a breath. What should he say? 'Yes, as beautiful as a snow cloaked mountain peak and about as cold and distant.'

Tolteal sat taller, his chin jutted forward. 'Distant, maybe, but not cold. And I thought the distance was because she was in love with another.'

'Ista? In love?' He had to stop repeating Tolteal's words like a *moros*. 'Who, in all the Five Lands, is the unfortunate sap?'

'Unfortunate? Rather say blessed, happy, most fortunate. How can you speak so? She is your sister.'

Had Ista changed, and he'd not noticed it? 'I've never seen her thaw with anyone in the Palace, except perhaps Mannok.' His eyes widened, 'Oh my ...' He chewed his lip, not sure what to think. Now that he thought of it, he could see the spark between them.

'Yes, Prince Mannok. I think he returns her affections. He has been shooting me smouldering looks and cutting in on me at the slightest opportunity. He is the most aggravating rude fellow.'

'I assure you, that relationship won't work.'

'Why not? Ista's father may be an unknown—I beg your pardon, I don't mean to be insulting—what I mean to say is that she has the grace and manners of a princess.'

'Yes, well that is precisely to the point. She is a princess, but not in any way that the Tamrin will acknowledge. Mannok's parents will never accept her as a daughter-in-law. The ocean might reach the top of Mount Pele before that happened.'

Tolteal's face brightened.

'Then there is hope for me? Can you give me any advice of how to win her?'

'I am rather inclined not to. I like you far too much.'

'You have the drollest sense of humour, Dinnis, but this is not a laughing matter. I'm dying here.'

'A terminal case indeed. If you insist; books are her weakness—and power. Promise her a library and a throne.'

'Those things I will have in time, but so will Mannok.'

'Make your offer, just don't pressure her. Be gentle and give her time.'

'I don't have time.'

'If your parents were to approach the Kapok? Though you will have to persuade them it is a good idea first.'

Tolteal groaned, putting his head in his hands. 'Not just them—my grandmother too. Is the path of true love always this difficult?'

Dinnis lifted a shoulder. 'I have no idea.' Rasel's face and willowy figure, her you-are-special smile came unbidden—though she was as remote and unreachable as the silver moon, Argenti. 'Sometimes you have to settle for the possible not the impossible. I've got to go, Your Highness.'

He stood up and strolled through the orchard, shaking his head in amazement at the thought of his prickly sister snaring the hearts of two hapless princes. The sight of the stack of charred journals tweaked his memory, and he paused beneath a spreading marosa tree. Maybe, she'd been using and developing her 'gift'. Should he warn anyone? As he pictured seeking an interview with the Kapok, or Sparak, or Lukarn, he grimaced. Besides, even amiable Kaptan Jakan probably wouldn't believe him, and, after all, it wasn't his problem. Though maybe he should warn Ista.

Chapter Fifty: Last Night

Ista

Ista smothered a yawn behind her hand and tried to ignore her aching limbs. It was the last night before the Siliseans set off to return to their far away home, so the Kupanna had enlisted her help in arranging the farewell festivities. She had been up since dawn picking flowers, running errands, ensuring all the details were to the Kupanna's satisfaction. During the meal, she'd sat at the high table during the banquet several seats down from the royal family and their royal visitors, tuning out the boring chatter of Lumi and Rizanna and the other young noblewomen. She wasn't included, anyhow. Prince Tolteal's eyes often drifted troop of traveling Shanti singers and acrobats to her. Then, everyone filed into the reception room for an extension of the festivities.

The large room crowded with noble ladies and men in brightly dressed tunics, cloaks and headdresses. As the night wore on, many wilted like overblown flowers. The candles burnt low in the candelabra. Against the tapestried wall musicians played plaintive tunes on drums, pipes and flutes.

The Kapok was deep in conversation with his cousin, prince Tannik, oblivious of the late hour. The Kupanna sat beside him, looking pale and drawn. Her drooping eyes and furrowed brow indicated a sick headache brewing. She would need some cold compresses when she could retire.

Mannok, Garvin and Tolteal had been cornered by a bevy of blushing beauties, mostly of the minor local nobility. Lumi and

Rizanna were flirting with other young scions from the Prince's band under the watchful eye of Lady Samara and Lady Taraya, Kaptan Kaspin's wife. Though the young ladies' families had returned to their regional capitals, they had remained to attend the Kupanna and learn courtly behaviour. Dinnis was nowhere to be seen, though he'd been at the Prince's table during the banquet. He often avoided too close a contact with the royal family, as though they had a contagious disease.

Ista noticed that the platters, once heaped with sweet delicacies, cheeses, and fruits freeze-dried by mountain frosts, were bare. Madomo Bitjarnan, who had imbibed beakers of maize beer, leaned against the wall in spirited discussion with Kaptan Kaspin, Garvin's bluff father. Ista stood up, smoothed out her long tunic and walked towards the Madomo. She waited for a break in their conversation about the local wrestling matches, before whispering to the Madomo that the platters needed refilling.

As she wound her way back she felt a hand on her elbow. Tolteal had extracted himself from the giggling entourage. Somehow, he looked eager and panicked all at the same time.

'Sweet Ista, could you spare me a moment?'

'In this press of people, Your Highness, it is a bit difficult.'

'I know, but this is our last night in Tarka.'

She allowed him to draw her into the shadows behind a large, overgrown pot plant. Out of the direct light of the multitudinous candles, the full orb of Argenti cast a silvery shimmer through the window beside them.

'This is for you Ista. I know it's not a big volume, but I think you will enjoy this selection of Meltan's poetry. It is my personal copy and belonged to my grandfather.'

Tolteal held the beautiful carved leather-bound book out to her, his hands trembling and his breathing rapid. Ista felt his anxiety. Her own heart fluttered. She was flattered by his attentions, had encouraged them even. But Tarka was now her home, and it was Mannok who inhabited her dreams.

'Ista?'

She dipped her head. 'I can't take such a valuable book, Your Highness. It would not be appropriate for an unattached lady to do so.'

He inhaled and squared his neat shoulders. 'But I hope we might become attached to each other. It's not just up to me, of course, but I want you to be my princess.'

He moved closer and catching her hand, placed the book in it, with his own then covering her hand and the book. Her treacherous heart began to beat faster. She could feel his breath on her cheek, the pounding of his heart. The soft leather and his warm skin encased her hand. She dropped her eyes and when she pulled her hand back he let go, leaving the book balancing on her palm. She caught it before it fell and then looked up at him.

'You honour me greatly, Your Highness, but I ...'

She didn't know what to say. She glanced across to where Mannok teased the girls, shocking them with outrageous tales, while loyal Garvin watched with amusement. He seemed oblivious to her.

Tolteal's breath, fragrant with mountain mint, tickled her cheek. 'I understand that you may have other leanings, my Kiprissa. I just ask that you think about it and perhaps look with favour on my suit when my parents to send a formal offer. I hope that will be in the not too distant future.'

He learnt forward and brushed his lips against her cheek. He stepped back, bowed and melted into the crowd, leaving his treasured book of poetry in her hands.

Chapter Fifty-One: Stolen

Mannok

Mannok looked up from where he was adjusting Shadow's girth strap. Yesterday's rain had left a legacy of mud and puddles. This morning only a few wispy clouds clung to the eggshell-blue sky. Mannok blew on his fingers to warm them in the early morning chill. The horse moved restlessly beside him and nibbled his hair. He stroked Shadow's velvet nose and found a guava to give him.

He glanced across to where Garvin saddled the blue roan gelding, Glacier. 'I'm glad the Silesians are gone and things are back to normal these last few days.'

Garo tilted his head. 'I don't know, Mannu. Prince Tolteal was good company.'

Mannok snorted as he pulled the cinch tight around Shadow's girth. It was sickening the way the Silisean Prince had wormed his way into Ista's good graces. He had seen Tolteal pull Ista behind the pot plant at the soiree on his last night in Tarka. It was just bad manners. And somehow conversations between Ista and himself had become awkward. A gallop outside the city gates in the crisp early morning air would surely brighten his mood.

The service gates creaked and swung open. A long string of pack yarmas, with huge panniers overflowing with hay, plodded through the opening. The driver flashed his credentials at the guards. Mannok was just about to give Shadow's tack one final inspection when the flicker of a shadow caught of his eye. He looked up in time to see Dinnis slip behind the groaning yarmas and out of the gate.

What was Dinnis doing, heading out of the Palace? Of course, lessons weren't for another hour or so and he could be running an errand for Kaptan Jakan. Just the other day Uson had sprouted some nonsense about Dinnis being involved in dishonest activities. He had dismissed the hints. Uson was sour to be left out of the Trial this year, when Dinnis was included in his group. The memory of Dinnis hunkered down near the bridge to Eagle's Rest intruded into his thoughts. Not that his age-mate had reason to want him dead and he had risked his life to get them across the ravine.

Yet there was something furtive about Dinnis' movements as he slipped out the gate.

Mannok threw Shadow's reins to a nearby groom and sprinted toward the gate. 'Come on, Garo.'

'What are you doing, Mannu?'

The guards saluted as he passed. 'Your Highness, do you need an escort?'

Mannok increased his speed. Dinnis was already well up the road, nearing the crest, in the direction of the Trade District.

'Hurry, Garo, we'll lose him.'

Garvin came abreast and gripped his shoulder. 'I don't think this is a good idea.'

'He's up to something, I'm sure of it.'

Mannok shrugged off Garo's hand and jogged after Dinnis, up the gentle pull of the hill, then down the steep descent. The fellow didn't alter his pace or turn around. As soon as he turned the corner into Upper Market Street, Mannok broke into a run, trying to close the distance between them. Garvin's boots pounded on the cobblestones behind him.

Catching his breath, Mannok pulled up in the busy street and scanned both ways to locate his age-mate. The early morning sunlight gilded the tiled roofs and awnings and gave the leftover puddles a golden sheen. Shop owners were setting up for the day, sweeping steps, opening shutters and hauling out their wares. A few early shoppers picked their way along the damp shadow-streaked street, examining the colourful woven baskets and the goods that spilled out in front of the shops.

Dinnis was nowhere to be seen.

As he hesitated, Garvin caught up with him.

'Why ...' Garvin placed his hands on his thighs and sucked in a breath. '... are we following Dinnis?'

'I want to know why he's sneaking around. I've lost sight of him, though.'

'Good, let's go back.' Garvin straightened up and turned toward the Palace.

Mannok grabbed his arm. 'And give up so easily? No way.'

'Really, Your Highness, you shouldn't wander around the city on foot and without a guard.'

Mannok ground his teeth. 'I'm not in my regalia. Who's going to recognise me? Especially if you stop calling me 'Your Highness.' I saw him turn left, let's go that way.'

'You really have been in a strange mood since the Siliseans left.'

'Come on.' Pulling his reluctant friend with him, Mannok sauntered down the street, peering around the piled-up wares and into the dim interiors of the shops. Food stall holders spruiked their hot food. Mouth-watering aromas of hot corn wraps overlayed the stale odours of wilted vegetables, last night's bean stew and mud. They had passed flower merchants, spice merchants, cheesemakers, vegetable sellers and chandlers when something caught Mannok's eye. He stopped, Garvin bumping into him.

'Did you see him?'

Mannok shook his head. The area outside the shop was piled up old furniture, utensils and tapestries in a disorganised jumble. A battered sign proclaimed 'Junok's Second Hand Wares: Find rare objects and old treasures. Satisfaction Guaranteed.'

He stepped closer. 'See that small tapestry of the hunting dogs there, doesn't that remind you of the one in the guest chambers?'

Garvin shook his head. 'How would I know what tapestries are like in the guest chambers?'

Mannok's eyes widened as he saw a couple of elaborately moulded silver candelabra and a set of carved bone-handled knives next to it.

'This is all stuff from the Palace—from the less used rooms in the guest quarters.'

'Maybe it just looks like it, Mannu. Why would a broker be selling royal furnishings? It's not like the treasuries are empty.'

'I recognise the dent on that embroidered foot stool, it is Palace stuff. I'm sure Bitjarnan wouldn't have disposed of it. Perhaps that is what Dinnis is up to, selling palace property. It would explain why he always has metal on him when he doesn't have any family.'

'I don't think Dinnis is a thief, Mannu. He does errands for Wasuk, Ralton and some of the others. We should go back and let Bitjarnan and Jakan know what we've found.'

Mannok was only half-listening. He was livid. Maybe Dinnis was in the shop right this minute selling the purloined goods.

Shaking off Garvin's restraining hand, he marched towards the entrance hidden behind the piled-up junk. A dark figure slipped out of the shop and disappeared around the corner into a narrow lane between this shop and the next one. Mannok didn't have to think. He chased after the escaping miscreant.

A door slammed as he turned into the muddy lane. After running a few paces, he stopped. The lane, steeped in shadows and choked with dead weeds and rubbish, was empty. There were several doors in the ramshackle buildings on either side. The windows were shuttered. The hairs on the back of his neck stood up. He didn't like the feel of this narrow laneway. Perhaps Garo was right. This was not a safe place to be. He half turned to see Garvin standing beside him, scanning the buildings and a hand on the hilt of his hunting knife.

'Prince Mannok, what are you doing here?' He jumped as a cultured female voice echoed off the peeling adobe walls.

Turning, he saw Ista's tall, slim figure glide into the alley. Her long white tunic and dark blue hooded cloak edged in silver were in stark contrast to the shabby surroundings. She carried a large basket over her arm.

'Ista, I could ask the same thing of you. Why are you here?'

'The Kupanna often sends me to the markets when she wants particular ingredients or finest quality spices. When I saw you, I couldn't believe it was you. This isn't a good place for you to be.'

He shrugged and stepped towards her. 'We were following someone, but he escaped. Surely you aren't on your own?'

'What, are you working for Sparak now? Stranger and stranger.' She laughed, a musical trill. 'The assistant cook and a couple of guards are back at Salik's Spice Merchants.'

He was several paces away, Garvin behind him, when a door slammed open, bouncing against the wall. A brawny, blunt faced fellow with a squashed nose burst out into the lane beside Ista.

Mannok quickened his pace. This wasn't good.

The fellow lunged, wrapped a brawny arm around Ista's chest and held a long knife against her neck. His close-set eyes gleamed, with the satisfaction of a peccary raiding a village garden. Behind him five other young men tumbled out of the door.

'Don't move, ya nobs, if you want the pretty lady to live,' the big fellow said. He was probably in his late teens or early twenties. His clothes were of coarse wool, his hands dirty and calloused. The other lads, gripping poles, rough clubs or knives in their hands, flanked him.

Mannok stood still. His breath caught in his throat, his mouth suddenly dry. He was such a fool putting himself and his friends in danger over a bit of old furniture.

He had only his hunting knife with him and Garvin to back him up. In his haste, he'd left his spear and club in their holsters on Shadow back at the Palace stables. It wasn't the mismatch in numbers or even weapons that worried him, it was that lethal looking knife pressed up against Ista's throat. Beautiful Ista standing deathly still, her eyes like beacons, locked on his. A small drop of crimson beaded at the tip of the knife and began to trickle down her soft neck.

A weight crushed his chest, turning his blood to sludge. It was too risky to try anything, yet unthinkable to do nothing. If those thugs harmed Ista he would tear them apart limb by limb.

Like a sunburst, he knew she was more precious to him than gold or any number of accolades.

Chapter Fifty-Two: Blinded

Ista

The point of the knife stung Ista's neck. The lout that held her smelt of old sweat, unwashed clothes and mouldy cheese. His body rammed against hers, pinning her arm to her chest and pressing her basket into her side. Mannok and Garvin stood still as boulders, eyes wide with shock.

'Grab them, gag and tie them up,' the big one said. 'Then get these nobs out of the lane fast.'

'Wouldn't it be easier to cut them here?' asked the shortest of the thugs, his voice a high-pitched whine.

'Orders are orders,' her captor snapped. 'Get to it.'

The other young men edged towards Garvin and Mannok, both in a wrestler's half crouch. The alley was empty and overshadowed by buildings on either side, yet help was just a shout away in the busy Market Street. Should she risk it?

An icy shiver ran down Ista's spine. It might help the boys, but she knew it would only take a second for the knife to slice into her neck.

'You would be wise to let the lady go,' Mannok said, a muscle in his cheek twitching. His face was pale under the tan, his eyes blazed like green fire. 'If you harm us, my father will hunt you down and destroy you. You do not know who I am—.'

The louts erupted into hooting laughter.

'Oh, we know who you be, Your Highness. Good of you to deliver yourself to us,' the big one said. 'Saved us a load of trouble.'

The Prince breathed in sharply. His eyes darted from the big man, to the underlings moving towards him, to Ista and back again.

Garvin licked his lips. 'What are you going to do with us?'

The big one hawked and spat. 'You'll find out soon enough. One move from you nobs, and the lady is dead.'

She had to act. They were going to kill her anyway. Kidnapping the Prince, they couldn't afford any witnesses. Once he and Garvin were tied up, their chances of fighting would be non-existent. She had to risk it. Her breath was ragged in her throat. With glacial slowness, Ista slipped her hand into the basket on her other arm, pulled out the wrapped-up chilli powder she had just purchased, loosened the package. Squeezing shut her own eyes, she flicked the red powder into those of her captor.

The man bellowed. Dropping the knife, he clawed at his eyes. Ista stamped down on his foot and ground her heel in. His grip loosened, she pulled away and staggered a few steps.

'Mannok, now,' she yelled. 'Guards, guards, help. In the lane.'

Mannok and Garvin whipped out their hunting knives and faced off the thugs.

She turned to run out of the alley, but the big one blocked her path. He gasped and writhed and yelped. The whiny voiced lad moved towards her, wielding a brutal looking club. Bending down, she caught up the fallen knife and held it and the bulky basket out in front of her, her back now to Mannok. Behind her she heard the scuffles and grunts, four thugs against Mannok and Garvin.

'Guards,' she screamed. 'In the lane.'

The whiner made a lunge at her, she jumped back, stumbled, his club missing her head by ninas. She slashed at his exposed belly with the knife, using the basket as a shield. He staggered backwards, a look of shock on his face, as though he hadn't expected her to fight.

Ista gripped the handle, slick with sweat, ready for his counter-move. A loud thunk. From the corner of her eye, she saw Mannok plant a powerful kick on one of the ruffians and dodge the swing of a pole from the other. Garvin too was holding his own.

She looked back in time to avoid another vicious swing of the club. She felt it lift her hair, that now straggled loose from its elaborate arrangement down her back. She examined her opponent for weaknesses, dredging up the lessons Hecton had given her as a child and a couple from Mannok. Maybe a more direct approach would be better. Ista reached out with her mind, pushing through the whiner's thoughts like a knife through yarma cheese. The man whimpered as she probed, her own mind screaming at the effort. His arm wobbled and began to lower, his eyes bulged. Sweat poured down his narrow forehead.

A tall figure loped towards them down the laneway. Her eyes widened. The grim-faced figure was Dinnis. He seized the unsuspecting thug from behind, grabbed his wrist in a vice-like grip, twisting his arms and pinning them behind his back. The club clattered to the ground. Dinnis kicked it towards her. She grabbed it and together they ran towards the Prince, Dinnis pushing the struggling lout in front of him.

As they neared the other combatants, Dinnis lifted the lout and threw him into the two thugs attacking Mannok. All three fell in a confusion of limbs and weapons. The assailants all scrambled to their feet and fled, leaving the large lad moaning in the mud. His eyes were fiery red, his face scratched from efforts to remove the chilli.

Ista staggered, her legs suddenly weak. Blood drained from her head. Strong arms caught her. Putting her hands on his chest, she pushed away from him.

'I'm fine,' she snapped, angry at her weakness, not liking to be touched.

'Beg pardon, my Lady.' Dinnis gave her a small crooked smile and a slight bow as he released her. She wobbled a bit and gripped his arm for a second before standing straight and tall, her chin lifted high.

Mannok and Garvin stood panting in the lane, their tunics dishevelled, bruises and scratches on face and limbs. Mannok half-turned towards the fleeing thugs, an avid look in jade-green eyes. Garvin grasped his arm, though too blown to speak.

The Prince kicked a rock. 'They're getting away.' He swung around. 'Are you unharmed, Ista?' he added in a softer voice.

She melted at the fire in his eyes. He took her arm and wiped the trickle of blood from her neck with his cloak.

Dinnis moved up behind the Prince. 'Doesn't look too serious. How about you, Your Highness? That's a nasty bruise.'

Mannok knocked Dinnis hand away. 'What business do you have in Market Street?'

Dinnis raised his eyebrow, putting his hands up in front of him.

'I was running an errand for Ralton that could not wait another second. He had to have a particular ink by yesterday.' He patted his tunic where the shape of a small parcel was obvious. 'Otherwise the whole world will end, or so it seems. I sometimes think he must be royalty, the way he demands instant obedience to unreasonable demands.'

Ista put her hand over her mouth. Her brother's face was bland as he met Mannok's searing glare. Mannok's hands tightened on her arm.

'That doesn't explain why you're in the lane.'

'I was just heading back to the Palace when I heard the lady calling for help.' Dinnis bent down, picked up the basket, brushed off the mud, and handed it to Ista with another small bow. 'I wouldn't have thought that street fighting was an appropriate pastime for a young woman of the court, though you seem to have been getting the gist of it.'

She gave him a withering stare. 'You seem rather practiced at it yourself,' she said through stiff lips.

'Some of those interminable wrestling sessions must have paid off.'

Garvin grinned. 'Rather an unconventional fighting style.'

Mannok loosened his grip, deflated. 'I guess we should thank you, though we were getting things under control.'

'So it looked.' Dinnis raised an eyebrow.

'You might wonder what we were doing here ...' Mannok lifted his chin. He had not let go of her arm. She could feel the warmth of his fingers through the thin fabric of her tunic, inhale his scent.

'None of my business, I'm sure,' Dinnis said.

'I saw some stolen palace goods in the shop back there.' Mannok continued as though he hadn't spoken.

He took a step towards her brother. 'You wouldn't know anything about that, now would you, Dinnis?'

Chapter Fifty-Three: Cross Purposes

Mannok

Mannok glared at Dinnis, furious with him and furious with himself. The insolent fellow looked at him with his usual unreadable face, not answering.

'Well, what have you to say for yourself?' His voice clipped from the effort of not shouting.

Dinnis grey eyes widened a fraction, his right eyebrow tilted upwards. 'Surely you don't think that I …? Where are these stolen goods, Your Highness?'

With a frustrated growl, Mannok let go of Ista's arm and charged down the lane towards Market Street, stopping as he reached the corner.

He turned to check that the others followed. Sauntering behind Garvin and Ista, Dinnis glanced at the moaning assailant against the far wall. Mannok had forgotten about the fellow. They should have secured him first. The thug pushed himself up on hands and knees. With a roar, his inflamed eyes still screwed shut, he heaved himself upright and staggered down the lane in the direction of his mates.

Dinnis paused and turned back to Mannok, a question in his eyes. 'Should we give chase, Your Highness?'

'Not a good idea,' Garvin said.

Mannok looked down the long length of the lane. Garvin was right; they could find themselves surrounded by ruffians and even further from the main street than before. He wouldn't put Ista in danger again. Might this be a ploy for Dinnis to make his own escape? If he was guilty. As the heat of the battle began to wane, Mannok realised that the shadowy figure darting into the lane couldn't have been his age-mate. Yet he could not shake the hunch that Dinnis was hiding something.

'Mannok?' Dinnis stood beside Ista and Garvin.

Gritting his teeth, Mannok shook his head. Feeling foolish, the embers of his temper stirred again. 'Look here. See if you recognise anything.' Mannok pointed with his chin at the stacks of furniture and knickknacks piled in front of the shop. 'Can you see the tapestry of the hounds, the silver candlesticks ...' he listed the items he had noticed.

Dinnis picked up the candlesticks. 'These are pewter not silver, and they don't have the royal mark on them.'

Mannok grabbed a set of eating knives, thrust them into Dinnis' face, then frowned. The handles were carved wood, not bone. A frantic search of the merchandise revealed not one single item that he recognised.

'They were here.' He swung around to look at the puzzled faces of his friends, a feeling of unease, as though the earth had moved, under his feet. Had he imagined it? 'They were here. I know they were.' He closed his eyes and ground his teeth. This was one of those days when things just got worse and worse.

Dinnis straightened, his enigmatic grey eyes thoughtful.

'There are scuff marks in the mud here, as though objects have been moved in haste. Perhaps they've been swapped.' He rubbed his chin with long fingers. 'Junok's does not have the best of reputations. Yet who would be so brash to steal from the Palace?'

Mannok was about to retort, 'Maybe you would,' but thought better of it. He had no proof that Dinnis was involved and his story of getting ink for the Head Librarian could be true. Yet if Dinnis was not responsible who was?

Ista brushed her cool fingers on his arm. Her alluring perfume of mountain lilies and apple-mint filled his senses. He gazed into her eyes, like two grey mountain doves. She was lovely even with her clothes rent and muddied, her dark hair half cascading down her back. His slowing heart began to hammer again as he took in the soft curve of her cheek, her slender neck and willowy figure. He felt a chill seep into him. She could have been killed today. He could have lost her.

A soft blush spread across her pale cheeks as though she sensed his thoughts. She dropped her eyes and spoke softly.

'Please excuse me, Your Highness, the Kupanna is waiting on these spices. I need to replace the losses and return to the Palace.'

Dinnis' sardonic voice jarred into his thoughts.

'We should all return to the Palace, Your Highness. It would be wise to inform your father and Kaptan Jakan of your suspicions and the attack on your person. It was rash of you to wander about the lower city unguarded.'

'That's what I said,' Garvin muttered under his breath. 'I think Dinnis is right, Mannok,' he added in a louder voice.

As much as he wanted to take issue with them both, Mannok knew they were right.

* * *

A couple of hours later, Mannok hurried along the path, taking scant notice of the warm sunshine and summer scents wafting from the heaped-up flowers and verdant branches in the Palace gardens. The sun stood halfway up in the brilliant lapis lazuli sky, washed clean by the recent rain. Little woolly clouds had begun to pile up along the horizon. He would speak to Kaptan Jakan or his father later. Right now, he needed to speak with Ista.

On the walk back to the Palace, he'd been keenly aware of Ista's lissom figure and exhilarating perfume beside him. They had been good friends from the moment she had arrived in Tarka, almost as close as brother and sister. He could count on her to listen to his latest exploits and wild schemes, and he would empathize with her about the joys and challenges of her day. Over the years, they had talked to each other about the nightmares that had disturbed their sleep. She had spoken about her time in Akrad's Tower; he told of the horror of Naetok's attack on his father and the uncertain years that had followed.

Ista was reserved, yet she didn't pretend with him. She didn't giggle and simper like the young women his mother suggested as possible brides and who bothered him with their attentions. His heartbeat quickened. She was stately, almost regal. He loved that about her. He knew the other girls teased her because of her strange pale skin and exotic eyes, but he was captivated by them. Garvin thought he was mad, but then, Garvin liked Lumi.

Mannok strode along the curving paths, peering into the small garden courtyards and arbours, hoping Ista wasn't walking the maze. She rushed off as soon as they had arrived back at the Palace to deliver the spices to the kitchen and report to his mother. Yet about this time, she sometimes cut flowers from the garden for the Kupanna. If he didn't find her now, it was unlikely he would see her until that evening—and then only under his mother's watchful eyes. He had to find her, tell her how he felt.

A gust of wind carried the soft sound of singing towards him. He headed toward the sound. He picked up his pace and jumped over a low hedge. As he saw her across the grass-fringed paving stones, he stood still, his heart like thunder in his ears.

Ista was leaning over a garden bed of mountain lilies, cutting and placing them in a flat basket already half-filled with delicate dusky pink marosa flowers, snow blossoms and fern fronds. She had changed into a soft blue tunic encrusted with seed pearls, and her hair was caught up with an elaborate mother of pearl comb, leaving her slender neck uncovered. He savoured the pale rose on her cheeks and the sweep of her dark eyelashes.

Mannok stole towards her and clamped his hands over her eyes. She started with a soft exclamation and then stood still, her fingers tightening on the pruning knife.

'Mannok, is that you? Please, don't surprise me like that after this morning's escapade.'

'Hmmm, just as well you don't have any chilli powder in that basket.' He released her and turned her around to face him. Seeing the small scratch on her pale throat, the scene in the alleyway flashed in his mind. 'Sorry, that was thoughtless of me.' He felt himself falling into the depth of her misty grey eyes. Without thinking, he pulled her towards him and kissed her.

Chapter Fifty-Four: Declaration

Ista

Ista's heart hammered against her chest. Mannok's lips were firm against hers, almost bruising in their urgency, his arms encircled her and held her tight. Her lips tingled with delight. She breathed in his tangy aroma, excitement surging through her, both of power and surrender and fear.

This is what she wanted, what she longed for. He loved her and she hadn't had to use her power to entice him. He'd chosen her, even though she had little status among the Tamrin.

Like a dash of cold water, an awful thought intruded. What did he intend? Would he take her like a maid to be discarded later or were his intentions honourable? She wanted so much to melt into his embrace, but she would not be abused by anyone. She was a kiprissa, a granddaughter of Akrad. She would be treated as such. With difficulty, she pulled her hands up to his chest, and pushed herself back from him.

'No, stop it. What do you take me for?'

She stood panting in front of him, tears pricking her eyelids at the bewilderment in the smoky green depths of his irises. His eyes widened and his brow contracted. He had such an open face with strong lines and vibrant colouring. His russet hair whipped untidily in the wind, his hawk like nose almost as prominent as his father. She felt the maelstrom of his emotions, passion, anger, hurt, confusion.

'You weren't so coy with Prince Tolteal.' His voice was a mixture of ice and fire.

She started with surprise. She was sure he had not noticed anything she had done that evening before the Siliseans had left. Almost the same height, they stood glaring at each other.

'A chaste kiss on the cheek after declaring his intentions.' She was furious at how things were turning out. 'Would you treat any other lady of the court with such disrespect?'

'What intentions?' Then he flushed. 'Of course, not … I, I mean of course … Oh slide it, Ista. I don't want to kiss any of the other ladies of the court. It's you I want.'

'And is this how you would approach them if you did? Prince Tolteal has declared his wish to marry me. He seeks his parents' permission.' Treacherous tears began to brim on her lower lids. 'Which no doubt they will refuse. For why should a Prince marry a penniless orphan like me? But you, I always thought you understood and would treat me with respect—as a kinswoman if not as an equal.'

The anger leeched from his face and a look of horror replaced it. He grabbed her hands and cupped them in his own.

'Ista, my Lady, you can't think I meant to …' He scrunched up his face and his shoulders slumped. 'I've gone about this all the wrong way. By the moons, I'm an idiot.' He drew her towards him. 'I do want to marry you. Will you be my bride, my love? Do you care for me at all or has that wretched flatlander captured your heart?'

She did not resist. They stood with their bodies brushing up against each other.

'*Moros*, of course I love you, not some silly flatlander—no matter how tempting his book collection might be.'

It took a moment for her words to sink in. Then a ferocious grin so like his father's curved up his face. 'Book collection? Well if that is what it takes, I had better start collecting,' he teased.

Ista rested her head on his chest. He placed his hand around her waist, pulling her closer.

'I'm not sure your mother will approve,' she said in a low voice. 'You know how quickly she jumps on us if she sees us together.'

He stroked her cheek and gave a mock shudder. 'Papa has always insisted that I could choose for myself. Well, I choose you. Maybe Mama won't like it at first, but with time... Let me speak to her and Papa about this.'

'She has much grander plans for you —a princess, a Markan's daughter or at least the daughter of a clan leader.'

'Even if you don't have a grand dowry, you are of noble blood. Besides, Mama has really warmed to you in recent years. You are already more like a daughter than a servant to her.'

Ista ignored the warning chill at the back of her neck. She so wanted to believe this dream could come true. She pushed away what she knew Grandfather would say about love. In Mannok's arms, she felt safe and cherished.

She laid her hand on his heart. 'Very well, Your Highness. I am yours and no other's.'

When he bent to kiss her again, she savoured the touch of his lips before she pushed him away again, this time more gently. 'In the meantime, we will behave with perfect propriety.'

He grimaced, then stepped back and swept her a courtly bow. 'As you wish, my sweet Princess. I am at your command.'

* * *

Ista entered the reception room with the basket of flowers, humming under her breath and her steps light. Mannok had declared his love for her and asked her to marry him. Maybe, Dinnis was right about not forcing things.

She placed the basket on a low table and began to arrange purple, pink and white blossoms in the tall vases, all the while singing a pretty song she remembered from her childhood. An errant breeze, tiptoeing through the open doors to the atrium, stirred the fronds of the pot plants and caressed her cheek. For the first time in as long as she could remember, she felt happy right up to the brim. Whatever opposition the Kupanna might make to their plans, she and Mannok would prevail. She trusted the strength of his love, their resolution. Perhaps the Kapok wouldn't be so hard to persuade.

'Hussy!' She jumped when the Marra's cold voice, intruded on her thoughts. 'Do you think I didn't see you attempting to ensnare my son?'

Ista cheeks flamed. She swung around to face her accuser.

The Kupanna arms akimbo, her face like flint, two spots of crimson on her tan cheeks.

'Your Majesty, I didn't ... He approached me,' she stammered.

Her mistress pressed her lips together, her nose wrinkled as though she had discovered dung in the linen cupboards. In three strides, she crossed the room and slapped Ista across the cheek.

'Don't you dare try to shift the blame.'

Ista gasped, her hands flying to her burning cheeks. In all the years of servitude, from the harsh early years to the more favoured later years, Marra had never struck her. Tears pushed through Ista's eyelashes. She took a deep breath and steadied herself. She had known when she'd accepted the Prince's proposal that the next little while would be difficult. She just hadn't expected the hounding to start so soon. She lifted her chin and met the Kupanna's accusatory eyes.

'He says he want to marry me.'

Marra's nostrils flared, her pupils dilating. She lunged forward and grabbed Ista by the left wrist. 'This has to stop now!' She tugged and pulled Ista along after her as she strode towards the open door. 'Come with me!'

Ista didn't not resist and tried to keep her feet as the Kupanna charged ahead.

Marra headed for the atrium corridor, climbed the flight of stairs at the end and dragged Ista behind her toward the Royal sleeping apartments. They left a wake of gaping servants. The Kupanna reefed open the door to the antechamber, pulled Ista through and shoved her into the centre of the room.

Rokkan looked up, his eyebrows raised. He was dressed in a simple tunic and breeches, papers and maps spread out on the low table in front of him. He had a pen in his hand, ink smudges on his fingers, a document spread out ready for signing and sealing.

Marra pointed at Ista. 'I was taking a minute to relax on the balcony when I saw this young hussy kissing our son in the garden. Kissing, Rokkan. They want to get married, she says.'

The Kapok's eyes widened. The pen dropped from his slack hand, splattering over the document in front of him. He opened his mouth, looked from the Kupanna to her and back to the Kupanna.

Marra marched toward the door. 'I will not have her under my roof for even one more night. Do you understand Rokkan? This is all your fault, son of Martal. You fix it.'

And with that ultimatum, Marra stormed out of the room, slamming the door behind her.

Chapter Fifty-Five: A Hard Father

Ista

Ista pushed down the panic that threatened to envelop her. She had anticipated opposition from Mannok's mother but not his father. Maybe he wouldn't be overjoyed with the concept of their marriage, but she had not expected his blank-faced shock. The Kapok stared at the shut door, the stunned look still on his face. He glanced at her, then sunk his head into his large hands and groaned.

She caught her lip in her teeth, pushing back the tears. It didn't matter, she and Mannok wouldn't give in. But if they sent her away, what could she do? What could two sixteen-year-olds do against the full might of the rulers of the realm? Where would they send her and what would become of her? What hope was there for them? Rokkan had taken her part in the past. She needed to keep her wits about her. She needed to get him on her side.

'Why does she always blame you, *kuree*?' she asked keeping her voice soft.

Rokkan looked up at her words, his golden eyes almost tan in the shadows of the room. He seemed older, the sharp lines on forehead and at the corners of his eyes etched deeper, the few strands of grey at the temple noticeable. There was no softness in his eyes, not even the hint of a smile. He looked grim and tired.

'I'm afraid this time, *chia*, Marra is right. This is all my fault.'

She had expected accusations, reproaches, reprimands or pleas but not this muted regret. It unnerved her. He was going to do as the Kupanna had requested. She felt hollowed out, adrift. But she couldn't give up, this meant everything to her—love, position, safety. She sank down on her knees in front of him.

'Your Majesty, I know I do not have much to offer in terms of position and wealth, but I am not uneducated or without ability. My birth is noble. I would make a good wife for Mannok and a good daughter-in-law to you.'

'Your rank is not the problem, Ista. You are a Princess, a Kiprissa by birth. And if I thought you were a suitable wife for my son, and he truly loved you, neither your lack of position nor of wealth would be an issue for me, though I know they may well be for the Kupanna.'

His words cut her deeply. A tear slipped down her cheek, followed by another.

'If not my rank, then why do you think me unsuitable? I ... I thought you ... you were fond of me. Is it because I'm ... I'm Nolmec or Akrad's progeny?'

He leant forward and wiped the tears off her cheeks with a gentle finger, then sat back with a heavy sigh.

'My feelings for you are ... irrelevant, Ista. I have no prejudice against the Nolmec. Indeed, some would say that I've been far too sympathetic toward them in the past.'

He gave a wry smile.

'Then why?' she wailed, unable to keep the bereft tone out of her voice.

'You cannot marry Mannok, because he is your brother.'

The quiet words made no sense to her. They hovered somewhere above her head but would not penetrate her thinking.

'My brother? But, that is ridiculous. My mother is Gaia, daughter of Zowee. There is no way Marra could be my mother.'

He lifted his strong eyebrows. 'To be precise, he is your half-brother.'

'Half-brother? You mean ...'

Realisation flooded her mind, overwhelming her with a confusion of unnamed emotions. It was as if the mountains were quaking, bringing down the cliffs in an avalanche of rock, ice and snow. It was as if she had woken up and found herself in an underwater, upside down world. It was as if she'd woken up from a dream into a nightmare. Her vision smudged and darkened, her blood hammered in her ears.

The feel of his arms, the smell of chilli, the horses and the dogs. That was it. That was why this man had seemed familiar and safe to her all those years ago, when she had arrived as a frightened girl in the seat of power of her enemies.

'You are my father?' Her lips were numb, her voice strange in her ears. 'But, Dinnis said our father died at North Pass.'

'He told you that?'

'No, not to me, but to anyone else who asks about his father.'

She frowned. What did it matter what her brother said? Brother! Chills began to race up and down her body and she couldn't stop her trembling. Mannok was her brother. They could never get married. She felt a lump in her chest where once her heart had been, a lump now smashed and broken into pieces.

This was worse than the concerted opposition of all of Tamra. Her love could never, should never have been.

Rokkan's voice came as though from a long distance. She shook her head against its buzzing and wrapped her arms around her. She could feel nothing, nothing at all.

'Ista.'

There was compassion in his eyes, but she didn't want it. Marra was right, he was right, this was all his fault.

'How could you? It couldn't have been just a quick furtive tumble in the field … or … or does Dinnis have a different father than me?'

His eyes narrowed, and then he gave a bark of a laugh.

'Gaia and I had six glorious years together. Quick? Yes. But only as in far too brief. I was devastated when she died. If it had not been for Marra and you children, I am not sure what I would have done. My father would have killed me if he knew I had married, not just a Nolmec, but a *kiprissa* and the granddaughter of Akrad. I was supposed to be spying on the enemy, not consorting with them. Well, I did both. Gaia never agreed with Akrad's grandiose plans for conquest …' His voice trailed into silence. He sucked in a deep breath. 'Your mother was my life.' He sat back in the chair and closed his eyes, pain etched into his normally jovial face.

She tried to take in what he was saying. She latched on to one fact, one discrepancy.

'Married? But if you married why can't you acknowledge us?'

He brushed the side of the chair then brought his hands together. '*Chia*, I would if I could.'

'You are Kapok,' she snapped back at him, furious with his excuses.

'It's not that simple.' He leaned forward. 'My father arranged the hand-fasting between Marra and myself when we were children. He insisted the marriage go ahead despite my objections. The son of the Kapok is a mere subject like anyone else. My father was a hard man.'

'But he didn't know about us.' Ista clasped her cold hands to still the shaking. 'And Marra ...' She refused to call her Kupanna, now she knew it was a title her own mother should have borne. She drew in a breath. 'She doesn't know?'

'Marra found out after Gaia died.'

'Giving birth to me.'

'Yes.' He looked away, over her head.

The whirlwind of thoughts and emotions steadied into sudden clarity. Marra's and her brother Lukarn's hostility when she had arrived in the Palace. No wonder the woman had hated her, hated Dinnis. Why hadn't Dinnis told her that their Papa had come for him. Her fingers curled into her palms, the long nails biting. 'Because,' replied a sibilant voice, Grandfather's voice 'He didn't come back for you.' Rokkan had come, but he hadn't acknowledged them, hadn't given them the position their birth deserved.

Did Mannok know? No, he couldn't have. Her chest heaved. She wanted to scream.

'Marra hates us because we are a threat to her—to her son's claim on the throne.' She paused, feeling the words like acid on her tongue. 'I understand that now, but *you* refuse to acknowledge us? You are the Kapok.'

He met her gaze. 'I'm sorry, there is what I might want to do and then there is what is necessary for the good of Tamra.'

'By all that's right, we ...

'Since Princess Sil, women are unable to inherit the—'

'And Dinnis?'

His golden eyes narrowed. He was silent for so long she thought he would not answer. He stirred. 'That is what both Marra and Lukarn fear most, why they wanted me to ... eliminate ... the threat. I once thought it possible, but with the Nolmec incursions and Naetok's rebellion, the clans would never accept an heir of Nolmec blood, particularly the northern clans who would defend Mannok's claim to the last warrior. And my cousin Haka ready to exploit the slightest weakness. As Kapok, too often I find myself having to decide between the impossible and the unthinkable. I will not, cannot, plunge my country into civil war again.'

'Perhaps you should've thought of that before you consorted with my mother.' The words were out before she could stop them.

'Indeed. I was naïve, idealistic, stupid.'

'To protect your throne, you disinherit us, and now you send me away.' Her eyes stung. Her dreams of a future with Mannok now impossible, shredding away like spider silk. It's what Grandfather— her Master—had always said. Life was about power, everything else was illusion.

Rokkan stood up abruptly and disappeared into an adjacent chamber. He reappeared a few moments later, a small bundle in his hands. He gave it to her. Her hand clutched the soft material. Was he trying to buy her forgiveness for a few metal pieces?

'These belonged to your mother. Now, you best go pack your things as we leave within three hours, before the sun sets.'

'We ... you're coming with me? But what of the dinner tonight and the Soiree the Kupanna is planning in a five-day, and the council meeting and the harvest festival ...' her voice trailed away.

Rokkan raised his eyebrow. 'If the Kupanna wishes me to attend these things, she should not expect you gone before the evening meal.'

'She will be furious.'

'She already is. I intend to see you settled in a situation that befits my daughter, and there is no one else I can trust to do it as I would wish.' He grimaced. 'Not Sparak or Lukarn, for sure, at least in this matter.'

'Where are you taking me?'

'Silisea. I am sure you will have a warm welcome there. And you need not think you are penniless. I have my mother's dowry, much of it in Silisean property, to dispose of and I intend to settle the bulk of that on you. I'm long overdue for a visit to Silisea.'

'You ... you would acknowledge me?'

'Not publicly, I'm afraid. But I will make sure that Queen Suza is aware of our connection. With wealth and royal favour, you can make a life for yourself.'

'What about Dinnis? Could he come too?' However, provoking

her brother could be, he'd been with her from the beginning, the only one who had never left her.

A shadow flittered across the Kapok's face. 'I wish … but, no, it would be misinterpreted. Is there anything you would take with you? Ask, and if I can grant it, I will.'

She looked down at her long fingers encircling the purple cloth. Whatever baubles the cloth contained, they could not make her safe. She had been wrong to dream of love, wrong to trust in the Kupanna's good opinion or the Kapok's favour, wrong to trust anyone but her own self. Such things were an illusion, just as Grandfather had said. She could see the stack of Akrad's notebooks in a forgotten corner of the library as clearly as though they were in front of her. Dinnis had warned her from following that path but Dinnis was wrong.

'Some books from the library.'

He studied her, as though straining to discern her thoughts, though his mind, as always was like a wall of basalt. She tensed ready to throw up a shield, when he nodded his head.

'Whatever Ralton can spare, and you want, you can have.' He rubbed the ink stain on his hand. 'Why I have a feeling I might regret this, I'm not at all sure.'

'And I would like to say goodbye to Dinnis and …' Would she ever be able to face Mannok again? She wanted to, to see his face and hear his voice, but it was humiliating to think of their forbidden love, what they might have done. How would he react when he found out? Would he find her abhorrent? She lowered her head to hide the burn she could feel spreading across her face.

Rokkan thought for a few minutes then nodded again. 'Dinnis I will allow. Just keep your seditious plans to a minimum.'

She jerked her head up, just in time to see the faint remnants of his familiar teasing smile in his eyes.

Chapter Fifty-Six: Siblings

Ista

It didn't take long for Ista to pack her things and arrange with Ralton to transport Akrad's notebooks and one or two other treasured tomes to Silisea. She found some food in the kitchens, but could not swallow it. The Kupanna had sent Mannok on some invented errand to the Temple. She wasn't sure whether to be pleased or angry that she'd been prevented from seeing him. As the shadows lengthened, she decided to look for Dinnis for a final farewell, perhaps forever. In less than an hour she would be leaving Tarka for an unknown city far to the south. Tolteal's city.

She found Dinnis in the enclosed orchards of the Silisean Palace, sitting cross-legged under a tree with an open book on his lap. His grey eyes followed her as she walked towards him.

'To what do I owe the honour of your august presence, my Lady?' Dinnis lent forward, beginning to rise to his feet.

'Don't be silly.'

He tilted his head, then sank back down on the long grass beneath the guava tree.

His lips quirked at the corners. 'I've missed your tender words.'

She sat down in front of him, tucking her legs under her. She might get grass stains on the fine fabric of her tunic, but what did it matter? She shivered. If only she had known that Mannok was her half-brother, things would have turned out different, their friendship could have stayed within the bounds. Once the cavy escaped the box, it was hard to put it back in.

'Ista, something is wrong.'

Without warning, tears pooled in her eyes and streamed down her cheeks. 'Everything is wrong.'

His face softened. He reached out and took her hand in his. 'Tell me.'

'Mannok asked me to marry him. Kupanna Marra found out. She was furious and took me to the Kapok who said … who explained why it's impossible. He didn't die at North Pass, like you said. The Kapok is our father.' She pressed her hands against her mouth. 'So, he's sending me away.'

The wry amusement leached from his face, but not even a hint of shock or surprise flickered in his smoke-grey eyes.

'You knew! Why didn't you tell me he was our father?'

'How would it have helped? He didn't plan to acknowledge us. Insisted I keep it a secret.'

She brushed the tears of her face. 'I wouldn't have allowed my feelings for Mannok …' She stopped, humiliated. 'You should have warned me.'

'Sorry, *chia*. You are right, I should have.'

Ista sighed at the Nolmec endearment, then pulled out the bundle Rokkan had given her. 'He gave me this. He said it was our mother's.' She placed it between them and opened the soft leather to reveal a shimmering purple cloth bag, a leather-bound notebook and a small vial.

He leant forward, his face suddenly intense with emotion. He picked up the bag and emptied out the contents: a gorgeous jade and gold necklace with six pointed stars, double circles and, at the nadir, a beautifully carved translucent bird with a crest, long wings and tail, a phoenix. Matching earrings and bracelets slid out after it. His eyes gleamed like reflected water.

'I remember this. I remember her wearing it.'

He handed the jewellery to Ista, picked up the stone vial, carved with the bird on both sides and took out the stopper. A subtle scent of summer flowers wafted onto the soft breeze.

'That's her perfume.' His voice was choked with emotion.

He bit his lip, looked down at the book and opened it. They bent over so that their heads were almost touching and pored over the pages. It was full of drawings—many of Rokkan with his horse or dogs and often with a young boy. Underneath were swirling handwriting labels such as 'My love' and 'Dinnu with Tracer.' Interleaved were unattached pages with short messages and embarrassing romantic poems in their father's familiar precise writing. On the last page was a hasty sketch of a woman's face by a different artist and the same precise writing, wilder and untidy, with the words in Nolmec 'My evening star, my phoenix, my life. Today the world died. How can I go on?'

Dinnis choked back a sob then pulled a notebook from his tunic. Opening it up, he smoothed the page where another, more practiced sketch of a woman's face stared at them. It was the same. Both portrayed the dark, oblique eyes, high cheekbones, small straight nose, silvery blue skin and a curtain of black hair, the lines of carefree laughter.

'So, I did remember her face.' His face, so full of emotion, seemed unfamiliar to Ista. He abruptly caught the things up, wrapping them up in the cover and pushed them into her hands. He leant back against the tree trunk, 'And now you're leaving too.'

'She looks like you,' she said. 'She was beautiful,' she added after a pause.

He laughed without opening his eyes. 'Now that's a contradiction. You are right though, she was beautiful.'

'He loved her.'

'Maybe. Not that did us any good.'

'They were married, you know.'

He sat up straighter. 'No, I didn't.' Picking up a fallen twig, he shredded the leaves. 'I just thought ... but she was the Kiprissa. It makes sense.'

'Do you hate him for betraying us?'

He looked at her, his grey eyes so like her own. His face was hard to read, the emotion smoothed out of it.

'Hate is too mild a word for what I felt when he disowned me. I've thought of a thousand ways to get back at him.'

She took in a quick breath. 'Would you kill him?'

'It's tempting. I've thought about it a lot, but I'm not sure that would change anything. I'm not sure I like the idea of what I would become. Well, probably very dead for one thing.' He gave a lopsided smile.

'You could become the Kapok, you are his eldest son.'

'Hush, Ista. Such words are treason and will get us both killed.'

Her heart beat more insistently. She lowered her voice. 'But it's true.'

His mouth twisted. 'Are you blind? Look at me. Is this the face of a Kapok? Can you imagine a Nolmec on the Golden Throne of Tamra?' He laughed, a low bitter sound. 'No one would support my claim even if that is what I wanted. A Kapok cannot rule without the support of the clans or the temple.'

She thought for a moment, stroking the exotic necklace, her mother's. They were of royal blood through their half-Nolmec mother and also through their Tamrin father. They were the great-grandchildren of the great Arkon Akrad who was of another ancient royal line, or so he had told her. Yet they had been treated like slaves or *pioni*, made to fetch and carry and follow the whims of others. She should have been the one giving the orders, not the one receiving them. Ista didn't want to leave Tamra, certainly not forever. Perhaps there was a way. She smiled.

'Now that's a scary sight,' her brother said.

He was watching her with the same knowing look that Rokkan often had. If fact, if you looked past the Nolmec features, there were telling resemblances. His nose, not quite as prominent, the shape of his ears and his hands but particularly the way he moved, his gaze and, when he allowed it, his smile. She shivered. How had she not known?

Yet maybe deep down, she had. Why else had she felt so attached to Rokkan? He had been kind to her, but it was more than that. A shaft of anger pierced her. What a farce! He should have given her a place as his daughter instead of the left-over crumbs. He should have made her a princess, not a serving wrench to that usurping Kupanna. What he now offered would never compensate for what she and Dinnis had lost.

She reached out and took her brother's hand.

'Perhaps, it could be possible. If we made overtures to Markan Haka, he might well support our cause. Our knowledge of Rokkan's strengths and weaknesses could be of a great help to him.' She was careful to keep her voice low.

He raised his eyebrow in a gesture so like Rokkan.

'You may be right. Haka would see the potential in using our claim as a pretext for deposing Rokkan. He might have the troops and the backing of the southern clans to do it, but he would then just as swiftly get rid of us. He wants to sit on the throne, not stand behind it.'

'So, we dispose of him before he gets the chance to dispose of us.'

He sat back and sighed. 'You were such a sweet little thing before that Monster got his claws into you. You could be Akrad. You could be Haka.'

'But imagine it, Dinnis. You would be Kapok. Think what you could do.'

'What would that make you? You'd still be only a princess. And what about Mannok? He'd never make peace with his father—our father's—killers.'

Her cheeks burned. How could she hate Mannok when none of this was his fault? He was as much a victim as she was. She pulled her hand from Dinnis' grasp and traced the pattern of a fallen leaf with her finger. What did she really want? A world in which things weren't turned upside down by a whim, in which there was order, in which she wasn't at the mercy of the powers that be.

'I don't want to be Kapok, Ista. I've seen what it does to a man, that much power. And always looking over your shoulder, never knowing who will knife you from the shadows.'

'It was just a fancy,' she said, 'But don't you ever think what you could do with the power, how you could shape the world?'

Girls didn't inherit the throne in Tamra, but they could in Silisea or more to the point, Tolteal would. If she couldn't have Tarka, perhaps she would settle for another throne, but this time she would have done with sentiment, with softness and girlish dreams. 'You could come with me to Silisea.'

His eyes brightened, then clouded. 'I'd love to travel, to see all the Five Lands and beyond, but I doubt the Kapok would allow it. In case I started forming alliances, building armies, making invasion plans.' His smile was twisted, sad. 'Besides, I have a life here.'

The sunset gong sounded, distant and faint here in the orchards. She stood up, smoothed out her tunic. 'Well, if you're content with being a lackey to the Prince, I wish you the happiness of it. I have to go.'

'That's not quite the life I meant.' He jumped to his feet and handed her the bundle. 'Take care. Don't be too rough on Silisea.' He gave her an awkward sideways hug.

'Your concern is touching, dear brother.' She turned and walked towards the stables and a new life in the south away from Tarka and Mannok. She had no intention of returning while Marra lived.

Chapter Fifty-Seven: Message

Mannok

Three alume later, Mannok drummed his fingers on the solid junglewood table. Warm morning sun slanted in through the high arched windows of the Council Chamber, reflected in a dazzle of white by the plethora of documents scattered on the long table in the centre of the room. The small number of people present—his mother, the madomo, the Master of Scouts, the Kaptans of Palace and City Guards—seemed dwarfed by the large, high-roofed chamber.

Since Papa and hauled Ista off to Silisea with no explanation, he'd found it hard to be interested in the everyday business of palace life. A hard-to-contain simmering rage and suppressed grief were his constant companions. Mama either couldn't or wouldn't explain why Papa decided visit Silisea with Ista the same day that he'd proposed. The timing couldn't be coincidence. Mannok had expected opposition but not this highhanded action without giving him a chance to explain himself, to plead his case. And Papa's continued absence meant that Mannok was trapped in these interminable meetings.

Bitjarnan droned on and on and on about palace business, his nasal voice drilling into Mannok's head like a giant mosquito until he could barely restrain himself from howling. Problems with the levy staff, problems with the supply of this or that foodstuff, problems with birds befouling the lookout pavilion ...

'... and I'm investigating the disappearance of some—'

He sat forward. 'Yes, yes, well, maybe we could leave it for the next meeting.'

Mama placed her beringed hands on the table. 'The Prince has a point. We appreciate your diligence and concern, worthy Madomo, but the Palace is not the Realm. That will be all, thank you.'

Bitjarnan's double chin wobbled and his hands fluttered. 'Ah, yes … but, Your Majesty, Kaptan Jakan—'

Kaptan Jakan leaned forward. 'Meet with me this afternoon, Bitjarnan, we'll talk about it then.'

'As you wish.' Bitjarnan stood with an air of wounded dignity and bowed low to Mannok and the Kupanna. 'Your Highness, Your Majesty.'

The doors clicked shut behind his straight back.

'Thank you, Kaptan. And Mannok can you stop that annoying tapping.'

Mannok lifted his hand from the table and hooked them into his belt, his cheeks warming. 'Sorry, Mama.'

Mama turned to the Master of Scouts. 'Sparak, have you any news of note?' She smoothed down a curl in the scroll in front of her, her voice nonchalant.

Sparak in the middle of smothering a yawn, sat up straighter. He dipped his head. 'Your Majesty, indeed. Our border with the Nolmec remains stable with no incursions. One of the jungle tribes attacked a village in the East March but were repelled easily enough. Ah, and one of the villagers from Eagle's Rest claims to have seen three warriors on the road south of the village the morning of the bridge incident. One was wearing a Puma insignia.'

Mannok's ears pricked at the mention of Eagle's Rest. As much as he found it hard to care about anything since Ista's departure, he owed it to Redrik and his grieving family to find and punish the saboteurs.

'Why didn't the villager mention this sooner?' he said.

'Puma? It seems unlikely that anyone from my father's clan would harm the Prince.' Mama spoke over him.

Sparak traced a knot in the surface of the table. 'Agreed, Your Majesty. The Puma clan are invested in their Prince, given the strong ties with both your gracious self and Kupanna Suraya. Rifts caused by Naetok's rebellion were healed at the Council of Nakri. It may have been a fake insignia to divert suspicion.'

Mama inclined her head. 'And the Prince's query? It's been five alume since the attack. This villager ... why does he speak up now?'

'She. The widow was travelling south at the time. She'd just left the village for an extended stay with her daughter in South Ridge village and she has only just now returned.'

Mannok let out a frustrated sigh. 'Even if this woman's account can be trusted, it may be coincidence. Could she give any other identifying details?'

'She may remember more, but it had been raining for days, if you remember. She set out at the first break in the weather, before dawn. The light was poor and the travellers wrapped up against the chill and damp.'

Mannok slumped back into his narrow-backed chair. 'How could I forget the incessant rain.' Still, this was slim pickings.

Kaptan Kaspin cleared his throat. 'There have been no further attacks in five alume. It may just have been a terrible accident.'

Mannok squirmed. Maybe he should have mentioned the incident in the alley-way as Dinnis advised. In the chaos of his feeling about Ista, he'd forgotten to say anything and he was embarrassed about his impetuous dash. His stomach rumbled. He hoped the meeting could finish soon.

Kaptan Jakan glanced at him, frowned and opened his mouth, when Mama spoke first.

'Any news of travellers crossing the border from Silisea, Sparak?' She fiddled with the papers in front of her.

'No, no sign of the Kapok.'

'Forgive me, Your Majesty. I received a dispatch from His Royal Majesty a few days ago. I didn't realise ...' The Kaptan Jakan's cheeks darkened.

Heat rushed to Mannok's head as the simmering anger flared. Three alume and just brief notes saying he'd be staying longer than he'd planned and now this ...

Two pink spots bloomed on Mama's cheeks. She folded her lips together as though she didn't trust herself to speak.

Sparak growled. 'Spit it out, man.'

'Err ... nothing of great import. He is thinking of staying at least another alume, something about arranging transfer of property and the selection of promising foals from the royal Silisean horses. He's gone with the Royal family to their spring palace near the border with the Southern Wilderness.'

Mama rubbed her temples. 'No doubt, he'll deign to be back for the Prince's birthday feast.' Despite the blandness of her words, her voice was like cut glass.

'I ... er ... I believe so Your Majesty.'

That was it. His father hiving off to Silisea as though he had no royal responsibilities, as though Mannok's wishes were unimportant. And now Mama, despite everything, insisted on making his birthday into a gala event again.

Mannok jumped up, the chair tottering for a moment before righting itself.

'But isn't Papa's coronation and the establishment of peace in the realm the more important anniversary to celebrate. And if Papa is not here—'

'The two are not unconnected, Mannok. Until you marry and have heirs, you are the future of the realm.'

The blood roared in his ears. How could she talk of marriage when they had taken his sweet love from him? His hands tingled as he struggled for breath. He couldn't stay in this madhouse a moment longer.

He cast around for an excuse, a reason. 'I'm leaving tomorrow for a hunting expedition.'

Mama stood up. 'No, you can't. You're too young to go on your own.'

'I've passed the Trial. I'll be seventeen in two alume. I'm not a minor any longer, Mama. It's the hunting season. It's tradition.'

He caught his breath, excited. Yes, this was it. He could go to the lodge in the Southern wilderness, find out what had happened to Ista. It was perfect.

'Didn't you listen to Sparak? It's not safe.'

'I'll have my age-mates with me, more than two-tens of young blades, plus as many guards as Kaptan Kaspin can spare.'

'Mannok, I can't agree to you going.'

'I'm sorry, Mama—Your Majesty— I am the Prince Royal of Tamra and you can't stop me.'

ONE ALUME LATER
Hunting Lodge, Southern Wilderness

Chapter Fifty-Eight: Surprise Arrival

Dinnis

Dinnis leant back against a tree and suppressed a yawn. The young blades had been testing their mettle on the dirt practice yard at the back of the Hunting Lodge for most of the morning. All around them, birds chorused their enjoyment of the recent rain and the rustles of wildlife overlaid the neighs and nickers in the stables and the yelps of the dogs.

It was tempting to slip away and collect some elusive herbs that would fetch a good price in the city. The trouble was that Mannok had been in a foul mood ever since the Kapok left with Ista and he was hyper-vigilant since arriving at the Hunting Lodge. Choosing a lodge so close to the Silisean border had to be more than a coincidence. The Prince could be planning some wild scheme or other, though so far, he'd stayed within Tamrin domains.

A roar of approval cut into his thoughts. Dinnis looked up to see Uson slam Durrin down and pin him to the ground. Now that both lads were close to full-grown, the three-year age gap was not apparent. They were both of similar bulk and build. Uson had a self-serving killer instinct which Durrin son of Durak, Markan of the South March, lacked. Both were bullies and best avoided.

Uson lifted his clenched fist in triumph, a smug smirk on his face as the other blades congratulated him.

Estolik stepped forward and helped Durrin up. 'See if you can defeat Mannok, orphan boy,' he yelled.

The other lads began to thump their chests one handed, chanting.

'Uson. Uson. Mannok, Mannok, Mannok.'

The Prince did not need much persuasion. He had taken the situation with Ista very hard indeed. They had that in common. It was surprising how much Dinnis missed his sister, even though they'd not had much to do with each other over the years. He hoped she would make a good life for herself in Silisea. He shook his head. He didn't think Rokkan had told Mannok about their blood connection. There was no spark of recognition in the Prince's moody green eyes. Any closeness that had developed after the Trial of Tears had long dissipated. No, the only family he had in Tarka was Anna's.

A loud cheer erupted. Mannok was pulling off his tunic. The Prince strapped his wrists, slipped off his boots and faced off with the grinning Uson. They were of similar heights, Mannok a hand taller. Uson was stronger. Mannok had agility, skill and a flawless instinct. The two lads circled and feinted, testing each other. Normally, the Prince would hold himself back a little to give the other lads some face before going for victory. Today, he made the first move, his jade eyes narrowed and deadly. The bout was likely to be short with Mannok in this mood.

Dinnis turned his head at a faint thudidty-thud and jingle of metal of approaching riders competed with the hoots of derision, the yells of encouragement.

Mannok sidestepped Uson's lunge and put him off balance with a swift countermove. The hoof beats were getting louder, a couple of horses approaching at a steady pace from the south, but not in the direction of the path where the two age-mates on guard duty would be standing. Could this be another attack on the Prince?

Dinnis signalled Garvin and then Waren, but both were engrossed in the combat. No one noticed him and it was hard to be heard over the shouting. Mannok had Uson off balance and backed in a corner. The Prince moved in for the finishing move when a large horse emerged into the clearing in front of him.

Dinnis blinked, not sure he was seeing right. Plume's dapple-grey coat gleamed in the sunshine, the Kapok sitting at ease in his saddle. The Prince stood stock still, gaze riveted to his father, while the yells of their age-mates dwindled to a stunned silence. Uson, his back to the new arrivals, barrelled into Mannok, slammed him into the ground and wedged his knee on his neck, whooping in triumph.

'You are to be congratulated, Uson son of Yanak on your prowess,' Rokkan Kapok's amused bass voice sliced into hazy afternoon air. 'You may have killed your opponent on the battlefield, but your lack of peripheral awareness has earned you a spear in the back.'

The Head Groom, Wasuk rode up behind the Kapok on a red roan, the royal dogs weaving around the horses. There was no sign of the warriors, officials and servants that would normally ride with the Kapok.

Uson jumped up and spun around, his eyes as wide as an owl's. 'Your ... Your Majesty,' he spluttered and fell to his knees.

Mannok dusted himself off and sank on his knees before his father. Dinnis and the circle of astounded lads did the same.

Rokkan motioned them up. Dressed with a casual lack of ostentation more suited to the minor nobility or a moderately successful merchant or artisan, he was as unperturbed as though he had just turned up in his own stables after an afternoon ride.

'Papa ...Your Majesty, where is the rest of your party?' Mannok's look of astonishment transformed into a scowl.

'Oh, I sent them on to Tarka. I thought I might just collect you on the way home. We don't want to be late for your Birthday Banquet, do we? You know how upset your mother gets about these things.'

Dinnis bit his lip to stop the insane urge to laugh. Four alume and here he was, larger than life and as cool as a glacial stream.

Mannok edged closer to his father. 'Mama is already past furious at you for disappearing,' Mannok hissed in an irate whisper. 'And you can't travel about the countryside unprotected. You are the Kapok, someone might want to kill you.'

'Really? I can't imagine why? Still, I doubt anyone else knows where I am as we took a little-known route. If we are all packed and ready to go in the morning, I'm sure I'll survive. Especially with a troop of sturdy young warriors to protect me.'

He swung down from his horse, patted his favourite dog Ruse on the head and smiled.

'Please, don't let me interrupt your play.'

'Of course, to an old man wrestling must seem like playing,' Mannok shot back and then seemed appalled at what he had just said.

The Kapok's eyes narrowed. 'Old man, huh? I think I might remember a few moves from the distant past.' Then he grinned. 'I'll give best pick on the next shipment of Silisean horses to the first lad that can defeat me. I've picked out some beauties while enjoying Queen Suza's hospitality.'

It took a moment for the Kapok's offer to sink in, but soon about half the lads were lining up to have a go at what they thought might be an easy task. Dinnis grinned. He was glad now he hadn't snuck off and missed the morning's entertainment. He wasn't surprised to see that Rokkan was an accomplished wrestler. Although he had that reputation it was always hard to know the real abilities of royalty since it was generally considered impolite to best them too often or too well, a point Uson didn't seem to have learned.

Rokkan's style was unique and deadly. He was taller than everyone else except Dinnis, which could be a disadvantage in wrestling, but he also had broad shoulders and a muscular build. Nimble on his feet, he seemed familiar with all the Tamrin wrestling moves. When his strength did not suffice, he often surprised his opponent with unexpected moves that Dinnis recognised as Nolmec wrestling techniques.

After Rokkan had defeated three of the lads in quick succession, Dinnis knew that he could defeat all who challenged him, even Mannok; that is if he was fit enough and didn't exhaust his strength. For a man in his early forties he was in superb condition, but Dinnis was sure the Kapok would feel this day's activities tomorrow morning.

However this contest turned out, Dinnis was going to enjoy watching it.

Chapter Fifty-Nine: Ants' Nest

Mannok

Mannok frowned as he watched his father pin Uson down in under three minutes. So far, Uson had lasted the longest. His hands sweated. He was confident that he was the best wrestler among his age-mates but could he defeat Papa? It was galling to think that Papa was good at everything he tried his hand at. No matter what he did, Papa did it better and then some.

He wanted the satisfaction of pushing Papa into the dirt. He had expected Mama to oppose his choice of marriage partner, but the Kapok's high-handed approach of riding off with Ista without a word to anyone was infuriating. And now, after a handful of brief messages, Papa had turned up to escort Mannok back to Tarka. Apart from being galling, it was incredibly bad timing. Mannok had almost steeled himself to take a couple of his trusted age-mates with him on a mission. Garvin, Hasuk, Dinnis and possibly Waren. No, Waren was a stickler for rules. Mannok sighed. Maybe three companions would have been sufficient. Now his half-formed plans were shattered.

'Anyone else?'

Papa stood poised on his toes, breathing a little faster but not yet winded. He had stripped his tunic and boots like the lads and his torso was well muscled though criss-crossed with ugly battle scars both front and back. Mannok could see the jagged scar where Naetok had twisted in his blade.

'No one?'

'I will.' Mannok stepped out into the centre of the ring and crouched.

Papa was fast and he had the greater reach and strength. His best strategy would be to tire him out so he kept up a flurry of feints and withdrawals. He could see his opponent tiring, but it was not enough. Mannok used his greater agility to escape a couple of grapples and almost managed to take the bigger man down with a two-leg dive when with sudden explosive power, Papa disengaged then grabbed one ankle and arm and lifted him completely off the ground. Seconds later, he had Mannok pinned on his back. Defeated a second time that morning, but at least he had lasted longer than Uson.

He pushed down his frustration and, jumping up, he met his father's eyes. He bowed with as much grace as he could muster. Papa clasped him on the back, squeezed his shoulder affectionately and then grinned.

'Best effort yet,' he said. 'You almost had me. You are right. I must be getting old.'

'Not that I noticed,' Mannok said.

Whatever his differences with Papa, he had to admire him. Now he was here, it was harder to maintain his rage against him. Maybe he could still change his father's mind, show him that he wasn't about to forget Ista.

Papa released him and looked around the ring of subdued young men, his right eyebrow raised.

'So ... is that it? No one?'

Mannok walked back towards Garvin, stretching his sore limbs.

'How about Dinnis?' Estolik called out and grinned.

'Yes, that's a great idea,' Uson yelled and dissolved into derisive laughter.

Sniggers and smirks flashed around the circle. Hasuk began to chant, 'Dinnis, Dinnis.' Others took it up.

Mannok turned and saw his father frown. He glanced over to where Dinnis was standing, his face impassive. His taciturn age-mate had never shown much enthusiasm for wrestling.

'No one need fight unless they want to.' Papa stretched and signalled to Wasuk to bring him his tunic.

'I'll fight,' Dinnis said, surprising them all. He gave a crooked grin, 'Maybe I feel lucky today.'

Uson sniggered. 'You will need more than luck.'

Mannok bent to grab the drying cloth next to Garvin and watched Dinnis pull his tunic off. Though it was harder to see on his blue skin, the scarring on his back and upper arms was worse in many ways than Papa's. He remembered how shocked he had been when he had first noticed it, not long after Dinnis had arrived in the Palace.

'The price of annoying Akrad,' he had said with a shrug. He refused to say more.

Expecting the contest to be over before it even started, Mannok pulled on his tunic and boots and then went to grab a drink from the well. As he sauntered back towards the ring, he realised that that everyone was still there, their eyes trained on the two men grappling in the centre. The silence was eerie.

They were well matched in height, but Dinnis did not have the broad shoulders and muscled physique of the Kapok. Yet he was still on his feet. Every attack Papa made, Dinnis avoided as if he anticipated each move, even some of the more unconventional ones that had confused the others.

Papa was still smiling, but he was covered in a fine sheen of sweat and beginning to work for air. Dinnis had the advantage of being fresh. With unexpected speed, he lunged for Papa's ankle and began to pull up his leg, but Papa sprawled over him, pushing him down with his body weight. Dinnis pulled back. They circled each other again, testing each other's defences and attempting to gain control.

Once again Dinnis lunged forward, this time sweeping around Papa's left side. Kneeling, he grabbed behind Papa's left and then right knee, pulling his feet up and tipping him into the ground. In an instance, he was on the bigger man, trying to convert the pin, but Papa swung to the side, pushed up, rolled pulling Dinnis with him. Now on top, he leant back pinning the slighter man to the ground. Dinnis had lost the contest, but none of the other lads had come so close to besting the Kapok. The astonishment was thick in the air.

Papa helped his opponent up and bowed.

'You fought well.'

'Not well enough,' Dinnis said with a half-smile after returning the bow. He was sweating and breathing fast after the punishing round.

'Even so, you lasted seven minutes. Considering how many

training practices you miss that's impressive. I think as the contender that lasted the longest, you get first choice of the horses.'

'Thank you, Your Majesty, I'll pick something nice and docile.' Dinnis bowed and turned to leave the circle of packed earth.

Uson stepped forward. 'But Your Majesty, he had an unfair advantage. You were tired after so many other bouts, while this was his first bout for the day. Perhaps, Dinnis should compete against the runners up, Prince Mannok and me, to determine the true winner. A good horse is wasted on him.'

'Count me out, I'm happy to concede to Dinnis,' Mannok said at once.

He couldn't believe Uson's gall. Papa too was frowning.

Uson grinned, not taking the hint. He turned to Dinnis and raised his eyebrows. 'Are you up to it? I'll promise not to break any bones this time.'

Dinnis shrugged. 'Why not? I'm sure you will get the reward you deserve.'

The two age-mates squared off and began manoeuvring for position. Uson was shorter and stronger. Dinnis started defensively, giving ground to Uson consistently until he was almost backed against the far side of the ground, hemmed in by the trees of the surrounding forest. The style of play seemed so different from just minutes before that Mannok began to wonder what Dinnis was playing at. Was he exhausted or did he fear Uson's strength and aggression?

Dinnis took another step back and Uson lunged in low to grab both his legs but at the last minute, his opponent sidestepped, and he sprawled into the bushes at the tree line. Instead of jumping up and closing in on Dinnis, Uson began to thrash and scream. For the third time that morning, his age-mates stood gaping in astonishment.

Dinnis had stood back in a low crouch facing Uson's direction but, as the lad continued to thrash about, his screams intensified. Dinnis straightened up. With a short sigh, he stepped forward and grabbed Uson and dragged him into the clearing and began to pat him down. Large, vicious ants had covered the fellow and were leaving red welts all over his skin. Warrior ants. Horror thrilled through Mannok.

'Get them off me, get them off me,' Uson moaned.

'He's fallen into a nest of warrior ants,' Mannok yelled.

The lad was covered in them. Grabbing the drying cloth Mannok wrapped it around his hands and arms and joined Dinnis to brush the ants off the writhing lad's body. Others stepped in to help, but not before Dinnis and Mannok were extensively bitten. Every part of Uson's exposed body was crowded with bites, and he could barely open his eyes.

'Best get him back to the Lodge,' Papa said. His face was grim and he studied Dinnis with narrowed eyes. 'Do you have a medic with you, Mannok?'

'Fulik came with us. I will find him.' Waren rushed back toward the lodge.

They carried Uson into the common room, where he continued to writhe and moan with pain. Mannok could sympathise as the twenty or so bites on his own arms and chest were excruciating. Dinnis' arms, chest and even face were covered with them though he seemed oblivious to their fiery sting.

'Wet some cloth and lay it on the bites, that should ease the pain a little,' Dinnis said. 'Maybe Fulik has keka leaf. It's a powerful pain killer.' He grabbed his shirt and soaked it in water and laid it gently on the thrashing lad.

Uson slapped and snarled at him, landing a couple of hard blows on Dinnis arms and face. 'You did this on purpose, you little sneak. You couldn't defeat me fairly if you tried. You don't deserve the prize.'

Dinnis caught his flailing hands and held them securely.

'Peace, Son of Yanak. I'm willing to concede the contest. I'm sure you would value the prize more than I would anyway, but if you keep thrashing around like this you will only increase the pain. Let me put this cloth on you, it will help a little till better aid arrives.'

'Filthy bluey,' Uson spat back. 'Don't think your soft talking fools me.'

Nevertheless, he allowed Dinnis to apply the wet cloth, his moaning decreasing a fraction in volume.

Mannok watched Dinnis as his age-mate did his best to soothe the other lad's bites and then, once Fulik arrived, hovered behind the medic, watching and carrying out his instructions almost before he uttered them. Even though Mannok had lived in close quarters with the fellow for over nine years, he realized he didn't really know him. He was such a mixture of contradictions and enigmas. Had he manoeuvred Uson into falling into a warrior ant's nest in revenge for the ridicule and rough treatment that lout had heaped on him over the years?

After a while the keka leaf paste worked its magic. Uson's complaints and groans subsided and he drifted off to sleep. Fulik then turned and administered to Mannok's bites. When he insisted that Dinnis be tended to next, his age mate had deferred to Mannok's royal status. Fulik spread a green paste on the inflamed and gave him some keka leaf to chew. The medic turned to minister Dinnis, and Mannok jumped when Papa's hand thumped down on his shoulder.

'We need to talk, Mannu. Come, walk with me.'

Chapter Sixty: I Hate You

Mannok

Mannok followed his father out of the hunting lodge into the surrounding woods. They walked without talking. Tracer, Lead and the other dogs ran between them, licking their hands in happy excitement. When they reached a clearing with a few rotten old stumps in the centre Papa stopped and faced him.

'What has your mother told you, Mannok?'

'That you were against Ista and I marrying,' he said, being careful to keep the resentment out of his voice.

Papa raised both his eyebrows and exhaled.

'Is that all? Did she explain why?' He paused. 'No. I don't suppose she did.'

Papa took a step back and sat down on one of the old stumps, stretching his long legs out in front of him. The dogs circled and then settled down about him.

So, he was against their marriage. It wasn't just Mama's spin on it. Mannok pushed down the flare of anger and met his father's gaze straight on.

'Papa, I know Ista isn't a typical choice, but if you would listen. She ...'

His father held up a hand.

'Enough, Mannok. I know what you will say and to be honest I don't disagree. Ista may appear to be a fatherless orphan without a dowry, but she is an intelligent, capable, well-educated young woman. She has poise and beauty. She has ambition—maybe a bit too much for my comfort—and the capacity to be ruthless, but I must admit that I've noticed over the years you have the ability to bring out her better feelings. Noted it and been pleased by it.' He sighed. 'She has many of the qualities one might seek in a princess or indeed a Kupanna.'

'Then why do you object? Is it because she is a child of Akrad?'

'Great-granddaughter to be precise. But no, it is not because of that, or not directly so, for we have the same heritage. I need to tell you something.' He studied his hands, looked up and met Mannok's gaze. 'When I was not much older than you, my father sent me to spy on Akrad and his Nolmec friends.'

'Papa, I hardly see the relevance of ancient history—'

'Let me finish Mannok!'

'You haven't even let me get started ...' Mannok muttered but perched on one of the other stumps. If he listened, then maybe Papa would listen to him.

'I was able to gain access, because it suited Akrad's purposes to cultivate me and perhaps turn me against my father. I used that willingness to get the information we needed. Though I did not realise it at the time, I met Akrad's granddaughter, Kiprissa Gaia. We became fast friends. More than friends. Not unlike you and Ista, we decided to defy our parents' expectations and get married.'

Mannok wasn't sure he was hearing right. He knew Papa had been sent to check out the Nolmec. This was the first he'd heard of a Nolmec princess. 'But ... Was this before you married Mama? But that doesn't make sense.'

'It's not generally known. In fact, if we count you, there are maybe six people in the whole realm who are aware of it. My father wasn't one of them.'

'You married secretly.'

'Indeed. I had hoped to persuade him, but the snows of Mount Pele would melt before Papa would have agreed to any offspring of his marrying a child under Akrad's tutelage. He would have seen me dead first.'

Mannok was four when Martal Kapok died, just before Naetok's assassination attempt on Papa. He'd vague memories of a gruff, taciturn, but not unkind man. 'Perhaps he would have come around in time.'

Papa looked doubtful. 'Maybe. I'll never know.'

'Are you telling me this as some sort of object lesson? You can't be recommending that Ista and I marry in secret.'

Papa bent down and rubbed Ruse's ears. The old dog thumped her tail on the leaf litter and let out a long-drawn sigh of contentment. Lead sleepily opened his eyes and whined softly. 'I am explaining my objection, but I see I must spell it out to you.'

As Papa's golden eyes met his, the full implications of his words hit Mannok like a war club. The tips of his fingers began to tingle and a chill ran down his spine. He could see as clearly as he did that day, the image of Ista perched behind his father as he rode into the Palace courtyard fresh from the Battle of North Pass; the battle that had defeated Akrad. He could see the shock on his mother's face when she has first seen Ista in the garden afterwards. His father's words reverberated in his head 'I met Akrad's granddaughter ... more than friends ... married.'

'How many children did Akrad have?' Mannok pushed the words out through numb lips.

'Three daughters through our ancestress Sil, all dead long ago, and Zowee, Kiprissa of the Nolmec, and mother of Gaia.' Papa crossed his arms across his chest but did not break his steady gaze. 'My wife.'

'Ista's mother,' Mannok whispered, appalled. 'You are Ista's father?'

'Yes, I'm Ista's father and also Di -'

Mannok caught his breath. His heart smashed against his ribs. Papa had lied to him, to Ista. 'How could you? How could you not tell me that Ista was my sister? That I had a sister?'

'Your mother ...'

'And you allowed your own daughter be treated like a common servant? Do you know how miserable she was? You should have acknowledged her. Then, then we wouldn't have ...' his fist clenched against the nausea, the betrayal.

'If I had, your position would be compromised because Din ...'

'That's rubbish. How would having a sister compromise my position? Do you think I'm stupid?'

'No Mannok, I don't. If you would just stop yelling at me and let me explain. You also have ...'

'It's too late for explanations don't you think? I trusted you. I can't believe it. All those long lectures about acting in a 'princely manner' and 'living up to my position', yet you married against your father's will and weren't man enough to acknowledge your own daughter?'

Papa's eyes narrowed, a pulse beating in his temple. 'Long lectures? You have no idea ...'

'To think I used to admire you; that I wanted to be like you. My oh-so-perfect father. Good at everything. But you're not, are you? You're a sham.'

He took a step forward. Breaker and Lead lifted their heads and growled in their throats.

'You are upset, Mannok, I understand that. Perhaps one day when you have a son ...'

'I know I'll do a whole better job of being a father and a husband than you have done. You are a terrible father; do you know that?'

The muscles on Papa's neck corded. 'Then I pray you don't have an impetuous, empty-headed fool for a son like I have.'

The words slammed into him like a rockslide. They glowered at each other, both beyond speaking.

In the distance, he could hear the carefree shouts and thumps of his age-mates playing hoop ball and the closer tap, tap of a woodpecker. Papa dropped his eyes but not before Mannok thought he glimpsed the sheen of unshed tears. His father stood up.

'I'm sorry, Mannu, I didn't mean to say that.'

'But it's that what you think? Isn't it?'

'No, no, I think ...'

'Well, I hate you. I hate you. I wish you weren't my father. I wish you were dead. I—I could kill you.'

The words were out before he could stop them. But he didn't care. He meant them. All that he knew about his father now seemed mere smoke and haze, a mirage to deceive a weary traveller in the desert. He felt hollow and full of molten anger at the same time. So, angry that he didn't regret his words.

Lead barked, the other dogs sat up all on alert.

His father looked at Mannok, eyes narrowed, thin-lipped, his nostrils flaring. His balled his hands into fists. When he spoke, his voice was soft and clipped.

'You too, huh? Seems a common sentiment among my children. But Prince Mannok, whatever you may think of me as a father, I

336

would remind you that I am your Kapok. I advise you to keep your treasonous sentiments to yourself.'

He turned and stalked away with the dogs at his heels, leaving Mannok alone in the shadows that were beginning to stretch across the desolate glade.

The next day, they packed up and headed back to Tarka, nothing resolved.

ONE ALUME LATER
Tarka

Chapter Sixty-One: Questioned

Dinnis

Dinnis whistled tunelessly as he strode through the Great Hall. Sunlight and shadows filtered through the high skylights onto the mosaic floor as the early morning rain clouds tussled with a clearing wind. The place seemed empty after the recent crowds. Following the festivities of the Birthday Banquet and the Rain Festival, most of the nobles' families, including age-mates like Waren, Yalik, Estolik and Durrin, returned to their clan lands for the wet season, leaving just the perennials behind, Uson, Hasuk, Asik, Garvin and himself. The Prince remained moody and volatile. He had lost interest in afternoon practices and went on long horse rides with Garvin or, as often as not, on his own.

Dinnis pulled a sunfruit from a fold in his tunic, he bit into the sweet fruit. There was no reason he should be concerned. The situation gave him time to pursue his studies with Laetil and spend time with Anna, Tilli and the others. Uson kept his distance following his painful ant-bites. The Kupanna seemed too distracted to worry about him. He missed Ista but, after all, she had barely spoken to him over the last few years. The Kapok's arbitrary ways still rankled, though the man had treated his sister well enough.

Dinnis popped the rest of the juicy fruit into his mouth and licked his fingers before striding towards the stairs leading to the upper levels of the Library Atrium. He could get some work down for Ralton this morning before sharing the midday meal at Anna's Herbal Shop. He was keen to escape the Palace for a few hours. An icy formality had settled over the place since their return from the Hunting Lodge and Dinnis couldn't shake a sense of foreboding.

* * *

'Dinnis, do you have a moment?'

His hand jerked, splattering ink across the drawing the parts and usages of maika plant. 'Slide it.'

He'd been so engrossed in and so used to being left alone while in the library, he hadn't noted the sound of boots on the polished stone floor. He looked up into Lutan Jakan's leaf-green eyes, eyes that were unusually serious. Was one of the man's young children ill?

'*Kuree*?' The old Nolmec word slipped out without thinking.

'On your feet, lad, when you address an officer.'

Dinnis blinked, puzzled at the level of formality in the older man's voice. Not a sick child then. As he jumped to his feet. Had he done anything wrong or rather where had he been caught out? At least it wasn't Sparak or Lukarn glowering at him with barely buried homicidal hostility.

'Sir?'

'Report to the Northern Audience Room at once.'

The old throne room, before the newer far grander one was built by Tellek Kapok, and one that Rokkan often used to receive petitioners from among the common folk and minor nobility. Dinnis picked up his book and followed Jakan along the book stacks to a side entrance of the library. He would normally have let the ink dry, but the drawing was already ruined.

Dinnis moistened his lips. 'Why am I needed?'

Jakan heaved out a sigh. 'For once in your life, could you follow orders without endless questions and obstruction?' He beckoned two guards waiting outside the entrance. 'Escort the lad to the Kapok.'

Dinnis swallowed hard and his whole body prickled with alarm. This was no ordinary errand. Surely if there were to be retribution following Ista's entanglement with Mannok or for his prank against Uson, it would have happened already. Assuming a nonchalance he didn't feel, he sauntered along the corridor to the Audience Room.

'Oh, Dinnis.' Jakan called at the entrance of the library. 'Just tell the truth, lad, and you'll be fine.'

* * *

The scrawny scribe stood with his stylus inked and hovering over the large codex open on the podium in front of him. Dinnis recognised him as one of Ralton's picks, a lad from one of the larger villages in the Tarkan Valley who'd shown promise while serving his annual levy at the Palace. Rokkan sat in the great carved chair on a small podium at the end of the room, crunching down on chillied castana nuts, his golden eyes hooded and brooding.

Dinnis clamped his teeth shut and waited. Was Rokkan trying to unnerve him? Well, he was succeeding. In all the time since that first interview in his office, his father had spoken maybe a half-ten words to him. It was as if Rokkan's eyes slid past him, as though Dinnis didn't exist, as though he was an unseen ghost or a fading memory. And Dinnis had done his best to keep it that way, to be invisible. A chill settled in his stomach. Except half an alume ago at the Southern Hunting Lodge. Had he stirred up more than one anthill with his pride? He rubbed his sweaty palms against his breeches.

Moments slid by like snow-chilled honey. Rokkan Kapok straightened. He turned to the scribe. 'Take a break, Mattik.'

The scribe eyes popped open. 'Your ... Your Majesty.'

Rokkan flicked his fingers. 'You heard me.' He turned to the guards. 'Wait outside and close the door. I wish to speak to this suspect in private.'

The guards, stirred and gaped, hands tightening on the shaft of their spears. Rokkan arched an eyebrow. In a rush Mattik left the room, the guards clumping behind and pulling the large doors shut with a boom.

This was it. He was going to be sent away, maybe sent to work in the mines or thrown the dungeons or given to the Nolmec now Ista was in Silisea. He had done nothing to threaten the Throne— except to almost beat his father in a wrestling match. His stomach hollowed out. *Moros*, all these years of cultivating a harmless image, turned to ash in a moment of madness. And after all those' fantasies about escape, it hit him that he didn't want to leave. What he'd said to Ista was true. His life, his home was here—with Anna, with Jakan, with grouchy Ralton, even with Mannok. Was it all going to be snatched away from him?

Rokkan leaned forward, placing his hands on his thighs. 'Do you know why you are here?'

Dinnis met his father's gaze defiantly. 'Yes, you brought me here after the battle of North Pass.' Slide it, maybe he should try some diplomacy.

'Son of Gaia, you know what I mean.'

A heart-beat. Breathe in, breathe out. 'No, I don't know why I'm here.'

'You are aware that items of value have been taken from the Palace and sold by a disreputable trader?'

'What?' Dinnis shook his head, disorientated. Was this about when the Mannok had been attacked the alleyway. That was old history. Why question him now? And why personally, when Jakan or even Lukarn would have done?

'Answer the question.'

'The Prince made that claim before ... some time ago, the day he was attacked by some local louts, but I didn't see any evidence of it. And since nothing further has been said, I thought nothing more of it.'

'The matter has only come to my attention since I returned from Silisea.'

What was he to say to that? It wasn't surprising that Mannok failed to mention that escapade to his father or Jakan. Rokkan had left with Ista the very afternoon of the attack. It must be an ongoing issue for Rokkan to pursue it now, but it seemed a lot of fuss over a bit of furniture.

'But you did report to Kaptan Jakan that you recognised the leader of the gang that attacked the Prince.' The Kapok's eyes bored into him. 'On the actual day of the attack.'

'Yes.' Dinnis swallowed. 'A young thug named Toban. I thought that Jakan should know ...'

'And how is it that you know this Toban?'

Dinnis clamped his mouth shut. He knew Toban because he lived in the same street as Tilli. In fact, he knew lots of the common folk because he'd treated them while working for Laetil or Anna, but he couldn't tell Rokkan that without giving away way too many secrets. If his father found out, would he be forced to give up his plans? Would that be enough for him to lose his freedom or even his life?

Rokkan stood up. 'This Toban, son of Rupak. He is Junok's nephew, but still not the sort with palace connection. But, somehow, he has had access to palace goods. Can you explain that, Dinnis?'

'No, sir. I can't.' Dinnis resisted the urge to lower his gaze. 'Why are a few sticks of furniture important?'

'Not just a few and we think it's a cover for a more serious operation. You don't deny that you are rather adept at creative ways to acquire metal; running errands for Jakan or Head Cook or doing some scribe work for Ralton when you are supposed to be serving your Prince?'

'Serving my Prince,' Dinnis' mouth twisted. His younger and privileged half-brother. 'Yes, well, I do know how to make myself useful, but I'm not a thief,' he glared at his father, 'like some people.'

'Is this where you start yelling at me?'

'No, it's hardly worth the effort.' Nine years he'd restrained his anger, worked as best he could to fit in and now this? To be accused of stealing furniture and consorting with the likes of Toban!

'So, what did Haka have to say to you? Do you commune with him often?'

Did Rokkan mean that day on the archery range after the feast of New Beginnings? 'I told him to get lost,' Dinnis spat through clenched teeth. 'He's as big a criminal as you are. You are all the same, hungry for power with no concern for the common people.'

Rokkan's eyes flickered. He paced the length of the room, turned to face Dinnis, his voice as cold and brittle as ice. 'So now we get to the real Dinnis. You hide your feelings and thoughts better than anyone I know. And Lukarn is right, you're devious as Naetok—or Akrad. Presenting a smooth exterior while all the time plotting against your betters—whether it's opening a postern gate or dumping an age-mate in a nest of warrior ants.'

Feelings that Dinnis thought he'd buried long ago welled up inside him. All the bulwarks he'd built, fluttering away like dead leaves before the wind. It was happening all over again. Bile seared his throat.

'And then there was the sabotage of the bridge at Eagles Rest. Each one of these things is nothing by themselves but added together, they present a damming picture, don't you think?'

Dinnis shoved his hand deep into the fold of his tunic and felt something hard—

The Kapok took a step back, his eyes narrowed, watchful.

—the token Rokkan had given him a long time ago. And with it a feather. He pulled them out and rolled them around with his fingers. What had Rasel meant? About taking a different path. About hope and seeds of love. Perhaps it didn't matter that others thought so little of him. What mattered was the choices he made, the person he wanted to be.

He looked up, meeting the distrustful eyes of his father and folded his arms across his chest. 'I guess it is, when you list it like that.' He took a deep breath. 'And no doubt you won't believe me. I … I admit the anthill was a mistake and that Mannok can be annoying …'

Rokkan's eyebrows shot up.

'… and that is nothing to the anger I've felt against you.'

'You admit to seditious thoughts?'

'Thoughts, yes.' He blinked, took a deep breath. 'It didn't matter, never mattered what Akrad said. I loved you, I believed in you. I would have followed you anywhere, but that meant nothing, less than nothing to you. So yes, I hated you.'

'And you admit— '

'No. I know nothing about this furniture. Toban is no friend of mine, and I'm not aware of any contact he might have within the Palace. I did not sabotage the bridge. I haven't any plans of assassinating either the Prince or … you.' He could have added that he'd saved Mannok's life at least once, but he didn't. Instead, he executed a perfect bow. 'I am a loyal subject and yours to command, Your Majesty. Perhaps, no more than that a minor piece risked and sacrificed for greater ends, but no less than that either.'

Dinnis could hear his heart hammering against his chest, his breath pulling in and out of his lungs. He could feel his father's eyes on his, his strong mind probing against his defences. He wouldn't let him in, he couldn't, but he wished he lived in a world where that was possible, where Rokkan was his Papa again and not his Kapok. But whatever happened, he would not be bent by the choices of others.

He couldn't stand the silence anymore. 'So, are you going to arrest me? Lukarn will be pleased.'

Rokkan stood very still, not a muscle moving, his face remote and eyes looking to a point above Dinnis' shoulder. He stirred, a shadow passing across his face. 'Not at this time. I have a few more people to interview.' He cleared his throat. 'Just stay in the Palace grounds until you are needed.'

346

Then he was still a suspect. A shiver ran through Dinnis. 'I have a meeting with— '

'Then best to rearrange it. You are dismissed.'

'Your Majesty.'

Dinnis backed out of the audience chamber. Clamping his teeth against the rage roiling inside of him. He returned to the library, but as much as he tried, he couldn't focus. He kept blotting the paper and having to start again. It was midday, he'd been up early this morning and his stomach was rumbling. Packing up his equipment, he headed towards the Palace kitchens.

A team of cooks and assistants were in a flurry preparing the midday meal due to the unexpected arrival of the Lord Lukarn. Dinnis nodded at the Head Cook, grabbed a round of maize bread from a heaped-up tray and a piece of roasted duck from another dish. He wandered toward the herb garden, then pulled up at a troubling sight.

A tray stood unattended on one of the long tables. The finest maizebread, roast duck, yarma cheese, greens and a bowl of blueberries lay beautifully presented on a cloth woven in gold thread with the royal emblem, a prowling jaguar. A goblet of guava juice stood uncovered. The Kapok's favourite cup reputed to have been in the royal family for generations. Anyone could slip poison into the food or drink.

A few heart beats later, a serving man pushed past Dinnis, picked up the tray and walked out of the busy room.

Chapter Sixty-Two: Breathstill

Dinnis

Dinnis raced up the stairs and past the startled guards at the door.

'State your business. Stop!' they cried, running after him.

'I need to save him,' Dinnis yelled. 'This is important. Don't drink the juice.'

Rokkan Kapok sat in the end of the sundrenched room, a golden cup to his lips. He gulped, half-choking on the mouthful of guava juice, a startled look on his face. Bitjarnan stood beside him, mouth hanging open and eyes round as dishes.

'What is this?' Rokkan demanded, lurching from his seat.

'Don't drink it,' Dinnis panted, knowing it was too late. He struck the goblet from his father's hand and, unable to slow down, collided into him.

The cup clattered against the mosaic floor, spilling its contents in a crimson arc.

Dinnis could smell the juice on his father's breath. Rokkan's movements slowed, becoming jerky and tight. His legs stiffened, his eyes bulged. Hands outstretched to grab Dinnis, he staggered backward and collapsed to the ground, taking the chair with him.

'What are you doing?' the Madomo yelled. 'Grab the traitor.'

Rokkan tried to speak, but only garbled nonsense came through stiff lips. His flesh set to stone like frost expanding on the surface of a pond.

Breathstill, it had to be. Dinnis dropped to his knees. If he could make his father vomit to void the rest of the poison and get Akrad's remedy from his satchel in time, he could save him.

Rough hands grabbed him, reefed him up. 'Got you, you blue dog.' The guard Lantil growled in his ear. The other guard took his other arm, blunt fingernails digging into his skin.

'Let me go. You don't understand. I can save him.'

Bitjarnan knelt beside the Kapok's stiffening form, his face slack with shock. His pudgy hands fluttered over his chest, his face. 'He's not breathing.' He looked up, horror in his faded brown eyes. 'He's dead.'

'No, not yet, let me save him.' Dinnis pulled against the hands clamping on to his arms. His heart hammered with the hollow beat of funeral drums. Who had done this?

Bitjarnan's face contorted. 'Traitor. You will die for this. Get him out of my sight.'

The guards hesitated, then dragged him off to an alcove while Bitjarnan pulled the Kapok onto his back, the worst position, and tidied his clothes.

'He's not dead. He need's medical help. I can save him.' Dinnis panted and pulled against the strength of his captors.

Bitjarnan pushed himself upright. He strode towards the alcove, rage masking his normally mild features. 'You mock us.' He spun around to a guard. 'I told you to keep him quiet.'

A meaty hand clamped over Dinnis' mouth. Tears started in his eyes, blurring his vision.

Slide it, what did it matter that this man who had disowned him, scorned and ignored him would die? Yet a dark grief stole over him like a thief. Whatever his faults, whatever his denials, Rokkan was his father.

A choked noise came from the doorway. Mannok stood staring at the Kapok.

'Your Highness!' Madomo Bitjarnan rushed toward the Prince. 'Your Highness, I'm so sorry. The Kapok is ...' The old Madomo's voice slide upwards. '...He's dead.'

'No,' Mannok glared at the small rotund man. 'You must be mistaken.'

'Your father's not breathing. I...' Sweat beaded Bitjarnan's wrinkled forehead. 'I'm so sorry, Your Majesty—'

'Don't call me that.' Mannok swung to face the Madomo. 'I'm

not…not yet.' He shook his head, his gaze darting around the room. 'What happened?

'He …Your Highness, the Kapok was taking a meal break between petitioners.' Bitjarnan's pudgy hands flapped. 'We were discussing some irregularities in the Palace inventory when Dinnis rushed through the door. Before he could be stopped, he leapt at your royal father and struck him down. Your father fell like a toppled tree. We … I mean the guards grabbed Dinnis …'

The Madomo pointed with his chin at him. Dinnis pulled against the guards, his eyes meeting Mannok's horrified stare. Surely his age-mate would listen, for the sake of his father, their father.

Mannok stiffened, outrage written across his features. 'Guards, is this true? Dinnis attacked my father?'

Lantil, dipped his head. 'Yes, Your Maj … ah, Highness.'

The other guard nodded. 'He said he had something important to tell the Kapok.'

'I …' Bitjarnan glanced at the guards.

Lantil shook his head. 'We couldn't find a weapon, only his hunting knife, but it was still sheathed … and the old battered satchel he always carries.'

Mannok strode across the room, stopping in front of Dinnis. 'I thought you a friend, loyal to the throne. You owe everything to Papa, your life, your home, your position.'

Heat rushed through Dinnis. His face twisted with bitterness. Perhaps, he did owe what he had to the Kapok, even if it fell far short of what he could have expected from his father. *Rakka,* I am trying to save him, you fool,' he shouted, but his words were muffled.

Mannok waved his hand. 'Let him speak.'

'Yes, of course, Your Highness. He wouldn't stop shouting.' Bitjarnan stuttered.

The guard dropped his hand. Dinnis licked his bruised lips. 'Mannok … Your Highness, you must listen, I didn't kill him. …'

Mannok raised his eyebrows, his mouth twisting into a sneer. 'Do you deny the claims of three witnesses?'

'No, but you don't understand …'

'How did you do it? What trick did you use?'

'I didn't… Slide it, Mannu, that's not what's important right now …'

Mannok balled his fist and slammed it into the stone pillar

beside him. Dinnis' heart accelerated. If Mannok would not listen, then no one would.

Bitjarnan tugged at the Prince's cloak. 'Your Highness, shouldn't we ring the alarm ...'

Mannok spun to face the old madomo, nursing his hand. 'No, not yet. 'Fetch my uncle Lukarn and get a physician. And have the guards clear the Great Hall. No one is to enter until we confirm ... that my father is dead and how it was done.' Mannok pushed Bitjarnan towards entrance of the audience room. 'Hurry!'

Dinnis tried again. 'Mannok, please, your father ...'

Mannok swung around. 'Your excuses and lies can wait.' He spat the words. 'Gag and bind him.'

Despair filled Dinnis as the guards gagged him and tied his hands behind his back. It was urgent that he administer the herbal mixture before it was too late. If only Mannok would listen. If ever there was a time to dig up his latent gift it was now, but he couldn't think, couldn't focus through the confusing turmoil of emotions.

Mannok turned his back and dropped to his knees beside the Kapok laid out like a corpse on the stone flagged floor.

It was too late. Dinnis had risked his life for no reason. He hadn't saved his father, he had just condemned himself.

* * *

'He's alive!' The Prince jumped up and spun around, jubilation and terror warring on his face. 'He's breathing. Slide it, where is the physician?' His eyes flicked to the empty doorway then back to Dinnis and the guards.

The weight pushing him down lifted. There was still a chance Rokkan could live, but for how long.

The clatter of boots on stone boomed from the stairs outside the audience room. Moments later the burly figure of Lord Lukarn burst into the room. The Markan's blunt face paled, his breath hissing between his teeth, at the sight of the Kapok stretched out on the floor.

'Mannu, is he ...?'

'He's still alive, Uncle. Dinnis attacked him!'

Lukarn's thick eyebrows contracted into a scowl. He spun around and, in a couple of steps, stood nose to chin with Dinnis.

The blow hit him like a landslide, slamming into his jaw and rocking his head sideways. Pain exploded, taking his breath for a heartbeat. Dinnis swallowed the salty metallic taste of blood. As his head cleared, he realised the gag had slipped. He pulled in a breath of air and shouted.

'You got to listen to me. It's poison. I know the antidote.'

'Taken a trick out of Naetok's quiver, have you?' Lukarn backhanded him across the face, this time with less force. 'I'll make you pay with your last drop of life's blood.'

Dinnis shook his head against the dizziness. He had to persuade these thick-headed Tamrin. 'No, it wasn't me. I have to give him the antidote before it's too late.'

'Ha, do you think we'll give you a chance to finish him off. I always warned Rokkan that you were a danger, a snake. If he'd listened to me ...'

'*Rakka, moros*, idiot. You will kill him with your stupidity.' Dinnis' eyes sought Mannok. 'Your Highness, if you want to save your father, you must let me help you.'

Two sets of hostile eyes stared back at him; one pair of translucent jade, the other, coffee brown. Not even a flicker of mercy in their implacable scrutiny. They were not listening to him any more than the foolish Madomo or the plodding guards had done.

Insulting the Markan and shouting at the Prince were getting him nowhere. Anger would not help him. He closed his eyes and focused on his breathing. A stony calm seeped through him, loosening the tension in his muscles. There must be some way to persuade these Tamrin fools.

Just as he took a breath to speak, three more people clattered into the room. Dinnis recognized the young garrison surgeon, Fulik. He was a good man but would be out of his depths with anything that couldn't be fixed with cautery or yarmagut and needle. Behind him came his young assistant carrying the medical paraphernalia. The third man was obscured by one of the guards.

Prince Mannok's gaze whipped from Dinnis to the newcomer. 'Fulik, quick. You must save him.'

Fulik bowed low and knelt beside the Kapok, examining him while the Prince paced the room like a caged jaguar.

'It could be a heart seizure,' he said eventually. 'I don't think it's a stroke. He is alive but only by a heartbeat. I am sorry, Your Highness, but there isn't much I can do. Bitjarnan send to the

Greyhaven Street for the Royal Physician, but even Master Galan can't help now.'

Mannok gripped the back of his neck. 'The Nolmec said something about poison.'

Oh, great! The injustice of it slammed into Dinnis again. When it came down to it, he would always be an outsider. He was surprised at how much it still hurt. He could have been that forlorn boy standing in the Kapok's study, his whole world ripped apart by the cold, callous words, 'Your father is dead to you.'

Fulik moved to the cup and dipped his little finger into the red contents spilled out onto the floor. He smelt then tasted it with the tip of his tongue. He shook his head.

'I can't detect anything. It could be in the food.'

Moros. 'It is in the drink. The poison has no colour, the juice disguises the taste.' Dinnis strained against the brute strength of the guards. 'It's most likely Breathstill. I have the antidote.'

'And how would a rascal like you know?' Lukarn sneered.

Dinnis quailed. There was brutal murder in the Markan's eyes.

The third man stepped forward, his burly figure and nuggetty face coming into Dinnis' line of sight. He almost scraped the floor with his bow to the young Prince and his uncle. Uson.

'My Lord Lukarn, Your Highness, pardon my interruption, but I saw Dinnis hanging around old Anna's, the herbalist in Crooked Street the other day. And he was in the kitchen while the Kapok's meal was being prepared.'

Dinnis swallowed a groan. Any chance he'd had to convince Mannok and the Markan that he hadn't poisoned the Kapok was now buried under a mountain.

Another explosion of pain, a fist slammed into his face. Blinking his eyes and swallowing blood, he shook his head to clear the ringing in his ears. Mannok's face was only ninas away from his own, accusation swirling in opaque depths of his green eyes.

'Do you deny your guilt now? That you repaid my father's kindness with poison?'

The breath seemed to freeze in Dinnis' chest. He was supposed to be grateful? If only the Prince knew.

But it didn't matter, none of it mattered.

Dinnis closed his eyes a moment, tensed his muscles. 'Fine, whatever. Say I did—'

Markan Lukarn growled. 'You admit it? Before the night is ended you will join whatever foul gods of death you believe in.'

'Yes, okay, I did it.' He might as well admit it. It was the only way to get them to move on. 'I am telling you, I know how to reverse it. It is his only chance to survive.'

'Why should we trust you?' The Prince bunched his hands into fists.

A smirk spread across Uson's face. 'He wants to make sure the Kapok dies.'

Dinnis took a steadying breath against all *morona*. 'Because you have nothing to lose. The Kapok will die if you do nothing. I am giving you the chance to save him.'

Mannok swung to face Fulik. 'There must be some other way ...'

Fulik ran his hands down his tunic, his face grave. 'Any possibility of saving the Kapok seems doubtful.'

A fraught silence descended on the room. Mannok tugged his already mussed up russet hair between two hands, his face contorted.

Lukarn's scowl deepened. 'You can't be thinking of doing it? I'd sooner trust a crocodile.'

Dinnis held his breath. Please, please let him accept the offer. If there was a Maker, he would have been pleading for his influence. The image of the Rasel, white skin gleaming in the starlight, niggled at his memory. She would council hope even when there was none.

The Prince's hands dropped to his side. He took a deep shuddering breath. 'Give him the antidote. But know this—the moment he dies, so do you.' He signalled the guards. 'Release him.'

The older guard whipped out his hunting knife and sawed through the bindings. The last rope curled to the ground. Dinnis staggered forward, his arms flaring to life with needling fire.

'What, not even a mock trial with a foregone conclusion?' he couldn't help saying. He muted the scorn in his eyes and rubbed his hands to bring back the feeling in them. 'Fulik, get me some medicinal wine and a clean cup.'

He knelt beside the corpse-still form of the Kapok. Fulik gave a hesitant nod and signalled for his assistant who fetched the items he had asked for. His hand trembling, Dinnis got some lifeleap herb from the small herb pouch and crumbled it into the wine. Best results required steeping it in hot water but he had no fire and no time. He just had to hope it worked.

Beneath Dinnis' fingers, Rokkan Kapok's heartbeat was less than a whisper. He dribbled a few drops into the Kapok's slack mouth. Once the man stopped breathing that would be the end—for both of them.

Chapter Sixty-Three: Seize Him

Dinnis

Dinnis placed his hand on Rokkan's big chest and felt a steady heartbeat strengthen. The gentle rise and fall of his rib cage more noticeable than before.

Mannok stopped his pacing. 'Is he ...? Is it working?'

'I think it is, Your Highness.'

Fulik, hovering behind Dinnis, moved forward to check the breath from the Kapok's lips and the pulse in his neck. A small hopeful smile twitched at the corners of his mouth. He nodded first to the Prince and then to Dinnis.

The Kapok's frame eased, no longer stiff and still as a statue. It was as if a small flame was sweeping across a sheet of paper. Colour ebbed into Rokkan's waxen face, his chest expanded with growing volume and force. A few moments later his fingers twitched. He opened his eyes, staring at the ceiling.

A collective gasp went around the room. Uson shuffled his feet again. Dinnis turned and tried to engage the lad's dun eyes, but his gaze slide away. He squirmed. Annoying as he was, Uson would have no motive to act against the Kapok. This could not be a case of mistaken identity as had been the case with the thorn under Plume's saddle so long ago. Whoever had placed the poison in the golden cup had meant to kill the ruler of Tamra.

A heavy hand fell on his shoulder. Dinnis met Lukarn's rock-hard brown eyes and tightened his lips.

Lukarn cleared his throat. 'Let's get you were you belong. Guards, take this lad to one of the lower holding cells in the dungeons.'

Dinnis looked toward Mannok, who looked away.

He wasn't surprised. He'd confessed to poisoning the Kapok. Having once made the admission, it was going to be impossible to convince them otherwise. It had done him no good interfering. Yet, instead of fear, he felt a warm glow at saving the Kapok's life.

Lukarn gave him a shake. 'Get a move on, lad. Or the guards to drag you out.'

Uson sniggered. That twerp would love to see Dinnis hauled off to the dungeons. He stood up and took one last look at his father's face. Rokkan stared straight at him. Dinnis shivered. He had forgotten how intense and penetrating the man's gaze could be.

His father's mouth worked. 'Sssst ... staaa.'

'Don't worry, Rokkan. We have things under control here.'

The Kapok moistened his lips. 'Nooo ... Lissss ... en.' His hoarse whisper strengthened as the antidote took hold and reversed the poison. His eyes sought Dinnis again, staring with an unblinking intensity. 'Waaait ... dooon ...go.'

Mannok knelt and put an arm around his father, supporting him. His gaze locked on Dinnis and his eyebrows contracted together. 'You don't want Dinnis to go?' he asked. 'You want to speak to him?'

His father nodded. He closed his eyes.

Lukarn's hand weighed down on Dinnis' shoulder, and the man's breath was hot on the back of his neck. Would Rokkan throw accusations and outrage at his supposed betrayal like Mannok and Lukarn had? Dinnis could feel fate closing in on him.

The sounds of normal palace activity drifted through the open doors. News of the Kapok's dire condition couldn't have spread yet. Bitjarnan must have held his tongue, following the Prince's orders. So how had Uson known? The burly fellow's eyes darted from side to side, his breathing was rapid. He licked his dry lips, his voice nub bobbing up and down as he swallowed. Why was he so nervous? Unless ...

A guard's hurried steps came from the balcony leading to the room, followed by the distinctive gait of the Madomo, some moments before they came through the door.

Bitjarnan cleared his throat. 'Healer Galan will be here soon.' He blinked, wonder seeping across his face. 'Your Majesty, ... it is good to see you conscious.'

The Kapok sat up higher, the colour returning to his face. 'You are … hol … holding the wrong lad,' he said, his voice stronger. 'Lukku … think …'

'I don't understand, Rokkan.'

'Him … seize him.' Rokkan pointed his chin. At first Dinnis thought he was the target, then he realized that the Kapok was pointing to his left and behind him.

Uson gave a strangled cry, then turned on his heels and began to barrel towards the door. Lukarn caught him and held him firm. He dragged him closer to the Rokkan. Uson moaned. He dropped to his knees, and then fell flat on the floor.

'Do you mean the two lads were in collusion with each other?' asked the Markan, his eyes almost popping out of his head.

Mannok laughed. 'I couldn't think of a less likely alliance, uncle.' He turned to his father. 'Dinnis confessed, Papa. Besides a witness placed him near a herbalist shop and in the kitchen when your meal was being prepared. Bitjarnan saw Dinnis run into the room and attack you.'

'Yes, yes, I could hear what was said.'

Mannok and Lukarn looked puzzled.

Dinnis almost laughed. 'Breathstill stops movement, but it doesn't affect the mind or the hearing. It kills by suffocation when heart and lungs stop working.'

Fulik nodded. 'The lad's right.'

'Then Papa you would have heard Dinnis' confession,' Mannok said.

'You are not thinking, Mannu.' Rokkan shook his head, his voice sharp. 'Why attack if …you have already poisoned? Advantage of poison is to be … distant and undetected. He ran in and knocked the cup over, though not before I had drunk half.'

'And he offered the antidote.' Mannok's green eyes brightened. 'He was trying to save you.' Then his brows contracted again. 'But how could Dinnis know what antidote to use unless he knew the poison.' He looked up and met Dinnis' eyes. 'And how did you know the cup was poisoned unless you put it in? You said it was colourless and the sweetness of the juice masked the taste. Well?'

Dinnis held the Prince's gaze. Why should he have to explain himself? If the Kapok had, for some miraculous reason, chosen to speak on his behalf did it matter what the others thought? Yet he still needed to keep on reasonable terms with the Prince.

'Well, answer me,' Mannok demanded.

Chapter Sixty-Four: Culprit

Mannok

Mannok glared at Dinnis. The fellow was taking a long time answering what should have been a simple question.

'I didn't know, Your Highness.'

'Ridiculous! Why would you take the risk otherwise?'

Dinnis gave an ironical half bow. 'Indeed, idiotic, suicidal even. I had a hunch, a strong premonition is all. When I was in the kitchen I noticed that the juice had a slight soapy look and some of it had been split on to the tray. I tried to dismiss the discrepancies but, as much as I tried to, I couldn't ignore it. So, against my better judgment, I acted. As to knowing which poison,' he folded his arms across his narrow chest and raised his eyebrow, 'from the Kapok's reaction it was obviously a fast-acting toxin that causes muscles spasms and rapid paralysis of the muscles, and it was masked by the guava juice. It doesn't take much nous to work that out.'

Mannok bit his lip, controlling his rising irritation. The fellow was taking a jab at him. How did Dinnis know so much about poison? Something didn't add up. Perhaps he had poisoned Papa, but then, just as his ploy with Uson with the ants, he'd regretted his actions.

'And you just happened to have the antidote on you?'

Dinnis spread his hands. 'So, it seems.'

Mannok felt the heat rising in his face. He jumped at the weight of Papa's hand on his shoulder. Papa's lips tweaked up in an amused smile. He was looking better by the second. His breathing and colour had returned to normal, and he moved his limbs with more ease.

Then the joy of it hit Mannok. His father was alive. That was all that mattered. He dismissed Dinnis' annoying antics and smiled back.

'I suppose that does make sense, Papa. Besides, as irritating as he can be, I can't imagine why Dinnis would wish to attack you.'

'I can,' said Uncle Lukarn. He had the tall, gangly fellow clamped by the shoulder, with a watchful eye on the prostrate form of Uson.

'Your Majesty, I saw him put the poison in the cup,' Uson whined, his face pressed against the floor. 'It wasn't me.'

'Like you saw him place the thorn under my saddle?' Papa grimaced as though he had tasted something bitter. 'Still trying to shift the blame to Dinnis for your wrongdoing?'

'Why would you suspect me, Your Majesty? I swear I'm innocent.'

Papa pressed his lips together, his eyes narrowed. 'You admit that you were near a herbalist's shop and in the kitchen at the time the food was tampered with.'

'No, Your Majesty, I didn't.'

'Then how is it you saw Dinnis at those places if you weren't there?'

Uson opened his mouth then shut it again with a small pop. Papa turned to Mannok.

'Guilt is written all over his face and actions. Why did he run? Why is he here now? Couldn't resist coming to see how effective your handiwork was, could you Uson?'

'No, no, Your Majesty, I would never—'

Papa lunged forward and pulled a small satchel from the folds of Uson's tunic. He handed it to Fulik.

'Open it and tell me what's in it,' Papa said, catching his breath.

The big lad sobbed as the surgeon opened the leather satchel and searched inside. He pulled out a thick dark gum wrapped up in a scrap of paper with a list of measurements.

'Breathstill,' breathed Fulik.

Once again, Uson had been caught red handed. Mannok shook his head.

'But, why would he?' Uncle Lukarn growled.

Papa smiled grimly. 'To cover up the racket he has been conducting— reselling purloined palace good and supplies. It has been happening on a small scale for a while, but the volume increased while I was away visiting Silisea. Jakan and I had worked out how it was being done a few days ago, through something Dinnis reported the day I left for Silisea. Once I'd eliminated another suspect, Uson was on top of the list.'

'Your Majesty, Ha … Hak … A … Asik is the one who organised it. He tricked me into it. It isn't my fault. I … I'll tell you everything. Please, I'm not to blame.'

'Lukarn, take this pathetic creature into custody. One of the upper cells will be sufficient.'

The Markan puffed out his cheeks, then gave a slow nod. He let go of Dinnis, hauled the shivering Uson to his feet and handed him over to the guards.

'Oh, and restrain from hitting the prisoner. I would prefer we wait until after a proper trial before punishment is delivered. Personally, I'm not in favour of summary executions.'

Mannok looked down at his hands, then quickly shoved them into his tunic to hide the abrasions on his knuckles. He looked up and saw Dinnis standing as cool as new snow, one eyebrow raised a fraction and a thin smile on his bruised face.

Uncle Lukarn cleared his throat. 'As you say, Your Majesty. Guards, you heard the Kapok. Follow his instructions to the letter.'

'Perhaps, Papa we should get you into a more comfortable situation,' Mannok said, hoping to change the subject.

Uson twisted back, his face distorted with hatred and rage.

'You think you are so high and mighty. You are all going to die.'

'Get him out of here,' Mannok said, an acrid taste in his mouth. The guards dragged the kicking, screaming, spitting lad as he alternated between pleading for his life and cursing them all.

'Just one more thing,' Papa said, rubbing his chest. 'Dinnis, we—I—owe you an apology and a debt of gratitude for saving my life …. You are, as you said, a loyal subject of the throne and … more than that. Some recompense is appropriate.'

Mannok's face warmed. Papa was right. He owned Dinnis both thanks and an apology. 'Yeah, sorry …'

Dinnis glanced at him then stared at Papa. The minutes dripped by, the fellow's face as impassive as a cliff. Just when his silence would have been unforgivable, the fellow gave a quick mocking bow.

'Not at all, Your … Majesty. Your Highness. I only did what any loyal subject would have done for the good of the realm.'

Papa sat straighter, his face troubled. He glanced at Lukarn, then back at Dinnis. 'If we could speak alone.'

'Rokkan, that's hardly wise,' Uncle Lukarn said, stepping forward.

Papa closed his eyes, 'Markan, the lad just saved my life—for perhaps the second time.' He looked back at Dinnis. 'When you are ready, we should talk. For now, let Fulik attend your injuries.'

Dinnis touched his grazed cheekbones and lifted his narrow shoulders. 'A few bruises, nothing broken. It is hardly worth wasting the good surgeon's time.' He dropped his hand. 'Maybe ... maybe we could talk but, if you would excuse me, Your Majesty, I am late for an important appointment and am liable to get an ear full if I don't hurry. I am no longer a prisoner?'

'You are free to go.'

Dinnis raised his fist to his chest and strode out of the room.

'That lad is insufferable,' Uncle Lukarn burst out.

Papa raised his eyebrows. 'He just saved my life, Lukarn. Didn't I just say that a minute ago?' He leant forward and rested his forehead in the palms of hands. Mannok thought he saw something deep and unspoken in his father's eyes. 'He is as stubborn as ...'

'His father.'

Golden eyes met Lukarn's brown ones.

Mannok hated it when he sensed undercurrents in Papa's conversations. The anger and frustration of the last few alume simmered up. He missed Ista and loathed the way she'd been treated. Papa wasn't the paragon he'd imagined. He had flaws, he'd made mistakes and Mannok needed to work through what that meant.

He could still hear the words he had shouted in the forest by the Hunting Lodge. "I hate you. I wish you weren't my father. I wish you were dead."

Guilt twisted his thoughts like dark smoke. He'd barely spoken to his father since hurling them at him like hot rocks. They'd both said things that were hard to forget that day at the Hunting Lodge. And, sometimes, Mannok would catch a look of sorrow or weariness on his Papa's face as he saddled his horse for his frequent long rides, or did paperwork in his office near the Throne Room. Yet, Mannok didn't retract his words and pretended not to notice Papa's efforts to repair their relationship.

Now he knew with cold certainty that he would take them back, if he could. However angry he felt, Mannok didn't want Papa to die.

Suddenly, his father's arms were around him in a tight hug.

'You did well today, Prince Mannok. I'm proud of you. You

are a good man to have around in a crisis.' He gave him a squeeze and let go.

Unbidden, a grin spread across Mannok's face as joy bubbled up to the surface.

'Thanks, though I should have listened to Dinnis earlier.'

'Perhaps. I must say, we have to stop doing this.'

'Doing what, Papa?'

'These life and death dramatics on the floor.' Then he turned his head as though listening and groaned. 'Quick, give me a hand up. She'll never let me live this down. The less said about what happened the better.'

Mannok took Papa's arm, but paused when he heard his mother's voice.

'For the sake of charity, what are you two doing sitting on the floor?'

She stood at the door, one arm akimbo, her fine brows contracted together in a frown as she scanned the room. Markana Samara hovered behind her, her eyes rounded.

'This is ridiculous, Rokkan. You are the Kapok. Isn't it time you acted like it?'

Papa leant back and convulsed with contagious laughter. Mannok joined in. Papa was right. His mother would not soon let them forget this breach of etiquette, though surely she might make allowances for an assassination attempt? Still, the look in Mama's eyes set him rolling around the floor in helpless laughter with his father.

Chapter Sixty-Five: Coming Home

Dinnis

Dinnis stood at the top of the stairs, wondering the best way to get out of the Palace complex. Sunlight from the front windows and skylights threw patterns on the flagstone floor below. The Kupanna and Lady Samara walked out from the Royal Quarters.

He ducked back into the shadows of beneath the balcony that circled the Great Hall and waited for them to pass by. He wasn't in the mood for more confrontations.

Perhaps he should have accepted the Kapok's offer to talk. Yet nine years couldn't be scrubbed out just like that. Dinnis rubbed his aching face, stretching his jaw. A couple of teeth felt loose, his head throbbed, and his right ear was ringing, but Anna would have some keka leaf. He'd used all his supply on Uson.

The women turned along the balcony, heads together in deep conversation, and strolled towards the Lesser Audience room. The Kupanna to stopped at the door, hands fisted on her hips, her voice strident. Laughter erupted from the audience room. Dinnis had no idea what was so funny, but that wasn't his concern.

He was even later for Anna now, but he needed an excuse to get past the Palace gates. Kaptan Jakan might have an errand for him. The duty officer directed him to the small offices off the Throne Room.

Jakan was running his finger down an inventory list in the outer room of the Kapok's office, seeming unaware of the drama in the

Audience Room. Mannok probably should have sent for him, as well as Lord Lukarn.

Dinnis cleared his throat.

The Kaptan looked up. 'Ah, Dinnis.' He tilted his head. 'Been in a fight?'

'You could say that. I was wondering if you needed anything from the city.'

An apologetic look spread over the good Kaptan's face. 'I'm sorry lad. The Kapok ordered extra security. We arrested some thugs in the city earlier this morning, and about to arrest some more. Only essential errands in and out of the Palace.'

Of course, he should have known. He'd just have to go over the wall, though it would be risky with the heightened security.

A heavy hand landed on his shoulder. He jumped, his heart tripping an erratic beat. 'Give the boy a pass, Jakan. And you better send someone to arrest Asik.'

Jakan jumped to his feet. 'Your Majesty. Of course. So, the lad was involved in the scam? What about Uson?'

'Lukarn is taking Uson to the dungeons. The charges are more serious than purloined furniture now. We'll need to interrogate both lads, as I doubt they acted on their own. You wouldn't know anything about that would you, Dinnis?'

Heat climbed up Dinnis' neck. He swung around, shrugging the hand off his shoulder. 'Shouldn't you be resting, Your Majesty? A near-death experience like that shouldn't be taken lightly.'

Jakan's jaw gaped. 'Near death?'

The Kapok grinned and waved a hand. 'Yes, yes, now you sound like Lukarn. I'm about to totter off to be coddled upstairs, but I had a crucial appointment first.' He leant over and picked up the pass Jakan had scrawled and gave it to Dinnis. 'If you could track down Asik, Jakan, and, meanwhile I want double guards at the atrium entrance. I need privacy.'

'As you wish, Your Majesty.' Kaptan Jakan saluted and left.

Dinnis tucked the pass into his tunic. 'I'll get out of your way then, sir.'

'If that's what you want Dinnu, but we have a few minutes before Lukarn realises I'm not in my quarters and comes charging in here like a wounded peccary.'

'But your guest...'

366

'Is you.' The Kapok indicated the door to his office with an open hand. 'Please, we need to talk.'

There was a note of pleading in the voice that Dinnis had never heard before. He could refuse, but maybe he did want to hear what Papa had to say. Dinnis walked into the book-lined office that felt even more cramped that it had when he was eleven.

Rokkan perched on the corner of the desk, one leg swinging. 'So, thank you for agreeing—'

Dinnis gave him a sceptical look. 'You're not about to acknowledge me, are you?'

'No, not publicly. I can't. If things were different ...' A look of pain flashed across Rokkan's face.

'But they're not, are they? Or you are not willing to make them so. What the point of talking? So you can feel better about it?' Dinnis picked up the small pot of chillied nuts on the desk, put it down.

'I want to thank you for saving my life.'

'You've done that already.'

'And to apologise.'

'I didn't think a Kapok ever apologised.'

Frustration leeched into Rokkan's face. 'You don't make this easy, do you? A Kapok may not apologise, but a father should.'

A shudder ran through Dinnis. He gripped the edge of the desk. He wanted to believe it, but it was a trickle when a flood was overdue.

'My father died at North Pass. Or maybe even before then.'

Rokkan winced and then nodded. 'He died in the Throne Room, at the point of Naetok's knife. Marra and Lukarn both think I don't worry enough, but I'm not sure that's true. Sometimes I don't know if I can trust anyone, not even my closest friends, not even my own sons.'

Not even me, you mean. 'Mannok would die for you.'

'You should have heard him sounding off after I told him about Ista, but you're right, of course. And I am deeply sorry for not according you the same trust. Sorry for the way I've treated you.'

The walls Dinnis had built up over the years shivered a little as though they might crumble, and it scared him. 'I've thought about it.' He paused. The room felt stifling, curving around and enclosing him. He took a breath. 'The Tamrin would never accept a part-Nolmec heir, especially the northern clans. And despite the rebellion, that's your major support base, with Haka eying off the throne and Durak his loyal shadow. So, to protect the Kapok, you sacrifice an inconvenient pawn. Small price to pay, right?

'Not such a small price, Dinnu, but how could I risk more conflict after three years of bloody war?'

It hurt like the twist of a knife to hear his father admit it. 'I get it, but why totally ignore me all these years?'

'I wanted to make you my heir, to bridge the rifts between two warring peoples and seeing my eldest son on the Golden Throne. Idealistic madness. It would've destroy the Realm.'

'I don't care about being a Prince. I wanted a father.'

'Sparak knows how close we were, he was with us in Epinaos and later in Pylonis. And Lukarn knows me too well. Any sign of affection or attention would have been taken as weakening of my resolve.' Rokkan rubbed his chest, sorrow etched deep on his face. 'But it wasn't just that. My own father feared me, because when he looked at me he saw Akrad.'

Dinnis frowned. 'You don't look like him at all.'

'No, but I have his gift. I can read surface thoughts and emotions, some more than others. I can block intrusion into my own. I can't read you, not after Akrad took you from me. I can skim Ista's thoughts, but I can't read you.'

'I ... I had to keep the Monster out.'

Rokkan looked up towards the door and the sound of approaching footsteps, the sound of the guards. 'Lukarn, I'm guessing.' He gave a crooked smile. 'I should've given you a chance, son, but Akrad had you for three years and I was afraid he'd twisted you like he did Naetok.' He held up a hand. 'I feared you in the same way my father feared me. You've proved me wrong. I'm sorry, so sorry.'

Dinnis nodded, his chest tight, his arms pressed against his side. 'I can understand why, but it doesn't make it right.'

'No, it doesn't.'

His father's words splashed like rain on parched soil, softening the hardness yet soon soaked up and longing for more. He wanted to respond, to make things as they once had been, but he needed time. Time to know it was real, time to discover trust, time to rebuild scattered and discarded ruins into something new.

There was a pounding on the door. Dinnis lifted his chin. 'I have to go.'

The Kapok nodded, his eyes like burned amber. 'If that's what you want, duck out the back. I'm sure Anna will have kept some bean stew for you.'

It was only when he was walking out the Palace gate that Dinnis realised what his father had said. He knew about Anna and the Herbalist shop. How? Sparak, most likely. He should have been worried, but he wasn't. He felt light, as though he were floating. Papa had apologised, he'd shown feeling, expressed regret, maybe even more than that. It didn't change his situation, but it was a seed from which more could grow.

But now he had to hurry, for he was late.

* * *

Dinnis slipped through the door, careful to step at exactly the right spots to avoid setting the bell ringing. He breathed in the thick smell of guavamint, briarweed and other herbs that permeated the long, low room. As he turned, Anna's matronly figure appeared in the doorway to the living quarters, a heavy scowl over her wide face.

'You be late!'

He stood still. 'So I am, Mater. I got caught up with some business at the Palace. Have I missed dinner?'

Delicious smells emanated from the doorway. Like many in the lower city, Anna's family ate at midday to conserve the expense of candles at night.

'Humph. We waited for you. Better hope the pot hasn't burnt.'

He grinned. 'I'm ravenous.'

Dinnis followed her through the door into the family room at the back. Tilli, her hair in one long plait down her back, was wiping sweat off her brow as she stirred a large simmering pot of chilli beans. Her sister Nikki was taking the flat rounds of thin corn bread out of the charcoal oven. Aska pulled wooden bowls from the chest onto a tray and then set to pouring creamy yarma milk into wooden cups. Norak, the only boy, and Anna's youngest, was bent over a cracked clay tablet, practicing his letters with chalk, his tongue peeping out between his teeth. He was a solidly built lad with a coppery tinge to his shock of hair. Anna's brood.

Dinnis slipped into the room and grabbed a sunfruit from a

bowl of fruit on a side table, taking a bite before Anna could scold him. Tilli looked up and frowned.

'Didn't your Ma teach you common manners?' she said, standing up straighter and stretching her back before taking a large ladle and dolloping out the aromatic bean stew into the bowls provided by her sister.

He shrugged. 'Maybe she did, but I can't remember. I'm not sure how many manners a three-year-old can learn.'

Finishing the sunfruit, he moved over to the boy and looked at the laboriously formed words on the clay tablet.

'Good work, scamp.'

Norak scowled. 'Why do I have to learn my letters, anyways? Most of the other boys aren't learning.'

'Because one day you will be a physician,' Anna snapped, 'Not a common labourer. Your sisters are all literate, so there's no excuse for you not to be.'

'I'd rather be a warrior. You're good at fighting, Dinnis. Can't you teach me?'

'If you can finish Elsid's exercises, I'll teach you some moves.'

'Dinnis, don't encourage the lad.' Anna's eyes narrowed as they took in the grazes and bruises on his face. 'Have you been in a fight again?'

'An altercation with one of the young scions up at the Palace.'

She snorted. 'You have to stop insulting lads that are bigger than you.'

'I didn't insult ... Hmmm, I suppose I did call him an idiot.'

Dinnis recalled Mannok blazing eyes and the risks he'd taken. If he hadn't acted, his father would be dead. He fingered the token in his pocket.

Tilli placed the ladle next to the filled bowls before wiping her hands on her apron. She moved across to him and bent in close to examine his face.

'I'll get something to put on that black eye after the meal,' Tilli said, her hand resting on his cheek for a moment.

He breathed in her closeness, his heart stirring. She turned to her younger brother.

'Norak, go wash your hands before you eat.'

Norak rolled his eyes. Dinnis followed him to the basin, sluicing cool water on hands and face. They sat down on the eating mat on the floor with Anna on a low stool, her walking stick resting beside her. Tilli settled beside him, leaving only a few ninas of space between them.

He took the bowl with a smile to the shy lass and scooped up the beans with the corn bread. 'I know you don't like fighting, Anna. Neither do I but it doesn't hurt for the lad to know how to defend himself from louts like Toban and his friends.'

'Maybe,' Anna said. 'Fighting makes more problems than it solves, as often as not.'

Norak pulled his arm. 'Did you hear, Dinnis? Toban and his gang were arrested. Something to do with stealing from the Palace. Toban would steal from his own grandmother if he had one, but how could he ever get access to the Palace?'

'He was working in with one of the Prince's Age-mates—Uson— who was also arrested today.'

Uson and Toban, who would have thought it. It explained a lot but not everything. Without a doubt, that rope bridge had been cut at Eagle's Rest. Dinnis was sure Uson had almost named Haka this morning, but had been too frightened. The thefts were, no doubt, Uson and Toban's idea, but the attacks on Mannok and poisoning the Kapok were a different matter. Dinnis would not be the only disaffected person Haka had approached with tempting promises. He manoeuvred others to act and take the risks while he sat back in the shadows biding his time, like a crocodile lurking beneath the water's surface. Or was there someone else—

With a start, he felt the point of Anna's stick in his ribs. 'You seem deep in thought, son.' Concern crinkled her wrinkled brow and softened the normal cantankerous snap in her eyes.

He pushed the stick away. 'Just thinking of the importance of love and family.' He bent forward to scoop up another mouthful of the rich red bean stew before it cooled.

'You will always have a home with us, lad.'

Dinnis looked around at the simple kitchen, the smells of simple home cooking and the warmth of acceptance. He smiled at the lively conversation that swirled around him. The ethereal vision of the silver lady in the predawn light filled his inner vision. 'Plant seeds of love.' He nodded his head. Hate was bitter food. The more he hated, the more Akrad haunted his dreams. His father had betrayed him for political expediency. What he had done was wrong, but

Dinnis wasn't going to hold on to that anymore. He would put what he had lost to one side and focus on what he did have – his apprenticeship, his place in this family, his contrary though now distant sister, the uncertain friendship of an irascible prince, and yes, perhaps even a connection with his father.

He grinned, and realised the others had moved on to a spirited discussion about whose turn it was to clear out the vat—a task none of them enjoyed.

'I know, it's Dinnis' turn. He hasn't done it for a ten-day or more,' Norak shouted, his copper brown eyes shining with triumph.

'No, it's not. Dinnis is helping me clear up the kitchen. Besides, cleaning the vat would take a whole afternoon and Dinnis is due at Laetil's.'

'Overdue,' he said, 'but that's nothing new.'

Tilli placed her work roughened hand over his and instead of pulling his away, he interlaced fingers and smiled.

He didn't know what the future held but, he knew he had found a home.

Author's Note

The story continues in *Rasel's Song*, Book Two of *Akrad's Legacy* series.

For the latest news on releases, events or extras and receive a free copy of a short story set in the world of Nardva, sign up for my email letter sign-up here http://eepurl.com/bbLJKT or on the website JeanetteOHagan.com).

Reviews help authors, so if you've enjoyed this story, please share the love and leave a fair and honest review on Amazon, Goodreads and/or your favourite reviewing site.

Coming Soon

Lumi's Allegiance, Book 3 in Akrad's Legacy series
Mannok's Betrayal Book 4 in Akrad's Legacy series

Character List

Akillis, Palouma of the a Nolmec phalanx at North Pass.

Akrad, Arkon of the Nolmec (also call the Betrayer or the Westerner by the Forest Folk and Deceiver by the Tamrin) of unknown origin but who has dominated the politics of Tamra and the Five Lands for over to seventy years.

Anna, the old Herbalist in Crooked Street, Tarka; mother of Tilli, Nikki, Aska and Norak.

Amaruk of the X clan, wife of Princess Lakwi and Markan of the Eastern March.

Asik son of Lutan Turak, orphaned in the war and given a position as Prince Mannok's companion.

Bitjarnan, the madomo (head of palace staff, household steward) to Martal Kapok and his son Rokkan Kapok

Challak, son of Waruk, cousin of Lukarn and Marra, Head of the Puma clan, who sided with Naetok.

Durak, father of Durrin and Markan of the Southern March.

Durrin, son of Markan Durak, best friend of Estolik.

Dinnis, the son of a Tamrin warrior and of Kiprissa Gaia, granddaughter of Akrad.

Estolik, son of Markan Haka and Markana Yuta and older brother of Lumi.

Fulik, one of the garrison surgeons of the Royal Guard.

Galen, royal physician.

Garvin, the son of Kaptan Kaspin and childhood friend of Prince Mannok.

Haka of the Dolphin clan, the grandson of Tellek Kapok and cousin of Rokkan Kapok. He is Estolik and Lumi's father and Markan of the Eastern March.

Hasuk son of Kaptan Maikwi, orphaned in the war and given a position as Prince Mannok's companion.

Hecton, a Nolmec warrior.

Ista, younger sister of Dinnis, and daughter of a Tamrin warrior and of Kiprissa Gaia, granddaughter of Akrad.

Jakan, a warrior, a Lutan and then Kaptan, in the Palace Guard.

Jati, daughter of Princess Lakwi

Kimsak, a medic in the Tamrin army.

Kimsak, a younger son of Markan Lukarn

Korak, Kinleader of the Forest Folk and grandfather of Rasel and Semian.

Kolik, son of Derik, Markan Lukarn's younger brother and a Brigan in the Kapok's armies.

Lakwi, Princess of Tamra, younger half-sister of Rokkan Kapok, and son of Martal Kapok and Kupanna Suraya and married to Markan of the Western March.

Lukarn of the Puma clan, son of Derik, older brother of Kupanna Marra, nephew of Kupanna Suraya and best friend of Rokkan Kapok. Rokkan appoints him and Markan (or governor) of the Northern March after Prince Naetok's treachery.

Lumi, daughter of Markan Haka and Markana Yuta and younger sister of Estolik.

Mannok (Mannu), Prince of Tamra, son of Rokkan Kapok and Kupanna Marra

Marra of the Puma clan, Kupanna of Tamra, wife of Rokkan Kapok, mother of Prince Mannok and sister of Markan Lukarn

Martal Kapok son of Tellek Kapok and father of Rokkan Kapok, Prince Naetok and Princess Lakwi.

Mattik a royal scribe, originally a villager

Prince **Naetok** (Naetu), younger half-brother of Rokkan Kapok, and son of Martal Kapok and Kupanna Suraya. Before he dies, Martal appoints him Markan (or governor) of the Northern March.

Keloumen **Nikoris** the commander of the Phalanx of Nolmec supporting Akrad. Nikoris is under the command of the Nolmec General Nuktis.

Ninak, retired Kaptan of the Palace Guard, nephew of Pirak and father of Redrik.

Pirak, son of Kusin, of the Grey Fox Clan spoke against Rokkan at Nakri

Rasel, youngest daughter of Jazadek and granddaughter of Korak of the Forest Folk.

Redrik, youngest son of Kaptan Ninak and grand-nephew of Pirak

Rokkan (Rokku) Kapok son of Martal Kapok and Kupanna Tula (princess of Silisea).

Markana **Samara**, wife of Markan Lukarn and mother of Waren, Rizanna, Kimsak etc.

Kupanna **Suraya,** second wife of Martal Kapok, stepmother of

Rokkan Kapok and mother of Prince Naetok and Princess Lakwi.

Ralton, head librarian in the royal library.

Rizanna (Rizzi) of the Puma clan, eldest daughter of Markan Lukarn and Markana Samara, brother of Rizanna and Prince Mannok's cousin.

Semian son of Jazadek and brother of Rasel, one of the Forest Folk

Princess **Sila** of Silisea, wife of Tannik and mother of Tolteal; Sila is also Rokkan's cousin as her mother and his (Tula) were sisters.

Markana **Samara**, wife of Markan Lukarn and mother of Waren, Rizanna, Kimsak etc.

Sanak, Head Cook at the Golden Palace of Tarka

Kupanna **Suraya**, wife of Tellek Kapok, mother of Princess Lakwi and Prince Naetok and stepmother of Rokkan Kapok

Queen **Suza** of Silisea, mother of Princes Tannik and Asok

Prince **Tannik** of Silisea, husband of Princess Sila and father of Prince Tolteal.

Lady **Taraya**, Kaptan Kaspin's wife and mother of Garvin

Tilli, daughter of Anna the Herbalist.

Toban, a young ruffian and leader of a street gang.

Prince **Tolteal** of Silisea, son of Prince Tannik and Princess Sila.

Trasin, Lord Challak's second son and age-mate of Mannok.

Uson son of Lutan Yanak, orphaned in the war and given a position as Prince Mannok's companion.

Waren (Waro) of the Puma clan, eldest son of Markan Lukarn and Markana Samara, brother of Rizanna and Prince Mannok's cousin.

Wasuk, head groom of the royal stables, originally from Silisea.

Markana **Yuta**, wife of Markan Haka and mother of Estolik and Lumi and a good friend of Kupanna Marra's.

Zaven, Lutan in Rokkan Kapok's guard and later in the Palace Guard.

Peoples, Time and Measurements

People, Titles and Words

The Filane people consist of the people of the Five Lands (Mokka before the invasion by the Nolmec, Tamra, Shanta, Silisea, Limar). The Five Lands are in the southern hemisphere of the world of Nardva.

In Tamra, the king and queen are called Kapok and Kupanna while in Limar they are called Sulkan and Sulkana. In Tamra, the Lords of the Four Marchs (North, West, South, East) are known as Markan and their wives as Markana. The major household steward is known as 'madomo'.

Among the Nolmec a princess is called Kiprissa, a prince Kiprisson or more commonly Alfeas; a commander of a Phalanx (or Brigade) is a keloumen; kuree is a general honorific meaning 'sir'; moros means idiot or fool; pioni is foot soldier or servant; chia is a term of endearment.

Some Eldar words: rakka means fool or idiot, saba means grandfather, baba is father and matu is mother.

The Moons and Time

Nardva has two moons, the bigger golden hued moon Alumi and the smaller silver hued moon Argenti. The Filane (unlike the Nolmec) base their calendar on the cycle of Alumi with 12 months of 30 days. Thus an **alume** is 30 days (the cycle of Alumi); an **argen** is 20 days or two ten-days (the cycle of Argenti). Time is also divided into tens (e.g. a half-ten; a ten-day; two ten-days etc.)

Among most of the Filane nations at that time, **the day** is divided in two sets of ten 'hours' each - sunset to sunrise, sunrise to sunset. Thus, the first hour begins at sunset while the tenth hour ends at sunrise, and so also during daylight.

Filane measurements:

A **lek** (plural also lek) is the equivalent to 1.2 kilometres; a **tana** (plural, **tanis**) is equivalent to 1.2 metres; nina (plural, **ninas**) equals about 1.2 centimetres.

Map of the Five Lands

Genealogies

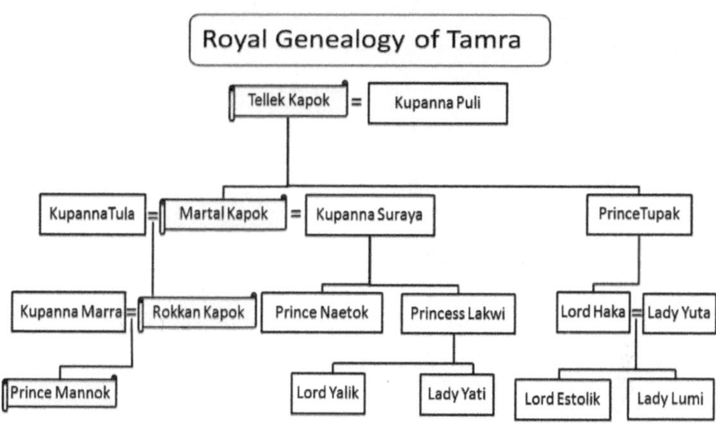

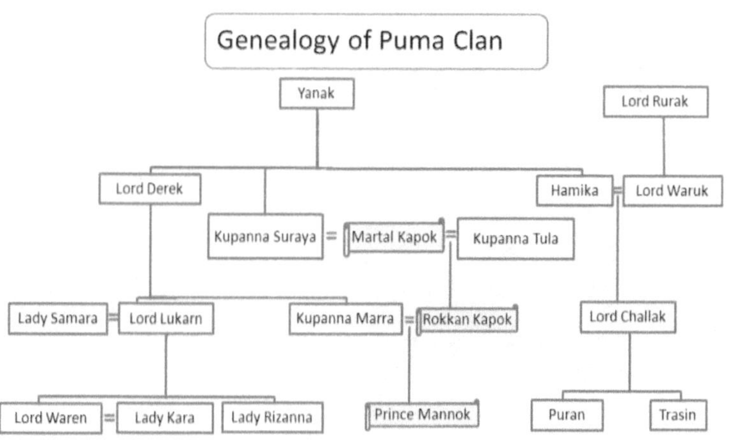

Acknowledgements

Akrad's Children is the first published novel in the Akrad's Legacy series. The series follows the lives of four young people caught up in the unrest and political machinations following a bitter war. *Akrad's Children* became Dinnis' tale.

I started writing this story six years ago, but the origin of the story began many decades before this. In my late teens, I dreamed of a young girl holding at lantern near a fountain and her story continued as into a waking dream. That dream became *Adelphi* (now titled *Finding Elene*), which I wrote down and revised in my early twenties and connected with my earlier preteen imagings in the world of Nardva. Then my life took another turn and it was only when I started postgraduate studies in creative writing that I dusted off the old manuscript, plus the notes I'd written for a sequel. In the process of rewriting these, I found myself writing the prequel to *Adelphi*. I had a dilemma. Which should I publish first? In the end, I chose the prequels and I've enjoyed exploring the lives, loves and adventures of Rasel, Mannok, Ista and Dinnis. I hope you do too.

The events of this story occur many years after 'Ruhanna's Flight', the Under the Mountain series and even the Tamrin Tales ('The Herbalist's Daughter' and 'Lakwi's Lament'), though a savvy reader may recognise some familiar names and references.

My heartfelt thanks to my wonderful editors Nola Passmore (of The Write Flourish) and Rowena Beresford, and to my redoubtable critique partners and beta readers Nicky Nugent, Christine Barrett, Suzanne Hay-Bartlem, Paula Vince, Julian Green, Ruth Bonetti, Gwendolyn Gage, and Kathleen Hillenberg.

I'm especially grateful for my family—my loving husband Tony, my precious children Kathleen and David, and my parents Tom and Jean Curtis—who instilled in me a love of faith and fantasy— and siblings, Tom Curtis, Frank Curtis, Chris Curtis and Kathleen Hillenberg, with whom I've shared many wonderful adventures.

As always, I'm grateful to my Maker in whose creative and imaginative footsteps I can only hope to follow.

Jeanette O'Hagan, June 2017

About the Author

Jeanette O'Hagan has spun tales in the world of Nardva from the age of eight. She enjoys writing fantasy, sci-fi, poetry, and editing.

Her Nardvan stories span continents, millennia and cultures. Some involve shapeshifters and magic. Others include space stations and cyborgs.

She has published over forty stories and poems, including the *Under the Mountain Series* (5 books), *Ruhanna's Flight and Other Stories, Akrad's Children* and *Rasel's Song*, the first two books in the Akrad's Legacy series - and the latest short story in the *Starlit Realms: Fantasy anthology.*

Jeanette has practised medicine, studied communication, history, theology and a Master of Arts (Writing). She lives in Brisbane, Australia, with her husband and two cats. She loves reading, painting, travel, catching up for coffee with friends, pondering the meaning of life.

Website

Jeanette O'Hagan Writes http://jeanetteohagan.com

Social Media

Jeanette O'Hagan is most active on
Facebook, Twitter, GoodReads, Bookbub and Instagram

Publications

Under the Mountain 5 novella series

Heart of the Mountain: a short novella
Blood Crystal: a novella
Stone of the Sea: a novella
Shadow Crystals: a novella
Caverns of the Deep

Akrad's Legacy Series

Akrad's Children
Rasel's Song
Lumi's Allegiance (Coming 2023)
Mannok's Betrayal (Coming 2023)

Short Stories and Collections

Ruhanna's Flight and Other Stories
Treasure in the Snow

Short Stories (in Other Anthologies)

'Space Triage' in *Challenge Accepted* Anthology
'Project Chameleon' in *The Quantam Soul* anthology
Maroon's Sanctuary in *God's of Clay* Anthology
'Full Moon Rises' in *Like a Woman* Anthology
'Shadow Queen' in *Starlit Realms* Anthology